JEOPARDY

A NOVEL

SURFACE

PERPETUITY

· PUBLISHING ·

© 2016 Sheri Leigh Horn

Published by Perpetuity Publishing, LLC

P.O. Box 3128, Stafford, Virginia 22554

www.PerpetuityBooks.com

Printed in the United States of America

This is a work of fiction. Some of the events in this story are based on actual events which are a matter of public record. Except in those cases, the names, characters, places, and incidents either are the product of the author's imagination or are used fictitiously, and any resemblance to actual persons, living or dead, to business establishments, events, or locales is entirely coincidental.

Paperback: 978-0-9981326-0-0

Hard cover: 978-0-9981326-1-7

eBook: 978-0-9981326-2-4

Cover design by Damonza Design

Author photograph by Dori Ottaviano

GEOGRAPHIC PROFILING is an investigative support technique that analyzes locations connected to a series of violent crimes to determine the most probable area in which the offender lives.

The three-dimensional output of this analysis is known as a jeopardy surface.

SHERI LEIGH HORN

JEOPARDY

A NOVEL

SURFACE

CHAPTER ONE

November 14

Triangle, Virginia

38°32'40.87"N, 77°19'32.87"W

FOG ROLLED AND shifted like a living thing, prolonging my confusion. *Cold. Wet. Dark.* A streetlight's feeble yellow glow illuminated the Tahoe and Jeep parked in the driveway. *My* driveway. Great, that explained *where*, but certainly not *how* or *why*. I'd been in bed, mentally clicking through a macabre slide show, my version of counting sheep. I must've fallen asleep, but my body felt too heavy to be dreaming. How had I gotten from my bed to the front yard? My sleep patterns hadn't exactly been normal lately, but somnambulism was a new one.

Think. Start with a couple of facts. Okay. Fact: Bare feet. Fact: Damp grass. Fact: Mid-November.

It was November when I'd gotten in bed, but I couldn't rule out the involvement of a space-time continuum. It was apparently that kind of night. Chilly temp, damp grass. Hence, cold wet feet. Cold wet everything. My hair was undoubtedly a Medusa-like mass of dark, wet tendrils. *Time?* My gut said it was the witching hour, sometime between midnight and zero-three-hundred when most law-abiding citizens were asleep and the insomniacs and serious miscreants were not.

Sounds. Chattering teeth. Crickets. Yipping—incessant, at that grating octave unique to the diva breeds. This little shit, a tiny mop with legs, belonged to Mrs. Schroeder and barked at anything that moved. *Skipper? Skippy? Really? You gonna stand here shivering all night in thin pajama pants and a tank top?* A porch light came on. Skittles must've woken a neighbor.

When I raised my wrist to check my watch, intense white light bathed my lawn. The weight in my left hand registered a moment before I realized what I was holding. *Sonofabitch.* Cool to the touch. No odor of burnt gunpowder, which would've lingered in the fog. A slide check revealed a round in the chamber. I'd obviously meant business. The motion-sensing security lights were timed to shut off after ten minutes without motion. They'd been off. *Well, this is fucking great. You've been standing here for at least ten minutes, oblivious, holding a firearm.*

No neighbors had come out to investigate the sound of a gunshot, a good sign. On the other hand, sounds of violence often went unheard in the middle of the night, especially in neighborhoods like mine where half of the potential witnesses removed their hearing aids before bed. For the first time, I considered what I might find inside my house. The front door was wide open, and the fact my alarm wasn't going off didn't exactly put me at ease. I'd managed to enter the six-digit code, apparently while sleepwalking.

A methodical check of each room revealed nothing out of place, with the exception of my bedroom. Assuming I hadn't traveled through a wormhole, I'd fallen asleep a little after midnight, which would've been about three hours earlier according to the alarm clock on the nightstand. The nightstand drawer where I kept the Glock was open, and the bed looked like the aftermath of a WWE match. After smoothing the fitted sheet, I released the magazine and counted each round as I ejected them onto the bed. Thirteen, plus one in the chamber. *Well, that's one thing to be thankful for.* I'd have to do something about this, but I was too tired to figure it out.

After reloading the pistol and returning it to the drawer, I stumbled to the bathroom through an obstacle course of strewn bedding, ungracefully shedding my wet pants in the process. My hand blindly explored cold tile, found the switch. Fifteen pounds of perturbed feline glared at me from the vanity.

"Sorry, Stell."

Ignoring me, she yawned, arched her back, and smoothly transitioned to the cat version of downward dog.

Random thoughts flitted like gnats. *What day is it? Saturday. God, my legs feel like someone beat me with a stick. What else had I done in my sleep? Was this the first time, or just the first time I hadn't woken up in my bed? Jesus, what if I'd fired my weapon! What in the hell is wrong with me? And what am I going to do about it? It's not like I can call a damned hotline. Why now? Things had been better until… until what? Until your partner went on leave and your workload doubled? Until Erin started reminding you that December 21st is right around the corner? No.* Yes, but there was something else, something that might explain the nightmares and, apparently, some kind of fucked up sleep disorder.

Dame Stella resettled and began half-heartedly grooming herself. Stella's a survivor. It takes one to know one, I suppose. One night seven years ago I was dumpster diving behind a Greyhound station. Ridiculous, I know. In a blind rage, I'd tossed out a couple of things, and after calming down I was ass-deep on a mission. The object of my frantic rooting was forgotten when I discovered a skinny gray kitten curled up inside a Stella Artois beer box. I'd abandoned a cat before, in Scotland, when I was a kid and didn't have any say in the matter. *Oh, quit being so dramatic, Regan. It's not abandonment. Mrs. Naughton will give Galileo a perfectly lovely home.* In retrospect, my aunt had been a tad busy burying my parents and relocating Erin and me to the States. My tabby was understandably low on her priority list, but try explaining that to a distraught six-year-old.

"We're a sad pair, Stell." Two quick tail swishes. Translation: *Speak for yourself, woman.* She resumed lick-swipe-licking.

I avoided the mirror like I'd managed to avoid my sister since we moved my niece into her dorm weeks, shit, *months*, ago. Erin, my ever meddling sister, would take one look at me and offer her diagnosis, undoubtedly something involving rapid weight loss and sleep deprivation with some complicated clinical terms thrown in. A check-in with my supervisor loomed, but at least he wouldn't be so goddamned clinical about it. *Jesus Christ, Ross. You been on a bender?* is more Harry Spielman's style.

Not surprisingly, Stella bolted at the mere suggestion of running water. The hot water did nothing to revive me. Shit. Zero-three-thirty. Chance of getting back to sleep: nil. It was supposed to be my day off, or at least the closest I got to a day off. I'd planned to unpack, then find something relaxing to do, but there would be no relaxing until I did something about my sleepwalking problem. Vincent Tomaro, a friend and former colleague, owned a private security firm. Video surveillance was one of his many specialized skills. He could set me up with cameras and a DVR so I could monitor myself. No one else needed to know. With the exception of my insurance company, Vincent was one of only four people who knew what was parked in my garage. He'd assume I was finally taking his advice to upgrade my security.

After that was taken care of, maybe I'd go for a long run or to the shooting range. I turned off the faucet and had another idea. *Chang's gym.* I was preparing to test for fourth *dan* rank soon and my sore legs begged for activity. Was there a better stress reliever than going for a run then kicking and pounding the hell out of a heavy bag? Nope. As I was drying my face and hands, I heard metal bouncing on tile. My Virginia Tech class ring. *What the hell?*

It slid back onto my finger too easily. Shit, had I lost more weight? As I stashed the ring in a drawer, I imagined Erin staging her version of an intervention, like she tried to do seven years ago. That had gone *so* well.

She was a single parent dealing with a resentful kid while managing a surgeon's schedule, and she'd wanted to add her moody, jobless sister to the mix. Had her offer not felt like an ultimatum, or had I been a little more gracious in refusing it, things might've gone differently. Maybe I wouldn't have become so evasive. Maybe I would be the kind of aunt my niece deserved. It wasn't fair to Erin or Lanie. Hell, it wasn't fair to me for that matter, but I didn't have the first clue what to do about it.

I'd changed into shorts and a t-shirt, and was sitting on the edge of the bed lacing up a Nike when my phone vibrated. *Shit.* As it continued to rattle obnoxiously on the nightstand, I ran through all the possibilities. If it couldn't wait until Monday, it probably meant a helicopter or plane ride to God-knows-where less than twenty-four hours after returning from Seattle. Or, maybe it was Erin commencing another voicemail barrage. She'd been obsessed with my plans for the holidays, as if this year might be an exception. We'd spend the anniversary like we always did, binging on booze and Turner Classic Movies and not talking about our dead parents. My participation was a given, but Erin apparently had something else in mind. It occurred to me, like it always did, that something bad had happened to Erin or Lanie.

The name on my missed call log was equally perplexing and unnerving: *Haskins, Robert.* When I returned the call, a tired, familiar voice answered. "Hey, Regan. Sorry to call so late."

"Early." Nonchalant. That's what I was going for, anyway.

"What?"

"It's early, Rob, not late. It's three-thirty in the morning."

"I haven't slept, so it's all the same to me."

Tell me about it.

"So, to what do I owe this howdy-do at the ass crack of dawn?" I said, trying to keep things casual.

"Well, you never sleep anyway, so I figure now is as good a time as any. You at home?" he asked, because I often wasn't.

"Yeah, what's up?"

"I need your help."

"Uh-huh."

"With a case."

"How many locations?" I asked, hobbling one-shoed into the living room, where I found a notebook and pen in my messenger bag and sat on the sofa.

"One so far, but we really don't know what we're dealing with yet."

Ominous.

"Where? Baltimore?" The locus of his field office's jurisdiction seemed a logical guess.

"Nope. Farther east." Though we hadn't spoken in several months, Haskins' need to constantly test my patience clearly hadn't waned.

"What the hell is east of Baltimore besides water?" I conjured a mental map of the North Atlantic region.

"The Eastern Shore, near Chestertown—"

"Jesus," I blurted, "is it Abbott?"

"Looks like it, but we can't make a visual ID. We're waiting for a dental comparison."

My hand paused over the notebook as images of Jennifer Abbott flashed. Her disappearance from a small college campus was national news. "M.O.?"

"That's just it. There's a certain element to this one, and, well, let's just say it seems like your bailiwick."

Why call me if he wasn't dealing with a series of crimes? *That* was my bailiwick. He didn't give me a chance to ask him to elaborate. "What do you know about geocaching?" he asked.

The left-field question took me a few seconds to process. "Well, it's basically GPS-assisted scavenger hunting. Geeky outdoorsy types hide caches filled with random, cheap shit and post the coordinates on geocaching websites for others to find. There are caches all over the world. Probably hundreds of thousands of them."

"Sounds like you have firsthand knowledge."

"You think I'm the geeky-outdoorsy type?" I asked, feigning incredulity.

"Outdoorsy, yes. Geeky only when you talk about algorithms and probability models." When I didn't respond, he added, "Geeky in a hot way. It totally works."

Cheeks burning, I chose to acknowledge the first half of his comment. "Jesus, Haskins, I believe that's the first time you've ever used the correct terminology and not 'mumbo-jumbo' or 'black magic.' I geocached years ago, back before smartphone apps, when we had to use handheld GPS devices. These days, you can't find a cache without tripping over somebody. Too crowded for me, even if I had the time. What the hell does geocaching have to do with your case?"

"That's what I'm hoping you can tell me. I'd rather you see for yourself."

"Who's leading the investigation?" I asked.

"Yours truly. I'm at the scene now, but the M.E.'s about to release the body. I'm huddling up with the Kent County Sheriff's Office and Maryland State Police investigators in an hour, then I'm heading to Baltimore for the autopsy."

"It'll have to be off the books. You know I haven't been officially—"

"Yeah, I know. Listen, I just need you to review my notes, take a look at the scene, and let me know what you think we're dealing with. Just do the voodoo that you do."

There it was. Yes, he was teasing, but I heard it too often, and it irritated the shit out of me, especially from someone who knew better. "There is no *voodoo,* and I'm not fucking clairvoyant. It's statistical modeling, not a carnival side show. It sounds like, assuming the victim is Abbott, you've probably only got a couple of associated locations at this point. So, I'm not gonna be able to give you anything specific."

"I know, but like I said, there's an element to this one that you're uniquely qualified to interpret. You'll be in and out."

That, I did not believe.

"I'll take whatever you're able to give me."

I sighed. Loudly. "Where's the body?"

"There's no address, per se. The place is abandoned. Locals call it the Garrett Farm."

"Garrett Farm. Right, I'll just plug that into the GPS. Seriously, do you have coordinates? A big red 'X' on a map? Something helpful?"

"You're awfully testy this morning, Munch."

Munch. Short for munchkin. Clearly, he was trying to push *all* my buttons.

"You're lucky you're not here. Your nuts would be in your throat, courtesy of the Lollipop Guild."

"Lullaby League."

"What the hell?"

"The Lollipop Guild is all-male. The Lullaby League is made up of the cute ballerina munchkins, which is—"

"What in God's name would make you associate me with *ballerinas*? Right now, I'm feeling more like the Wicked Witch of the East. How are you so chipper at this ungodly hour?"

"*West*, not East. Have you even seen *The Wizard of Oz*? There's a mailbox at the farm across the road from the Garrett place. No big red 'X,' but it does have some big white numbers painted on it. I can give you those."

He did and I jotted them down.

"There's also a hunting lease sign in front of the Garrett place. You can't miss it."

"Send me the scene photos, video if it's available," I said.

"Already did. Check your inbox."

Son of a bitch. Apparently, it was a foregone conclusion I'd drop everything and rush right out there to help him.

"Well, the good news is that it's November and the weather's shitty so there won't be any beach traffic," I said. "The bad news is that it's November and the weather's shitty."

Time check. *0350.* I still had all my gear with me from my trip to Seattle, which would save me a trip to Quantico and at least thirty minutes. I mentally ran through a to-do list: review Haskins' notes and crime scene photos; take a look at the satellite images of the area; shower; get dressed; and call Vincent, with a coffee fix in there somewhere. "I can be there mid-morning," I said.

"Perfect. I spoke to the Kent County sheriff. Nice guy. Give me a head's up when you're thirty minutes out and he'll have a deputy meet you at the scene."

I was being manipulated. The shitty part, the reason my jaw ached from grinding my teeth, was that it was my own damn fault. Residual guilt. The last time I'd refused Rob Haskins had been, well, epic.

"Anything else I should know?" I asked him.

"The specifics regarding M.O., what he did to her, it's all close-hold. Only three of us—well, four now—know about the cache."

"You found a cache *there*? At the scene?"

"Yeah, and it gets better. Or worse, depending on how you look at it. He posted the coordinates of the cache on a popular geocaching website. Maybe on other sites too, we've just started to look into it."

"Jesus."

"It's all in the notes. It's bad, Regan."

"They're all bad."

"Some are worse." A heavy sigh, then he said, "Listen, I appreciate it. I owe you one."

I'll take whatever you're able to give me.

It won't be enough. It never has been.

I ended the call and discovered two voicemails. They could wait.

Well, hell. So much for not thinking about death for the next twenty-four hours. As promised, Haskins' field notes and the crime scene photos were in my inbox. It didn't take long to understand why he'd called me, and after looking at the photos, it was obvious why a visual identification wasn't possible. Haskins was right. Some *are* worse than others.

CHAPTER TWO

November 14

10:23 a.m.

Chestertown, Maryland

39°.12'16.02"N, 76°.0'24.40W

I T WAS MIDMORNING on a wet, gloomy Saturday. Most folks were probably inside their warm homes reading the paper, watching *College Game Day*, or doing whatever farmers do on rainy days during harvest season. Thanks to steady drizzle and fogged windows, visibility was shit as I slowed to a stop on the shoulder of the two-lane blacktop. Despite popping Tums like pub snacks, acid roiled in my stomach—the result of too much caffeine, too little sleep, and Haskins' phone call.

Willing the dull ache behind my right eye to remain manageable, I rummaged through the glove box. My efforts produced a bottle of Excedrin. I downed two gel-caps with tepid coffee and checked my messages. Vincent had sent a couple of texts letting me know he was installing cameras at my house and asking for the keypad code for the garage. *Only you, V. No one else,* I replied, along with the code, reminding myself to change it at the first opportunity. There were four more voicemails from Erin, which I ignored. Lanie had called three times. She hadn't bothered to leave a message, but had followed up with two texts. The first: *Call me plz.* The second: *Aunt Regan, where r u?* I suspected her persistence had something to do with her mother.

I lowered my rain-streaked window to get a better look at the mailbox across the road, an obvious Louisville Slugger target. The post canted so far left I could only make out a couple of numbers on the side of the box. The marked Crown Vic parked in front of me and the hand-painted "Hunting Leases Available" sign told me I was at the right place. The cruiser was unoccupied. Had my designated escort from the Kent County Sheriff's Office gotten bored? Had nature called? A gravel driveway leading to a two-story farmhouse bisected an overgrown cornfield. It didn't take a historian's eye to deduce that the decaying house didn't have working plumbing. That third cup of coffee had been ill advised.

I'd noticed only a couple of cars since turning onto MD-544, but that didn't mean there hadn't been others. My mind had been on other things. With the engine idling and heater cranked, I watched and waited. After five minutes, a newer model Ford truck, a loud heavy-duty diesel with four tires on the rear axle, headed my way. The driver slowed when he spotted the patrol car, or the crime scene tape marking the perimeter, or both. He raised two fingers from the steering wheel in a lazy wave. Preoccupied with mental maps and traffic patterns, I didn't think to return the gesture until he was well past. One truck in five minutes constituted little traffic in my book. Low traffic volume meant less chance of someone noticing activity on the property and lower risk for the perpetrator. It was worth noting, so I did.

I cut the engine and glanced down at my clothing: khakis; down vest over corduroy shirt; and ancient hiking boots. Though more weather-appropriate than my usual Fed chic, the outfit made me look like I was dressed for an L.L. Bean photo shoot. After pulling my hair into a sloppy ponytail using a rubber band from the collection ringing the gearshift, I threaded it through a black ball cap. I swapped the vest for a black jacket that matched the cap and concealed the Glock on my hip.

After retrieving my scene bag from the rear of the Tahoe, I walked toward the house, where I assumed the cruiser's driver was waiting for me. No matter how much time I spent looking at maps, studying geospatial features—topographic elevations, ingress and egress routes, waterways, roadways, and terrain—the ground-level perspective always surprised me in some way. The brown stalks were casualties of a particularly hot and dry summer and winter-like fall. The satellite shots I'd pulled from Google Earth that morning had been captured in June, before everything had burned up. The corn had appeared as large benign swathes of green on the satellite images, and now the brown neglected stalks towered over me.

A boom sounded somewhere in front of me.

What the—

Another blast echoed over the corn field. Reacting without conscious thought, I dropped my bag, knelt, and drew my weapon. The corn completely blocked my peripheral view. I focused on movement in front of me. Eighty yards away, tattered curtains flapped in windows void of glass.

My breathing was ragged. White stars skittered across my field of vision, which narrowed to the diameter of a straw. I focused downrange, tightened my grip on the pistol. *Calm down, Ross. Breathe.* My pulse rushed in my ears. Finally, sounds penetrated. Someone called from far away. Two more shotgun blasts in quick succession sent several geese into flight. *Hunters. Damnit, calm the hell down. There's no threat here.* I slid my firearm into the holster, willed my heart rate to slow.

"Agent Ross?"

My head whipped toward the baritone voice. A large uniformed man hopped off the porch and began jogging my way.

When he got closer, I could make out the Kent County crest on his jacket. "Special Agent Ross?" he asked again. He was smiling— a good sign. Still, it occurred to me he'd likely been watching from the farmhouse while I acted like a neurotic asshole.

"Hi!" he said, reaching out a bear paw. "Deputy Chris Reynolds, Kent County Sheriff's Office." His eyes were so blue they commanded most of my attention.

"Hi. Yeah, Regan Ross, FBI," I offered, shaking his hand. The oversized letters across my cap and jacket made the introduction redundant. Reynolds actually looked happy to see me, which was curious. He'd been waiting on a Fed in shit weather while his fellow deputies were investigating a murder. I'd half-expected annoyance or outright resentment.

Jennifer Abbott had last been seen ten days ago in Chestertown, on the Washington College campus, approximately four miles from the Garrett Farm. The victim found that morning would likely be identified as Abbott. If not, she was a Jane Doe, and Jennifer Abbott was still missing. One thing was clear. For the second time in my FBI career, I was involved in a high-profile case that would be all over CNN, Nancy Grace, and every checkout stand tabloid by nightfall.

The single chevron on Reynolds' sleeve confirmed he hadn't been a sheriff's deputy long. I'd done some research before driving out. This was the third murder in Kent County since the Reagan administration. The last, a domestic turned murder-suicide, had occurred almost ten years ago, probably before Reynolds hit puberty.

It hadn't been so long since my rookie days that I'd forgotten what it felt like to be green, especially on a case this big, but the clock was ticking, and I'd never claimed to be a patient person. My priorities were to assess the scene as quickly as possible, provide Haskins whatever insight I could, and get back to my weekend. If

I could manage all that without coming across as an entitled bitch, then bonus.

"I appreciate you meeting me, Deputy. I know the scene has been processed, but I'd like to check out the surrounding area, take a few photos of my own, and maybe ask you some questions." When another series of shotgun blasts sounded, I did not flinch.

"Hunters," Reynolds explained. "Canada goose season opened this morning. I'd be trying to bag some myself today if I wasn't working."

"Sorry to bring you out here on a Saturday, but I'm sure the geese are thankful."

"It's no problem, ma'am." Reynolds' smile didn't register on my bullshit detector. He was prepared for the weather, clear plastic protected his Smokey the Bear hat. My cap, on the other hand, was soaked and rain hit my face every time I looked up to meet his eyes. Story of my life.

"Mind if we walk and talk?" I didn't wait for an answer. "You were one of the first officers on the scene, correct?" I'd read as much in Haskins' notes.

He nodded. "I was on patrol not too far from here when I got the dispatch. As soon as I saw what we were dealing with, I radioed it in. Another unit arrived about five minutes later. For a few minutes it was just the hunters and us, then all hell broke loose, every cop in the county, state police, and the media, the place was a fuckin' circus." Quick as a blink, Reynolds' cheeks and ears turned crimson and I pegged him as a fellow emotional blusher.

"Excuse my mouth, ma'am." He actually hung his head.

"It's fine, really." I was practically double-timing to keep up with his long strides. "You were saying?"

"It was all we could do to keep the media back. I mean, can you imagine if they got her on camera, strung up like that? Jesus, they'll put just about anything on TV these days."

Reynolds probably would have referred to the victim by name, but for the time being we were limited to "she" or "victim" or "decedent." Although her race, estimated age, height, and weight were consistent with Jennifer Abbott, the killer had completely obliterated her facial features. Abbott had no identifying marks and none were found on the body, so until a forensic odontologist compared Jane Doe's dental x-rays to Abbott, we wouldn't know for sure.

"How'd the hunters find her?" I asked.

"Walked right up on her. They got here last night, parked in front of the house, and walked around back. They were planning to camp and set up on the pond early this morning."

"This was at about a quarter to nine last night?"

"Yes, ma'am."

"And you said goose season started this morning?"

"The season officially opened at dawn."

"So they parked right here in front of the house and didn't notice anything until they walked around back?"

"Right. They found her on the back porch and one of 'em called 911. A detective from the Maryland State Police arrived on scene a little after we did and started barking orders. Santos got here about that time, and I thought he was gonna blow a gasket."

"Santos?"

"Sorry, ma'am. Detective Tomas Santos. He's the lead investigator from the Sheriff's Office."

"Gotcha. Go on."

"Well, while Detective Santos argued with the MSP investigators, two other deputies and I set up a perimeter, taped off the scene, and tried to keep the reporters back. A couple of Feds from the Baltimore Field Office showed up an hour or so later."

Interesting. Haskins hadn't mentioned a partner.

"With all due respect, Agent Ross, I'm not sure what you wanted to drive all the way out here for. The FBI team crawled over every inch of this place collecting evidence. From what I could tell, they did a pretty thorough job of it. Hell, the SAC even had a couple dozen fire academy cadets out here searching the woods."

I ignored the question Reynolds hadn't quite asked. "The Special Agent in Charge with Haskins—male or female?"

"Male. Name started with an E, I think."

"Eberley?" I offered.

"Yeah, that's it."

What a shit show. Haskins probably hadn't mentioned this tidbit because he'd known it wouldn't have helped his cause. Reynolds wanted to know what the hell I was doing there, fair enough. With Eberley running things, the Bureau had undoubtedly stormed in like the cavalry and hadn't provided much information to the locals. Some fences probably needed mending.

"Ever heard of NCAVC, Deputy?"

"No, ma'am, but sounds like government alphabet soup to me."

"The National Center for the Analysis of Violent Crime. It's located at Quantico," I explained.

"Where the FBI Academy is at?" He kept his eyes in front of him.

"Right, same complex," I said.

"Are you a profiler, like Jodie Foster in that movie? You look a little like her, as a matter of fact. The character, I mean, not Jodie Foster now. Shit, she's gotta be what, like fifty?"

Just. Fucking. Stop.

After an icy beat, I said, "Not exactly. I'm a criminal intelligence analyst specializing in geographic profiling and predictive analytics. I approach a series of crimes from geospatial angle, rather than a strictly behavioral—"

"Sorry, geographic profiling?"

"Yes," I explained, "I'm concerned with *where* crimes occur, crime location features and patterns and what they tell us."

"What patterns? This is the only location so far, right?"

"The only *known* location, but there are at least two—the

initial contact site and the murder site. So far, it looks like the victim was killed and left on this porch, which means the kill site and disposal site are the same. If the victim is Jennifer Abbott, there's at least one more location—"

"Where he kept her."

"Yeah, and we can't rule out that she was kept at more than one location," I added.

The path ended at a small clearing in front of the house. A thick layer of vines climbed the two-story farmhouse and blanketed the roof. Red bricks peeked through plaster. I counted ten windows in front, five on the first story and five on the second, each a gaping hole. A sheet of plywood sat next to the opening where a front door must've once been. The place was abandoned, remote, located off a quiet rural road, and surrounded by a natural sound barrier. From the offender's point of view, I understood the appeal.

We stepped onto the plank porch that spanned the entire length of the house. "The owner of the property is in a nursing home in Annapolis?" Haskins' notes had included this detail, but not much else. I set my scene bag next to the sheet of plywood, and both knees popped when I squatted next to it. After retrieving the digital range finder and laptop from the bag, I connected the DRF to the laptop and powered both on.

"That's right. Eddie Garrett. Special Agent Haskins sent me to conduct an initial interview with him to see if there was anything worth a follow-up by detectives."

"What's Garrett's story?" I asked, focusing on the hunting lease sign through the DRF lenses. Distance: 89.611 meters/294 feet.

"Eighty-two years old, a widower. He's the last of the Garretts, and the family has owned the house and land for three generations. He wants to have the structure demolished so more crops can be planted, but he'd have to pay a huge fine for damaging a historical building. Once you get him started, he's all piss and vinegar. Says he hasn't set foot on the property in ten years. What are you doing?"

"I'm using a range finder to determine exactly how far the house is from the road," I said as I exported the data from the binoculars-like device to the geospatial application running on the laptop. "You said he's the last of the Garretts. So, there are no relatives who might be familiar with the property?"

"Wife died about fifteen years ago. They had one son and he was KIA in Desert Storm. No other living relatives. Why do you need to know the exact distance?"

"Since the location of the road doesn't change, I can use its position for mensuration to precisely plot where the body was found."

He gave me a look like I'd just asked him to run into CVS and buy me a box of tampons. "Let me guess. I lost you at mensuration?"

"Yes, ma'am."

"Measurement. So, if it's just Garrett and he's holed up pissing and moaning in a nursing home, then who planted the corn?" Satisfied that the data was saved, I returned the devices to my bag and followed Reynolds into what had been the living room in another life.

"The Mitchells. They own the acreage across the road. Garrett leases the fields to them. Nice couple, forties, no kids. They've been trying to buy this land for years, but the old man won't sell. They don't live over there, in case you're wondering. They're in North Creek Estates, that newer subdivision on the north side of town. Brent Mitchell says he only comes out here to tend the corn and hasn't been out here in a few weeks. You can see what kind of shape the crops are in. Course, with the weather and all, I can see why he hasn't been in too big of a hurry."

Not too shabby, rookie. "What do we know about the hunters who leased the land?"

"I'm not sure. The detectives are probably following up on that."

The odors of mildew and something earthy pervaded as we

walked through the lower level of the house, which was empty save a few boards and disintegrating cardboard boxes. I tested the floor in a few places with my boot and found it generally intact. The fact that Reynolds hadn't fallen through told me enough. As he opened the screen door to the porch, I was assaulted by the lingering odor of burnt flesh. Hands fisted, I focused on breathing through my mouth. Once on the porch, I took my time scanning the property.

A field, clearly fallow for years, stretched for several acres, and a large pond sat in the middle of it. A small wooden shed that looked as old as the house fought to remain standing about twenty yards away, to the left. According to Haskins' notes, the scene techs had found nothing in the shed except small animal bones that had been there for months.

I retrieved the hand-held GPS from my bag and walked down the porch steps. Before leaving my house, I'd programmed the coordinates where the geocache had been found into the GPS. Following the GPS' guidance, I walked until I was standing on the plot of the coordinates, about two feet in front of the steps.

Based on the scene diagram Haskins had sent, I was standing within a meter of where the cache was found beneath the steps. Although I wanted to get a closer look at where the cache was placed, no one else was supposed to know about it. Reynolds was watching my every move.

I paused on the third step, directly over where the cache had been, and recorded the coordinates in the GPS. After returning the device to my bag, I took a close look at the porch and steps. At first glance, the yellow scene tape appeared to be the only sign that a young woman had been violently killed here, but I'd studied the photos and knew where to look.

Two support posts flanked the steps. I sat on the top step where the victim had been found and studied the posts until I spotted quarter-inch gouges about four feet up. I removed my cap and yanked the rubber band out of my hair, letting it fall past my shoulders. Next, I took my jacket off, faced forward, extended my arms, and grasped each of the posts just below the gouges. Short of stripping, it was the closest I could simulate the victim as she'd been found.

"Jesus Christ," Reynolds blurted behind me, and at first I thought he might've noticed the raised, pink scars covering the back of my left hand. *No, Ross, Jesus. He's reacting to you.* I was within an inch of the victim's height, with a similar build, and similar hair color.

"I spend quite a bit of time in a martial arts gym and run frequently, so I'd say I'm pretty fit and flexible. If the victim is Jennifer Abbott, she's an athlete, so let's give our girl the benefit of the doubt and say she was. The ropes tying her to the posts were taught. She had no slack. Deputy, could you come stand in front of me?"

I lowered my left arm so he could get past. He stopped two steps below the one my feet were resting on, beneath which a state police crime scene tech had discovered a cylindrical canister, the geocache probably left by the killer.

"Which step do you want me on?"

"That's fine. Just stand directly in front of me and face me, please," I instructed.

Ignoring his obvious unease, I studied his position for a moment. "There's not much you could do to me from that position. I can still kick out."

To demonstrate my point, I fully extended my right leg. My hiking boot was directly beneath his crotch. "And if I'm able to get one foot under me to support my weight, I can lift my body up, then I've got a lot more range of motion."

He nodded. "Her face—you think he did that while she was still alive?"

My gut said probably, my mouth said, "I dunno. I'm not a pathologist. But I sure as shit hope not."

"What about the brand on her chest?" he asked. "I didn't see it, but I heard Santos talking about how the son of a bitch branded her like a steer."

Reynolds was referring to an area on the victim's chest, just above the sternum, where the killer branded what looked like the letter 'A,' pointed at the top, the legs curled up, like a crude version of the University of Alabama logo. Though I doubted it, I hoped the branding occurred postmortem.

"I don't understand how someone—it just seems so personal, you know, like something she did got him worked up. Maybe like a jealous boyfriend, or… was she gay? Maybe this fucker's homophobic." He blushed. "Sorry."

Reynolds was grasping at straws, at anything to make sense out of what he'd seen. The sadistic things the killer had done to her suggested certain *proclivities,* not the result of pent-up rage or jealousy. It wasn't my job to speculate, especially with a deputy who might preach it as gospel to a reporter. It occurred to me he might interpret my silence as agreement and spew his theory to the first journalist who asked.

"No, I don't think so," I said. "It seems like a sexually motivated murder to me, but that's purely my opinion, based on what little information I have right now. I'd appreciate it if you didn't repeat it."

"Sure, but why do you say sexually motivated? Did he rape her?" he asked.

"Not that we know of, but I wouldn't necessary expect penetration. Sexual motivation often manifests in unusual or subtle ways, such as the postmortem mutilation, the bindings, the fact that he undressed her and left her nude."

"You sure talk like a profiler," he said.

"Well, I've seen *Silence of the Lambs* a half-dozen times," I deadpanned.

"He took his time, didn't he? You think he wanted to make it last a long time?" he asked.

"I do. He went to a lot of trouble, assumed a lot of risk. In the photos, there are several thin ligature marks around her neck. I think he probably tightened the ligature until she was on the verge of losing consciousness, then loosened it, letting her recover, dragging it out."

The M.E. would be able to verify that.

"So, if he left her legs free and she could kick out, maybe he strangled her from behind," Reynolds offered.

You're not here to speculate about this shit. Do your job. In and out, remember? Still, something was bothering me, and would continue to bother me until I had some idea of how this had played out. "Deputy, could you move behind me and kneel down on your knees, please?"

When Reynolds was behind me, I realized how vulnerable I would be if my arms were actually tied to the posts. My head was my only weapon, and unless my attacker's face or other sensitive area was directly behind my head, it wouldn't do me much good.

Reynolds must've come to the same conclusion. "He would've been slightly to the side."

He scooted left behind me and removed his jacket.

"You're right-handed, correct?"

"Yeah, how'd you know?"

"Watch on left wrist, firearm on right hip. And you opened the door with your right hand," I said. "Assuming she was alive when he branded her, show me how you think he did it," I instructed. "But please, don't get carried away."

As Reynolds tentatively reached over my right shoulder, I caught the faint scents of soap, starch, and cigarettes. I thrashed my head violently while keeping my arms locked in place to simulate being tied.

"Shit!" Reynolds gasped.

As intended, I'd caught him off guard.

"Do it!" I barked.

I struggled as much as possible while keeping my arms in position. To his credit, Reynolds managed to pin my head tight against his chest with his left arm. His right arm was over my shoulder, his fist turned toward my chest as if clutching a branding iron. Intent on freeing myself, I wasn't prepared when he suddenly released my head and pulled his arm back. With only imaginary restraints holding me up, I slid down his chest.

"That's it. You're nuts!" He was panting.

Breathless, I spun around to face him.

"Thank you, Deputy."

"Jesus. You've got a red mark over your eye. Must've been my watch or my nametag. You okay?" he asked.

"I'm fine. I've had much worse, believe me." His eyes darted to my hand, then quickly away.

Oh, that's nothing, buddy.

"Are all FBI agents crazy?"

"I wouldn't want to generalize. That just told us several important things. You're obviously no stranger to a weight room. Was it easy holding me still?"

"Hell no. You're small, but stronger than you look."

"Well, thanks for that."

"You fought me like hell," he said.

"She did, too. Yet, he was able to tie her to these posts, brand her, and strangle her. He knew she would fight, in fact, I think he wanted her to. He was confident he could overpower her. What does that say about him?"

"I dunno. That he had help?" Reynolds suggested.

"It's not out of the question, but for now let's work under the theory that it's one guy. What else?"

"He's a cocky bastard?" Reynolds suggested.

"Yeah, probably," I said. "What I was thinking, though, is that he's physically strong."

"Maybe she didn't put up a fight. Maybe she was unconscious."

I walked to the bottom step and gestured for Reynolds to join me. When he was standing next to me, I pointed out the bloodstains and scrapes in the center of the third and fourth steps. "See that?"

"Yeah."

I pointed to the gouges in the porch posts where the ropes had dug in. "And those?"

"Yes."

"An unconscious person didn't do that."

"No, obviously not," Reynolds said, shaking his head.

Something was bothering me and I concentrated on it.

"What're you thinking?" Reynolds asked.

"So, the more she's terrified, the more she fights. I think he gets off on that. He loses the benefit of *seeing* her terror if he's behind her."

I had Reynolds change places with me so that he was sitting on the top step with me behind him. I pretended to hold a rope at the back of his neck. The angle was totally off because of our height difference, but that wasn't what bugged me. He couldn't have been in front of her while he was strangling her. *Think, Ross.* I stood and looked around the porch, trying to make sense of it.

How could he have strangled her from the front? Could he have manipulated a rope? I couldn't see how. The rope would've had to have been extended down at an angle, and I didn't see anything a rope could've been fitted through or over to create the angle required. *You shouldn't be worrying about this. You have what you need. You were supposed to be in and out.* My eyes were scanning the ceiling anyway. Had it been any darker, I would've missed it.

I quickly retrieved a flashlight, ruler, and digital camera from my bag. The ruler went into a pocket, the camera around my neck. I shined the light on the area where I thought I'd spotted something, but I was too vertically challenged to get a good look. Reluctantly, I asked Reynolds to boost me up. He interlaced his hands and I stepped into them with my left foot. The spot I was interested in was just about in the center of the ceiling. There was nothing to hold onto. I stood slowly and had to crouch so my head didn't hit the ceiling.

"Need me to squat?" Reynolds asked.

"If you can, yeah."

"I'll be damned," I muttered, already taking pictures. I held the ruler below the holes with my left hand and clicked off several shots with my right.

"What do you see?"

"Four holes, evenly spaced, in one of the support beams. They look like screw holes."

"Okay, why are we interested in screw holes?" he asked.

I slid the ruler into my back pocket, braced myself with my free hand, and took two more photos. "I wouldn't have given them a second thought, but they were definitely drilled recently."

"So?"

I zoomed out with my thumb and clicked off another shot.

"So, Deputy, aren't you just a little curious why the hell there are fresh screw holes in the porch beam of an abandoned house?"

CHAPTER THREE

November 14

Chestertown, Maryland

39°.12'16.02"N, 76°.0'24.40W

"THE HOLES WEREN'T mentioned in Haskins' notes," I said. "No one noticed them?"

"I guess not. I was working the perimeter most of the morning." He didn't sound like he was straining in the slightest, and he was steady under me. "It's not like I was privy to everything that was going on here. What do you think they mean?"

I didn't answer, letting him connect the dots on his own.

"He wasn't behind her when he strangled her," he said.

"No, I don't think he was. I think he had a noose around her neck and fed the other end of the rope over or through whatever he attached to this ceiling. Then he stood in front of her on the steps and pulled the rope, tightening the noose, so—"

"—so he could see when she was about to lose consciousness, to know when to give the rope slack and let her recover, like you said."

"Yeah, and he could've carried on like that for a long time," I said.

"How long you been doin' this?" Reynolds asked.

"Acrobatics? First time."

"I meant—"

"I've been with the Bureau about seven years. I'm done. Thanks, you can put me down." Reynolds squatted until I could put my right foot onto the ground and step out of his hands. I thanked him and put the ruler and flashlight back into the bag.

"I can't believe you saw those tiny holes up there. All those crime scene techs went over every inch of that porch and didn't see them. Pretty impressive, Agent Ross."

"Instincts, maybe. I looked closer and I got lucky."

After pony-tailing it and putting my cap back on, I shifted my attention to the tasks I was actually there to accomplish. From the porch, I took several photos of the extended scene: field, small pond, and tree line that formed the far perimeter of the property. This took several minutes, and I flinched slightly when Reynolds broke the silence. "Mind if I smoke?"

"They're your lungs," I said, heading toward the tree line. I planned to work my way back from there to the farmhouse. Reynolds followed a few paces behind. The trees were mostly pines, spaced closely together. A thick layer of pine needles covered the ground. Fallen trees and thick brush made the woods virtually impassable. A quick study of satellite images earlier had told me that the pine copse bordered the field on three sides, separating it from other plots of land. Small creeks ran through the woods, but didn't join with any major rivers or tributaries.

Reynolds' boots on soggy ground announced his presence. I said, "A person could walk through these woods, but it would be slow going. He'd have to step over a lot of branches and weave through the trees. That's a chore in itself, but he was also dragging a terrified woman here against her will."

Beside me now, Reynolds exhaled a stream of smoke as he worked the cherry from his cigarette. When it fell, he ground it out with a boot toe and slipped the butt into his jacket pocket. "Yes, ma'am. I figure he drove the vehicle off the main road and around the house and parked in the back."

Reynolds' return to the formal "ma'am" did not go unnoticed.

"I've got what I need here. We can head back," I told him. As we started walking toward the farmhouse, I asked, "Was the plywood on the door when you arrived?"

"Yep. We took it off after the techs finished their photos so we could get through to the porch."

"Then no one could have seen anything from the road. You can't see the porch through the front windows."

"Right. And the way she was gagged, there's no way anyone could have heard her unless they were really close."

He was referring to the fact that the killer had gagged the victim with her own panties, which had still been in her mouth when he torched her face. If that hadn't been enough to muffle her screams, the corn would've provided a natural buffer. She was killed at least forty-eight hours prior to the opening of hunting season. No one had any reason to be near the farmhouse. Perfect time and place to torture and strangle someone to death.

We walked in silence, and I kept my head down so the rain flowed away from my face. When we reached the porch, Reynolds asked, "You think he installed whatever those screws were holding up there when he brought her out here or before?"

My gut said he watched the farm for a while, made sure no one else was using the property. Once he decided it was a suitable kill site, he purchased the items he would need to rig a pulley and cable, or he had them already. He would've tested the rig. Though informed by facts and experience, it was still speculation. Cops talk. There was a decent chance the inexperienced deputy would want to impress his buddies with insider information. I was concerned my preliminary thoughts about M.O. would become "the Feds' theory."

"What do you think, Deputy?" I asked, opting for redirection.

"Before. He's too careful to leave anything to chance."

I nodded. "Well, I think I've gotten everything I'm going to from this place. I appreciate you meeting me out here." He grasped my offered hand.

"My pleasure, ma'am."

"I thought we were past ma'am."

His smile was quick. "Sure. Sorry. I just thought maybe I had overplayed my hand. Didn't want you to think I was unprofessional."

A crimson blush spread across Reynolds' cheeks, and I laughed before I could help myself. "I assure you, I think you're perfectly professional."

He was smiling. "Well, that's good. But could you do me one favor?"

"What's that?" I asked, a little annoyed that Reynolds was still holding my hand.

"The next time you ask me to wrestle, at least let me buy you dinner first."

Heat spread across my cheeks. Certain my ears were about to spontaneously combust, I quickly reclaimed my hand.

Reynolds caught me off guard. "It was hard, you know."

Yeah, buddy, not exactly comfortable for me either.

When Reynolds continued, I realized I'd misinterpreted his comment. Again. "Seeing her like that, I just wanted to cut her down and cover her up. Give her dignity back, you know? I've got a sister. Christ."

I thought of Lanie, as I inevitably do at crime scenes. I tried to stay detached, to keep family and work separate, but, just like now, someone would say something, or there would be some little detail that reminded me of my niece or my sister. I practically forced Reynolds to go there, relive it. Shit.

I pulled my credentials wallet from my back pocket, removed

a business card, and handed it to him. "My desk and cell numbers are on here. If you come up with something and can't reach Special Agent Haskins, give me a call. I'll make sure he gets it. One more thing. Don't mention anything we've discussed with anyone, especially the media. Details like the screw holes and what they might mean absolutely can't get out. Understand?"

"Sure. Okay."

We walked back to our vehicles in silence. As I watched his cruiser pull away, I had so many questions. I was considering my next steps when my phone vibrated on my hip.

"Ross."

Her voice was a rush of breath. Dr. Erin Ross, cardio thoracic surgeon with nerves of steel, couldn't put two coherent sentences together. Only one thing could bring my sister to that level of panic. *Lanie.*

CHAPTER FOUR

November 14

1:12 p.m.

Triangle, Virginia

*38°32'40.87"N, 77°19'32.87"*W

L *ANIE IS FINE. She's camped out at the library studying. She'd gone to a party, crashed on someone's couch. Dead phone, no char-ger.* Plausible, maybe, but obvious bullshit to anyone who knew my niece. Elane Ross didn't go to parties, and she sure as hell wouldn't spend the night away from her dorm without telling someone.

"Small green star tattoo on the inside of her left wrist," I recited into the phone to the ER nurse as I rolled through a stop sign. I added, "She has an eyebrow piercing and a half-inch scar above it."

"Left or right?"

"Left, same as mine. The scar, not the tattoo," I told her, but it was too late. Clearly, I'd managed to confuse the hell out of her.

"Hair?" she asked.

"Auburn, shoulder length."

"Build?"

"Petite," I said. "Five-two, a hundred and fifteen pounds."

She would let us know, let *me* know, at least, if she was in trouble. Why hadn't she left a message? Oh, but she had. *Call me ASAP. Aunt Regan, where R U?*

"No, ma'am, I'm sorry. No one matching that description has been admitted." ER number four was a strikeout.

According to Johns Hopkins campus security, my niece's roommate hadn't seen her since Thursday. Erin had finally calmed down enough to tell me she'd last spoken to Lanie on Wednesday. Aunt Tabitha received a Facebook message from her over a week ago, but she hadn't talked to Lanie in three weeks. When her roommate talked to her Thursday morning, Lanie had seemed fine. All calls to her cellphone were going straight to voice mail. She either couldn't answer her phone or didn't want to, and she'd been a no-show for a biology exam.

I'd instructed Erin to file a missing person report with the Baltimore PD. My plan was to email my notes to Haskins, drop Stella off next door with Mrs. Radzimoski, and head to my sister's. Driving on autopilot and thinking about tortured, petite, athletic girls, I clipped the curb pulling into my driveway. I practically fell out of the Tahoe, managing to catch my bag before it crashed to the concrete.

Several stimuli registered at once—light from the kitchen, anomalous aroma, and voices. Moving on pure instinct, back to the wall, I drew my firearm and aimed toward the sounds and motion to my left. My security alarm should have been echoing the claxon blaring in my head. Had Vincent not armed it? My mind finally processed—voices from the TV, something tomato-based simmering in the kitchen, water boiling, and finally, a familiar voice. "Shit! Aunt Regan, it's me!"

Her hair threw me off, and it took me a moment to realize the young woman in the sights of my .40 caliber pistol was my niece, whole, unharmed, startled, hands in the don't-shoot position.

"Jesus Christ, Lanie!" I blurted, holstering the Glock. We

Rosses were not huggers, but I made an exception. My niece had always been fit and athletic, but this was something new. She was all hard lines and angles. Well, maybe some of that was me.

"Where the hell have you been?" Ignoring the smell of cigarette smoke lingering in her recently dyed hair, I pulled back and conducted a quick inventory. Short, black hair, cut asymmetrically, longer in the front and obscuring her right eye. The steel bar piercing her left eyebrow wasn't new, but the small silver stud through the cleft below her bottom lip was. She was wearing a *Siouxsie and the Banshees* tee, identifiable as mine by the ripped collar. The shirt had sentimental value, and I would've remembered giving it to her. If she'd been raiding my drawers, she obviously wasn't trying to hide it. There were bigger fish to fry.

"You wanna tell me what you're doing here?" I'd given her a key when we moved her on campus in case she wanted to get away for the weekend to study or decompress, but I couldn't imagine what had possessed my normally level-headed niece to skip her exams and go incommunicado for two days.

"You know you're welcome here, but shit, Lanie, you've got to let someone know where you are. Your mother is worried sick."

"Please hear me out. Two minutes, then you can call her," she pleaded.

"No, *you* will call her. Water's boiling. What is that, *spaghetti*?" How the hell had she found the required ingredients in my kitchen?

"Rotini, canned tomatoes, and ketchup. I improvised."

As I followed her to the stove, where she added petrified spirals to the pot, I noticed a Post-it stuck to the keypad next to the garage door, *CALL ME* scrawled in black marker. *Vincent.*

"You've got until the pasta is done, then you're calling your mother," I informed her. "Start with where you've been and why the hell you weren't answering your phone."

"My phone was charging and I was busy. How was I supposed to know Mom would lose her shit the second I didn't return her call? And you're one to talk about not answering phones. I sent you like a thousand texts this morning. Where have you been? I thought you might still be in Washington," she said, as she searched my cabinets. *Shitty aunt card. Well played, kid.*

"I got back yesterday. I've been in Ass Neck, Maryland, all morning. What are you looking for?"

"Spices."

"Pantry. Rack on the left."

She was bitching under her breath, something about Mother Hubbard's cupboard, and I'd had about enough of her blowing off the fact that she'd sent her mother and—by extension me—into a panic.

"Look. Salt, pepper, garlic, and chili powder. You want more than that, you can go stay with Rachel Ray. You missed your bio exam, Lanie. What the hell's going on?"

"I dis-enrolled." She sounded so casual as she added garlic to her improvised marinara I thought I might've misheard.

"You did what?"

"I'm not going back, Aunt Regan. And before you freak out, just hear me out, okay? I have plenty of time for college, and there are other things I want to do first or I'll never get the chance."

Be cool. "What *things*?"

"Travel, for one. And before you say something like, that's what summers are for, I'm not talking about boozing it up in Cancun over spring break. I mean *really* travel, learn a language, serve."

"You sound like a Peace Corps brochure. Just stop for a god-damn minute and tell me where this is coming from."

Conveniently, the pasta was done. She dumped it into a colander, her back to me. "I joined the Army."

"You did wh—"

"I enlisted."

Don't be reactionary. Don't be impulsive. She'd come to me, not her mother. She had her reasons, most of which I understood.

Several things I might say came to mind, but they all seemed, well, reactionary and impulsive. Finally, I skipped past everything Erin would say and settled on pragmatism. "Have you signed a contract?"

"Well, that's the tricky part. The contract won't be valid until I swear in. And I can't, yet."

Of course. She wouldn't turn eighteen until January and couldn't enlist without—

"You're a minor. You need Erin's formal consent."

She was facing me, hands behind her, gripping the edge of the counter. "If she'll sign, I can swear in on Monday."

Young. So goddamned young. My instinct was to oppose anything that could possibly put her in harm's way. I thought about Jennifer Abbott, snatched from a small college campus, and realized I didn't know what *safe* meant anymore or if there was such a thing. Lanie came to me because she needed me to convince Erin to permit her only child to give up an academic scholarship and join the Army. That was never going to fucking happen, whether I got involved or not. Lanie shifted her weight from one foot to the other, gnawed at a nail that was already chewed to the quick.

"Stop that," I said. "So, let me get this straight. Your plan was to drop out of school, ship off to boot camp, and just, what, send us a shitty post card?"

"Of course not. That's why I'm here. I thought we could hang—"

"No, Lanie. You came here looking for an ally. Your mother just filed a missing person report! Jesus Christ, selfish much?"

"Yes, damnit! For once in my life. My God, I've practically been pre-med since kindergarten."

"That's bullshit and you know it. Hoping you'd choose Hopkins and forcing you are completely different."

It dawned on me that I hadn't seen a car outside and had no

idea how Lanie had gotten to my house from Baltimore. I voiced my confusion.

"I sold the Camry. Ren drove me down. She's heading home for the weekend and it was sort of on her way."

"Who's Ren?"

"Um, my roommate, Ren Saito. Dementia much? You met her when you helped me move into the dorm, remember?"

Right. I wondered if, *hoped*, the Asian girl with the spiky blue hair and prolific tats was the smoker, but the car issue seemed more pressing. "Why in God's name would you sell your car?"

"It's not like I'm going to need to drive for a while. Once Mom finds out she'll cut me off, and I needed the cash."

I suspected selling the car was a half-baked effort to demonstrate her level of commitment. I let it go. Lanie carried her hobo lunch to my living room. I followed.

"That's ridiculous. Your mother isn't going to cut you off." *Unless she thinks it'll keep your ass in school.*

"Oh, come on, Aunt Regan. You know she envisioned a fucking surgical legacy the day she abandoned me for med school." She sat cross-legged on my sofa and blew on her food.

"Stop being so melodramatic. You know she didn't abandon you. And watch your language." The look-who's-talking eye roll was admittedly deserved, but it didn't mean I had to appreciate it.

"Really? What would you call it? She might as well have dropped me off at the circus."

"You may have a point about Aunt Tab," I admitted. We both smiled. Erin, Aunt Tab, and I were a sorry excuse for the perfect nuclear family. Somehow, despite the trifecta of parental incompetence, Lanie had somehow grown into a smart, well-adjusted kid bound for a top-tier university. Or so we thought.

"Lanie, you've worked so hard for Hopkins," I said, sitting next to her. "You've wanted this for so long."

"No, *she's* wanted it. When has she ever asked what I want?"

"The Army, Lanie? *Really?*"

"It was good enough for you."

"You have options that I didn't."

"That's bullshit. Mom told me you were offered soccer scholarships, a full ride to UNC. You *chose* the Army."

It was true. "This will kill Erin."

"Why is it always about *her*? Do *you* even care what I want?"

"Yes, Lanie, I'm just trying to understand where all this is coming from."

Of course. All the questions last spring about FBI qualification requirements. Physical fitness, diverse skill sets, military experience, foreign language, law, accounting, cybersecurity—hell, I'd practically rattled off a Bureau pamphlet on ideal candidacy. The running, the advanced French classes over the summer, it all made sense. She'd obviously keyed in on the military experience, the path I'd taken, intentional or not. Erin would never forgive me.

"What MOS are you guaranteed in your contract?"

"Thirty-five Papa."

Thirty-five. Military Intelligence.

I said, "My knowledge of enlisted occupational specialties is limited. What—"

"Cryptologic Linguist."

Sergeant Tim Andrews, Arabic linguist. Twenty-two years old, second week in country. Having to write that letter to his parents… Christ. No.

I wasn't aware of having gotten up, but I was standing.

"Aunt Regan?"

Linguist? Well, fluency in French and four years of Latin, which Erin had suggested would give her a leg up in med school, probably hadn't hurt her.

"This is a four-year commitment, Lane. Are you sure about this?"

"Six years, actually. And I'm totally sure."

Six years. She had no idea what she was getting into. For a moment, I seriously considered dropping trou and showing her the worst of it, not to scare her, well, okay, yes, if that's what it took. I wasn't above shocking her back to reality. Maybe seeing proof of how skilled hands put me back together graft by graft would inspire her to reconsider that *fucking surgical legacy,* but I knew what my niece was like once she made up her mind. Lanie wouldn't listen to me any more than I would have at her age, because at seventeen you're bulletproof until proven otherwise.

She'd been watching TV before I'd gotten home, and her attention was on the projector screen. A local news anchor was giving an update on the Eastern Shore murder.

A grisly scene early this morning in Kent County, Maryland where hunters discovered the nude body of a young woman, whom the Office of the Chief Medical Examiner of Maryland has just identified as Jennifer Abbott. The Washington College freshman had been missing since late Sunday night…

"Ren's cousin goes to Washington College. I wonder if she knows—shit, that's where you were this morning, isn't it? You were at that crime scene. That's why you didn't call me back."

I nodded.

"She was murdered?"

"You know I can't—"

"I know. Active investigation, blah, blah, blah."

"You got it," I said, unclipping my phone from my belt and handing it to her. "Time's up. Call your mother. Make sure you tell her to call Baltimore PD and campus security and let them know you're safe." I headed to the kitchen, making it clear she was on her own, but I eavesdropped while searching bare cabinets for an energy bar. The conversation was short and mostly one-sided, and I imagined a lot of jaw clenching and eye-rolling on Lanie's end. She ended the call with a defeated "*Fine.*"

"She's on her way."

"What, *here?*" I'd been reaching for a Diet Coke, suddenly wanted two fingers of Bushmills, but settled for an Amstel Light.

"Yep. The surgeon has cleared her schedule. Prepare for Armageddon." Lanie was clicking through channels while I tried to come up with something to change Erin's mind. Nothing. Shit. I put the beer back and grabbed two waters, which I carried to my bedroom and tossed into my gym bag. From the closet, I heard Lanie fall onto my bed. "Your food is getting cold," I told her, adding my Nikes to the bag.

"That's what microwaves are for."

"If your mother agrees to sign, and that's a big if, when would you report?" Two of my drawers hadn't been closed completely, evidence of Lanie's pilfering.

"In ten days. Can I stay here? *Please,* Aunt Regan."

"You can stay through the weekend. After that, you can either go back to school or stay with your mother, depending on what Erin decides. If you're leaving in ten days, you should spend that time with her."

"God, *fine.*" Teen-speak for: this sucks, you suck, life sucks.

"Move the boxes out of your way in the guest room. There are clean sheets in the linen closet. I probably won't be around much the next couple of days, I'm sorry."

"It's okay."

"And you've seen how little food there is. You need any money?"

"No, I sold the car, remember? I'm flush with cash."

"You're going to put most of that into the safe while you're here. I don't want you getting mugged or heading to Atlantic City."

"Very funny."

"Take the Jeep if you need to go out. It's gassed up and the keys are on the hook. Stay out of the garage and don't touch my beer," I instructed.

"I wouldn't dream of drinking your beer, Aunt Regan," she assured me. She wouldn't, and despite her fascination with the vehicles parked in my garage, she didn't know that particular alarm code and couldn't open the door without dispatching the cavalry. Still, it was the obligatory aunt thing to say.

"I want you to check on Mrs. Radzimoski next door. See if she needs groceries or a ride anywhere. Knock on the garage door, she won't answer the front. She'll probably think you're me, and if she does, she'll give you hell about this goth look you have going on."

"*Goth*? Jesus."

"Goth, punk, emo, whatever you kids are calling it these days." She snorted. "You sound like Mom."

"Whatever. My point is, you should just roll with it and not try to explain it. And FYI, there are about five years' worth of delivery meal containers stacked in her garage. Be careful of them. She gets upset if they're disturbed."

"Hoarder with Alzheimer's. Got it. Aunt Regan, if Mom signs, will you be there for my swearing-in Monday?"

"If you manage to get Erin to even consider this, I want you to do some serious soul searching over the weekend. Then, if you still want to do this on Monday, we'll talk. By the way, does Ren smoke?"

"Yeah, why?"

"Do *you*?"

"Ew! No! I borrowed one of your shirts because all my shit smells like an ashtray from being in the car with her."

She was telling the truth. Some people could get their heart into a lie. I'd seen some people, both suspects and cops, sell a lie better than the truth. My niece was not one of those people. She was an honest, conscientious, heart-on-her-sleeve kind of girl, and iron-willed like her mother. There was a stellar twenty-year Army career waiting for her, if that's what she wanted. Sure, it would be easy enough to take Erin's side, but it would be a lie; a sellable lie, but a lie all the same. If this was what Lanie truly wanted, who was I to stop her? Hell, a big part of me envied her.

Lanie was watching me in that intense way that had always scared me a little. "Right. Well, you might want to shower and wash your hair before your mom gets here. She might jump to conclusions."

"*Might?*" She snorted. "She'll totally lose her shit. You know she has no chill. Where are you going?"

"To work."

"It's Saturday."

"Yep."

"And you're packing your gym bag."

"I'll probably stop at Chang's on my way home."

Her eyes were wide. "You're leaving me here alone to deal with her?"

"Oh, you bet your ass."

CHAPTER FIVE

November 14

4:25 p.m.

Quantico, Virginia

38°31'34.94", 77°26'52.65"W

’D GOTTEN TWO hours and eighteen minutes of peace before my sister arrived at my house, heard the word *Army*, discovered my absence, and lost her shit because, apparently, somehow this was entirely my fault. "You didn't need to drive down here, Erin, really."

The offices of the Behavioral Analysis Unit—the BAU for short—were practically empty. Preferring a cave-like habitat, I'd cut the lights, shut the office door, and put Erin on speaker. Satellite images of eastern Maryland filled the two 27-inch monitors on my desk. I added a red dot at the coordinates where Jennifer Abbott's body had been found, then inserted a green dot where her car had been parked near the swim center, where we believed she'd been abducted.

Haskins was working with AT&T to obtain Abbott's cellphone records. Based on cell tower hits, the Bureau techies would attempt to determine where she'd been when she made her last calls. Her killer had removed the battery at some point and placed it in the cache, but when? If he hadn't taken it out of the phone right away, it might be possible to use cell tower hits to track her movements after she'd been abducted. Doubtful. The whole point of the cache was to prove he was at least one step ahead of us.

"It's under control, Erin."

"It most certainly is not. You obviously didn't talk any sense into her. The Army? I should've known." My sister's normally subdued Scottish accent functioned as a linguistic barometer, ratcheting up when she was excited, angry, or inebriated. A high-pressure system was definitely moving in.

"What's that supposed to mean?" The mouse took the brunt of my annoyance as I forcefully clicked on an overlay, highlighting the waterways within fifty miles of the Garrett Farm.

"She's following right in your goddamn footsteps. First it was the karate, now—"

"Hapkido. If you're going to blame me for something, at least be accurate. Just take a breath, E. It's not like she's dropping out to join a cult or deal meth. She wants to serve her country."

"I'm not sure she hasn't joined a cult. Have you seen her hair and this thing through her lip? At the very least, she'll end up with a scar, if not paresthesia, rejection, implantation, hepatitis—"

"It's a labret piercing, Erin, not a liver transplant. I had one when I was a teenager."

"Predictably, that's almost exactly what Lanie said. She needs to get her arse back to Hopkins."

"Maybe what she needs is to figure out what *she* wants," I suggested, clicking an icon. The roadways near the Garrett Farm were highlighted in electric blue. The closest major road was MD-213, a two-lane highway that ran through Chestertown and bisected the Washington College campus. Most likely, the killer would've taken 213 to MD-544—the road the Garrett Farm was on, but where had he taken her between the red dot and the green dot? These were rural roads, suggesting he was either a local or as comfortable as one.

I heard my refrigerator door open and imagined Erin's reaction at seeing my meager food stock. "She's seventeen, for Christ's sake. She doesn't know what she wants. She doesn't have to declare a major yet, but she needs to stay in school, not run off and play war."

"Is that what I was doing, Erin, *playing war?*" My voice was surprisingly neutral. Erin's not so much.

"I wouldn't know what you were doing, Regan. You cut me out, remember? Both of us, actually, but you wouldn't know it from the way Lanie kept right on wanting to be just like her hero aunt. When you were over there, do you know she wrote you countless letters that she never bothered to mail? She would set her alarm every goddamn morning for four thirty so she could check to see if you'd sent an email. When you had, she'd print it, read it at the table between mouthfuls of fucking Fruit Loops. She still has them, you know, took them with her to Hopkins, all neatly organized in a scrapbook. She just…"

Her voice trailed off, and for a moment I wasn't sure if she was still on the line.

"And then out of the blue, you called her on her birthday, those goddamned rockets, or mortars, or whatever in the background. Remember what you told her?"

My heart was in my throat.

"Fireworks. Not the shit from the roadside stands, but the big aerials all the way from China, you told her, special ordered for her birthday. It was all she talked about for weeks. You always knew what to say to her, Regan. Tell me, though, what should I have said to her when the letters and emails stopped coming, when she sulked and wouldn't eat, didn't want to leave her room?"

"Erin—"

"Her happiness has always been tied up in you, Regan, even

when you were breaking our hearts. She orbits you like you're the goddamn sun."

"The only thing she's ever wanted is a normal family. She wanted her mother. She wanted *you*, Erin. Instead, she got a teenager and a flake who fucked up her upbringing six ways to Sunday with our surrogate bullshit until you were ready to be a parent."

"Fuck off, Regan." Our typical argument ender, when a major nerve had been struck. There was no real fire in it. She sounded tired, mostly.

"Can we not do this now? I'll be home in a couple of hours. I'll pick up dinner," I suggested.

"Fine. If you can manage to find something with vegetables, that would be brilliant. Nothing fried. God knows what you two have been eating," she remarked, as if Lanie and I had been holed up in a crack house. A few replies came to mind, but she hung up before I could really put my foot into it.

Vegetables? I was at a loss. Louie, the bistro guy, would be shocked when I ordered something besides pizza and asked about vegetarian fare. I was searching for bistro coupons in my inbox when I noticed an email from mspears@CapitalHerald.com. That got my attention. A few years of silence had left me with the impression that the woman had finally taken the hint. An excellent example of why one should never assume. I should've deleted it. I knew better. Monica Spears was nothing but trouble.

Special Agent Ross,

You've been quite elusive! I must say, I'm not surprised you ended up at the FBI given your counterterrorism background and military heroics. You've been reluctant to speak to me in the past about your experience in Iraq, and I respect your wishes. I'm producing a documentary about Lockerbie and want to give you the opportunity to discuss it, in light of

Abdelbaset al-Megrahi's death in Libya. I can ensure your anonymity if you prefer. I'd love to speak to your sister as well. Please reply at your earliest convenience to arrange an interview.

Regards,

Monica Spears

P.S. - I trust you received the package.

What package? Why was Monica Fucking Spears suddenly interested in al-Megrahi? He'd been dead for three years. Scowling, I read it again. After the third time, I was still bewildered. My history of interview dodging with Monica Spears began the day I was discharged from the Army when one of her contacts at the Pentagon had tipped her off that a general was to present a female Army captain with a particularly distinguished medal at Brooks Army Medical Center.

I hadn't been thrilled about the distinction to begin with, and the last thing I'd wanted was to see it all over the papers. After my discharge, various journalists followed me from Texas to Virginia in an attempt to get the "real story" of what had happened in Iraq. The official, highly classified version was on file somewhere in the bowels of the Pentagon. Lacking the requisite "clearance and need-to-know," believing me to be the only survivor, and unsatisfied with the Army's watered-down press release, reporters and journalists hounded me for details.

Producers from CNN, Fox News—hell, even Oprah's reps— had flooded my phone with calls. I'd been careful. Monica Spears, a reporter with a practically unheard of D.C. paper, managed to get my personal phone number, forcing me to change it. Was it starting all over again, another media frenzy? If Spears had found out I was involved in the Abbott case... Hell, maybe Lockerbie was just a ploy to get me to talk. Package? What the hell? Had she mailed something to my house?

I hit reply and furiously typed:

Ms. Spears,

I appreciate your interest but, as always, I have nothing to say to you about al-Megrahi, Lockerbie, or anything else. I'm sure my sister feels the same. Do not contact us again.

R. Ross

I sent the email, praying M.F. Spears would crawl back under her rock. My phone chimed. A text from Lanie: *Plz come home. Mom is on the warpath. Need backup.*

I replied: *Sorry, kid. Busy. For now u r on a solo mission. Army of One. Hooah!*

I'd gotten a lot done: typed my notes from the scene; emailed photos to Haskins; and transferred data to the GIS software. The whiteboard that took up almost an entire wall of my office was covered with diagrams, photos, and notes. I'd also been listening to media coverage.

There was nothing new to report, so talking heads were crawling out of the woodwork like roaches, eager to speculate. They kept replaying a montage of Abbott photos—her high school yearbook picture, a family portrait that might've been on a Christmas card, a shot of her Washington College relay swim team. It was depressing. In need of distraction, I called Vincent Tomaro.

"Hey, Ross." He sounded like he was in a wind tunnel. Either he had me on speaker or he was using a shitty Bluetooth earpiece. Knowing Vincent, it was the former. Vincent didn't do shitty when it came to technology. "The horse hair was unexpected."

What the hell?

"I mean, I knew the car was historically accurate, but shit. The foam padding should add a level of protection and keep the module away from the metal frame."

"What the fuck did you do to my Porsche, Vincent?" My blood pressure jumped toward a hazardous level.

"Before you go ballistic on me, let me just say that with such a limited number of '57 356s, especially as cherry as yours, if it's stolen, there's going to be incentive to move it out of the country quickly. If that happens, you're fucked."

"Vincent, seriously, what did you do?" I hated surprises, especially when they had something to do with my car. "Those are three-thousand-dollar seats. *Each*."

"Jesus."

"If you fucked up the leather and I have to replace—"

"One of these days, you're going to tell me how you can afford a car like that on civil servant pay."

"Legally and ethically, I assure you. What kind of *module* did you put in my car and why? I swear, Vincent, if you—"

"Give me some credit, I went in through the seam. You won't even notice."

"Now you're a professional upholsterer?"

"I have many skills, Ross. It's not the first time I've hidden something in a seat."

As tempting as it was to go there, I decided to leave that one alone. "You were just supposed to upgrade the sensors in the garage and install cameras. What are you up to?"

"A combination DR-GPS, micro, I'm talking nineteen by nineteen millimeters," he informed me. "Not much bigger than a postage stamp, with global positioning."

"A tracking device."

"*The* most advanced tracking device on the market," he added. *Black market, probably.*

"You said DR-GPS. Dead reckoning?" I asked.

His enthusiasm was evident. "Kick-ass dead reckoning. I've been road testing this baby on one of my company vehicles for a couple of months. Virginia Beach tunnel, Shenandoah, Skyline Drive, spots where GPS tends to get flaky—that's where the DR kicks in and estimates, I mean accurately estimates, position based on heading and distance traveled since last known position."

"DR is great as long as heading and speed are constant, but that's rarely—"

"Right, accuracy is dependent on correct speed, time, and heading inputs. The GPS has on-board gyro that continuously calibrates based on data input from the vehicle's sensors. Refresh rate is twenty-five nanoseconds, which is unheard of. It's accurate as hell," he assured me.

"Sounds expensive as hell. I didn't sign up for this."

"Eh, don't worry about that, Ross. Consider it research and development for Tomaro Security, Inc."

"Okay," I said. "So, the car gets stolen. How is it tracked?"

"Positioning data is displayed on a website, which I maintain," he explained. "Access to the data is completely secure, only you and I can see it. You can access real-time positioning data on your smart-phone, too."

"Yeah, Vincent, it all sounds great, but a serious car jacker can find your tiny, expensive tracker in less than five minutes with a three-hundred-dollar off-the-shelf scanner."

"Are you really playing stump-the-chump with me, Ross? Scanners work by detecting RF wave emission during transmission. The beauty of this device is that I'm able to program it to only transmit when the car is in motion. These guys won't be running a scanner over the car while they're driving it. The device can also be manually activated and deactivated remotely, using a four-digit code."

"I'm not sure I like the idea of being tracked while I'm driving the car," I said, though those occasions were few and far between.

"Just so you know, Ross, I've got better things to do than play Big Brother while you're out on a joy ride."

"How'd you manage to get this thing anyway?" I asked. "You didn't just run down to the spy shop."

"Shit, no. This baby is manufactured by a Czech firm whose primary consumer is the People's Republic of China. I managed to get four of them. The other three are on company vehicles, and it took some extensive retrofitting and programming to make them secure, plus custom waterproofing."

"I'm curious how you managed to get your hot little hands on them, but in the interest of plausible deniability, it's probably best I don't know."

"You have nothing to worry about," he assured me. "No illegal activity involved, at least on my end. I can't vouch for my Aussie supplier."

"As long as my Carrera is still pristine. So, I haven't had a chance to play around with the DVR, but it looks like you got all the cameras in. Any issues?"

"Nope, interior and exterior of the house, motion activated. You're covered. You can set the DVR parameters for how long you want the files to save. The software is intuitive, but if you have any questions just let me know."

I thanked him and ended the call, feeling a little better about being able to monitor my nocturnal activity. Vincent had me thinking about GPS technology, and I spent the next couple of hours immersed in Haskins' initial field notes and Interweb Geeklandia. After perusing several geocaching sites, I settled on the one where the killer—username Cacher in the Rye—had chosen to leave clues and coordinates for the caches he left at the Garrett Farm. Geocacher KMC67 left a comment about the cache at *39.121602 -76.0244*, or thereabouts: *Private property? Not cool.* Three other cachers concurred. Nasty weather, prospect of hunters on the property, and No Trespassing signs explained why no one had bothered to look for the cache.

My rumbling stomach informed me the energy bar I'd scarfed at noon had long since burned off. I decided to put in a little gym time, pick up some dinner, head home, and face the rest of my rapidly deteriorating weekend.

CHAPTER SIX

November 14

6:40 p.m.

Triangle, Virginia

38°32'40.87"N, 77°19'32.87"W

"THERE ARE LOADS of vegetables on here! Look, I even got extra mushrooms, onions, and green peppers."

"Mushrooms are a fungus, Regan," my sister pointed out.

"Onions are bulbs," Lanie added.

Erin with the coup de grâce, "And bell peppers are the fruit of the capsicum plant."

"You two smart asses can suck it," I said, emptying the bags, producing a large garden salad, quart of minestrone soup, a six-pack, and a bottle of merlot. "I got one of every dressing they had because I didn't know what you'd want. I'm pretty sure there are vegetables in the soup, but you'll probably classify them as herbs, or weeds, or roots or something, and I'm sure you're gonna bitch that the crust isn't whole grain. Here," I said, sliding Erin a Sam Adams. "Wheat and barley."

Lanie informed us she wasn't hungry and would rather go for a run. Erin gave me the is-it-safe look.

I shook my head. "Treadmill. It's dark."

Lanie sighed dramatically, but seemed to remember what she'd been watching on the news earlier. She headed toward my guest room, leaving Erin and me alone. We transferred the food, beer, and wine to the table. Erin heaped salad onto her plate and conservatively added some no-calorie, no-flavor vinaigrette while I rid my pizza of fruit, bulbs, and fungi. Just as I was about to take a bite, Erin blind-sided me. "You've lost weight. Will you tell me why?"

"I've been busy, traveling a lot."

"That's nothing new. Are you eating and sleeping?" she asked, absently poking the tomatoes in her salad.

Annoyed with the line of questioning, I said, "I thought you were here to talk about Lanie."

Erin placed her fork on the table, and gingerly straightened it, as if it was a scalpel on a surgical tray. "Right. God forbid we talk about you."

She wouldn't meet my eyes. "I don't think I can do this." I wasn't sure if she was referring to me or Lanie.

"You just need to breathe. The vein in your forehead is doing that thing." I poured her a generous serving of wine and slid it toward her, earning a quiet, "Thank you." I reclaimed the beer and took a long pull, wondering what specific thing would be stuck in her craw next. I didn't have to wait long.

"Her hair. My God, she looks like one of those *Twilight* vampires."

"Not really. I'm pretty sure the Cullens have reddish hair, closer to her natural color." At least, for the moment, we weren't talking about me.

"She's thin and pale, too. There seems to be a lot of that going around." She shot me a look over the rim of her wine glass.

Of course she wouldn't let me off the hook that easily. "It's not exactly beach season."

Her next point of contention was Lanie's piercings, which,

from where I was sitting, should've been the least of our worries. "They're temporary, Erin," I pointed out. "If she goes through with this, she'll have to take them out soon enough."

"They're going to scar."

"Really? That's what you're worried about?"

"You know what I'm worried about."

"I do. But I think you have to let her do this because she's going to turn eighteen in a couple of months, and you know what? She's going to do it anyway. The only thing you can really control is how you spend the days before she leaves. She'll be an angry, sulking nightmare if you don't sign the consent form."

"I just don't understand why she's doing this now."

"Not once have you ever stopped to consider what she wants for her future or that there are other options. And there are, Erin. Lanie's future doesn't have to fit into your neat vision of what it should be."

"I never forced her into pursuing medicine."

"You've never encouraged any alternatives either. Medicine and the military are not mutually exclusive, Erin."

"I'll be damned if my only child is going to enlist in the Army!"

"Why? Is the Army not good enough? Christ, am I that big of a disappointment?"

"Yes! No! I've never been *disappointed*, Regan."

"Then *what?*"

"Terrified. Every minute of every day. You almost died, and *years* later, I still don't know how or why. Why do you insist on shutting me out?"

"I'm not. Shit, Erin, we're talking about Lanie. I'm not the crisis." I'd never been *her* crisis. Why couldn't she see that?

"Do you know how hard it was for me to gain her trust, to show her that I was ready to be her mother? How relieved I was that she decided to stay close to home for undergrad?"

"Yes, I know."

"I can't lose her, Regan. I can't."

"The only way you'll lose her is if you don't let her go. Jesus, that sounds like the chorus of a shitty country song. I'm trying to say I think maybe you have to let her do this, Erin. And whether she sticks it out or decides it was a mistake, when reality sets in, she's going to need you."

I'd started on my second Sam Adams and was taking my third bite of barren pizza when my phone vibrated.

"I'm sorry," I said. "I need to take this."

* * *

I'd been more than ready to bust Haskins' balls for making me wait, but he sounded exhausted. I cut him a break.

"The victim's ID is all over the news."

"No shit. I just got off the phone with the deputy director. He not-so-subtly hinted that if we don't close this case quickly, I'll be lucky to land a mall security job."

"We'd better come through, then. I'm not sure they'd let you wear your crazy-ass socks with your security guard uniform," I teased.

Haskins' wardrobe was a study in utilitarianism. I was amazed the first time I peeked into his closet. It contained several identical, beautifully tailored, black Hugo Boss suits and ten or so starched white shirts hanging next to the suits. He owned a dozen ties, all black. His rationale was that it saved him the trouble of picking out his clothes. He made up for the lack of variety in his attire with his seemingly infinite supply of novelty socks, featuring everything from Tabasco bottles to Yosemite Sam.

"The only good news is that the Kent County Sheriff's Office and MSP are cooperating and providing all available resources. The bad news is that every time I turn around someone is hounding my ass for a status report."

"At least you have your Girl Friday. Lucky me. Reynolds said Eberley was with you."

"Unfortunately."

Special Agent David Eberley, the Special Agent in Charge, or SAC, of the Baltimore Field Office made quite an impression on me during the Sanchez case. His tenure in the BAU ended abruptly under mysterious circumstances. According to the rumor mill, it had something to do with a beef with Supervisory Special Agent Harry Spielman, my direct supervisor. Word was, their feud reached boiling point right about the time Spielman and his wife filed for divorce. The biggest mystery was how someone hadn't kicked Eberley's sorry ass off the Bureau career ladder.

"Reynolds referred to you as the lead agent this morning. That means Eberley is letting you run the investigation?"

"Of course. That way, if this thing goes south, he can blame me. On the other hand, if we catch the guy, he can take all the credit. It's a win-win for him and a cluster fuck for me. Oh, and you're gonna love this—Eberley is convinced we're dealing with either a hate crime or an opportunistic lust killing."

"You're shitting me. What in God's name would make him think this is a bias-motivated crime? As far as I know she's straight, white, and Christian. Statistically, her killer probably is, too. Is there any evidence she was gay?"

"None. In fact, by all accounts she and her boyfriend have been hot and heavy since early summer."

"And this murder wasn't opportunistic. She was targeted. She didn't just happen to wander into his hunting area. It goes without saying, but I'm going to anyway, Eberley likes to hear himself talk."

"You're preaching to the choir. I asked him to take charge of the geocache angle, because that piece is relatively straightforward. He's got a team searching geocache sites. I'm concerned that there are more out there because this bastard is obviously committed to fucking with us."

"Yeah, about that, are we going on the assumption that he placed the cache there a few days before he took Abbott there to kill her?"

"That's what it looks like. We found the site where he posted the cache information, Go—"

"GoGeocache dot com. If someone found the cache before Abbott's body was left there, they didn't post anything about it online, which would go against geocaching protocol. I mean, it's kind of the whole point. Anyone sign the log in the cache?" I asked.

"Nope. The log is an index card and it's blank."

"Geocachers communicate details about the cache online, they chat about it in the website forum, and leave notes in the physical log inside the cache. There's a social aspect to it, a kind of community among strangers. If no one signed the log or posted about it online, we should assume no one found it," I said, then added, "That's good though."

"What, good that he made a mistake leaving it where no one would find it?"

"Good that no one found it before the scene was processed. Can you imagine the contamination and confusion we'd be dealing with if geocachers had been traipsing all over the scene, taking items from the cache and leaving shit of their own?"

"It'd be a nightmare trying to determine what he left and what others left." He added, "At least we know he's the one who put the three items into the cache."

"That's highly unusual, by the way; not just the cache itself, but that he intentionally left something at the scene. I'm assuming the lab didn't get anything off the cache or the items in it, or you would have mentioned it."

"You'd be correct. Not a goddamned thing. No prints, no DNA, nada."

"What about the hair?" I was referring to the lock of dark hair found in a snack-size Ziploc bag in the cache.

"It's synthetic. The kind used on Barbie dolls."

"Maybe a knock-off or some other kind of doll, but it didn't come from a Barbie," I said.

"What makes you say that?"

"It's too long. The only Barbie I can think of with eight inch hair is Rapunzel, but she has blonde hair, not dark."

"You're such a girl."

"I have a niece, jerk. Jennifer Abbott has long, dark hair. Probably not a coincidence. The Kent County Sheriff's Office magnet is obviously a fuck-you. It'd be easy enough for him to get one. It's the kind of thing handed out at school assemblies and county fairs. What are you thinking about the Brazilian coin?"

"Who the hell knows? It's common currency that any Brazilian would have in his pocket. Could mean he's been to Brazil, or he likes Brazil, or he collects coins, or—"

"—or he's fucking with us and it doesn't mean anything. That leaves the cellphone battery," I said.

"It fits a Samsung, the same model as Abbott's phone, which hasn't been recovered. The two usable prints found on the battery are hers. He was careful not to leave his own prints when he removed the battery, but he didn't bother wiping it clean."

"Sure, because he wanted us to find her prints so we'd have no doubt he left the cache. He probably made her remove it."

"The Bureau techies are going to get jack shit on her location after she left the pool house because he was smart enough to remove the battery, and he wants us to know it."

"So, what has the brilliant Eberley come up with so far on the geocache website account?" I asked.

"Not much. Basic membership is free, so he wouldn't have to provide credit card information, just a username and email address. The email address associated with the account is going to be difficult to track, but not impossible. His handle is Cacher in the Rye."

"Saw that," I said. "Very fucking clever."

"You think Salinger's novel has any meaning for him, or did he just pick something punny that wouldn't attract attention?"

"I have no idea. I haven't read the novel since high school, and I don't have time to even think about it at this point. There's plenty of other shit to worry about. Listen, I'll talk to Spielman Monday morning, but unless NCAVC officially accepts the case, I'll be working it on my own time. For the time being, I'm the only geographic profiler on staff at the moment and I have a serious backlog. That said, there's gotta be some major political bullshit in play with this case, so who knows."

"Shit!" My left hand was shaking so badly I'd spilled beer down the front of my shirt.

"What's wrong?"

"Nothing. I'm a friggin' klutz." Something was obviously wrong with me. Nightmares, panic attacks, and now hand tremors. *What next? Why now?*

I heard a muffled TV in the background on Haskins' end as I rummaged in my nightstand for a pack of Kleenex. "Are you watching a football game? You better not be watching TV while I'm putting in uncompensated overtime. Every hour of sleep deprivation takes days off your life expectancy." I mopped beer with a wad of tissues.

"Nope, I'm in a shitty motel in Redneck Central, Maryland. My extremely intoxicated neighbors apparently shot half the ducks in the state and are in quite the celebratory mood. They came over a while ago and invited me to join them. I was half-tempted. Lord knows I could use a drink right now."

"Geese, not ducks. Goose season opened this morning. You get the photos I sent of the screw holes?"

"Yes. Shit, how in the hell did we miss them?"

"I almost did, too. It didn't make sense for him to position her like that and strangle her from behind. I started thinking about how else he could have done it, got lucky. They were made recently.

Eddie Garrett and Brent Mitchell both say they have no clue who would have drilled any holes, or why. Mitchell's only purpose for being on that land is the corn, and it's a lost cause. He told Deputy Reynolds he hasn't been there in over two weeks and has never set foot on the porch. At this point, there's no other explanation for those screw holes except that the killer put them there."

"So he must have attached something to the porch ceiling, then removed it and taken it with him. The M.E. said that the ligature marks are at an upward angle. The force that caused the strangulation came from above and behind the victim. Are you thinking rigging?"

"Yeah, I am. I think he attached a pulley to that ceiling beam, put a noose around her neck, and fed the rope through the pulley. If he stood in front of her and pulled the rope, the force would have been from above and behind her, and he could've watched her face the whole time."

"Makes sense. See, I told you I need you on this case. Did I ever tell you that I love you, Ross?"

The comment was off-hand, rhetorical. Still, it took my breath away. He *had* told me, in no uncertain terms, and I'd run. Literally. Six months ago, I'd left him sitting in a fancy restaurant with questions I still didn't know how to answer.

Please don't bring that up. I can't deal with it right now.

He finally ended the torturous silence. "Speaking of love, I know someone else who's got a little crush on you. I spoke to young Chris Reynolds earlier."

"Oh, yeah?" I tried my damnedest to match his nonchalance.

"You made quite an impression on him. Were you aware that this is his first homicide investigation?"

"I suspected. He handled himself well."

"He asked if you're single," Haskins informed me, obviously amused.

"What'd you tell him?"

Are we seriously having this conversation?

"I said as far as I know, you aren't dating anyone. I wished him luck."

My eyes stung. My ears burned. Why did I care that Haskins didn't seem bothered?

"Well, he would need it, right?" The more I tried to keep the emotion out of my voice, the worse it was. "I mean, I'm a total bitch."

"Nah. That cat of yours, on the other hand…"

His tone was joking. He hadn't picked up on the fact that I was upset. *Why are you upset, Ross?*

"It's not Stella's fault you hate cats," I said.

"I don't hate cats, Regan. Your cat hates me. She's evil. She's got red eyes, for Christ's sake."

"Orange, not red, and she's *not* evil. She's just *particular.*"

"Just like that damn Stephen King cat, the one that wouldn't die."

I sighed. "Okay, I get it. You hate my cat. The feeling is probably mutual."

We were quiet for a moment. The brief levity we'd mustered quickly dissipated. When Haskins finally spoke, he was all business again and I was glad to be back on solid ground.

"There is one thing. According to the M.E., the ligature marks on her neck are consistent with something like steel cord, not rope like her wrists were tied with. The ligature cut into her neck, and there are injuries at the back of the neck where something pinched the skin. The M.E. said he's seen similar injuries when one end of a steel cable was threaded through the looped end of the other, forming a noose, which was placed around the victim's neck. He actually showed me a photo of the injury in the case he referenced, which happened to be a suicide. Regan, it was identical to Abbott's injuries."

"Okay. So he used steel cable around her neck, ropes on her wrists. What about the victim? Tell me about Jennifer Abbott."

"After the autopsy this morning, Eberley and I interviewed her friends, classmates, and professors. Like I said, long day."

I grabbed a legal pad and pen from my nightstand. "Give me the highlights, anything I might not have read in your notes."

"Well, she wasn't just a pretty face. She's the captain of the Washington College swim team, broke a bunch of records in high school. Brains, too. She was offered academic and swimming scholarships to several universities, some as far away as Texas. She chose to go to a small local college to be with her high school sweetheart. Stable family life. Her parents are real estate agents and live in Gaithersburg. I'm going to talk to them tomorrow. Jennifer had an older brother. He's a rescue diver with the coast guard, stationed in Alaska. Can you imagine? Worried every day about their son's safety and their daughter gets snatched and murdered right here at home."

"I know. It's awful." Awful didn't begin to describe it. "She was last seen in the swimming center parking lot on campus?"

"Yes. Her best friend, Brooke Crawford, had chemistry lab with her on Friday, the sixth. Class let out at four thirty, then they walked to the Aquatics Center together. Crawford says Jennifer climbed out of the pool and was heading toward the locker room at about five thirty. That's the last time she saw her. Crawford didn't leave the building until about six fifteen. Jennifer's car was still parked next to hers. Jennifer told Brooke that morning that she was planning to leave after their swim to drive to Gaithersburg to visit her parents over the weekend, which we verified with the Abbotts. She apparently never made it off campus."

"So, he grabbed her on campus or she left with him willingly," I said.

"Taser marks on her throat," he informed me. "Don't know if I mentioned that."

He hadn't.

"She also has two round contusions, about two inches apart, on the side of her neck. The M.E. says he's pretty sure they're not from the Taser, at least not the same one that made the other marks."

"He doesn't know what they could be? Puncture wounds? From a syringe?" I suggested.

"Apparently not. The skin's not broken, and the contusions are about the size of a pencil eraser. Looks like something might have been pressing into her neck, right at the pulse point, just above the ligature marks. The M.E.'s stumped."

"Weird. Well, if Jennifer showered, changed, and left the pool around, say six o'clock, it would've been pretty dark. He must have parked near her car and gotten close enough to use that Taser. Marks are on her throat, so she was probably facing him when he juiced her. Unless he reached around from behind."

"Yeah, I figure he zapped her and dragged her into his vehicle, which—like you said—must have been parked next to hers."

"He may have used a ruse to convince her to approach his vehicle," I said.

"The old Bundy trick—faking an injury, asking for help, something like that," Haskins added.

"Or, he posed as someone in a position of authority, someone to be trusted like a postal worker, security officer, someone in uniform," I suggested. "Regardless of his approach strategy, the Taser doesn't surprise me. He knew she would fight him and needed to be sure he could subdue her before she had an opportunity to resist."

We were falling into old patterns, thinking out loud, bouncing around theories. I hadn't realized how much I'd missed it. Missed *him*.

"What about the autopsy? I haven't seen the report," I reminded him.

"The M.E.'s examination confirmed that Abbott doesn't appear to have been sexually assaulted. That's another detail that doesn't support Eberley's hedonistic lust killer theory."

"We don't even use 'lust killer' in the BAU anymore," I said. "And just because there's no evidence of sexual assault doesn't mean it wasn't sexually motivated. It often manifests in subtler ways. He stripped her down, bound her, shoved her panties into her mouth, and left her on display. There may have been interactions we don't see evidence of. He could have fondled her, masturbated, a whole list of things that wouldn't necessarily leave evidence. It sure looks sexual to me."

"Cause of death is asphyxiation due to strangulation," he said. "Fractured hyoid and damage to the strap muscles are what you'd expect with that, and she has deep lacerations around both wrists."

"From struggling against the ropes," I said.

"Yeah, the M.E. found abrasions around her ankles. They had apparently been tied at some point. The injuries are consistent with the rope ligatures that her wrists were bound with. Maybe he had her ankles tied during transport, then untied them so he wouldn't have to carry her from his vehicle to the porch?"

"Are you thinking out loud or asking for my opinion?" I asked.

"Both"

"Well, yeah, maybe he had her ankles tied in the vehicle, then untied her so she could walk. The bruises on her neck could have something to do with the way she was bound during transport, though I'm having a hard time picturing something that would leave marks like that. Another possibility is that he untied her ankles to convince her that he was going to let her go. He would've gotten off seeing her hope turn to terror when she realized she was never going home. I think he's big on mind games, maximizing the suffering."

"But why leave her tied to the posts? He knew he was leaving evidence."

"Leaving the body at the murder site is the most common disposal method. Transporting her elsewhere would've actually increased the risk, and he gets the added benefit of shock value. If our theory is right and he rigged a pulley, the cable needed to be a certain length. He may have used hardware on the cable to create the noose. It took some time and effort to get it just right. I think he kept it because he plans to use it again."

"You think he's done this before, don't you?"

"I'm almost certain of it," I said. "He's practiced, skilled."

"Well, on that you and Eberley agree. He said the same thing. Shit." He sighed, said, "Abbott also had lacerations and wood splinters embedded in her heels."

"I saw where she kicked against the porch steps. Hey, earlier you said ligature marks, plural. There were multiple marks on her neck?" I asked.

"Yes. At least three and all probably made with the same steel cable. The M.E. thinks that the killer may have released the tension a few times as he was strangling her."

I didn't mention I suspected as much. "What about her face? Was the torching ante or postmortem?"

"Post, thank Christ. Can you imagine being on fire and unable to do a damn thing about it?"

I didn't have to imagine. I cleared my throat. "How could he tell? That it was postmortem, I mean."

"No evidence of inhalation. The panties in her mouth were almost completely incinerated. Had she been breathing, she would have inhaled smoke and debris."

"Jesus."

"Yeah. The M.E. also found several tan fibers in her hair."

"Well, that's something," I said.

"Maybe. Keep your fingers crossed that the lab can tell us something useful."

"What's the estimated time of death?" I asked.

"He thinks she was out there for three to five days."

I mentally calculated the time. "Okay, it's getting late and I'm tired, so check my math. She was found late on the thirteenth. If she was out there three to five days, it means she was killed between the ninth and the eleventh. If he took her on the day she was last seen, the sixth, he would've needed a secure place to keep her alive for at least a couple of days," I pointed out, furiously scribbling notes.

"That's the assumption I'm going on unless we find someone who spotted her after the ninth."

"It also means we've got at least three sites associated with this crime: approach site; hold site; and farm house, where he killed her and left her. Where's the evidence being processed?"

"Quantico. One of our lab techs drove it down this morning. It's been logged in, but I don't know if they've started on it yet. I was hoping you could check on it tomorrow."

"The one good thing about all the attention on this case is that it should mean some expediency in the labs. I'll stop by and see Odette first thing in the morning. I'm turning into your lackey, not exactly good for my career progression."

"Hey, Ross, I've got another call coming in, probably the tech guys. I'll call you if anything else comes up. Jesus, it's been a long day. Listen, thanks for your help. Really, I appreciate it."

I imagined Jennifer Abbott's legs, powerful from training in the pool, kicking against wooden porch steps until they were bloody while she looked into the eyes of her killer, steel cable constricting her throat. Who did she think of in those last moments? Her brother? Her parents? Her boyfriend? Did she think about the wedding that would never happen? The children she would never have?

There was a knock on my door followed by a muffled, "Aunt Regan?"

"Yeah?" I said. The scent of lavender preceded Lanie into the room. She'd combed her damp hair into a pompadour and her face, still pink from the shower, was free of heavy eyeliner.

"Good run?" I asked.

"Yeah. I meant to tell you earlier, this came for you," she said and tossed a padded FedEx envelope onto the bed before flopping down with teenage abandon. Thankfully, I'd removed the handcuff from the foot rail. That would've been a tricky one to explain. Lanie was scratching Stella's ears. I was always surprised by how much tolerance the cat reserved solely for my niece.

The return address confirmed my suspicion. The envelope contained no note, only a small bundle wrapped in a carefully clipped square of newspaper. I recognized the article immediately.

"Is that a Purple Heart?" Lanie asked over my shoulder.

"Uh-huh." I quickly wrapped the medals in the paper and tucked the bundle back into the envelope, postponing a closer examination until Lanie wasn't looking over my shoulder. *Are they my medals? How would she know I haven't had them in my possession? Did she stalk me at the bus station? And then what, gone dumpster diving herself? Why would she keep them for seven years? Why send them now?*

Like it or not, I was apparently the focus of Monica Spears' goddamn mysterious agenda.

CHAPTER SEVEN

November 16

8:35 a.m.

Quantico, Virginia

38°31'38.94"N, 77°27'8.63"W

THE CONCENTRATION OF scientific brainpower in the most sophisticated forensics lab in the world never ceased to amaze me. Every scientist in the lab was hunched over a microscope, meticulously comparing and analyzing all manner of trace evidence. The names of the equipment: mass spectrometer; gas chromatograph; fuming chambers; and comparison microscopes were vaguely familiar. Honestly, I would've been hard pressed to tell one apparatus from another, and was perfectly happy leaving the details to the diligent men and women around me, each an expert in his or her forensic field. As Odette had instructed, I made my way to the lab within the Trace Evidence Unit that specialized in the analysis of automotive carpet fibers. Though most of the evidence examiners in the TEU were wearing lab coats, their director was not. Odette DeSaulier wore whatever the hell she liked. I headed for the splash of color in the center of the clinical setting. Odette had both eyes on the lenses of a microscope.

"Special Agent Ross!" Odette drawled, eyes still focused on the task at hand.

"How'd you know it's me, Odette?"

"I can tell by your walk, Honey. You always sound like you're on a mission, always in a hurry."

Odette was the only person on the planet I let get away with calling me "Honey," with the possible exception of Aunt Tabitha.

"But I'm even wearing my stealthy boots," I said.

"Special Agent Haskins called this morning and said you'd be stopping by."

"Why'd you have to ruin it for me, Odette? I like to think you have a sixth sense."

"Wish I did. Then I could tell you whose vehicle these came from," she said, gesturing toward the microscope.

"Are those the fibers Haskins sent over?" I asked, practically bouncing.

"Yes, indeed. The specimen on the left is the evidence from your case. The one on the right is the comparison sample."

I set my messenger bag onto the floor and eagerly occupied the stool Odette rolled in front of the microscope. She handed me a two-page report detailing the results of the analysis. Nine fibers had been submitted for comparison. The diameter measurements and color characteristic descriptions were straightforward, but the extensive list of search parameters and associated results become more foreign the farther down the page I scanned. Cross-sectional shape, polymer class, striations, presence or absence of delustrant? Illuminate values? The colorful peaks and valleys of the charts on page two might've been more aesthetically pleasing to look at, but were no less foreign.

"I gotta be honest, Odette, this might as well be written in Chinese."

"Well, that's okay, Honey, because that report just validates what you can see plain as day with those pretty green eyes of yours. Take a look."

The tan fibers looked identical, and thanks to Odette's expert tutelage during the Sanchez case, I was able to identify them as synthetic.

"So, you were able to determine that these are from auto carpet?" I asked, turning to face Odette.

"Yes, ma'am, that was the easy part."

"Did you get a match to a specific make of vehicle?"

By way of reply, she cocked her head.

"Of course you did. I forgot who I'm dealing with," I said.

"Well, now, I can't take all the credit. FACID did a lot of the work."

The lab's Forensic Automotive Carpet Fiber Identification Database held an impressive number of sample carpet fibers provided by auto manufacturers. Evidence fibers could be cross-referenced against the database holdings to identify a match and, potentially, determine the type of vehicle the carpet fibers came from. FACID played a big role in the Sanchez investigation.

"According to FACID, these little guys came from carpet used in several Ford trucks and vans manufactured between 1998 and 2003," she informed me.

"That probably excludes Abbott's vehicle. She drove a 2005 Civic," I said. "If neither her boyfriend nor her other friends drove an older model Ford van or truck, we can assume the fibers came from the offender's vehicle. This could turn out to be a decent lead, Odette. Listen, I appreciate you putting a rush on this analysis."

"Oh, I'm not done, Honey. We've got some rope to discuss."

"Right. What can you tell me?"

"Not me," she said, then called out, "Dr. Harrison! Do you have a minute?"

A beaming auburn-haired man all but ran over to us.

"Scott Harrison, this is Special Agent Ross."

I shook the analyst's offered hand, unable to get over the man's resemblance to a young Ron Howard, but with sideburns straight out of the eighteen hundreds. His eyes didn't stray south. Points for Harrison.

"Nice to meet you, Special Agent Ross."

"Likewise."

"Scott, could you walk Agent Ross through the results of the analysis of the rope from the Abbott case?" Odette prompted.

"Absolutely. The rope removed from the victim's wrists is of the polyamide variety."

"That's nylon, right?" I asked. That tidbit might have come from Discovery Channel.

"Very good, Agent Ross. Nylon is the generic designation for a family of synthetic polymers. In fact, nylon is one of the most commonly used polymers."

Common was about as useless as *approximately* when dealing with evidence or data.

Harrison didn't pause for a breath.

"Nylon is one of the strongest materials used in the construction of rope, but it does lose some strength when it's wet. This particular type of rope, polyamide, is often used by boaters for anchor and towlines because of its ability to absorb shock loads."

"Okay, 'nylon rope, often used by boaters' sounds like something sold at every Walmart in the country. Please tell me I'm wrong."

"Patience, Honey, and have a little faith," Odette said. She gave a slight nod, presumably indicating the small cross necklace I was wearing.

I snorted involuntarily. "Patience is definitely not one of my strengths, Odette. Neither is faith, for that matter."

Harrison continued his analysis, oblivious to our sidebar. "This particular rope happens to be three-quarter-inch, white, twelve-strand, braided nylon with a fifteen-thousand-pound breaking strength intended specifically for maritime use. It's known as Iron Braid by its manufacturer, Trident Marine. They're located in Boston."

Harrison wasn't conveying much via facial expressions, but Odette looked awfully smug.

"There's no other twelve-strand, braided nylon rope with a fifteen-thousand-pound breaking strength out there?" I asked.

"Oh, sure, many varieties," Harrison told me.

Fucking fantastic. I might've said that out loud.

"But this rope was manufactured by Trident Marine in Boston after April seventeenth, 2014."

"How can you know when it was manufactured?" I asked.

"Because this rope sample was treated with a HAPS-free, eighty-percent epoxy coating."

"A haps what?"

"Sorry. HAPS stands for Hazardous Air Polluting Solvents. The regulations regarding HAPS-containing coatings became stricter last year, and in April 2014, Trident Marine began using a new epoxy coating within the required parameters according to HAPS regulations. The reformulated epoxy coating is consistent with the sample I tested."

"Okay. So you're able to say that the epoxy coating on this sample was produced sometime after April 2014. But is this type of epoxy coating available for purchase to the public? Could someone have, say, purchased the rope prior to 2014, then bought the epoxy solution at like a marine supply store or Home Depot or something after April of last year and coated the rope themselves?"

"Epoxy coatings are available from several retailers."

Opie was killing me.

"But not this particular coating. This composition is specific to the type of coating used by Trident Marine."

"So you're saying that, based on the particular composition of the epoxy shit on the rope sample, you can tell me not only who made it, but also that it was made sometime between April 17, 2014, and now?"

"No, I didn't say that."

I was about ready to locate the rope in question in the lab and strangle Harrison with it. He added, "I'm telling you that the rope sample submitted was manufactured between April seventeenth, 2014, and July twenty-seventh, 2015."

"Right, and how do you know that?"

"Because Trident Marine again altered their coating composition to adhere to HAPS standards on July twenty-eighth of this year." Muttonchops sounded rather pleased with himself.

"So this rope could only have been manufactured during a fifteen-month period?" I asked.

"Correct."

"Is Trident Marine a retailer, or do they manufacturer and sell their products to retailers?" I asked.

"The latter."

"So, *now* you're gonna tell me that Trident Marine sells Iron Braid to every Walmart in the country."

He paused, obviously enjoying himself, and I wondered if he and Haskins might be related. I waited, making a concentrated effort not to huff. Or roll my eyes. Or threaten him with violence. After a tortuous pause, Harrison told me Trident Marine sells Iron Braid nylon rope to several retailers worldwide.

"Fucking great," I muttered.

He clarified, "But to only one retailer in the United States. Boater's World."

"Definitely not every Walmart in the country," Odette added.

"Well, there aren't as many Boater's Worlds as there are Walmarts, so I guess that's something," I said. But, I realized, there were probably quite a few in eastern Maryland, still a pretty considerable haystack. I pitied the poor bastards who would have the monumental chore of checking out every retail location.

"I've already taken the liberty of printing a list of Boater's World locations within a hundred miles of where the rope evidence was collected," Harrison informed me.

"Thanks, Dr. Harrison."

"So your offender probably works in the maritime industry. Or has a yacht," Harrison continued.

"Why do you say that? Half the guys on the Eastern Shore probably have a boat and shop at Boaters World."

"True. But this particular rope is primarily intended for anchor and dock lines, for boats over forty feet. That's serious overkill for a recreational fisherman. No pun intended. And there's something else. We discovered a substance on the surface of the rope."

"Substance?" It was like pulling teeth with the guy.

"It appears to be paint."

"I didn't see any paint on the rope in the photos," I said.

"White paint on white rope is hard to detect with the naked eye, and it's a fine coating, consistent with paint mist rather than drops."

"Mist, like from a sprayer?" I asked.

"Could be, but I wouldn't want to speculate."

No, we couldn't have that. "Can you tell what type of paint?"

"No," he said. "But the Chem Unit might be able to."

Right. The TEU doesn't do paint analysis. The common perception was that "the lab" was one big room where every type of evidence was analyzed. While the FBI Laboratory was a single organization, it consisted of multiple units spread throughout a five-building complex. Each unit may have upward of a hundred scientists assigned, responsible for conducting specific types of examinations. One piece of evidence, the rope, for example, might make its way through multiple units and undergo several types of testing. Meaning, it might be days or weeks before we knew everything the rope was going to tell us. Odette had apparently read my thoughts.

"We'll let you know as soon as we know anything, Honey," she assured me.

I took a few moments to process everything Harrison said.

"What are you waiting for?" Odette asked, nudging my shoulder.

I met her eyes.

"There's a bogeyman out there and you've got somethin' to go on."

"Oh, yeah. I've got tons to go on. White male, late twenties to late forties. Above-average intelligence, from an unstable family, abusive or absent father and domineering mother. Was most likely sexually, physically, and/or emotionally abused throughout his childhood and probably tortured animals and wet the bed past the age of twelve. He's a strong guy who drives an older Ford van or truck with tan carpet, and probably works a menial job involving big boats. He might own a paint sprayer, but that would be speculating."

"See, you're all over it," she said.

"Shit, Odette, that's the standard Google description for a 'serial killer,' and the half that isn't myth probably applies to about a third of the males on the Eastern Shore."

"Look on the bright side. You know more than you did before you came in here this morning, right?"

"Yeah, you're right. You usually are," I admitted.

"Thanks so much, Dr. Harrison. Don't let us keep you any longer," Odette said.

"Yes, ma'am. Nice to meet you, Agent Ross."

"You, too. Thank you for working up the sample so quickly. I really appreciate it."

He blushed. Another blusher. We were apparently everywhere.

"My pleasure."

The analyst nodded once before scurrying back to his corner of the lab.

I turned back to Odette. "I'm sorry. I didn't mean to sound

ungrateful. You've been a huge help, and I appreciate you expediting the analysis."

"You're welcome."

Odette touched my cross pendant, and I wondered why she was suddenly fascinated with my jewelry.

"Have a little faith, Regan," Odette finally said.

I snorted.

"And yet you wear the cross of our Christ, the symbol of a believer," she pointed out.

"It was a gift." I met Odette's eyes. "And I didn't say I don't believe. I just think prayers are rarely answered. Too much awful shit happens to people who don't deserve it."

"Like your parents?" Odette asked.

Had I ever told her about my parents? We'd talked a lot during the Sanchez case. I knew quite a bit about Odette. That she was from New Orleans, the Lower Ninth Ward. Her husband died right after Katrina. Two sons, both grown. One was in the Army. We'd only missed each other by a couple of weeks in Iraq, I'd learned. As for what Odette knew about me, that was a different story. I'd never told her any specifics about my life in Scotland. So how could she know about my parents?

Harry.

They were tight. It shouldn't have surprised me that they'd talked about me. Before I could say anything, Odette took my hand, catching me off guard. I didn't think it was a coincidence she was holding my left hand, the scarred one. It was the first time in a long time someone had touched me with affection. When I finally answered her question, I was surprised by the emotion in my voice.

"Like my parents. Like Jennifer Abbott, like all those women who were raped last year, and it never stops."

"No, Honey. It never does stop. So you do what you can," she said.

"And what? Leave the rest to God?"

"That's where the faith part comes in."

"Well, then, I think I'm screwed, Odette."

"You know, I remember the Lockerbie investigation like it was yesterday. I analyzed some of that evidence."

I'd still been drinking from a sippy cup when Odette began her FBI career. I suddenly had an image of her gloved hands holding a piece of the plane debris that killed my parents.

"I think your parents are proud of you, Regan. Have faith in that," she said, squeezing my hand.

When she finally let go, I felt more than a little sad.

CHAPTER EIGHT

November 16

9:48 a.m.

Quantico, VA

38°31'34.94"N, 77°26'52.65"W

SUPERVISORY SPECIAL AGENT Harold Spielman's office door was closed, but his blinds were open just enough for me to gauge his mood before stepping into a potential tempest. He removed his reading glasses, tossed them onto his desk, and rubbed his hands over his face. His hair looked a little grayer since I'd seen him two weeks earlier. I knocked twice and was greeted with a muffled "Come in."

"Nice work in Seattle. The King County Sheriff is singing your praises," he said, replacing his glasses. "Jesus, Ross. You look like hell."

Without replying, I plopped down in one of the leather chairs in front of my boss's desk and plucked several M&Ms from the bowl he kept filled. Ours was not a typical supervisor-subordinate relationship. I'd often imagined what a therapist would say. *Surrogate father* would probably come up. It wasn't as if I'd intended to have a mentor in the Bureau, and if I'd realized what was happening, I probably would've fought it. My assignment to NCAVC had been Harry's doing, and after four years, I wasn't sure whether to curse or thank him.

During my second year at the Richmond Field Office, five men robbed nine banks within our jurisdiction over several months, resulting in my first assignment to a major task force. There were several locations throughout Richmond and Henrico County associated with the robberies, and I decided to analyze the data using the same geospatial analysis software I'd used in the Army.

Aiming to statistically characterize the areas near the targeted banks, I pulled in every bit of geospatial data I could get: locations of parks, bus stops, churches, police stations, social gathering places, convenience stores, ATMs, public toilets, and census and demographic data. In all, I used more than 350 different geospatial factors in my analysis. Then, I fused this data with the geo-coordinates of the banks and locations where the cars had been abandoned. This provided a statistical portrait of where the bank robbers preferred to operate. Using that profile, I was able to identify other geographically similar banks that had a likelihood of being hit next.

Unfortunately, the twenty thumbtacks stuck in the map covering the wall of the task force office didn't corroborate my findings, and, God forbid, the task force supervisor pay any credence to a rookie. Pissed off, overwhelmed, and frustrated, I back-doored my supervisor and sent the BAU my assessment and the modeling data to back it up. After a month of hearing nothing but chirping crickets, I figured they'd come to the same conclusion as my supervisor: an inexperienced agent couldn't possibly know anything about analyzing serial crimes.

Two days later, when the Chief of Behavioral Analysis Unit-4 arrived in Richmond with my report in hand, I started planning career alternatives. Maybe the post office was hiring? Wasting no time, Spielman presented the task force with a tactical surveillance plan for the high probability areas I'd identified. The task force supervisor went ballistic, and I imagined being reassigned to some cold, remote field office. My saving grace was that my analysis proved accurate. Within forty-eight hours of staking out the four banks I'd identified, the suspects were in custody. My reward was an ass chewing from my supervisor for jumping the chain of command.

A few months after the case was closed, I received an unexpected call from Spielman. He was expanding the use of geographic profiling and predictive analytic techniques in BAU-4 and wanted to know if I was interested in joining the team. I'd been equal parts flattered and apprehensive. Members of the BAU were usually supervisory special agents with at least ten years of investigative experience under their belts. I'd only been with the Bureau for three years. I voiced my concerns more than once, but Harry had been persuasive.

At the time, his confidence in my abilities swayed me. I'd actually looked forward to the challenge, but soon after arriving at Quantico, I realized just how far in over my head I was. Special Agent Beth Schiller, a Bureau of Alcohol, Tobacco, and Firearms veteran was the only reason the entire endeavor hadn't been a disaster. Beth had a decade of experience as a criminal geographic analyst, the last six years in BAU-1, which specialized in bombings and counterterrorism, among other things. She'd trained with the best geographic profilers and environmental crime analysts in the world and proved to be an amazing trainer herself.

Harry had asked me something, I realized. "Sir?"

"I said you look like shit. Have you slept?" Harry also called it like he saw it, which I appreciated most of the time. I didn't answer him because I wasn't sure where to start.

"Of course not," he said. "You never sleep. When was the last time you ate?"

"I'm eating right now," I told him, loudly crunching an M&M.

"Seriously, you alright?"

"I'm fine. My weekend was sabotaged by unexpected guests."

"Well, you look like shit. Did I mention that?"

"Yes, sir." I picked out two blue M&Ms. My mind was on the unknown blue data point, the place where the killer had held Jennifer Abbott before torturing and killing her. "All due respect, Sir, you're one to talk. Do those Samsonites under your eyes fly for free?"

"Smartass." He took a deep breath. He was about to shift gears. "So. Jennifer Abbott."

"Yes, sir?"

"You've talked to Special Agent Haskins?"

"I took a look at his notes, as a favor."

"Bullshit. You went to the crime scene and the lab."

Damn.

"On my own time. I didn't—"

He held up a large hand. "Cut the shit, Ross. It's good you're familiar with the case, because as of now, it's your number one priority."

Wait. What? Too easy. I'd come in prepared to plead my case and hadn't even had to ask.

"I want you to focus on the geographic profile. Give Haskins all the help you can, he'll welcome it. David Eberley is a different story. I offered to have the Unit staff work up a psychological profile, but apparently he's decided to take that upon himself."

"You've got to be fucking kidding me." I hadn't meant to say it out loud, but there it was.

"He apparently doesn't want to crawl back to the BAU for help, so he's going to muddle through this thing solo. The only thing that might keep this entire thing from turning into a complete cluster fuck is that Rob Haskins is running the investigation. He's got a good head on his shoulders. Give him any assistance he needs. You'll be my eyes and ears when it comes to Eberley. Don't let him run you all down a rabbit hole, understand?"

"Yes, sir," I said. "It appears Eberley's preliminary assessment is that we're dealing with either a hate crime or a hedonistic lust killing."

"Jesus Christ. That's about as accurate as saying either a gorilla killed her or a goddamned circus clown. What have you got so far?"

I held up the file I'd brought. "Please keep in mind that I haven't had a chance to add what Trace Evidence came up with on the rope and carpet fibers."

"Give me the *Reader's Digest* version, Ross. I've got a teleconference with the director in ten minutes."

"Sure. At this point, we're basing our assessment on a combination of victimology, M.O., forensic results, and the offender's choice of disposal location. I'm focusing on the latter, but I can give you a summary of the other aspects."

"Let's hear it," he said.

"Jennifer Abbott wasn't a partier, didn't drink or do drugs. She was on athletic scholarship and was diligent in her studies and training. She was fairly security conscious and was rarely alone."

"In other words, she falls in the low-risk range for criminal victimization," Spielman said.

"Right. While circumstantial vulnerability factored somewhat, she was likely targeted because the offender found her physically attractive or she appealed to a specific intrinsic need, or both."

"Sexual aspects?" he asked.

"There's no evidence of sexual penetration or other overt sexual interaction, but the bindings, state of undress, particularly sadistic torture, strangulation by ligature, and postmortem mutilation indicate the murder was sexually motivated," I said.

Spielman checked his watch. I was apparently taking too long.

"The offender chose an isolated disposal site and left Abbott 'as-is' at the scene, and kept her at a different location for several days, suggesting he was familiar with the area. This familiarity would have come, at least in part, from surveillance conducted in the days or weeks before he abducted her. He operates from a single, local anchor point and is mobile. Tan carpet fibers found on Abbott's body at autopsy are consistent with a Ford van or truck manufactured between 1998 and 2003. Analysis of the rope used to bind the victim's wrists tells us it's intended for tow lines for boats over forty feet and is only sold domestically and only at Boater's World retail outlets."

"I'm assuming that lead is being checked out," he said.

I nodded.

"Good. Anything else?"

"A fine coating of paint was also found on the rope. It's being analyzed now. The offender may own or work on a large boat or work somewhere that does maintenance on them. Abbott was athletic and she put up a fight. He initially Tased her, but was later able to overpower her at the scene, presumably when she was alert and fighting. It took a considerable amount of strength to strangle her the way we think he did, from the front using a cable and rigging. He may have some skill with his hands, mechanical aptitude."

"Does Haskins know about the lab results yet?" he asked.

"No, not yet, but I plan to call him this morning and suggest surveillance of marinas near where Abbott was abducted. The team should look for older Ford vans and trucks, run the plates, and see if anything stands out."

He nodded. "Good."

"Sir, there's something else, something that only a handful of investigators are aware of because Haskins doesn't want it leaked."

His hair turned a little greyer before my eyes as I informed him about Cacher in the Rye and the items found in the cache.

"An offender intentionally leaving an item at a murder scene is atypical," I said. "Leaving a geocache and posting the coordinates online suggests he wanted the body to be found. Have you ever seen anything like this?"

"Items left at the scene, yes, but nothing this ballsy. Despite the horseshit dished out by the pseudo-experts, offenders don't want to get caught. They typically attempt to delay discovery of the body, not expedite it. I don't suppose the lab was able to get any fingerprints, DNA?"

"No. He was wearing gloves, wiped it clean, or both."

"Also atypical. What about a geoprofile?"

"I only have two data points right now, not enough for a full analysis," I said.

He nodded and stood, my cue that it was time to go. When he was halfway to the door, he stopped and turned. I was right on his heels and had to pull up short.

"Remember, Ross. You deal directly with Haskins. Don't get into a pissing match with Eberley. I'm sure you've heard about his history with the BAU. He still thinks he's the next John Douglas. The worst thing that could happen to this investigation is for Eberley to kick you off it, and he has the authority to do it. Haskins is the lead. Let him deal with Eberley."

"I got it."

"Oh, and Regan—"

"Yes, sir?"

I met his eyes.

"For God's sake, get some sleep."

I almost laughed. Almost.

CHAPTER NINE

December 17

10:20 a.m.

Quantico, Virginia

38°31'48.74"N, 77°26'47.67"W

F EW OF THE National Academy students who filled the auditorium seemed to notice my entrance, and those who did quickly returned their attention to the speaker. Alisha Trent, the National Academy lecture coordinator, looked relieved when I slid into the front-row seat she'd saved for me.

"What?" I whispered. "Thought I wouldn't show?"

She smirked. "You always show."

True, but Beth and I usually rotated lecture duty and it was technically her turn. When Alisha had asked me to fill in for Beth, who was spending her maternity leave at home with Baby Schiller, I had no way of knowing I'd be assisting with a high-profile murder investigation. I'd wanted to cancel, but Haskins had argued that it would only be a few hours and the investigation would not come to a screeching halt in my absence. True, maybe, but it was slowing down enough on its own.

There's a point in any major case where tips flood in, thousands of them, and each one has to be followed to its end. Out of all those well-intentioned pieces of information, maybe five percent would lead to anything useful. Despite visiting seven Boater's Worlds, Kent County detectives hadn't yet turned up a single lead on the rope. Eberley's team was monitoring geocache sites all over Kent County, both physically and virtually. Cacher in the Rye had either been laying low or caching under a different username.

The MSP guys had set up surveillance cameras in the marinas near Chestertown, based on the locations I suggested. The mark branded into Abbott's chest was very similar to cattle brands associated with several ranches in the western United States, but so far that angle hadn't led anywhere. We'd spent a month tracking down leads and had very little to show for it. While the investigation was cooling off, the killer was probably out there, somewhere, ramping up, hunting his next victim. And he had every advantage. Predictive analysis relies on crime-related data. We likely wouldn't get more useful data until there was another murder. That truth sat in my gut like a lead weight.

I checked my watch. Ten minutes until I was up, plenty of time to refuel. When I rummaged in my bag and produced a protein bar and bottle of water, Alisha cut her eyes at me, as if to say, *really?* A girl had to eat. Other than the speaker's rather melodious voice, you could hear a pin drop in the auditorium. Gingerly, I unwrapped the PowerBar. It still seemed obnoxiously loud. After taking a bite and washing it down with water, I turned my attention to the lecturer.

A red visitor's badge was clipped to the lapel of her perfectly tailored skirt suit, which put my outlet mall ensemble to shame. A familiar accent colored her speech. Flat vowels, swallowed r's. UK, definitely. Not a Scottish brogue. Welsh? Irish? Wherever she was from, she clearly wasn't a stranger to public speaking. Though my scan of the audience was less than discrete, I doubt anyone would have noticed if I'd stood on my chair and taken my time with a pair of binoculars. The sharply dressed visitor with the dulcet voice had mesmerized two hundred people.

"How do the signatures manifest?" she rhetorically asked the audience. "Acts of domination or control during any aspect of the crime, the use of especially vulgar language, for example. The offender may use force beyond what is required to commit the crime, such as stabbing a victim repeatedly after he or she is obviously deceased."

She smoothed her French braid, and added, "The important thing to remember is that while M.O. will usually change through a series of crimes, you will see the signature repeated at each scene unless circumstances prevent it. The offender is interrupted, he sets off an alarm, the victim fights back and he is forced to change his plans. In some cases, deterioration of the scene or the body may prevent us from seeing the signature, though it was actually present. Rain might wash away blood, urine, or semen, for example."

The incongruity between her voice, which was perfectly suited to narrate fairy tales to a group of pre-schoolers, and the macabre subject matter, was unsettling.

"Who's the lecturer?" I asked Alisha.

She handed me a folded lecture program and tapped a manicured finger on the back page, indicating a photo and bio. Dr. Sheridan Rourke was smiling in her professional headshot, which appeared to be current. As I skimmed the bio, certain details jumped out. Dr. Rourke was a consulting forensic psychologist at the Police Service of Northern Ireland or PSNI. Apparently, her expertise led to the identification of several high-profile serial offenders throughout the UK.

I shifted my attention from the photo to the woman on stage. Her long, well-toned legs suggested Pilates or yoga, and her flawless fair skin indicated a disciplined skin care regimen, making her age hard to peg. She was close to Erin's age, early forties, if I had to guess.

Dr. Rourke directed the audience's attention to the large screen behind her and said, "These examples depict evidence of signatures at various crime scenes. This first image shows a message left by a serial rapist on the wall of his victim's flat. The letters went undetected until they fluoresced under UV light. They were written in the offender's semen."

I could make out a C, a U. An H? Nope, an N. Ah, yes. Zero points for originality.

"Similar messages, conveying the offender's general disdain for women, were observed at subsequent scenes," Rourke added.

The image that filled the screen next was an area of excised skin on what looked like a woman's shoulder. It was hard enough to look at, but the victim's short, red hair made me think of Lanie.

She's at Hopkins. Safe. Studying.

After a heated debate with Erin, Lanie had agreed to stay, finish her midterms, and defer her swearing-in until after the holidays. I'd managed to distance myself from the contentious two-party talks, and they were both still furious with me. The fact that I'd bailed on Thanksgiving dinner hadn't helped smooth things over. At least they were pissed at me and not at each other. I'd momentarily zoned out as the psychologist flashed through slides. I was now looking at a crime scene photo of a young man, apparently deceased, teeth marks visible over his heart.

"Robert Callahan stalked and killed homosexual males near Belfast. See the signature?" Rourke asked.

The next slide showed the same victim from a greater distance.

"There's another signature visible in this photo, the binding. It was used on three different victims, and while restraining his victims is certainly a component of his M.O., tying the victims in this particular way is his *signature*. The binding is excessive; the knots sophisticated, intricately tied in a way that caused more pain the more the victim struggled. This took time, thus increasing the risk."

The next photo caused me to utter a profanity loud enough to earn a disapproving look from the woman sitting to my right. My first thought was that Dr. Rourke had somehow obtained one of the evidence photos from the Abbott case. No, I realized, this was not Abbott. The scene was different. This teenage girl, or young woman, it was difficult to tell, was nude and bound to fence posts. Though her small frame and long dark hair were eerily similar to Abbott's, something else was causing a physiological response as my mind tried to put the pieces together.

My mind raced, as I tried to rationalize what I was seeing. Below the bridge of the nose, the soft tissue of the face had been reduced to blackened tatters of flesh, clinging to exposed skull. Charred cloth protruded from the gaping mouth. It could not be, yet it was.

* * *

"Alisha, don't let Dr. Rourke leave the building. I *need* to speak to her," I said, just as Rourke exited the auditorium.

Alisha nodded, then walked to the podium and introduced me.

Focus, Ross. There's nothing you can do about it now. You owe it to these students not to space out.

The polite applause was my cue the intro was over. Alisha headed to the door Rourke had exited through as I crossed the stage and took my place behind the podium. My three-inch heels compensated for my height deficit just enough for me to see over the podium.

"Good morning. Since you've been studying behavioral sciences, you're aware that my colleagues in the BAU provide several services to a wide range of law enforcement agencies—investigative strategies, profiles of unknown offenders, threat analysis, critical incident analysis, interview strategies, and major case management. BAU staff also assists at trial, both in strategy development and expert testimony. The Violent Criminal Apprehension

Program, or ViCAP, is also a component of the NCAVC, and Mr. Anthony Parillo will be providing an overview of that program later in the day."

What if Dr. Rourke left before I could speak to her? I had so many questions.

Focus!

"Think about your morning routine. You're on your way to work. You stop at a convenience store. Why? You're low on fuel. You need your coffee fix. Maybe you need to hit the ATM so you can pay the babysitter tonight. You like the coffee at this particular store, but there's no ATM. There's an ATM at this store, but the java tastes like swamp water and the gas prices are high. These specific attractors and inhibitors are unique to you and your needs, and will determine where you end up. Your choices result in various spatial and temporal intersections. We can model these intersections over time to see the patterns."

Rourke entered through the same door I'd used earlier, with Alisha right behind her. They occupied the two front-row seats Alisha and I had vacated earlier.

"A crime inherently involves the intersection of four elements: offender; victim; time; and space. Time and space are fixed and absolutely not random. Why? Because the offender *chose* them, whether five seconds before the act or five weeks, he chose them. No matter how disturbed the offender is, there will always be some discernible pattern from crime to crime and making mathematical sense of those patterns is what I do.

"I want to share a geographic profiling success story that occurred before I joined the FBI. At the time, I was an Army officer assigned to the Defense Intelligence Agency, halfway through a one-year deployment in Iraq where I commanded a small intelligence unit that supported counter-IED operations. Over several months, we analyzed a series of IED attacks in Baghdad determined to have been carried out by one insurgent cell."

I picked up a remote mouse controller from the podium and pointed it at my laptop. At the click of a button, a map of Baghdad filled the large screen behind me. I was pleased to see that the technology gods were cooperating.

"The first thing we did was geolocate the IED attack sites," I said, pushing the button on the controller again.

"The red dots represent those attack sites. The IED cell chose these locations because they are along known convoy routes in the city, so they didn't really tell us anything about where the cell was likely based. Fortunately, we did have the coordinates of the buildings where the particular components used in these explosives were assembled."

I brought up several blue dots on the map with a click.

"We also had locations where vehicles that had been observed at or near the assembly sites had been parked."

Another click brought up a series of green dots representing the parked vehicles.

"We input all these coordinates into our software, which used a sophisticated algorithm to give us this," I said, clicking. A new image replaced the map.

"This is what we call a jeopardy surface. It resembles a topographic map, but the 'elevations' you see are not topographic heights. These raised, color-coded surfaces represent the probability that our suspect cell is based at that location. The north-south comprises the 'x' axis, east-west is the 'y' axis, and the represented likelihood of our cell's base of operations, or anchor point, is the 'z' axis. For this to be of any use, we have to overlay our jeopardy surface on top of the area in Baghdad where the IED attacks occurred."

I clicked again and the graphic changed.

"Now we see the significance of our jeopardy surface as it is laid over a street map of Baghdad. The red 'peaks' indicate the highest probability that the location is our anchor point. In a criminal investigation, the anchor point is where the offender most likely lives or works. In this case, we have multiple actors, an insurgent cell, and we're looking for the locations where they typically meet. Notice that we have three red peaks within Baghdad."

"Are there any questions so far?" I asked.

The forensic psychologist raised her hand.

"Yes, Dr. Rourke."

She said, "I would imagine that if your coordinates were off in the slightest, it would skew the results of the algorithm. How did you ensure that your data was completely accurate?"

Is she asking because she actually wants to know or is she testing me? Why do I care either way?

I delivered my answer to the rest of the room. "That's a great point. Soldiers on the ground used a hand-held GPS to record the actual geo-coords at each site. We then used the coordinates as the input data for the pattern-analysis algorithm. We also used satellite imagery and mensuration techniques to help verify that our locational data was accurate."

When I called for additional questions, a blonde woman seated in the middle of the auditorium raised her hand. "What happened with the cell in Baghdad? Were you able to determine if the cell was operating from one of those peaks?" she asked.

Offering unspoken thanks for the unsolicited, perfectly timed segue, I said, "As a matter of fact, we provided the results of our analysis to the tactical team we were supporting and they conducted a raid on the three locations. The team found a cache of IED components and weapons at these two locations," I said, pointing to two of the peaks with the laser pointer that was built into the mouse controller.

"This third peak was a store where one of the cell members drove his truck to work every day."

"So, although we didn't give the team one definitive location, we narrowed down their search to the three most optimal areas.

The red areas were the first locations the teams searched, and fortunately they proved accurate. Had those sites not yielded the results we were looking for, we would have focused on the orange peaks, because those areas were the next most probable base sites. Had this been a criminal investigation, the same analysis could have been used to plan surveillance or to search addresses in a database."

I provided a few examples of cases where I had used pattern analysis and showed how distance perception affected the profile. Several audience members asked questions, and before I knew it, I'd been talking for over an hour. I asked for questions and a tiny woman with Asian features raised her hand. "I'm a supervisory detective in the Dallas PD. How would I go about requesting your services?"

At least it was an easy one.

"There are NCAVC coordinators assigned to each FBI field office that serve as liaisons with area police departments and typically handle requests. You can find a listing of the Bureau's field offices with contact info on the website. Someone at your local F.O. should be able to put you in contact with the coordinator."

My conclusion was rushed, but at least I remembered to display my contact information. If they needed geographic profiling support, they knew where to find me, which was kind of the point of me speaking anyway.

The audience was clapping, my cue to exit. I practically ripped the cords out of my laptop. Alisha was making her way to the stage. Rourke was still sitting in her seat. I held up a finger, mouthed *be right there.*

She smiled and nodded.

When I approached her, she stood and said, "Yes, Agent Ross? How can I help—"

"The photo of the woman, with her face burned, when and where was it taken?" I asked, trying to keep the strange combination of excitement and dread out of my voice.

Rourke took time to study me. For a moment I thought she might not answer at all.

"Near Crawfordsburn, July 2013," she said, her tone exuding nothing but detached professionalism.

The specificity of her answer both impressed and intrigued me. I asked, "That's Northern Ireland?"

She nodded.

"Were there others?"

Again, Rourke hesitated slightly before answering. "Yes. Four that we're aware of."

"Was anyone charged for the murders?" I asked.

Rourke wasn't nearly as quick with her answer this time and something cold flashed in her eyes. Finally, she said, "That's what I believe you Yanks call a loaded question, Agent Ross. James Ballinger was arrested and charged. As to whether he was responsible, well, opinions vary."

Her words were neutral. Her tone was not.

"Was Ballinger convicted?" I asked.

She shook her head. "Never made it to trial. Hanged himself in his cell. That spoke to his guilt for a lot of people."

"But not to you?"

"No."

I waited a beat or two, watching her weigh something in her mind. I'm not a patient person. "Care to elaborate?"

Rourke hesitated as she studied me. My pupils were probably dilated, face flushed, and she was trained to notice. When she finally spoke, she was cool and professional.

"They were organized, carefully planned murders. The man responsible possesses above-average intelligence. He managed to stay one step ahead of investigators for several months."

The same thing I'd said about Jennifer Abbott's killer.

"James Ballinger had an IQ of seventy," Dr. Rourke added.

"Were there any other murders after Ballinger's arrest?"

"No," she said, before quickly adding, "but it's possible the killer left the UK."

"Oh, I think he has." I hadn't necessarily meant to say that out loud.

"Why do you say that?" Rourke's scrutiny was intense.

Some of the details had intentionally been withheld, and I didn't want to inadvertently contribute to a leak. Leaning in a bit, I kept my voice low. "Because I have photos of a woman who could be your victim's double, tied almost the same way, underwear shoved in her mouth, and her face practically burned off."

"When and where were the photos taken?" Rourke asked.

"Maryland," I informed her. "Less than a month ago."

"Bloody hell. Show me."

CHAPTER TEN

December 17
11:50 a.m.
NCAVC, Quantico, VA
38°31'34.94"N, 77°26'52.65"W

W E WERE BOTH lost in thought, the sound of our heels clopping on tile accompanying the walk to my office. How the hell could the Northern Ireland victim be killed and posed so similarly and not be related? Either way, the torching was a unique ritual, and the only other possibility I could fathom was that we were dealing with a copycat. That scenario was problematic. The killer would have to know the specifics and, according to Dr. Rourke, the case hadn't made it to trial. Could there have been a leak? What about the cache? Had he left any in Northern Ireland?

I had many questions for Rourke, but there were complications. For starters, I was actively involved in an on-going murder investigation and under a tremendous amount of scrutiny. Sharing case information with a forensic psychologist three thousand miles outside her jurisdiction might not be the most prudent thing in the world. Rourke hadn't said a word since we'd left the auditorium. I stole a glance and caught her doing the same. How much information would she be willing to share? Despite my eagerness to determine whether or not Abbott's killer also murdered women in Northern Ireland, I needed to be selective about the information I shared with Rourke.

Oh, hell.

As we stepped into my office, I realized I'd been too lost in thought for my own good. Crime scene photos, notes, maps, and diagrams covered an entire wall. Before I could even think about damage control, Rourke was studying a group of photos featuring Jennifer Abbott. So much for being selective.

"One victim?" Rourke asked.

"So far, but I think it's only a matter of time."

"When was she killed?"

"Our best guess is between November ninth and eleventh. She was found on the thirteenth," I added.

"Where was she abducted?" Rourke asked, still intently studying the photos and notes.

I wasn't sure how I envisioned this would go, but I definitely didn't relish being on the receiving end of what was shaping up to be an interrogation.

"College campus, probably at or near her car," I informed her, not sure why I was still answering her questions.

Without taking her eyes off the photos, Rourke said, "Well, it appears his M.O. hasn't changed in that regard."

So, she's decided it's the same guy.

"In two of our cases, we found evidence of a struggle at the victim's car," Rourke said by way of an explanation.

"Two of the five cases?" I asked.

Rourke had taken the seat adjacent to the desk and was booting up her laptop. The momentum had shifted and, armed with legal pad and pen, I wasn't about to take the opportunity for granted.

"Aye."

"And the last murder was when?" I asked.

"Sioban McKinnon was found on the eighteenth of August. Ballinger was arrested about a week later."

I jotted this down, asked, "The killings stopped?"

"There were no more victims showing the same signatures found in the UK."

Not a no. Was she suggesting the true killer had been busy elsewhere?

"You were consulting on the case?"

"Aye, there were several veteran inspectors on the—you would call it a task force. The chief inspector running the investigation asked me to consult."

"Did he agree with you about Ballinger?" I asked.

"*She* did, though she never had the opportunity to do so publicly."

"How's that?"

"She was killed."

If Rourke noticed my head snap up, she didn't let on. She was focused on her laptop.

"Killed how?" I asked.

"Car bomb."

"Seriously?" *Shit, Ross. Of all the idiotic, insensitive...*

"Aye, Special Agent Ross. Seriously," she said, without shifting her attention from her laptop. "Catholic members of the police force are the primary targets these days."

"Jesus. I'm sorry. I guess I didn't realize that sh-stuff still goes on." She finally looked up, her expression unreadable.

"Most don't, but that *shite* does indeed go on."

My knowledge of Northern Ireland was limited to what I'd seen in movies and a couple of documentaries. I was sure I'd offended her, but I wanted to understand how and why a PSNI chief inspector had been killed by a bomb, especially if it could've had anything to do with what she'd been investigating. "IRA?" I guessed.

"Splinter groups mostly. Die-hard Catholic dissidents."

Pinning my hopes on the History channel, I said, "I thought the violence quieted down over a decade ago with the Good Friday Agreement."

Rourke huffed. "That's what most people outside of Northern Ireland think, that the Good Friday Agreement solved all our problems. Hardly."

"So, explain it to me. You said die-hard Catholic dissidents were responsible for the attacks. But you also said that Catholic police officers were the intended victims. Why would they attack their own?"

"They don't view police as their own. The PSNI has been very public and successful in their efforts to recruit more Catholic members. These splinter groups are bent on killing Catholic members of the force to subvert the recruiting initiative."

"But I thought Sinn Féin has publicly denounced armed attacks." Was that nugget from Tom Clancy? I needed to do some real research before I managed to cement Rourke's impression she was dealing with a complete fucking idiot.

"Aye, but these breakaway groups—Continuity IRA, *the Óglaigh na hÉireann*—they're based mostly in rural areas that border the Republic of Ireland where republicanism is deeply rooted. They believe Sinn Féin sold out by seeking a political solution in Northern Ireland."

"You said these attacks are fairly common?"

"The PSNI responds to at least one attack a month, and these groups use a variety of tactics: car bombs, pipe bombs, land mines, gun attacks. In 2013, about three weeks after Chief Inspector Grace O'Donnell was killed, a small dissident group that originated as the Real IRA now known as *Óglaigh na hÉireann* attempted to shoot down a PSNI helicopter with a rocket. Car bombs are more typical and the one that killed O'Donnell was particularly sophisticated."

"O'Donnell was the inspector in charge of the investigation? When was she killed?" I asked.

"Aye. She was killed on the fifth of August, two weeks before the last murder. We'd been making some headway in the investigation, but not quickly enough for some. The chief superintendent ultimately decided any viable suspect would do, whether or not he remotely matched the profile. They found someone with a criminal record for sexual assault who lived near two of the victims."

"Ballinger?" I offered.

"Aye, never mind that a pub full of people swear Ballinger was knocking back pints at the time two of the victims were killed. Lamping the ladies about is a far cry from the level of sadism exhibited in these crimes. Like I've said from the beginning, in my opinion, those murders were committed by a highly intelligent and organized individual."

"The women were all killed in Northern Ireland, I assume?"

She nodded. "The first victim, Dana Mullen, was found nude and hanging by her wrists from the rafters of an abandoned factory in Donaghadee." Rourke demonstrated by touching the insides of her wrists together and extending her arms straight up. "She was strangled with a garrote and gagged with her own knickers. No evidence of sexual assault. The factory was less than two kilometers from a marina. Based on the type of rope used, we thought our man might be a fisherman or some sort of laborer who worked the docks. Inspectors looked into every bloke in the area with a criminal record and turned up nothing."

"What type of rope was it?"

"Braided white nylon."

Sounded familiar.

"A common type sold all over the U.K," she added.

"What about mutilation? Did he brand or burn her in any way?"

"No. He didn't start burning them until Siofra Hayes, the third victim. She was also the first to be bound with her arms outstretched, each wrist tied to a post."

"It makes sense," I said. "A garrote would've been difficult to manage with her arms straight up like that, especially when she was struggling."

"His modus operandi was evolving at that point, and his signature was showing more sophistication as well. Hayes wasn't branded, but her chest was torched, probably with whatever he used to ignite the knickers. Siofra was gagged just like your girl there, Jennifer Abbott," Rourke said, indicating the photos on the whiteboard.

"Any thoughts on the significance of that?" I asked. "We've been throwing around a few ideas, but I'm interested in your opinion."

Rourke cocked an eyebrow. "We?"

"Special Agent Haskins and I."

"Haskins is your partner?"

"I don't have a partner per se. Rob Haskins is with the Baltimore Field Office and he's the lead investigator on the Abbott murder. I'm working with him."

"I see. Well, finding knickers in a victim's mouth isn't unprecedented, as I'm sure you know. It's usually a learned component of M.O. Gacy, for example, would shove his victims' knickers or socks down their throat after discovering that fluids tend to escape from the mouth after death. 'The Boston Strangler' used them to expedite strangulation, and I could cite cases from the UK as well, but these are examples of modus operandi. On the other hand, what 'The Boston Strangler' did to his victims after they were already dead—posing the body, tying a bow around the neck with nylons—that wasn't necessary or practical; it was his own special flourish. That's what we're seeing here. Gagging them, torching their faces—"

"He's signing his work," I said.

"Aye. The rest of it, though, everything he makes her *feel*, is about demonstrating his absolute power over her," Rourke added.

"Control. Manipulation. The psychological aspect is more your specialty, obviously, but don't you think he probably feels slighted or incompetent in some way and this is his way of taking control to compensate?" I asked.

"Mm, overcompensate," Rourke muttered. "But his inadequacy probably isn't sexual. There's no evidence of rape, stabbing, or penetrating mutilation, which we often see with sexual impotence. But something in his life or in his past causes him to feel like he has no control, and yes, his fantasies are his way of countering those feelings."

Rourke moved to the murder board again, added, "And at some point, the fantasies weren't enough."

"Dr. Rourke, were any of the details regarding signature in the Northern Ireland murders publicly disclosed?"

"No. We were careful about that. We withheld those details to help disprove the fifty or so local eejits who 'confessed' to the murders."

"So there's no way someone who wasn't involved in the investigation could've known the specific details?"

"No," Rourke said, turning back to the photos. "I don't see how this could be a copycat."

"I don't either."

She was attempting to read the various Post-it notes scattered around the photos. Most of the notes were written in shorthand, indecipherable to anyone but me. Even if she could interpret them, there were a lot of details she wasn't going to get from that board. Hell, it was way too late to hold anything back now. I gave Rourke a rundown of everything I knew about the Jennifer Abbott murder, including the cache, and hoped I wouldn't come to regret it later. She listened intently, occasionally taking notes, her face giving nothing away until I mentioned the screw holes and the theory the killer had installed some sort of rigging so he could strangle the victim while standing in front of her.

"If that's the case, then it appears his signature has evolved."

Her next question surprised me. "Is there a police station near the farmhouse where Abbott was killed?"

"Yes," I said. "A state police barracks about three miles away."

"Each of our crime sites was within two kilometers of a police station," Rourke informed me, not breaking eye contact. "I've always believed it intentional. A taunt, like this—"

She tapped a photo of the Kent County Sheriff's Office magnet. "He's saying, look what I did right under your bloody nose, and feck-all you're doin' about it. He's manipulative that way and probably harbors deep disdain for authority, law, and societal restrictions. This might stem from the feeling he was failed or overlooked by the system that was supposed to protect him when he was a child."

"Or," I said, "Maybe that system rejected him as an adult because he's a sack of shit. We see a lot of soldier or cop wannabes."

Rourke picked up a copy of Abbott's autopsy report and I made no move to stop her. The discretion ship had sailed.

A thought occurred to me and I asked Rourke, "What was the date of the first murder?"

"Dana Mullen was killed sometime during the first week of April, 2013. Her body was discovered on the fifth."

I pulled up the calendar on my computer and jumped back to the date. "And the next victim?"

Rourke was scrolling through the case information on her laptop. "Mary Delaney. She was killed around nineteenth of May, about forty days later. Then thirty-six days later, Siofra Hayes on about twenty-fourth of June. The fourth victim, Colleen Byrne, was killed one month later, on twenty-fourth of July. Sioban McKinnon, his last in Northern Ireland, was twenty-four days later."

"So the cooling off period between killings lessened each time. That's what we typically see," I said.

"Aye, decompensation. The need to fulfill the fantasy becomes stronger with each kill. And then they abruptly stopped. It's possible he went dormant for two years. Or he's been active elsewhere and the crimes haven't been linked."

"Exactly. It's a common myth that when there's a time break in a series it means the offender is dead, locked up, in a mental facility, or joined the military. It's just as likely he stopped killing for whatever reason or, like you said, he's been active somewhere we don't know about. We should check with Interpol to see if there are any international notices for murders with similar signatures," I said, already looking up the number for the Interpol National Central Bureau in D.C.

"After the murders stopped, I suspected our man had fled the country. I urged the PSNI to request Interpol issue a Green Notice, but that didn't go very far," Rourke informed me.

Interpol, the international police organization, assisted with cross-border police cooperation. The organization issued Green Notices to provide warnings and criminal intelligence regarding individuals who committed criminal offenses and were likely to repeat crimes in other countries. Essentially, a Green Notice was a worldwide heads-up that a serious offender was at-large.

"Haskins is lead, he should contact Interpol. Hell, I need to call him."

My stomach growled so loudly that Rourke looked up. It was going on two o'clock and we hadn't had lunch. The two cups of coffee and PowerBar had long burned off. I could call Haskins on the way.

"How about a late lunch? My treat," I suggested.

"Brilliant. But do you mind if we make a stop on the way? I need to look in on a mate."

"Sure. Where's your friend?" I asked, grabbing my jacket.

"Here at Quantico."

"FBI?"

Rourke shook her head. "PSNI. Retired."

CHAPTER ELEVEN

December 17

2:23 p.m.

Marine Corps Base, Quantico

38°31'48.73"N, 77°19'36.83"W

QUANTICO WAS THE home of major training organiza-tions for both the Marine Corps and federal law enforcement agencies. The one hundred square miles of secluded woods in rural Virginia made it an ideal location for sensitive training, yet its picturesque park-like quality was disarming. As we wound our way through the Marine Corps Base, I wondered about Rourke's retired PSNI "mate" and what possible business he or she had at Quantico. I was about to ask when her cellphone rang. She checked the display and immediately answered it, her voice low. "Jamie, hello." She paused. "Any news?"

News about what? I wondered. She didn't make eavesdrop-ping easy. Her tone was intimate and I was running through possibilities—relative, friend, colleague, lover—when my own phone vibrated.

Erin. Shit. Well, at least she was willing to talk to me. I hadn't heard a word from her since my absence on Turkey Day. Of course, it was possible she was calling to lay into me again.

"Hi, Erin—"

"She wants another tattoo."

Not what I'd been expecting, but on a positive note, she didn't sound particularly accusatory. "And?"

"I don't know what to tell her. I mean, the thought of a tatted-up stranger coming near my daughter with a needle makes my skin crawl. I keep thinking about what you said."

"You're gonna have to help me out here, E."

"She'll turn eighteen soon and she'll do it anyway. The only thing I might have some control over is her attitude these last few weeks. If I refuse... a sulking nightmare, I think you said."

"Well, then I think you might want to concede the tat, unless she's planning to go all Lisbeth Salander or something."

"Who?" she asked.

"*The Girl with the Dragon Tattoo.*"

"No dragons, thank God. She wants to add a couple of stars to her wrist."

"Sounds pretty harmless to me. If she wants to come down here, I know a couple of reputable shops a lot of the Marines go to. I'll even go with her, but she needs to give me some notice. My schedule is crazy. Unless she's still pissed at me."

"Call and ask her, Regan. I'm not playing intermediary."

Funny how neither one of them had any trouble asking me to be the peace broker. I let it go. "Okay," I said. "That it?"

"Eager to get off the phone, are we?"

"Well, I'm driv—"

"Who is Monica Spears?" Erin asked.

Had I not warned her? I'd meant to. "Did she contact you?"

"Several times. Email first, then phone calls. She wants an interview for some kind of documentary on the Lockerbie bombing from what I gathered. I haven't responded."

"Don't. Monica Spears is a fucking parasite."

"She mentioned you. She says you're key to the podcast she's producing—"

"What podcast? What are you talking about?"

"I don't know. Sounds like the *Serial* podcasts, you know, about that murder case in Baltimore and there was one about that Army deserter."

"Bowe Bergdahl?"

"Yes, he's the one."

"What the hell? I'm remotely familiar with the podcasts, but can't fathom how Spears factors or what any of it has to do with me."

"What's her angle, Regan?"

"I don't fucking know, and this is exactly why I don't like it that your phone number and email address are listed," I said.

"I'm a physician, Regan. It's important my patients be able to reach me. You know that. Every other physician's number is listed in the Hopkins directory, too."

"I know you're a doctor, Erin, but it doesn't mean I have to like it that anyone can easily find out your phone number and where your office is located. It's not ideal from a security standpoint. Take my word for it, Spears is bad news and she's obsessed with me, and you by association."

"Why is she interested in Lockerbie? I mean, why *now*? Al-Megrahi has been dead for three years."

"I have no idea what she's up to or what any of it has to do with a fucking podcast. Caitlyn Jenner, the Great Wall of Trump, Adele's new album, Charlie Hebdo, Greece's economy shitting the bed. Hell, I would think Americans would be more interested in any of those things than a dead terrorist associated with an event that happened over twenty-five years ago. Don't contact her, Erin. She's probably working against a deadline, and there's no telling what lengths she'll go to for an interview with a well-known surgeon and federal agent who are the daughters of two of the—"

"Christ, Regan. We made a pact. The two of us don't talk about it, so what makes you think I would ever discuss it with a stranger?"

"I know. I'm just saying."

"So, what about Christmas?"

I wasn't prepared for the holiday plans talk, probably the main reason for the call. I wouldn't have answered if it had occurred to me.

"Beyond the usual, what do you have in mind?" I asked.

"Aunt Tabitha flies into BWI on the evening of the twenty-third. I thought it would be nice if you came with me to pick her up."

"Whose idea was *that*?"

"Lanie's. She wants to see her before she ships out. It'll probably be a long time before we're all together again."

"I can't promise anything, Erin. I'm sorry. I'm heading back out to the Eastern Shore in the morning. I don't think I can swing it."

"You're not coming *at all*?"

Familiar patterns, but I couldn't help it. Five cases in Northern Ireland were probably connected to Abbott. After a month of dead-ends, we finally had a break. There was so much to do I couldn't even think about Christmas.

"Listen, Erin, I'll be there on the twenty-first, like always, but beyond that, I doubt it. The investigation—"

"You're being so goddamned selfish, Regan."

Really? It's selfish to try to stop a fucking murderer?

"I have to go, Erin." I ended the call as Rourke instructed me to pull into the parking lot on our right.

We parked in front of a building that was the kind of brown fugly unique to military installations. The plaque on the building said "Military Police Company, Security Battalion Kennel." Why the hell would a retired officer from Northern Ireland be at a U.S. Marine kennel? Baffled, I climbed out and practically sprinted to catch up with Rourke, who was halfway to the entrance.

Once inside, Rourke navigated her way through the building in a way that left no doubt she'd been there before. We walked through a rear door, into a grassy courtyard. A large, black dog clambered up ramps, darted through tunnels, climbed a ladder, and scaled a wall in blitzkrieg fashion while a uniformed female shouted commands from the middle of the course. At the final command, the dog trotted over to the woman and sat next to her.

The handler jogged toward us, the German shepherd trotting at her side. The handler wore desert fatigues with "Kennedy" stitched over her right breast pocket and "U.S. Marines" over the opposite one. My mind leapt to images of the dog blowing down pigs' houses and eating little girls in red cloaks. The association might've had something to do with the empty socket where the dog's left eye should've been.

"*Sitz*," the Marine ordered. The dog sat grinning next to her, eyes locked on Rourke, who knelt.

"*Dia duit*, Ripley."

Rin Tin Tin was apparently multilingual. The dog obviously wanted to go to Rourke, but obediently stayed put, its entire body vibrating with anticipation.

"*Hier*." At Rourke's command the dog practically jumped into her arms.

"Easy, girl. *Sitz*." The dog immediately complied, her tail wagging with enough force to propel a cargo ship.

"Special Agent Ross, meet Ripley," Rourke said.

Ripley watched me with one intelligent amber eye. I'm not easily intimidated, but she was managing to get the job done.

"Ripley as in *Believe It or Not*?" I asked.

She shook her head. "Sigourney Weaver's character in the *Alien* films. Her trainer was a fan."

"Ah. Nice to meet you, Ripley," I said. I liked having all my digits and didn't attempt to pet or shake. Ripley didn't strike me as a paw-offering kind of pooch.

Rourke, who was now standing and facing the Marine, said, "Looked like she was enjoying herself."

"She's doing great. Good to see you again, Sheridan."

"Likewise, Kirsten."

Sheridan? Kirsten? WTF?

"Special Agent Ross, this is the Kennel Master, Staff Sergeant Kirsten Kennedy."

"Hello, ma'am," Kennedy said.

"Nice to meet you, Staff Sergeant," I said, keeping my eyes on the dog.

"Well, Ripley, what did you do today, Love?" Rourke asked.

"We ran through some tracking and alerting. Would never know her sight is compromised. I'd deploy with her any day," Kennedy replied.

"When did you get back?" Rourke asked her.

"About six weeks ago."

"Glad you made it back safely."

"Thanks. Me, too. It's good to be home."

"So, this is your retired PSNI friend?" I asked Rourke. At least the kennel thing made more sense.

"Aye. Ripley was a tracker for the police service. She lost an eye trying to save an officer and was retired a couple of years ago. I adopted her. Or she adopted me. We're still sorting it out."

"You said she was a tracker?" I asked.

"Primarily. She's trained for tracking and victim recovery. She'll also alert on or subdue a subject, depending on the command."

"Subdue" sounded like a euphemism for *bite the shit out of.*

"So how do you two know each other?" I asked, still not clear why a retired K-9 from Northern Ireland was staying at the Marine kennel.

"Ripley's former handler attended the National Academy a couple of years ago. She brought Ripley with her and Staff Sergeant Kennedy offered to board her and let her do some training with the Security Battalion's K-9s," Rourke explained.

"I was the senior trainer at the time," Kennedy added.

"And she was kind enough to extend the offer again when I told her I would be visiting Quantico. Kirsten, if you don't mind, I'd like to run through a few exercises with her."

Kennedy nodded her consent, and it was my cue to call Haskins.

Surprisingly, he answered on the first ring. I wasted no time filling him in about Rourke and the connection to the other murders.

"You should contact Interpol."

"Absolutely. If he left Northern Ireland, there's a good chance he was active in another country. We need to have Interpol check previous notices, see if there were any homicides reported anywhere with the same signatures, and we need to get a Green Notice issued. Where are you, anyway? Do I hear barking?"

"Yeah. I'm at the Marine Corps Base kennels."

"Why?"

"Long story. Listen, with the Northern Ireland murders, we've got at least five data points, maybe more with confirmed abduction sites. It might be enough for probability analysis. At the very least, we should be able to cross-check a preliminary geoprofile against last known addresses of convicted men who worked the docks and marinas."

"Sounds like a plan. Is Rourke going to be able to stick around and help us out?" he asked.

"I don't know. We haven't discussed it."

"Well, if she has to go back across the pond, hopefully she can get some traction there. I mean, there's more evidence in Northern Ireland than here at this point."

"Yeah, but it's complicated," I said. "The PSNI wouldn't be

especially thrilled if they knew she was working the case. As far as they're concerned it's closed."

"Think they'll share their evidence?" he asked.

"That's going to be tricky. From what Rourke says, they're adamant they arrested and charged the man responsible. I can't imagine they'll be too eager to reopen the cases."

"They don't have to, at least not officially," he said. "They think they had the right guy, and he's six feet under. What's the harm in sharing evidence that's sitting on a shelf collecting dust? It won't hurt to ask. Sounds like a job for the SAC."

"Eberley," I said.

"He may be a jackass, but he's good at telling people exactly what they want to hear to get what he wants."

"You have a point. It's worth a shot, I guess."

"If they're not willing to play ball, then we fall back on the ol' MLAT," he said.

"Um, what the hell's an MLAT?"

"Mutual Legal Assistance Treaty. The attorney general sends a request directly to his British counterpart, the UK Central Authority. If the request is granted, which they usually are, the PSNI will be compelled to give us whatever evidence they have."

"Shit, you really did learn something at Harvard Law. How long will the request take?"

"I'm not sure, but if they drag their feet too long maybe you could go over there and work your charm on them."

"My *charm*?"

Haskins didn't miss a beat. "Oh, before I forget, I heard from the lab. The paint on the rope is an automotive type, a waterborne base coat not consistent with any paint composition used by any major auto manufacturer. This is after-market stuff."

"Interesting. So, maybe someone was painting a car, and the paint in the air came in contact with the rope," I suggested.

"Possible. Listen, I'm going to call Interpol. Let me know what you get from the, well, whatever that woo-woo thing is."

"Woo-woo? You mean statistical probability analysis?"

"God, it sounds so geek-sexy when you say it."

"Okay. Buh-bye Rob," I said and hung up.

It was going on three o'clock and I was ravenous. Ripley was lapping at a bowl of water. Rourke and Kennedy were chatting. Well, we were going to need Rourke to stick around for an indefinite period of time. I suggested to Rourke that she and Ripley stay at my place. I had a spare bedroom. Convenient. Free. Rourke finally agreed. Next, I proposed we pick up some take-out and head to Chalet Ross for some Chinese food and a round of connect-the-data-points. That one required less persuasion.

CHAPTER TWELVE

December 17

3:30 p.m.

Triangle, Virginia

38°32'40.87"N, 77°19'32.87"W

EFFECTIVE INVESTIGATION REQUIRED an objective eye, an open mind. If you got too close to something, you'd lose perspective. With this principle in mind, I studied the room. The furniture was sparse. The leather sofa and coffee table were high-end, but worn. A lone coaster sat on the coffee table. No obvious stains or crayon marks. Expensive electronics. No safety plugs in the wall outlets. No toys, children's books, or G-rated movies in sight. The dominating neutral tones suggested the decorator had been inspired by a bowl of oatmeal. Deduction: one single, childless, unsentimental occupant who tended toward functionality. I watched Rourke arrange Chinese food on my coffee table and wondered what the psychologist made of my digs. Besides my small family and Vincent, Rourke was the only person who'd been in my house.

"Whose feet?" Rourke asked, and for a moment I thought she might be referring to our dinner.

"Pardon?"

Realization dawned when Rourke nodded toward the largest of the framed black and white photos on the wall.

"Oh. My sister's and niece's. And mine. For some reason, Lanie felt the need to take a picture of our feet at the beach last summer. I've learned not to question her artistic notions."

"Lanie is your niece?"

"Mm-hmm," I murmured as I reached into my messenger bag and pulled out the laptop and notes I'd brought from the office.

"Did she take all of these?" Rourke knelt on the couch so she could get a better look at one of the photos, an extreme close-up of an American flag patch on a desert camouflage uniform. Lanie had snapped the shot just before I'd boarded the plane to Iraq.

"Yep. Lanie's the photographer in the family. Among other things."

Not for the first time that day, my stomach rumbled loud enough for Rourke to hear. Smiling, she passed the carton of sesame chicken.

"So Erin is the tall one?" she asked.

"Excuse me?"

"Well, one pair of feet is significantly longer than the other two," Rourke noted, licking sweet and sour sauce off a finger. "They're not yours. I'm guessing Erin." The woman didn't miss much.

"Oh, right. Yeah, that would be Erin, the Amazonian. Lanie and I inherited the short gene from my mother."

"Do you want to use plates or eat out of the containers?" Rourke asked.

"We don't have to act like total Barbarians," I said, realizing I only owned four plates and none were clean. "I have the best Dixie has to offer. I'll get them."

"No, I'll get 'em. Just tell me where. My laptop is in my bag."

"They're in the cabinet to the right of the fridge. There's soda, beer, and water in the fridge. Help yourself."

"Thank you. What do you fancy?"

"A Sprite is fine. Thanks."

I retrieved Rourke's laptop from its bag and connected it to the docking station on the coffee table, which was wired via carefully hidden cables to a projector mounted to the ceiling. A couple of remote clicks later and a large screen descended from a recess in the ceiling as the projector powered up. As the Windows logo and login prompt appeared, Rourke entered carrying the paper plates, two Sprites, and a roll of paper towels.

"Must be brilliant for watching films," she commented.

She made room for the plates and sodas on the coffee table and set the paper towels on the floor before joining me on the couch.

"I wouldn't know unless crime scene videos count," I said. "You'll have to log in."

Rourke leaned over and entered her password. A photo of Ripley, evidently her desktop background, filled the screen. She quickly navigated to a folder on her hard drive. When she double-clicked the folder, a long list of files opened.

"This is everything I have. Copies of interview transcripts, crime scene photos, investigation notes, and suspect lists. Chief Inspector O'Donnell shared virtually all of her personal notes with me. She attended four of the autopsies, and I have her notes for those as well."

I started to ask why O'Donnell hadn't attended all five autopsies, but then remembered the inspector had been killed before the fifth victim was murdered.

"I need a fork. You?" Rourke asked, heading back to the kitchen.

"There are chopsticks in the bag," I said.

"I'd still be eating this time tomorrow and you'd be picking rice out of your carpet."

"Silverware is in the top drawer to the right of the sink," I said, chuckling.

Rourke paused at the counter that divided the living room and kitchen where several framed photos were arranged. The photos were mostly of Erin and Lanie, but there were others, a few of Stella, one of my parents. No significant other. I was sure the psychologist noticed.

"This must be the entire family, then?" she said, picking up one of the frames. "This is Glasgow Cathedral?"

"Yep."

"You were on holiday?"

I shook my head. "Just a weekend trip."

Rourke looked confused.

"I was born in Edinburgh. Lived not far from there, in Livingston, until I was six."

"Your parents are Scottish?"

"My father was. My mother was originally from Virginia," I said, hoping that line of inquiry wouldn't go too far.

"So, you have dual citizenship?"

"Not anymore. I handed over my passport and renounced citizenship before my Army commissioning."

"Oh, I see."

"But Erin still has dual citizenship, technically."

"You spoke of your parents in past tense. They're deceased?"

"Yes," I said, hoping she wouldn't ask me to elaborate.

She didn't.

"You and your niece are the spittin' image of your mum."

"That's what everyone says," I said, everyone being Erin and Aunt Tabitha.

"Except the eyes. You all have your da's eyes."

"They say that, too."

"I detect no hint of an Edinburgh accent."

"Not for a long time. My sister is a different story. She was fifteen when we moved here and the high school kids immediately decided the Scottish thing was very rock-n-roll. She laid it on thick. I took my cues, told the other first graders that Annie

Lennox was my mother and our aunt was just looking after us while Eurythmics were on tour. But I was the tiny, weird girl who talked funny. Lay a brogue on 'Mickey Mouse' and it sounds like 'Mickey *Moose.*' The little shits at Colonial Forge Elementary couldn't get enough. It sucked slightly less to be laughed at than to be completely ignored."

"Children can be cruel," Rourke said.

"Children can be Machiavellian. So, I compelled my aunt to record *Who's the Boss?* and committed myself to hours of linguistic conditioning, courtesy of Alyssa Milano. Eventually, I ceased to be a novelty. Erin never needed to fit in. She was the cool chick from day one."

While Rourke rummaged in the kitchen, I clicked on a file. The photo of a young woman, maybe a high school yearbook portrait, filled the screen.

"Dana Mullen," Rourke said, as she re-entered. She filled her plate and settled on the sofa.

As eager as I was to start analyzing data points, my stomach reminded me of more pressing matters. I heaped fried rice and chicken onto a paper plate and dug in. As usual, Beijing Dragon didn't disappoint. We ate in silence, each lost in thought.

When our plates were empty, I collected all the take-out litter and deposited it in the kitchen. When I returned, Rourke was looking over the notes I'd left on the coffee table. I undocked her laptop and swapped it for mine. A few clicks later, as a satellite image of Northern Ireland began filling the screen, I said, "Okay, so what I thought we'd do is identify the location of each of your crime scenes. We can start with the general area and I'll continue to zoom in until we have the most precise location possible. Once you're satisfied that the location is accurate, I'll record it as a data point and mark it. Once I've entered all of the data points, the software will do its work and compute the most probable anchor point."

"The anchor point is the most likely location where the offender lives, works, or otherwise spends most of his time?" she asked.

"Clearly, you were paying attention to my lecture."

"Every word. This is the same software you demonstrated this morning?"

Was that this morning? Seems like days ago.

"Similar," I said. "The software we used in Iraq is a proprietary Department of Defense geospatial analysis program. It was sufficient for what we were doing in the area of operations, but useless for criminal investigations."

"Due to lack of access to data?" Rourke asked.

I nodded. "It's always been a challenge. Trend analysis and modeling requires access to a lot of data. The right data. Without it, we're working in a vacuum. The system I'm using now is the result of a joint Department of Justice-Department of Defense project we started working on about four years ago. Geospatial analysts, criminal investigators, geographers, mathematicians, 3-D modeling specialists, and software engineers were handpicked from several agencies for the project. The result is a kick-ass geospatial information system and visualization program powered by a suite of algorithms and predictive models."

"You said *we*. You were involved in the project?"

"Yeah, and I'm still not sure what they were thinking. I only had a couple of years of field experience at the time."

"That's being a wee modest, I think. Will this software produce the same type of 3-D display, what did you call it? Jeopardy something?"

"Yep, jeopardy surface. So, we have an analytic choice to make based on the data environment, status of the investigation, and the question we're trying to answer. Do we take a forensic approach or a predictive one? Are we asking where the killer most likely is, his anchor point, or do we want to know where he is most likely to strike next? In this case, we have a data rich environment."

"Access to all the geospatial data associated with crime locations for five murders," Rourke said.

"Exactly. And we know he's no longer in Northern Ireland, so running predictive analytics for the Belfast area wouldn't get us anywhere. But we can use probability algorithms to determine areas where the anchor point most likely is, where he lives or works or otherwise spends most of his time."

"So, based on the jeopardy surface, we'll be able to cross-check suspect addresses against the highest probability areas," she said.

"That's the idea. We'll digitally lay the 3-D probability model over the map of the Belfast area. But first I need to pull in geographic data for the locations associated with each of the murders."

I retrieved a laser pointer from my bag and handed it to Rourke. "So, the first victim, Dana Mullen. Can you show me where her body was found?"

She aimed the pointer at the screen and a red light appeared on the eastern coast. "Abandoned factory in Donaghadee."

I zoomed in until I could make out streets and their names on the annotated satellite image. Rourke was already looking up the location in her notes. She read the address off and indicated the general area with the pointer. It didn't take long to isolate the exact location.

"That's the place. You can make out the factory. The roof is larger than the buildings around it," Rourke said.

"Okay, I've got the coordinates and I'm going to mark this as the first data point. I'll tag it 'Mullen' and mark it with a red dot. Let's do the same for the second victim."

"Mary Delaney. She was found in the woods near Rathgil."

Rourke moved the pointer to the left, indicating a spot between the previous data point and Belfast city center. We repeated the same process as before to zero-in on the location and I marked the second data point with another red dot and labeled it "Delaney." We located the third data point, where Siofra Hayes was found, near Killarn, just south and west of the second point, and then we marked the fourth and fifth data points, representing Colleen Byrne and Sioban McKinnon's recovery sites near Crawfordsburn and Mount Stewart respectively.

"Are there any known abduction sites?" I asked.

"We couldn't narrow it down with any specificity. We got a hit on Colleen Byrne's cellphone after we believed she was abducted. I can give you the address for that, if you'd like," she offered.

"Not just yet. We don't know how close that cell tower was to her actual location, and that's too much variability. We have five solid data points, so I'd like to stick with those for now."

We studied the array of red dots, which started near the water east of Bangor, moved west, then slightly southwest, then almost due north, and finally to the southeast—in other words, all over the place. The pattern appeared random, but I knew better.

"Can you detect any discernible pattern?" Rourke asked. "Because I've been starin' at the same dots on a wall map for over two years and I can't."

"No, not really, but I can tell you whoever committed these murders had access to a vehicle. Those locations aren't accessible by water or public transportation. Two are in urban areas, one is on a farm, and the other two are in heavily wooded areas."

"Brilliant, we're no further along than we were before."

"We're about to be," I said.

Rourke raised an eyebrow.

With the mouse, I checked several boxes to the right of the image, selecting the output parameters for the probability analysis. Rourke leaned forward, watching what I was doing. "Ready for some mathematical mojo?"

"Dazzle me," Rourke said and smiled, *really* smiled, and for the first time since I'd met her, the cool professional mask vanished.

"It's a sophisticated algorithm. It'll take a few minutes," I informed her.

Rourke took the opportunity to check on Ripley. The dog had made herself at home in the back yard, to the dismay of the squirrels. As soon as Rourke opened the slider, the dog trotted in, tail wagging.

"She's enjoying the exercise," Rourke said. She'd brought in the bowl of water and Ripley lapped at it eagerly.

After resettling on the couch, Rourke said, "So, you've been with the FBI for seven years, military before that. How long were you in the Army?"

"About five years," I said.

"Why'd you give it up? I'm curious what made you decide to join the FBI." Ripley circled in front of Rourke before lying down. Her erect ears and one eye followed our conversation.

The answer to Rourke's first question was complicated. I ignored it and tackled her second.

"I'd worked with an FBI agent when I was assigned to the DIA. He was doing a rotation, sort of an agent-exchange, in the counterterrorism division. I taught him the basics of geospatial analysis, he taught me a thing or two about counter-terrorism operations. We became friends and kept in touch. When he heard I'd left the Army, he contacted me about joining the Bureau. Whatever machinations happened behind the administrative curtain are still a mystery to me, but I reported to Quantico for training about three months later."

Rourke opened her mouth to say something, but was interrupted by a ping from the laptop.

"Let's see what we've got," I said.

The screensaver had kicked in. I entered my password and we were looking at a three-dimensional topographic model.

"So the red area indicates the most likely area for the offender's... anchor point?" she asked.

"Right."

"And the orange area is the next most probable, then the yellow, then the green?"

"Yep. The highest probability for the anchor point is this area here," I said, shining the laser on the peak's highest point. "Of course, this doesn't do us much good right now. They just look like colorful mountain peaks."

From a pull-down menu in the application, I selected the Northern Ireland satellite image. Two mouse clicks later, a street map replaced the satellite image, and I zeroed in on the red area, the highest "peak" of the jeopardy surface.

"We've got about a three-square-mile area in the marina just north of Bangor, which is consistent with our theory that the offender may work in the maritime industry."

"That's one of the marinas we focused on," Rourke informed me. "Especially after Colleen Byrne. Crawfordsburn isn't far from the Bangor Marina."

"Well, based on these results, I think it should continue to be an area of focus. I don't feel like I have a good handle on the Northern Ireland victims. Would you mind walking through each of those murders? I need to get a feel for the victimology, as well as the areas where the victims lived."

She suggested we start with the first victim.

"Dana Mullen," I said, taking up a notepad and pen.

"Aye. My consultation didn't begin until after the second victim was found, so I didn't see the Mullen crime scene first-hand. What I know of her case was gleaned from the case reports, photos, and what the investigators told me. I can tell you that everyone who was at the scene was shaken up."

"I can imagine."

"All due respect, I'm not sure you can," Rourke said. "That's not to say you can't be shocked. But you're American. It's different in the UK when it comes to violent crime."

Right. I'm American and couldn't possibly know the first thing about—

"Car bombs, sure, but by the time the investigators reach the scene, there's not much left to look at."

And I couldn't understand the first thing about seeing people blown to pieces, either. Christ almighty. I bit down hard enough on the inside of my cheek to draw blood. *Don't blame her for what she doesn't know.*

Rourke went on. "Murders do occur, but not with the frequency that you get here in the U.S. Our homicides tend to be gang-related or the result of a domestic that got out of hand. What was done to Dana Mullen and the others, and particularly the way they were left on display, well most, if not all, of the investigators had never personally seen anything like that."

"So, why Dana Mullen?" I asked. "She was the first, at least in this series. I don't think she was his first victim, though."

"I agree. It suggests practice. He continued to adapt his M.O. after Mullen, but he already knew what he was doing by that time."

"No murders with any of the same signatures turned up?" I asked.

"Not that the investigators could find."

"He could have lived in another country previously, been killing, or at least working up to it," I suggested.

"Aye."

He was obviously familiar with Belfast, had been there for some time. "Tell me about Mullen," I prompted.

"Eighteen years old, middle class, stable home. She was a dancer, studied at a ballet academy in Belfast. You've seen the photos of her. She was built like a ballerina, slight, almost diminutive—"

"I prefer compact," I said.

Rourke smirked. "Well, she was about one hundred and sixty centimeters tall, weighed about forty-five kilos."

"That's about a hundred pounds, right?"

"Roughly. About your size."

I clicked a button on one of the remotes and the projector screen glided up, revealing a large white board. I walked to the board, snatched a marker from the tray, and wrote "Dana Mullen." Under the name, I listed several categories: physical characteristics; socioeconomic status; relationship status; education; hobbies; and so on. As Rourke provided the details of Dana Mullen's life, I added them under the appropriate column. Once we felt like we'd captured all the information we had for one victim, we moved on to the next. With a local channel on for background noise and occasional not-so-newsworthy updates on the Jennifer Abbott case, we continued filling in the victimology matrix for hours, only stopping for bathroom breaks.

When Jimmy Fallon started his *Tonight Show* monologue, I warned Rourke that I neither cooked nor shopped, ate most of my meals in the cafeteria at Quantico or in motel rooms, and if I couldn't buy it at a 7-Eleven, I didn't. The psychologist was going to have to get used to take-out during her stay if she didn't want to starve to death. We settled on my usual Italian delivery joint, Angelo's Bistro. Rourke ate a salad and the crusts from my pizza. Bellies full, fatigue hit us hard, and it occurred to me that my guest was probably experiencing some major jet lag. "You're probably exhausted," I said. "I am, and didn't just fly across the Atlantic. Why don't we get some sleep? We've got a lot of work ahead of us tomorrow."

Rourke didn't argue. We carried her bags in and got her settled in the guest room, which involved some rearranging of boxes. Ten minutes after checking the locks and setting the alarm, I was in bed, face and teeth freshly scrubbed. My mind zoomed as I associated a name and a face to each red dot on the Belfast map. Was the momentum finally beginning to shift in our favor? There was so much to do. That morning, I'd had one victim on my murder board. Now, I had six. How much longer before there was another?

The cameras and DVR Vincent installed had revealed that, although my nocturnal episodes didn't appear to be frequent—a couple of times in the last three weeks—the front yard outing hadn't been an isolated episode. Though I'd not ventured outside since November fourteenth, I couldn't trust myself not to go wandering around in my sleep while armed, and I wasn't going to let that happen with Rourke in the house.

The handcuff wasn't exactly comfortable on my ankle, but I didn't think it would keep me from sleeping. Before securing it to the iron rail at the foot of my bed, I tied the key to a long length of thread, which I secured to my nightstand handle. I prayed that remembering where the key was and retrieving it weren't things I could do while asleep. It didn't escape me that in the event of a house fire or other emergency, my response time was increased. What would the first responders think? *She burned up in the bed. Damn shame. What's with the handcuff? Sex games gone wrong? But why only on one ankle?* The rabbit hole of possible scenarios would keep me up all night. I dealt in probabilities. I was just going to have to take the chance that sleepwalking was more likely than a house fire or earthquake.

CHAPTER THIRTEEN

December 18

Triangle, VA

38°32'40.87"N, 77°19'32.87"W

A STRANGLED CRY HUNG in the room. Something acrid—*smoke?*—in my throat and—*oh God! Smoke! Get out of bed now!* A tug on my ankle. *What the hell?* I threw the covers aside and stared at the metal cuff, familiar, but not. *Focus, Ross.* No fire, no smoke. A dream. The clock's minute digit rolled over: 2:58. Hell, I'd never be able to get back to sleep. The key was right where I'd left it. Once freed, I clipped my phone to the waistband of my pajamas and ignored my numb foot as I headed toward the living room with the intention of studying the notes covering the white board. Instead, I found myself entering the code in the keypad next to the garage door.

As soon as I slid inside the car, I felt a little calmer. New leather scent in a car with an old soul was always a little surprising. I ran my hand along the seam of the cherry red leather seat, wondering exactly where Vincent had hidden the tiny GPS tracker. Head back, eyes closed, I managed to not think about anything for a few minutes. At some point, I must've fallen asleep because the rapping on the window startled me. My hand instinctively went to my hip and found nothing there. Rourke was watching me through the window. She might've been amused or concerned. Maybe a little of both, it was hard to tell.

"Sorry. You okay?" she asked, voice muffled through the window.

"Oh, yeah. Fine. Must've dozed off," I said.

And this doesn't look at all weird.

She walked around to the passenger side, checking out the car as she did. She was dressed for a Victoria's Secret photo shoot, silk robe, not a hair out of place. I was on the other end of the fashion spectrum in my faded flannel pants and Sex Pistols t-shirt. She opened the door and slid in. "It's beautiful. Porsche?"

"Yeah," I said, rubbing my eyes. "Fifty-seven 356 Carrera Speedster."

"Did you restore it yourself?"

Oh, God. I'm too tired to tell this story.

"It's kind of a long story," I said. "Especially in the middle of the night." *Morning. Whatever.*

"My hypothalamus didn't get the memo. I'm wide awake," Rourke said.

"Well, I don't know the full history of the car, but by the time I discovered it, it was a rusted shell of its former glory. It belonged to the mother of the guy I was dating at the time, who'd acquired it in a divorce settlement. She had just about as little affection for the car as she did for husband number four. I'd wanted a classic Porsche since watching Kelly McGillis drive one in *Top Gun*. I offered her five hundred dollars, every penny I had without touching my inheritance. She sold it to me for ten bucks and the price of a tow truck to haul it off her property. It sat in storage for four years until I could afford to have any work done on it and I put ten grand into it just to get it in drivable condition, but it still looked like a rusted bathtub on wheels."

I'd warned Rourke it was a long story, but she still looked interested. "A few years later, I was a rookie special agent assigned to
the Richmond Field Office and working with the Richmond Area
Violent Enterprise Task Force. Enter Raoul Mendoza. Raoul had a
couple of priors, minor drug charges. He owned a body shop and
was essentially a decent hard-working guy who got involved with
the wrong hombres. You familiar with MS-13?"

"The Latino gang? Aye, I've heard of them."

"Well, a sub-clique of MS-13 called the SLSW, Sailors
Loco Salvatrucha Western, was specializing in stolen cars in the
Richmond area at the time and got their hooks into Mendoza,
turned his business into a chop shop. The SLSW stole enough cars
that the Task Force got involved. We flipped Raoul, got him to
wear a wire and the whole enchilada. He was scared shitless. My
job was to talk him down when he started to freak out, which was
practically every other day. Long story short, the SLSW got jumpy,
saw Raoul as a liability."

"He was in trouble," Rourke said.

"Big trouble. The guy had four little kids at home. The Locos
don't mess around and Raoul knew it. The SAC was ready to pull
him out. As a last-ditch effort to keep the entire operation from
tanking, I basically forced Raoul to beat the shit out of me in front
of an audience of MS-13 thugs. Suffice it to say, I didn't give him
a choice. The idea was to convince the Locos that Raoul was a
badass and no friend of the Feds. EMS carted me off, and the Task
Force made a big show of arresting Raoul. We let the Locos think
Raoul was in custody for a while. He crashed at my apartment for
three or four weeks, and by then, the Locos were business as usual,
chopping and moving cars on the regular. Two months later, we
took them down."

"What happened to Raoul?"

"He spent a couple of months in prison to keep up appearances with the Locos, then went completely straight, started specializing in pimpin' rides and restoring classic cars."

"This is his handiwork?" Rourke asked, running a finger along the dash.

"Yeah, Raoul got it in his head that he owed me something. I tried to convince him a broken nose was temporary, and it's not like I would even notice a couple more scars. It was no use. He has three younger sisters, and messing up my face *really* bothered him. I felt bad for making him feel bad. We were stuck in a cycle of guilt. Finally, I made a deal with him. I'd pay for the material and parts, and he'd donate his time and talent."

"He did a wonderful job. I don't know much about classic cars, but the black paint is classy and the interior is gorgeous."

"If it didn't exist in 1957, it's not in the car. It's a hundred percent authentic."

"Must be worth a fortune now," Rourke said.

"Another restored '57 Carrera Speedster, not nearly as pristine as mine, sold at auction for just shy of a quarter million dollars last year."

"Jaysus."

"Only a few people know about the car. I'd like to keep it that way," I said.

"Of course. That a motorcycle under the tarp?"

"A Ducati. Sadly, I never have time to ride. My niece desperately wants to learn to ride and has been lobbying hard. Erin would kill me. She refers to a helmet as a brain bucket."

"Well, Agent Ross, you're certainly full of surprises," she said.

"Since you're learning all my secrets, might as well dispense with the formalities. Please, just Regan. Or Ross. Whichever."

"Right. Likewise, please call me Sheridan then."

"Okay, Sheridan."

"Well, Regan, in the interest of full disclosure, I have something to show you." She produced an evidence bag from the pocket of her robe, an *unlabeled* evidence bag that had presumably traveled across international waters. *What the hell?*

Rourke didn't seem eager to offer any clues, so I examined the contents through the clear plastic, a postcard hand-addressed to Dr. Sheridan Rourke at an address in Belfast. The photo side of the card featured Baltimore's Inner Harbor. The return address was a little more interesting, Baltimore-Washington International Airport. In the message block of the card, someone had carefully written a four-digit number that could mean any number of things: last four of an SSN, partial phone number, a date. Nothing stood out as particularly likely. As I read the series of numbers below that, realization settled like a lead weight in my gut. In the interest of maintaining plausible deniability, I didn't point out the obvious disregard for chain of custody protocols or my growing suspicion that the timing of her lecture at the Academy hadn't been entirely serendipitous.

"These coordinates are local, and by local I don't mean continental U.S.," I said. "In fact, right off the top of my head, I'd say whoever sent this to you was pretty much pointing to my fucking back yard."

"Aye, Quantico."

"Does this make any sense to you?" I asked, losing patience and willing the pieces to fall into place.

"I think he's pointing me to Maryland, connecting the murders," she said, absently spinning one of the silver beads on her necklace.

"And what, suggesting you visit the FBI? Or did he already know you were planning to?"

"The latter seems highly unlikely considering Alisha Trent added me to the lecture schedule at the last minute," she said.

"The Academy schedule isn't published," I pointed out. "Unless he had insider information. What about the PSNI? Did you tell any colleagues, post your trip to social media or—"

"Give me some credit, Regan. I didn't tell anyone. With the exception of British Airways, no one knew my itinerary."

"This other number mean anything to you? Four-oh-two-nine?" I asked.

"Grace O'Donnell's constable number."

"Like a badge number?"

"Same idea, but constables don't have badges. Officers wear their assigned number on their epaulettes."

"But O'Donnell was a chief inspector, not a const—"

"She didn't start out as one."

"Not to sound flippant, but a car bombing would have been all over the news over there, right? It wouldn't be hard to figure out where O'Donnell worked. Some creative cold calling probably could have produced her constable number. Realistically, anyone could have sent this." Even as it left my mouth, I didn't believe it. "Why you? Why would he address it specifically to you?"

"Because Ballinger was arrested after Grace O'Donnell was killed, within a week of Sioban McKinnon's murder. After that, I was the only one operating on the theory that the killer was still out there. I wasn't exactly quiet about it."

"Jesus, Sheridan. Assuming this was sent by the man who murdered Jennifer Abbott and five victims in Northern Ireland, he's telling you the cases are connected. He obviously wanted you to follow him to Maryland. I'm not gonna lie, I'm a little freaked out. Why didn't you tell me about this sooner?" I fought to keep my voice even.

"I probably should have, but it's complicated. As far as the PSNI is concerned, this case is closed. And I mean 'closed' with a finality I'm not sure you can understand. If the PSNI superintendent knew I was sharing information with an American federal agent right now, he—"

"Do they know about this?" I thumped the bag.

She hesitated slightly. "No one else has seen it."

The postmark was dated October twenty-fifth. By then, he was probably stalking Abbott.

"I'm just trying to wrap my head around the fact that you didn't bother to tell anyone at the PSNI that you received a postcard, addressed to you, from a possible serial murderer."

"That's just it, Regan. They wouldn't believe it was from a serial murderer. They believe Ballinger killed those women, and his timely exit provided the closure a lot of people were looking for. At this point, it's easier for them to believe I'd fabricate evidence than to admit that they accused the wrong man and allowed a psychopath to get free and kill in the United States."

"What would possibly make them believe you're capable of that?" I asked.

"Because they've banned me from touching the case. They would believe that I am so desperate to have the case reopened that I would fabricate this postcard."

It still seemed far-fetched, but I let it go for the moment. "Have you had it tested for DNA? Fingerprints?"

"No. Like I said, you're the only person I've shown it to."

"I can have it analyzed by our lab, but I'll be surprised if they find anything. No fingerprints have been found on any of the cache items, and I don't know if I mentioned it, but Jennifer Abbott's fingernails were cut short. Her best friend and boyfriend both insist she always wore them long and had gotten a manicure three days before she went missing."

"He clipped them to remove any trace evidence that might have been under her nails," Rourke said. "It was the same with the Belfast victims."

"My point is, if he's that particular about removing trace evidence, he's not going to leave prints or DNA on a postcard unless it's intentional. We're not going to find anything he doesn't want us to find on that card or anywhere else. It makes me wonder about the fibers."

"We suspected he washed their bodies. Siofra Hayes had damp hair the weather didn't account for. Yet he missed the fibers in Abbott's hair," she said. "Was that a mistake?"

Doubtful.

"I don't know. There was nothing rushed about this crime. If he was going to make a mistake, wouldn't you expect it to happen much earlier in the series?"

"Aye, before he became proficient."

"It's possible he planted fibers to throw us off," I suggested.

"I've never seen a case where the offender planted evidence," she said. "It's much more common to see items removed."

Rourke's lone wolf bullshit bugged me. This wasn't going to work if she was inclined to withhold information. I said, "Listen, Sheridan, we're obviously going to have to work together. If there's anything else you're not telling me…"

"Aye, well, shite." She sighed heavily, obviously resigned to another revelation, and I wondered what other evidence might be stashed in her Louis Vuitton.

"I'm not exactly on holiday," she informed me. "And I'm not just at Quantico to present a lecture."

After a nonverbal prompt, she looked away, and quietly said, "As of three weeks ago, I no longer have a professional association with the Police Service."

Not even close to what I'd been expecting. "Why?"

"A month ago, the PSNI discovered that I was investigating the murders on my own after I had been explicitly ordered not to. Remember I told you that I'd attempted to have Interpol issue a Green Notice?"

I nodded.

"Well, I contacted them directly after I received that," she said, nodding at the bag I was still holding. "Someone from Interpol contacted the station to follow up and a PSNI inspector took the call. He happened to be the inspector who arrested Ballinger, and he wasn't pleased that I was investigating on my own, to say the least. In fact, he took it as a personal affront, as if I was questioning his judgment or ethics. Which, I suppose I was."

"So how did you end up lecturing at the Academy?" I asked.

"I attended a working group at NCAVC a few years ago and became acquainted with Anthony Parillo."

"ViCAP Tony?"

"Aye. A few months ago, I contacted him to see if he could check for ViCAP records of any crimes that had been committed in the U.S. matching the Belfast Strangler's M.O. and signatures. He casually mentioned that the Academy was lining up presenters and asked if I was interested. One thing led to another and a few days later Ms. Trent called and invited me to speak."

"Belfast Strangler?"

"That was the media's doing. Not very original. They probably would have capitalized on the alliteration and dubbed him the 'Belfast Burner' if the bit about the torching had been released. I had other choice names for the bastard, but they weren't appropriate for public utterance."

"So, your PSNI contract was suspended and you came to the U.S. to guest lecture at the Academy."

"And to follow up on the postcard."

I was about to reply when my cellphone vibrated. This early in the morning, it wouldn't be anything good.

"Ross."

"It's Haskins. Ross, we—"

"The more Dr. Rourke and I compare notes, the more obvious it is that our guy committed the murders in Northern Ireland."

I held the plastic bag up and asked for permission with my eyes. After a brief pause, she nodded.

"He sent Rourke a postcard, Rob, with O'Donnell's badge number on it. It was sent on October twenty-fifth."

"Slow down. Who is O'Donnell?"

"The PSNI inspector in charge. She was killed during the investigation."

"Jesus Christ. How? No, you know what? Tell me about it when you get here."

"Get where?"

"Another woman is missing, Regan."

"Fuck. Who?"

"Allison Brightwell. Last seen about twenty miles from where Jennifer Abbott was found. Twenty years old, petite, athletic, long dark hair. Sound familiar?"

"Son of a bitch," I muttered. "I'll stop by Quantico and drop the postcard off at the lab. When do you need us?"

"Right this goddamn second, but ASAP will have to do."

CHAPTER FOURTEEN

December 18
7:58 a.m.
Eastern Shore, Maryland
38°59'29.37"N, 76°22'26.24"W

T HREE HOURS LATER, we were cruising two hundred feet above the Chesapeake Bay in a lane all to ourselves, thanks to the Tahoe's emergency lights. Rourke had a white-knuckle grip on the *Oh Shit* handle, and I didn't think it was entirely due to our speed. She hadn't dared to peek out the side window since we'd merged onto the Bay Bridge. My other passenger was much more relaxed. Ripley seemed content to watch swooping seagulls through the back window.

"So, your sister Erin is a physician?" Rourke asked.

"Yeah, a cardio-thoracic surgeon. How'd you—"

My eyes were on the road, but I felt her watching me and sensed her embarrassment at inadvertently intruding into my personal affairs.

"We were in the same car, Sheridan. You don't need to apologize for overhearing."

"Your sister must have a grueling schedule. Does her husband work at hospital too?"

"Husband?" I snorted. "No, she's never been married." *Never dated anyone long enough for me to bother remembering a name, come to think of it.*

"Oh, I see. She has a daughter, and… Sorry. It was daft of me to assume."

"I don't know all the details because Erin has never wanted to talk about it. She got knocked up her third year of medical school. I get the impression he wasn't much more than a one night stand."

"Does Lanie have any contact with her father?" Rourke asked.

"No. When she was born, baby-daddy's family insisted on paying the medical bills, but Erin wouldn't accept a dime from him. Or any of them. I think he and Erin both preferred he stay out of the picture."

"Lanie's never asked about him?"

"Not really, but I suppose it's naïve to think she won't want to know about him at some point."

"How in the world did your sister manage to raise a daughter on her own while going to medical school?" Rourke asked.

"She didn't. My aunt and I took care of Lanie. The University of Virginia is about an hour from Lexington, where we lived. Erin would come home on the weekends, whenever she could get away. When she started her surgical residency at Johns Hopkins, we moved to be closer to her."

"You must've been a teenager."

"I was fifteen when Lanie was born."

"That's an incredible amount of responsibility."

"We managed."

"What led you to the Army?"

"Love," I said, automatically and without an ounce of sincerity.

"You know you're going to have to elaborate."

"My lifelong dream was waiting for me, a full-ride athletic

scholarship to the University of North Carolina and a place in a premier soccer program. The only problem was that my boyfriend, whom I was convinced I couldn't breathe without, was set on becoming an Army officer. So, I hung up my cleats and followed him into the ROTC program at Virginia Tech."

"Shite, what a loss. You could've been the next Mia Hamm," Rourke said. "He the same ex-boyfriend whose mother owned the Porsche?"

"Yeah, as a matter of fact."

"And you followed your man into the Army?" Rourke asked, clearly amused.

"Oh, God no. Daniel flunked out by the middle of our sophomore year. He's a welder now, works for some offshore outfit, last I heard."

"You must have liked the military if you stuck with it," she said.

"I loved it, pretty much from day one. The discipline and structure..."

"I don't imagine you'd ever really had that."

"Nope. Your turn. What's your story? How'd you end up a forensic psychologist?"

"Well, it certainly wasn't my original plan. I initially followed in the family tradition. My da, uncles, brothers, they're all with the Police Service. I put in three years."

"You were a cop? Seriously?"

"Aye, worked the beat in Belfast," she said. "Is it difficult to imagine?"

"Yes and no. So, how'd you go from cop to shrink?"

We were nearing the shore and Rourke finally let her gaze venture outside the Tahoe.

"Don't get me wrong, I love my da and brothers, but everything with them is a feckin' competition. I made rank faster than my oldest brother, Sean, and it caused a lot of tension between us. I never had the same passion for policing as my brothers. I quit the

Police Service and moved to Liverpool to attend university. A master's degree in forensic psychology and criminal investigation didn't sit well with my family."

"Why the hell not?" I asked.

"Da was livid I'd disgraced the family by leaving the Police Service, and my brothers resented me for getting an education. I decided to leave the UK to pursue a doctorate."

"Where?" I asked.

"San Diego."

"California? Why'd you come here?"

"I was interested in psychopathology. Frankly, the best place to study the subject is the United States, particularly UC, San Diego. There's more research opportunity here. My dissertation was on the criminal brain. Specifically, psychopathology of violent criminals."

"Well, we've definitely got more than our share of those," I said.

"Exactly. The number of incarcerated persons in the U.S. is seven times that of all of Europe combined. My research thesis focused on the question of whether criminal behavior can be considered a psychological disorder, like depression or anxiety, or a neuropsychological disorder directly linked to identifiable abnormalities of the brain. I wanted to study—"

"—the brains of our most violent criminals. You wanted to see if their noggins are different."

"Essentially, yes. My research was based on twenty-three neuroimaging studies that indicated abnormalities in localized areas of the frontal lobes in subjects with violent or aggressive behavioral histories."

"Wait, are you saying that sick fucks like Dahmer and Gacy got a bump on the head and that excuses the fact that they tortured and killed young men?" I asked.

"Not Dahmer and Gacy, necessarily. I don't happen to know the details of their neurological history. And you're oversimplifying it. I was interested in what's going on in the brains of 'sick fucks,' how frontal lobe damage correlates to their 'sickness.'"

My grip tightened on the steering wheel, and I was sure she noticed. She continued, undeterred. "As a child, Ken Bianchi fell off a jungle gym and landed on the back of his head. He began having epileptic—"

"Are you serious? Bianchi gets a bump on the head and that's supposed to excuse the premeditated murder—"

"I never used the word *excuse*, Regan, nor would I. It's not my belief that prefrontal cortex abnormalities, nor any other neurological abnormalities for that matter, excuse violent behavior. But they could *explain* aggressive, violent, or impulsive tendencies. The frontal cortex is extremely vulnerable to injury, and injuries to this area are often devastating and sometimes lead to disorganized, asocial, and even violent criminal behavior."

"So, if you compared your brain to Ted Bundy's, you'd see a definite difference?" I asked.

"No, actually. Extensive x-rays and brain scans were performed on Bundy and revealed no evidence of brain disease or trauma."

"Doesn't that contradict everything you've been saying?" I asked.

"Not at all. I never said that every violent serial offender is going to have an abnormal brain. I believe I said, or at least intended to say, that we see it often. And in cases where we do, there's a direct linkage between neurobiology and behavior. Research, including some of my own, has shown that a high percentage of death-row inmates in this country have had severe head injuries. And approximately seventy percent of brain-injured patients develop aggressive tendencies. As you know, many violent serial offenders suffered physical abuse by a parent. In many cases, that abuse included some form of head trauma. That said, obviously head trauma doesn't guarantee a serial killer."

"I sure as hell hope not," I said, rubbing the scar over my left eye.

"There's no one singular factor that makes someone a serial rapist or killer, but it's my job to ask the question, 'Why did he do it,' no matter how complicated the answers, or the fact that I'll probably never be entirely sure. The answers to those questions inform decisions regarding the best way to—"

"Please spare me the mental health rehabilitation versus punitive incarceration debate. The person who tortured and killed your Belfast girls and Jennifer Abbott, well, I couldn't give two shits *why*. He deserves the needle, and I'll gladly be first in line to shove it in his vein. Brain trauma, or childhood molestation, or whatever the fuck happened to him, you know what? I don't care. It doesn't give him license to—"

"Of course not. Mitigating circumstances to criminal behavior don't excuse the behavior, but they do help us make sense of the factors that contributed to it—Jayzus, is that what I think it is?" Rourke blurted as a truck brazenly passed us in the right lane.

My gaze followed the truck, which almost qualified for monster status. I snorted when I realized what had caught her attention. Rourke was gawking at the object dangling from the rear bumper, which was at about the level of the Tahoe's hood.

"Yep. That would be a big ol' rubber scrotum," I said.

"Jaysus, Mary, and the Rolling Stones. What in God's name?"

"I don't understand it either," I admitted. "I see them occasionally, and almost exclusively on large trucks."

"Must be an American thing," Rourke said.

"More like a redneck thing."

Rourke was grinning around her fist. Before I knew it, we were both laughing. The more we tried to stop, the more impossible it was. I was still trying to catch my breath and avoid running us off the road when my cellphone rang.

"Ross."

"Hello, Special Agent Ross. This is Monica Spears. I just wanted to follow up regarding our email exchange."

The mirth instantly evaporated. "Not much of an exchange, Ms. Spears. It was you requesting an interview and me declining. I'm past being polite." My abrupt change in tone earned Rourke's full attention.

"I understand, Regan, I just thought your sister might want–"

"We're not on a first-name basis, and you obviously don't understand. What my sister wants is to be left alone. I'm telling you right now not to contact anyone in my family again. Doing so will constitute harassment, which I will absolutely respond to with every recourse available, legal and otherwise. You do not want that, Ms. Spears, trust me."

"Have you had a chance to speak to Dr. Ross about–"

"You and I are done. You and my sister are done. And if you ever send something to my home address again, I swear to God… Final warning, Ms. Spears. Do not attempt to contact us again."

"Fucking reporters," I muttered, ending the call. Rourke started to say something, but was interrupted by my buzzing phone.

"Jesus, lady. What the hell is your problem?" I barked into the phone.

"Whoa," a familiar voice said.

"Sorry, Haskins. Thought you were someone else."

"Apparently someone you're really fond of. Where are you?"

"Just got off the Bay Bridge. We should be there in fifteen minutes," I informed him.

"Great. You'll be glad to hear that Eberley actually came through. He went to the deputy director, who spoke to the superintendent at the PSNI. They've agreed to reopen their cases and cooperate with the FBI in any way they can, so there's no need to get the attorney general involved. They've also agreed to reinstate Rourke's consulting contract and loan her to us for the duration of the investigation, so long as she's willing."

"How the hell did Eberley manage all that?"

"Well, I wouldn't give him all the credit. It was mostly the deputy director who mentioned how unfortunate it would be for their little blunder to be picked up by international news networks."

"You mean the little blunder that resulted in their killer going free and becoming a threat to the international community?"

"Exactly. He also emphasized how much better this would be for everyone if it was handled discreetly. Interpol issued a Green Notice thirty minutes ago."

"That's good news. I'll let Rourke know."

"Great. I'll fill you both in when I see you."

"Where are we staying, anyway?" I asked.

"Shady Hill Motel. Drive through town and you'll see it. Just don't blink. We've pretty much taken over the place. There are only eight rooms. I'm sorry, but you and Rourke are going to have to room together."

"Do I at least get my own bed?" I asked.

"Yep, and your own little patio with a lovely view of a horse pasture. Listen, there's a K-Mart at Kent Island, you should be close to it now. It would behoove you to purchase some bedding."

"Why?"

"You'll see. See you soon."

Rourke looked at me expectantly. I informed her she'd been reinstated and would have the pleasure of my company for the foreseeable future.

"Well, now that we apparently have the PSNI's cooperation, I need to contact my colleagues and have them start an inquiry in the area you identified with your..."

"Jeopardy surface," I said.

"Right. I'll have them start with men in the area who did any sort of marine or fishing work during the time of the murders."

"You can narrow it down to those who were in the area through last August and focus on those who may have tried to enlist in the military or law enforcement," I suggested.

"Aye, and he's probably mechanically inclined."

"A handy Popeye."

"So, who's this Spears woman? And what does she want with you and your sister?"

"I'll tell you about her, Sheridan, but not now. It'll take a while and probably involve some liquor on my part."

CHAPTER FIFTEEN

December 18

8:22 a.m.

Centreville, Maryland

39°2'25.27"N, 76°4'17.95"W

IT WAS HARD to tell what overall theme the owners of the Shady Hill Motel were aiming for. Rustic, maybe. No aspect of Room 102's décor appeared to have been altered since the motel had been built, which had to have been in the forties? Fifties? Several ancient oil paintings depicting waterfowl in various stages of flight adorned the wood paneling. The artists' versions were slightly less depressing than the mounted specimens, which had probably met their demise during the early days of the Cold War. The original color and pattern of the threadbare carpet was anyone's guess. Someone had sprayed entirely too much Lysol in an attempt to mask an unidentifiable funk. I was contemplating the feasibility of donning a Tyvek suit and gloves for the duration of my stay as Haskins began the introductions.

"Ladies and gentlemen, we're joined by Special Agent Regan Ross and Dr. Sheridan Rourke. Agent Ross is with the Behavioral Analysis Unit and is on loan from Quantico and Dr. Rourke is a consulting forensic psychologist from the UK. By now, you're all aware of the connection between Abbott and the murders in Northern Ireland. We're fortunate to have the benefit of Dr. Rourke's expertise. Having previously worked with Special Agent Ross, I can tell you that her unique skills are especially suited to this investigation."

Haskins actually winked at me, and a hot blush spread across my cheeks. Heart's "If Looks Could Kill" played in my head.

He didn't miss a beat. "Ladies, allow me to introduce sheriffs Paul Banks and Kerry Wagner."

Like a scene from an old western, the lawmen simultaneously tugged the brim of their hats. Physically, the two men couldn't have been more different. Wagner, the Queen Anne's sheriff, was standing next to Chris Reynolds and had a couple of inches and about forty pounds, mostly gut, on the deputy. He removed the toothpick he'd been working long enough to nod in our direction. Banks, Kent County's sheriff, reminded me of a young Billy Dee Williams. The four detectives in plainclothes could've been from either sheriffs' office or the MSP. Haskins introduced Marisol Fuentes, who was heading up the Baltimore F.O.'s Evidence Response Team, and Kimberley Graham, one of Odette's forensic operations specialists charged with overseeing the transport of evidence from Centreville to Quantico. Eberley was MIA, which could mean any number of things detrimental to the investigation.

It was just as well. You couldn't squeeze a fart in that motel room, much less another person. The beds had been replaced by two long folding tables, which held several laptop computers, a fax machine, a printer, and four handheld radios. Directly across the room from me, a whiteboard had been hung over the dresser. My eyes were drawn dead center to a photo of a young woman at a track meet. She had the well-defined musculature of a world-class athlete, and she was in mid-clap, beaming. Celebrating. "Nice to meet you both. Allison Brightwell?" I asked, pointing at the photo.

"Yup," Wagner confirmed.

"How recent is that?" I asked.

Wagner chewed his toothpick for a moment, thinking. "Four months or so. It was taken in late summer, I believe. Appearance hasn't changed much, except she may be a little less tan and her hair's longer, according to her mother."

"What do we know so far?" I asked.

"About eight o'clock last night, Lynn called the Sheriff's Office in a panic, said Allison was supposed to meet her and her husband for dinner and never showed up. Allison wasn't returning her calls."

"Sorry to interrupt you, Sheriff. Lynn is Allison's mother?" I asked.

He nodded.

"Do you know her personally?"

"Oh, sure. Allison's father, Doug, is minister of Calvary Baptist, right out on 50 East, near the college. Lynn's a teller at one of the banks in town."

"How long did Mrs. Brightwell wait before calling to report Allison missing?" I asked.

"Couple of hours. She called around and checked all the places she could think of that Allison might be—apartment, gym, library, what have you. She even drove the route that Allison usually runs."

"Allison runs competitively?"

"Oh, yeah. She placed first in the hurdles at the national championship this summer—"

"—high jump, I believe, Sheriff." The interrupting plainclothes detective sported a military high and tight haircut.

"Maybe it was the high jump," Wagner said. "There are so many different events in the decathlon or whatever it is, it's hard to keep them straight."

"Heptathlon," the detective offered. His jaws worked hard, giving a wad of gum the business.

"Well, hell, Sergeant, you seem to know all about it, why don't you tell 'em?" Sheriff Wagner suggested, sounding slightly irritated.

"Yes, Sir. Miss Brightwell competed in seven events at the national championships in June. I believe she placed first in the high jump and fourth in the hundred-meter hurdles. She's got a shot at the U.S. Olympic team for Rio next year. There was a write-up in the local paper about it three or four months ago."

Wagner jumped back in. "She attends Chesapeake College now, when she's not competing, which is often. According to Lynn, she plans to transfer to the University of Maryland next semester on a full athletic scholarship."

Heptathlon. Agility, speed, explosive strength. The young woman in the picture clearly benefited from a sophisticated training program, and I couldn't imagine a local community college providing it. I voiced my puzzlement.

Surprisingly, Haskins provided the answer. "She trains with a coach, a former Olympian, Davis LeMarc. They use the Queen Anne's High School facilities. So far, LeMarc is clean and well-alibied."

"Does Brightwell live alone? What about a boyfriend?" I asked.

The sheriff shared a sideways look with his knowledgeable detective.

Wagner finally replied, "No and not exactly."

I waited for him to elaborate.

"She has a roommate, Rachel—what's her last name, Bill?" the sheriff asked the detective who was apparently also schooled up on Allison's personal life.

Detective Bill consulted a small notebook. "Rachel McAlester."

"It appears that Allison and Miss McAlester are, well, more than friends," Sheriff Wagner added.

"They live together?" I asked.

"Evidently so. Her parents didn't realize the, uh, nature of the relationship until we started asking questions. We talked to some of her high school teammates. A couple of them said that they quote, 'kinda knew that Allison wasn't into guys,' but she was private about it."

"What's the timeline? When do we think she was abducted?" I asked.

Haskins approached the whiteboard and pointed to a line drawn across the bottom of the board, bisected by smaller lines annotated with times.

"Allison's whereabouts were last accounted for at three-thirty yesterday. She attended class from nine to eleven yesterday morning and from one to three o'clock in the afternoon. That was her last scheduled class of the day. She logged into a computer in the campus library at three-eighteen and logged off about twenty minutes later. She had plans to have dinner in Kent Island with her parents at six-thirty. McAlester said Allison mentioned her dinner plans that morning. It was a regular thing and she hadn't forgotten about it."

"So at three-thirty she was on campus intending to meet her parents in Kent Island at six-thirty. How far is the restaurant from the campus library?" I asked.

"About fifteen miles," Haskins said.

"How did she get to campus? She has a car?" I asked.

Wagner answered. "Yes. It was found at her apartment."

"Which is where?"

"She and McAlester rent a townhouse right here, downtown," Haskins said. I got the impression Haskins was trying to maintain control of the meeting, so I addressed my next question to him. "So, she apparently drove home after going to the library. Was Rachel home? Did she see Allison?"

"No," Wagner answered. "Rachel was working. She waits tables part-time at the bar next door. She should be there now, matter of fact."

"Anyone else see Allison that afternoon? Any sign of forced entry?" I asked.

"We haven't identified anyone who saw or heard from Allison after she left campus," Haskins informed me. "Rachel said the doors were locked when she got home. Allison apparently changed clothes when she got to the apartment. We found the clothes she wore to class folded on a chair in the bedroom, her purse hanging on a chair in the kitchen. Her key and ID were the only items missing."

"Cellphone?" I asked.

"In her purse," Haskins said.

Rourke chimed in. "What about her trainers?"

Rourke had captured the attention of just about everyone in the room from the moment she'd walked in. Her foreign accent only heightened the captivation. Captivation and *confusion*, I realized.

"Trainers—her running shoes," I clarified. "Are they missing?"

There were shrugs and raised eyebrows all around. Apparently, no one had thought to check or ask.

"We're assuming she went for a run and never made it back," I said. "Knowing for certain whether or not she was wearing running shoes would lend some credence. You said her mother drove the route she usually runs. Do we know what that route is?"

Wagner jumped back in. "McAlester would be the best one to answer that. It's our understanding that she and Allison frequently run together. We didn't get a chance to ask her last night. She's pretty shaken up, suspects the worst. We had to cut the interview short."

I turned to Haskins. "I'd like to review Rachel's statement. And I'd like to talk to her."

He nodded.

It appeared that Allison likely encountered her abductor while she was running. Determining the most likely ambush points was my first priority.

"So what's the game plan, Special Agent Haskins?" Sheriff Wagner asked.

Haskins addressed the group. "For now, we're treating Ms. Brightwell as a missing person. The victimology is consistent with Abbott and the Northern Ireland victims. Let's be clear. We have six known murders committed by the same man. Allison may well be the seventh. Personally, I believe Allison was abducted by our offender and that she's still alive. Obviously, time is not on our side. Dr. Rourke, could you give us a rundown of the working profile?"

She cleared her throat. "Statistically, there's an eighty percent chance that we're looking for a white male, roughly between the ages of twenty-five and forty, though I tend to believe he's closer to the middle of that range. He may very well have been in a long-term relationship with a woman in the past and may currently have a girlfriend or wife. He's intelligent, likely has at least a secondary education, possibly post-secondary. He attends to detail and may have worked in some kind of menial maritime job. We should continue to focus on docks and marinas in the area. He chooses petite, athletic victims and derives pleasure from exerting physical and emotional power over them. He has a deep disdain for law enforcement. He believes he's smarter than you all and wants you to believe it as well."

Sheriff Banks cleared his throat. "Abbott and Brightwell, they're athletes. Hell, Brightwell could outrun any of us. Grabbing her while she was running would be like trying to take down a thoroughbred. Seems like a big risk."

Haskins beat me to a response.

"You're right. We have to consider that he ambushed her, either from a place of concealment or by gaining her trust and luring her to him."

"Based on his M.O., he likely uses a well-practiced ruse to gain the trust of his victims," Rourke added.

"We believe he hit Abbott with a Taser at her car," I said. "World-class speed and strength wouldn't have helped her. You all know what happens when the voltage hits you. That's his ace in the hole."

"Which is why we've got to have a town hall meeting as soon as possible to warn the public," Haskins said.

"But the information must be carefully controlled. There are certain details that we don't want the public to know," I added.

"That's right," Haskins said. "Nothing gets disseminated without my authorization. I'll be consulting with Special Agent Ross and Dr. Rourke. We'll provide the guidance for what is and is not released to the public."

Banks, the Billy Dee look-alike, stepped forward. "Now, just a minute, Special Agent Haskins. These people need to know what we're dealing with. I can't get up there and not answer their questions. I'd lose their trust."

"I understand, Sheriff. We'll answer most questions, but not to the detriment of this investigation. Our main objectives are to let the public know what precautions they should be taking and to enlist their help in finding our offender. Someone works with this guy or lives next to him. Are there any questions about that?"

There weren't. He continued, "In the meantime, Dr. Rourke will be coordinating with her colleagues in Northern Ireland. Now that we know about the connection with the murders there, the PSNI has agreed to reopen those cases. She'll keep us updated regarding any new details. Deputy Reynolds, what do you have on the list of hunters who leased the Garrett property?"

"Nine hunters have had leases over the last five years, including the three who found Abbott's body. All three had solid alibis for when Abbott was killed, and none of them could've been out of the country when the murders in Northern Ireland were committed. Pete Jensen signed a five-year lease a couple of years ago, but he died last year. Plus, he was seventy-one, so he doesn't quite fit the profile." Reynolds smirked, cut his eyes to me.

"That leaves five," I said, hopefully.

"Kent Spann, twenty-eight years old. Had a lease in his name for the last two seasons," Reynolds informed us. "Might'a been a stretch for him, though. He's been on a military deployment the last four months."

Reynolds consulted his list.

"Willie Williams. Thirty-five years old. Doesn't have an alibi for the night Abbott was murdered."

"*But.* There's gotta be a but, right?" I asked.

"Yep. He's lame and walks with a pronounced limp. He's also a small guy. Doesn't exactly fit the profile," Reynolds said.

"I agree the physical disability is probably a disqualifier, but we shouldn't rule someone out just because they don't fit the profile," Rourke said. "The profile is a guide, not the rule."

"If someone's on the hunting lease list and doesn't have a solid alibi for the week leading up to November seventeenth and could have possibly been out of the country during the Belfast murders, we've got to check him out completely. Or someone on that list may have ties to someone who doesn't have an alibi. We can't take anything for granted," Haskins said.

"Now you're going to tell us that the other two on the list are eighty-year-old women, right?" I said.

"No. Well, one's a woman," Reynolds informed us, "and she was eight months pregnant."

"Pregnant hunter. Nothing surprises me anymore," I muttered. "And the last candidate?"

"That would be me," Sheriff Banks said. "I've had a lease with Garrett for four years."

An image of Lando Calrissian hunting ducks came to mind. Banks needed to be checked out, too, to cover our bases, but the list of hunters was looking like a bust.

Haskins checked his watch. "It's getting late. Special Agent Ross, why don't you and Dr. Rourke get on the phone with the PSNI investigators, help them focus their Belfast canvas."

"Sure," I said. "I was able to generate a jeopardy surface, which we're ready to pass along to the PSNI. Sheriff Wagner, you mentioned that Rachel McAlester is waiting tables next door?"

He nodded.

"I'd like to talk to her. Maybe I can catch her at the end of her shift. Tomorrow morning I'd like to check out the route that Brightwell ran, see if there are any places that stand out as possible ambush points."

"Sounds good," Haskins said. "Dr. Rourke, we'd appreciate your help planning the town hall. We could use your expertise."

"Absolutely," Rourke said.

"Good. Well, let's get to it. We'll meet up here at seven a.m tomorrow and see where we are."

Thus concluded the first official meeting of the Eastern Shore Task Force.

CHAPTER SIXTEEN

December 18

9:14 p.m.

Centreville, Maryland

39°2'25.46"N, 76°4'16.25"W

MY FAMILIARITY WITH the interior of the Shady Hill Motel should've prepared me for the ambiance of its neighbor, the Shady Hill Bar and Grill, yet the décor still managed to bewilder. Mounted animal heads competed with random sports memorabilia for every available inch of wall space. The patrons packing the place on a Tuesday night didn't seem to notice. As I made my way to the bar, a blonde waitress hurried by, her taut white t-shirt barely containing her 38 Ds. Hooters meets hunting lodge. Nice.

When the bartender finally made eye contact, she asked, "What can I get you, Hon?"

Hon. Oh, how I *love* terms of endearment from perfect strangers. I reciprocated with my best well-hi-there-Sugar smile. "Hi. Is Rachel McAlester working?"

"Oh, yeah. You can go on back. Dining room, corner booth."

Her appearance and voice gave the impression of fifty or so years of smoking and hard living.

"Thanks."

A pretty blonde waitress sat in a booth in the back corner of the dining room. She was lost in thought, rolling silverware in paper napkins, oblivious to my approach.

"Miss McAlester?" I asked.

"Yes?" Startled, she dropped the fork and knife she'd been holding. Swollen eyes and smudged eyeliner had a marginal effect on Rachel McAlester's girl-next-door good looks.

"Hi. I'm Special Agent Regan Ross," I said, flashing my credentials.

Her eyes widened, and she was suddenly up and grasping my arm. "Oh, God, did they find her?"

Stupid, Ross. Shit. I could feel her hand trembling as she gripped my arm. The opposite of how I wanted this to go.

"No, no. I just wanted to ask you some questions if you have a few minutes."

She looked simultaneously relieved and disappointed. "Oh. Oh, okay. It's pretty quiet back here. Do you mind if I roll this silverware while we talk? I gotta finish before I leave."

"Sure. I can help if you want," I offered.

"No, that's okay. It won't take long. I've already done most of it." Her hands were efficient, but the gold bracelet with the jittery crab charm around her left wrist gave her away.

"I understand you and Allison are close," I prompted, emphasizing the last word.

She met my eyes.

"You're..."

"Allison is my girlfriend. That doesn't begin to cover it, really. She's my *person*."

"How long have you two been together?" I asked.

"Two and a half years, but we've been friends since, well, forever."

"Rachel, has Allison acted differently lately? Has her routine changed? Has she seemed preoccupied or mentioned anything out of the ordinary?"

"Yeah, preoccupied, you could say that."

"What makes *you* say that?"

"She's been looking over her shoulder a lot. Literally, like she can't relax. I thought she was being overly paranoid, you know, because of what happened to that Washington College student, Jennifer. She said she thought someone was following her."

Had she mentioned this to the investigators before they cut the interview short? It hadn't come up at the meeting.

"A specific someone?" I asked.

"Yeah, a guy in her sociology class. He asked her out several times. She kept telling him no, but…"

"He was persistent."

"Very."

"Do you know his name?"

"Justin something. He's from Centreville, was a year ahead of us in school. I tried to get her to tell him the truth, but she wouldn't. He knows her parents from church. She was afraid he'd tell them."

"That she's gay?"

"They don't know. It's complicated. They're bible-thump— they're very religious."

"Her father is a minister?" I asked.

"Yeah, God, they're going to find out, aren't they? I mean, the police know and it's a small town. We've been so careful."

"Who does know, Rachel?"

"Some girls we knew in high school, I'm sure. Girls talk in the locker room as much as guys, maybe more. Except Al doesn't, and I'm sure they wondered. Most of them went away after graduation, though. My family has known for a while. I came out to them when I was sixteen."

"That must've been hard."

"Not really. My parents are basically the opposite of Al's. They didn't like that it would make my life harder, especially around here, but they accept it, and they love Allison to death. She's so strong in every other aspect of her life, but, I don't know. This is different. She needs their approval, especially her dad's. She's afraid they'll be ashamed of her. Her own parents have no idea who she really is, and it kills me to see her so stressed all the time. It's the only thing we ever argue about, really." Her eyes were brimming. It was time to change tacks.

Justin Something seemed too young to be our guy, and if he was a local boy, he couldn't have been killing women in Northern Ireland. I needed to establish whether or not he'd been following Allison. If not, maybe someone else had been.

"When did Allison start acting jumpy?" I asked.

"About a month ago, maybe."

"Before Jennifer Abbott went missing?"

"Yeah. She started asking friends to walk her to her car on campus if I wasn't with her. I wanted to talk to the guy, to tell him to back off, but Al wouldn't let me. She was afraid to be by herself after dark."

Smart girl.

"But she went running by herself?" I asked.

"Yeah, but, she's so fast, you know, and she carried pepper spray. She was smart about it."

"It wasn't a judgment, Rachel," I said. "Plenty of women run solo. I do."

"Why hasn't she come home?" Her eyes were wide. "He has her, doesn't he? The one who killed Jennifer Abbott has her."

Probably.

Hope was the only thing allowing her to keep it together, and I wasn't about to destroy that. Nor would I blow smoke. I reached across the table and lightly gripped her arm.

"We don't know yet, Rachel. Right now, we're treating Allison as a missing person. We're doing everything we can to find her."

"Oh my God." She was sobbing. My hand still on her arm, I fished a travel pack of Kleenex out of a pocket and kept her supplied. After a few minutes, she sat up straight.

"Promise me, please, just find her," she said, wiping her nose. "Please, Agent Ross, I need you to promise me."

Her eyes pleaded with me to say the words. Unwilling to make a promise I wasn't sure I could keep, I gave her arm a final squeeze and focused on my notes.

"Rachel, you were in the house before the police got there. Did you notice if her running shoes were missing?"

"Yeah, I checked," she said, dabbing her eyes. "She has a dozen different pairs, for different events. Lately, she's been wearing a newer pair for her night runs. They weren't in the apartment."

"What route does she run?" I asked.

"She usually runs four miles each night. Most nights I run with her. Three nights a week, at the end of our run, Al stops at the high school track and usually runs sprints for a while, sometimes hurdles. She has a key to the equipment shed. She keeps her shot-put weights and javelins in there, too."

"She runs at the track alone?" I asked.

"Sometimes. If I don't have to work, I stay and keep time and log for her. If I have a shift, I jog back to the townhouse and she logs herself."

"What exactly goes into this log?" I asked.

"Just her run times, heights, distances, so she can track her progress."

"Okay. What time do you start your run?" I asked.

"Usually about five o'clock, as soon as we get home from class and change clothes."

"How long do you run?"

"If she goes to the track after, usually around seven. If not, then usually about a quarter to six. Monday nights, she always skips the track and runs by herself, a long route. She runs hard for an hour, like she would have done last night. I was on campus at study group."

"Allison's serious about running, huh?"

"You have no idea. That's just what she does on her own. She's in the gym lifting weights at zero dark thirty, does agility training after that, then goes to classes, then works with Davis in the afternoon."

"Davis is her coach? Does she work with him every day?" I asked.

"Four days a week. The other days she always checks in with him. She has a nutritionist, too."

"How does she afford her trainers? Do her parents pay for it?"

She shook her head. "New Balance sponsors her. They pay for her training and competition fees. You know, Al is the top high jumper in the country right now, and she's pulling a three point eight GPA. She could be in any elite track program in the country or living in Colorado Springs at the Olympic Training Center."

"But she stayed in Maryland to be with you," I said.

Rachel nodded, getting weepy again. "We're transferring to the University of Maryland in the spring."

Hang in there, Rachel. A few more minutes. I pulled a map of Centreville provided by the Shady Hill Motel out of my back pocket and spread it out on the table. "You've been great. Just one more thing, and we're done, okay? Could you show me the route Allison would've run last night?"

"Sure." She took a pen out of her apron pocket and outlined a route on the map.

"You've been a huge help." I handed her my business card. "My office and personal numbers are on there. If you think of anything, give me a call. Any time."

"I will. Thank you, Agent Ross."

"Oh, Rachel, one other thing. Does Allison listen to music when she runs?"

"No way. She says it throws her off her pace and distracts her. Plus, she doesn't do anything in training that she doesn't do during competition."

A purist. She should've been able to hear someone approaching. Maybe she had, but it hadn't done her any good.

CHAPTER SEVENTEEN

December 19
10:56 a.m.
Grasonville, Maryland
38°58'34.88"N, 76°18'47.51"W

A QUEEN ANNE'S SHERIFF'S deputy had managed to find a lead—in fact, a potentially big one, so my plans to run Allison's route would have to wait. As we walked across the shopping center parking lot, Haskins asked, "What do you think, Dr. Rourke? Are we wasting our time?"

"Perhaps. But if four people purchased the exact type of rope used to bind Jennifer Abbott at this location within two months of when she was killed, I can't help but be cautiously optimistic."

There was a slight chance the golden ticket could be inside the Boater's World in Chester, Maryland. Another data point would be fantastic, but I knew better than to get my hopes up. As we entered the store, it struck me that it might've been prudent to dress down. "Hell, Haskins. We stick out like Shaquille O'Neal at a jockey convention. Who wears a suit to buy fishing lures, for God's sake?"

"Aye," Rourke agreed. "You two practically scream government agent."

I snorted. "You're one to talk, with your haute couture."

"It's hardly haute—"

"Hi, there!" Haskins bellowed to the ill-groomed man at the register. His eyes went wide when Haskins flashed his credentials.

"I'm Special Agent Haskins, these are my colleagues, Dr. Rourke and Special Agent Ross. A deputy sheriff was in a little while ago, he should've told you to expect us. May we speak to the manager?"

"That would be me, Carl Patterson." He extended his hand, which Haskins shook. The man's polo was embroidered with the "Patterson Charters" logo, presumably his moonlighting gig. As he leaned across the counter, I couldn't help notice his muscled arms, which had probably reeled in their share of marlins or whatever they fished for in the Chesapeake. He was too busy ogling Rourke to acknowledge Haskins' proffered badge.

"We're trying to track down the source of some evidence related to an investigation," Haskins informed him.

"This is about the Abbott murder, ain't it?" Patterson asked.

"We can't comment on that," I said. He finally peeled his eyes off Rourke.

"Right. Well, I suppose you folks are here about that rope the deputy was asking about?"

"That's right," Haskins said, passing Patterson a slip of paper.

"That's the product number for a type of Iron Braid rope manufactured by Trident Marine," Haskins explained. "We're looking for that lot number sold within the date range listed there."

"Let me see what I can do." Carl spent several agonizing minutes hen-pecking the keyboard. Haskins, Rourke, and I exchanged glances and checked for messages on our phones. Finally, Patterson looked up and smiled at Rourke, obviously proud of himself. "Rope from this lot was sold on four different days during this timeframe."

"Can you tell if the purchase was made with a credit card or cash?" Haskins asked.

"Nope. This just shows the item and quantity sold."

"What about a time?" I asked.

"Yep. There's a time stamp for the sale."

Moderately helpful.

"If it's not too much bother, would you mind printing us a copy of those records?" Rourke asked.

"Sure, Hon. That's no problem."

Hon. For the love of God.

"What about your video cameras? Do they record, or is it real-time feed only?" Haskins asked. Investigators had already determined that security systems were inconsistent from one store to the next. The cameras at some locations didn't record at all. Some of the stores that recorded their feed didn't keep the recordings long enough to do us any good. In other words, it was a crapshoot.

"They record," Patterson said.

"How long do you maintain the recordings?" I asked.

"Ninety days."

Praise Jesus.

Haskins asked to see the video for the four crucial days.

"Sure. Just give me a minute to find Bobby to take over for me at the register. He's doin' inventory in the back."

When Carl headed off to find his sales associate, Haskins turned to Rourke, obviously amused. "Well, it looks like Carl's got a thing for you, Dr. Rourke."

"Not my type," Rourke said.

"What, too old?" Haskins teased.

Unfazed, she shook her head.

"Too *young?*" he pressed.

She studied an imaginary blemish on a perfectly manicured nail.

Unable to resist, I chimed in. "Too rugged and outdoorsy?"

Her lips pursed ever so slightly.

"Too American?" Haskins continued.

Rourke gave him her full attention. "No, Special Agent Haskins, too *male*." She actually winked at him, and I witnessed a rare phenomenon: Haskins at a complete loss for words. As I pondered that little nugget, a skinny teenager walked up to the counter. His nametag said 'Bobby,' and his reaction when he saw Rourke suggested he was running through mental files trying to remember which movie or issue of *Maxim* he'd seen her in.

"Carl said you all can go on back to the office," Bobby stammered.

We took Carl up on the invitation, and Haskins diplomatically requested he not join us in the office so we could freely discuss specifics without a civilian lurking over our shoulders. The three of us crowded around the monitor in the cramped office and I ended up at the controls of the DVR. Haskins instructed me to fast-forward to September twenty-third, the date of the first rope purchase. When the clock counter was a few minutes before the time of purchase, I let the video play at normal speed. When a customer approached the counter lugging a spool of rope, we were hopeful. The man was stoop-shouldered, and I pointed out that he looked too old and frail to be our guy.

"Could be a disguise," Haskins offered.

"If it is, it's a brilliant one," Rourke added.

We noted the time before I sped through video until the date and time corresponded to the next purchase of our rope. We watched a young black man buy a short section of rope and tackle. Not our guy. The next customer was more promising. A white male took his time perusing the shelves, finally selecting four items: a spool of rope, a small item from the hardware section, a flashlight, and a soda.

"We may have something here," I muttered.

Haskins called for Carl and asked him who was on video working the counter.

"That's Bobby," he informed us.

"Could you send him back here? We need to ask him a couple of questions."

Patterson walked to the office door and bellowed Bobby's name. A few seconds later, Bobby was huddled with us in front of the monitor.

"You remember this guy?" Haskins asked him.

"Sort of."

"Describe him to us. Anything you remember," I encouraged.

"I don't remember anything that you can't see in the video," Bobby said.

"Anything is helpful, Bobby. No detail is insignificant," Rourke said, leaning toward him.

Bobby swallowed audibly. "He's a white guy. You can see he's pretty jacked, like he spends a lot of time in the gym."

Strong. White. So far, so good.

"What about his voice? Did you detect an accent, similar to mine, maybe? Or anything else that stood out?" Rourke asked.

"I don't remember an accent."

"Ross, pause it right there," Haskins instructed, and I did.

"He says something to you here, Bobby," Haskins prompted. "Do you remember what it was?"

"As a matter of fact, yeah. Because it was kind of strange."

Strange is good.

"What was strange, Bobby?" Haskins prompted.

"He asked where the closest gas station is. Only he didn't say *gas* station. I remember it because he said *petrol* station. I mean, who says petrol?"

Rourke and I shared a look. *A foreigner.*

"That's helpful, Bobby," Rourke said. "Looks like you might have given him directions. Do you remember what you told him?"

"I told him to go to the Exxon station right down off the service road. You can see it from here."

"Most gas stations have exterior security cameras monitoring the pumps," I said.

"Bobby," Rourke said, "I could kiss you."

Lo and behold, another blusher.

CHAPTER EIGHTEEN

December 19
4:52 p.m.
Centreville, Maryland
39°2′42.64″N, 76°3′57.91″W

THE EXXON STATION was a complete bust. The two surveillance cameras aimed at the gas pumps had been promising. One may have actually captured a good shot of the driver or a license plate. Even if it had, turns out it wouldn't have done us a damned bit of good. Unfortunately, management only retained video recordings for thirty days and we were more than a month behind the investigative curve. If the same individual who'd purchased the rope at Boater's World filled up his tank with "petrol" at that particular station, we wouldn't be able to confirm it with video.

On the off chance the Boater's World customer had paid for gas with a credit card, Haskins tasked an agent to cross-check credit card transactions at the gas station occurring within an hour of the rope purchase. That poor bastard would also have the task of following up with each of those credit card holders to rule them out, a lot of effort for what was probably a pointless endeavor. Rourke and I agreed that the offender likely dealt in cash to leave as small a digital footprint as possible. Still, every lead had to be followed to its end, which was why I was sucking lungfuls of cold air and fighting to maintain my footing on an icy sidewalk in downtown Centreville.

With the map of Allison Brightwell's route provided by Rachel McAlester burned into my mind, my strategy had been to simulate conditions at the time she'd been abducted. According to Rachel, Allison always began her run at five p.m., which would have been right at dusk. Six days before Christmas, sunset occurred about fifteen minutes earlier. I'd begun my run from the doorstep of Allison and Rachel's townhouse promptly at a quarter to five.

The amount of sunlight, I had some control over, the weather, not so much. Temps were in the mid-thirties and falling, with snow impending. This was one reason I'd opted for layers instead of Allison's choice of short-sleeved compression shirt and running shorts. I was also armed and not particularly keen on advertising it to the world, so I'd gone with leggings and moisture-wicking shirt with built-in sports bra, beneath which a padded pouch secured a subcompact pistol, credentials, keys, and phone. A wide, breathable elastic band held everything against my abs and kept it from bouncing around. After years of running with the custom rig, I barely noticed it.

MD-213 split into two one-way roads, northbound Commerce and southbound Liberty, which remained divided through downtown Centreville. The small townhouse complex where Rachel and Allison lived was situated at the southern tail of this split. Less than a minute into the run, I was jogging past quaint buildings, mostly businesses with a few private homes mixed in. The hodgepodge of architectural styles represented the last three centuries. Markers at two small, Colonial frame homes, "Wright's Chance" and "Tucker House," indicated they were built in the mid- and late eighteenth century, respectively.

Hand-painted signs urged folks to be sure to visit these local treasures during the annual Holiday Historical Tour. I crossed Commerce Street at the signal and ran along "Lawyer's Row," which was appropriately named. The row of attorneys' offices were conveniently located across from the courthouse plaza, as I suspected had been the case for more than two hundred years.

I made a right onto Liberty, then left on Broadway, past the volunteer fire department. I'd been an all-weather runner since high school. In the Army, our mantra was, "If it ain't raining, we ain't training!" I was feeling fatigued and breathless, and it had nothing to do with the cold air. Frustrated to be winded after only a mile, I pushed myself into another gear for the next two miles, until I reached one of the possible ambush points.

At least when studying overhead photos of the area it had seemed like a good place to lie in wait, with plenty of natural cover. In mid-November, the trees and bushes would have been bare like what I was seeing, providing much less cover than I'd expected. Chesterfield Avenue was residential and, because of the proximity to the board of education, elementary school, and only Catholic church in town, would have been heavily trafficked. The school zone meant drivers would be taking their time, more likely to notice anything out of the ordinary. Nope. Not the place.

Things began to change as Chesterfield Avenue split, becoming Watson Road, and I veered right, as Allison would have. As I neared the Corsica River and the landscape transitioned to rural, the houses were spaced farther apart, with much longer driveways, many situated on several acres. Most of the lawns sloped away from the road, restricting the view, appealing from the offender's perspective. Across the frosted field to my right, several deer grazed at the tree line. Distracted, I didn't see the patch of ice, didn't realize what was happening until I was in a penguin-style belly skid. The pain registered about the same moment I came to a stop in the middle of the road.

Painfully, I pushed myself to hands and knees and crawled to safety. My tights were torn and bloody at my left knee, but I could bend my leg without too much pain. Both palms were badly scraped, and half a dozen places stung or throbbed, but nothing seemed sprained nor broken. Banged up, but functional. Still, I wasn't exactly gung-ho about walking the two and half miles back to the motel. Frustrated, I called Haskins and arranged a pick-up, not telling him why because he'd vehemently tried to talk me out of "running around alone in the dark like a dumbass." He'd gone so far as to suggest that I was putting myself out there as "bait." I wasn't, but it was pointless to argue.

Admittedly, he did have a point. A killer was at large and stalking women who were alone and vulnerable, whether they felt that way or not. I was armed and thought I'd been aware of my surroundings, yet I'd managed to become distracted by wildlife long enough to be surprised by black ice. Not a single passerby had witnessed my crash and burn, and I was lucky my injuries weren't more serious. A lot could happen here without anyone noticing. The only house in sight was the large Victorian across the road where, I noticed, a tall woman was beckoning me over from the front porch. Someone had noticed after all.

* * *

My Good Samaritan's home was warm and fragrant. Aromas—cinnamon, vanilla, and something citrusy—permeated the living room. After introductions, Lenore Zimmerman insisted I "make myself at home." When she was satisfied I was no longer in danger of "catching my death," she asked what possessed me to run in weather like this. "Oh, your poor chin," she added. Apparently, the heels of my hands and left knee weren't the only abrasions. "Let me just run and get something to take care of that," she said, retreating down the hallway and leaving me awkwardly trying to keep my blood off her floral print sofa. I'd just sent Haskins a quick text to let him know where to find me when she returned with a first aid kit in hand.

"Thank you, Ms. Zimmerman–"

"Lenore."

"Lenore. I'm fine, really. I appreciate you letting me wait inside for my friend."

"That was a nasty fall. Still, not too worse for wear," she noted, opening a packet of gauze, "considering." She doused a pad with hydrogen peroxide and offered it to me. I dabbed at the painful area on my chin and she indicated her approval with a nod. We traded gauze for antibiotic ointment. When chin, knee, and hands had been dressed to her satisfaction, she declared that the mulling spices and cookies were just about ready, as if we had plans to go a' wassailing.

"I've opened a bottle of merlot, but if you're on duty or take it with something else, well, I also have some Dr. Pepper. My late husband wouldn't touch it with anything except warm Dr. Pepper or R.C. Cola." I was hung up on the "on duty," because I'd offered nothing but my first name by way of introduction. She blinked expectantly.

"Oh," I said, "whatever you're having, thank you."

She was off to the kitchen before I could ask whether she was clairvoyant or possessed some sort of insider knowledge.

Left alone, I studied her living room. An empty easel and chair sat on top of a drop cloth where a TV might otherwise have been. A wheeled cart displaying a variety of paints and brushes was within reach. All of the furniture in the room faced the large bay window. Curtains were pulled open, revealing a wide view of the yard, the road, and the field beyond. A pair of binoculars sat on the windowsill. Seashells were arranged on a tray in the middle of the coffee table, and the homeowner's affinity for the ocean was further reflected by the artwork on the walls. They were all oil on canvas and appeared to be originals; well done, but not particularly inspiring, the sort of thing you'd expect to see in a dentist's office or hotel room.

There had been no car in the driveway and there was no sign that Lenore Zimmerman lived with anyone. I wondered who she'd been baking for. The first cold, hungry stranger who jogged by?

When she entered the room bearing a tray of steaming mugs and a plate of cookies, I asked, "How did you know?"

"Pardon?" She set the tray next to the conch assortment.

"Before, you suggested that I might be 'on duty.' What did you mean?"

"Oh, well, honey, I was married to a police officer for forty-five years. You just struck me as, well, most people don't have that kind of awareness of their surroundings. Until right before you fell, I saw you taking everything in. Well, I don't know, something about the way you carried yourself. I got the impression you're either police or military. Am I wrong?"

"No. You're not wrong."

"State police?" she asked.

"No, ma'am. FBI."

"Well," she said, "at least they're taking this seriously, after what happened to that poor Washington College student. It's just so awful. This kind of thing happens in big cities. Girls go missing all the time, many of them are never found. It's just not something that happens *here*. But I suppose everyone thinks that until it does. I just feel terrible for the families. The Brightwell girl is real sweet and quite the athlete. You know, when I first saw you, for a moment I thought she's not missing at all. She's right there, running like always. I guess sometimes we see what we want to see."

Lenore Zimmerman struck me as someone who always had her ear to the ground and eye on her neighbors, the type who tended to make a particularly helpful witness. For the first time in days, I felt the tiniest flicker of hope. "Lenore, how often do you see Allison Brightwell running on this road?"

"Well, until she went missing, I would say every evening, though I can't vouch for Saturdays because I volunteer at the library on Saturdays. The rest of the week, though, you could set your watch by her."

"Do you happen to remember seeing her around five-fifteen to five-thirty last night?"

"No, I didn't. Doesn't mean she didn't jog by, but I was cutting up a roast, would've been in the kitchen, I'm sure."

"What about vehicles?" I asked. "Did you see any vehicles that looked out of place yesterday or maybe a few days before?"

"As a matter of fact, yes. A van," she said, pushing the plate of cookies toward me. Wanting to keep her focused and talking, I politely took one. As soon as it was in my mouth, I knew I'd made a terrible mistake.

"What do you—" I choked out, "remember about it?" The thing in my mouth had instantaneously absorbed every bit of moisture and I wasn't sure I'd be able to get it down. I reached for the only liquid available, a steaming mug of aqueous incense.

"Well, it was white. Had an electrical company's information on the side. There are three or four electricians in town, and that van didn't belong to either of them. I can't tell you what the number was, but I remember thinking the area code wasn't local. Saw it Friday evening and again on Sunday, parked at the same place, about where you fell. It was parked there for at least twenty minutes. I never saw the driver, but the motor was running because I noticed the exhaust. It just struck me as strange."

The "cookie" burned its way down, chased with a healthy slug of spice-infused wine. Had she forgotten sugar? Confused flour with plaster mix? The only thing I could think to compare it to was a military Meal-Ready-to-Eat cracker, which required a canteen's worth of water to make it down a human gullet.

"Any logo on the truck?" I asked, mouth still dry.

"No, just the lettering. Nothing fancy, like it was stenciled on."

"Do you remember anything else?"

"There was no ladder on the van. You know, I don't think I've ever seen an electrician's van that didn't have a ladder on top."

Lenore was on a roll. "Anything else?"

"The hub caps didn't match. I could only see the wheels facing me, of course, but one had a hubcap, the other one didn't. And the van just generally looked the worse for wear, needed some body work, rust around the wheel wells, that sort of thing."

"I gotta say, Mrs. Zimmerman, your memory is amazing."

"Lenore, honey. Well, I play brain games on the computer when things are slow at the library. Keeps my mind sharp."

"Well, a detective will probably follow—"

The doorbell interrupted us. I thanked Lenore and she walked me to the door, where I expected to be met by Haskins. Instead, we were greeted by a Queen Anne's County deputy sheriff. He wouldn't tell me anything in front of present company except, "There's been a development, ma'am."

His eyes and body language told me it wasn't the good kind.

CHAPTER NINETEEN

December 19
6:17 p.m.
Church Hill, Maryland
39°8'42.61"N, 75°58'4.50"W

THERE WAS SOMETHING to be said for chaotic scenes. Flashing lights and pumping adrenaline fueled our belief, however thin, that we would be in time to help, to save. When we failed in that, things stopped happening in real time. The scene transformed into a macabre diorama, a collection of rotting artifacts to be excavated and studied. We observed, we documented, and we analyzed. The tether of humanity that anchored us to the living also cruelly bound us to the dead. We thought about ligatures and strangulation during sex. Laughter felt foreign and guilt always followed. We saw the results of primal rage and fear up close and wondered if we were capable of the same. Some of us didn't have to wonder. We knew. We coped. Some days it was less impossible than others, and sometimes hope glimmered. Not this time. We were too late for Allison Brightwell, and hope wasn't on my radar.

The Tahoe dug fresh ruts into the mud as I wedged behind a

dark panel van. Frozen pellets bounced off the windshield. The intermittent drizzle had evolved into a full-on wintery mix. After fishing a couple of Excedrin out of the glove box, my awkward, half-dive into the back floorboards for a bottle of water was interrupted by Rourke, who managed to open the passenger door and slide into the seat while juggling two steaming cups of salvation. She appeared unfazed to have been greeted by my ass, which I promptly planted onto the seat.

"Sweet Jaysus, are you roastin' a turkey in here?" She waited until I was settled before handing me one of the cups.

Water forgotten, I had the coffee to my lips before I considered thanking her. My scraped palms necessitated cautious handling of the cup. She noticed.

"Can't get warm," I said, turning down the heat only slightly.

"Well, it's no wonder. Perfect jogging weather for the mentallers. Seriously, you alright, other than the obvious?"

"Scrapes and bruises. I'm fine." The coffee was some kind of amazing gourmet blend, rich and smooth, with a chocolaty undertone. The cream was the real deal. She'd pegged my version of heaven in a cup.

"I won't say I told you so," she said. "You're flushed."

The pills went down like shards of glass. "Turkey roasting will do that," I said, my voice cracking.

"Special Agent Haskins asked me to let him know as soon as you arrived. He's been in there a while." She tilted her head slightly to the right, presumably indicating some location in the woods beyond the lit clearing.

"How'd you manage this? It's obviously not local," I said, trying to make out details through increasingly foggy glass. Two dozen law enforcement vehicles and several media vans lined both sides of the road.

"Mm, Sumatran beans. One of the CNN guys had it brought in."

"A fucking miracle," I said. "Obviously a bribe."

"They were rather disappointed to learn I'm not FBI." Her smirk wasn't subtle.

"They weren't curious why a foreigner is working with the Feds? What'd you tell 'em?"

"Feck-all beyond how exceptional their organic Gayo is."

"Please tell me *organic* doesn't mean this was made from those beans they dig out of monkey shit," I said.

The smile reached her eyes. My second glimpse of this effect was as startling as the first.

"Asian civets, not monkeys," she informed me, obviously amused.

Bewildered by the rare levity and dubious contents of my cup, I asked, "Jesus, do I want to know what a civet is?"

"Similar to a cat, and no, I can assure you these beans were harvested the traditional way. A pound of Kopi Luwak beans would cost as much as a Prada bag. I can't imagine a cameraman springing for it."

Rourke sobered. "The civets are treated terribly, kept in cages and force-fed the beans. Torturous, really."

Torture. There's a lot of that going around. I swiped my arm across the fogged side window and through streaked condensation made out a dozen tents along the road venting steam from portable heaters. A dozen reporters primped for cameras. The solemn vibe on our side of the road felt surreal in contrast. Two men huddled under an umbrella at the rear of a dark blue van, the tall thin one trying to block the wind for his physical opposite who struggled to light a cigarette.

Rourke followed my gaze. "Morgue techs waiting for the M.E. to clear the body. Your eyes are glassy and you sound knackered."

Knackered didn't begin to cover it, and the Excedrin likely wouldn't touch what felt like a team of tiny construction workers going at it with jackhammers behind my right eye. It was a shame to waste the best coffee I'd had in weeks, but it wasn't exactly soothing my throat.

A narrow path, worn by foot traffic and perhaps the occasional ATV, began at the blacktop and snaked its way through high brown grass before disappearing into the trees. "How far back in there is she?" I asked. Like ants returning to the colony, half a dozen crime scene techs trudged along the path, arms loaded with evidence bags, headlamps bobbing in the dark. One of them might be holding that one little thing that could break the investigation wide open, but I wasn't holding my breath. It usually didn't work that way.

"About fifty meters, I'm told."

I sipped, tried not to wince, and did my best to force visions of a hot shower and warm bed out of my mind. "You haven't seen her yet?" The shivering and headache had less to do with the fever I probably had than with what we were about to face in those woods.

"No," she said. "I was waiting for you."

"Thanks. Do you mind if we..."

Promise me, please, just find her.

"I just need a minute," I said.

Rourke's eyes moved from me to the woods. "Of course. We'll go when you're sorted."

We watched the crime scene techs in silence for a few minutes before Rourke asked if my run had been worthwhile, wipeout notwithstanding. She stoically sipped her coffee as I filled her in on the probable ambush point, suspicious van, and Lenore Zimmerman's amazing attention to detail, right down to the goddamned hubcaps.

"He's comfortable and he's clever. Watching, unnoticed until he wants to be." She paused a beat before adding, "But it wouldn't be terribly hard, would it? Who would notice a utility van, something an electrician or odd job man would drive?"

"Mrs. Zimmerman, for one, because she's got nothing better

to do than spy on her neighbors and bake cookies that should be illegal."

"Well, he wouldn't be expecting that—someone spying on *him*."

"I've got a feeling, Sheridan. I think he was following her for a while until he figured out the best place to ambush her and get her into that van."

"Well, your man's certainly got some bollocks. But this is what he prefers." She nodded toward the woods. "A quiet, hidden place to work. A place where he can take his time. They found a cache. I don't know what they've told you, you probably know more than I do. I'll be surprised if he didn't leave something for us."

Of course he had. For the same reason he sent Rourke the postcard and left the cache under the porch steps at the Garrett place. He enjoyed fucking with us.

I said, "What I've been told is that a geocacher found a body in those woods—female, late teens or early twenties. A cache obviously complicates things. Footprints, fingerprints, trace evidence all multiplied times the number of cache-seekers who've been traipsing all over the scene. All of it will have to be analyzed, all those people tracked down and ruled out. He's intentionally pre-contaminating the scene. It's fucking ingenious."

Although we'd have more coordinates to work with, it wasn't exactly a silver lining.

I retrieved my parka from behind the seat and handed it to Rourke, who had yet to purchase appropriate outerwear. She waved it off, declaring she wasn't about to let me catch my death on her account. She agreed to wear my FBI windbreaker over her fleece pullover, but balked at the umbrella.

"Take it, Sheridan. I won't use it. I like to keep my hands free."

She wasn't persuaded until I tossed the umbrella onto the back seat and put on my FBI cap. As I was digging a pair of rubber boots out of the back of the Tahoe, I remembered Ripley. Rourke informed me she was dry and cozy in a heated tent with the state police K-9s. "Lucky bitch," I muttered. Rourke's calfskin riding boots were equally practical and fashionable, and my grumbling commentary on her uncanny knack for making me look like a slob was interrupted by the sound of excessive horsepower. I let a string of obscenities fly as a familiar blonde exited a sporty red Mercedes and stalked toward us.

"Agent Ross!" she yelled, her three-inch heels sinking into the mud.

"Is that—"

"Monica Fucking Spears," I said, silently praying for a full-on face plant. As I slung the strap of my scene bag across my chest, Rourke surprised me by calling out to the morgue techs, "Say, lads, could you do us a favor and inform that woman that the press is not permitted past the yellow tape?" She stopped just short of batting her lashes before spinning on her heel and hauling me by the elbow toward the tree line. By the time we made it across the field, I was having a hard time catching my breath. Neither our attempt to flee nor the warning had deterred Spears in the least. She was closing in on us fast.

"Bloody persistent, that one," Rourke muttered.

"Agent Ross! Wait! Just a few minutes of your time." Spears mistakenly thought she'd compelled us to stop and was obviously pleased with herself. Rourke placed a warning hand on my arm. Spears opened her mouth to say something, but I didn't give her a chance.

"You need to leave," I snapped. Not fazed in the least, she inserted herself in my personal space and launched into what she undoubtedly believed to be the intro of a Pulitzer-caliber story. "A young girl survives the Lockerbie bombing, grows up to become an Army officer, overcomes life-threatening combat injuries, and becomes only the third woman to receive the Silver

Star in almost seven decades. Can you blame me, Agent Ross? It's one hell of a story."

Had Rourke not tightened her grip on my arm, I would've lunged. "I don't know what the hell is wrong with you, but I've made it perfectly clear more than once that you were not to contact me again."

"Well, since we happened to run into each other, I thought you might—"

"Are you kidding me? You just chased me across a god-damned pasture!"

"How about a short interview, at your convenience, of course, strictly focused on what you do? Geographic profiling is unique. As intriguing as your tie to the Pan Am Flight 103 disaster is, your transition from decorated Iraq War veteran to FBI profiler more than warrants a story, Regan."

"I have a job to do, Ms. Spears, and I'm not about to be in the middle of a goddamned Barbara Walters special."

Spears didn't let up. "I'm sure the Bureau would endorse the positive publicity. Frankly, I'm surprised they haven't thought to put your face on recruitment posters already, even if you do appear a little worse for wear. What happened?"

Rourke's tether was easily broken, and I found myself close enough to Monica Spears to smell peppermint gum and vanilla body lotion. Deploring the need to look up to meet her eyes, I took a deep breath, trying to maintain some semblance of calm. A mistake. The resulting coughing fit felt like my lungs had detached themselves and were bouncing off my ribcage like dice.

Once able to talk, I said, "Listen to me, because I'm only going to say this once. You will turn your ass around on those ridiculous heels and get on the other side of that yellow tape or I'll cuff you, march you past all those cameras, throw your ass into a patrol car, and charge you with obstruction." It probably would've sounded more convincing if I hadn't nearly choked to death on my own fluids getting it out.

Behind me, a deep voice said, "The M.E. is finishing up." When a large hand, obviously not Rourke's, grasped my shoulder, I nearly jumped out of my skin.

Rounding on him, I said, "Jesus, Haskins."

"Apologies, Special Agent Ross." The formal address was a reminder to get my shit together. He placed shoe covers in my hand and leaned in close so Spears couldn't hear. "If you hurry, you can see the body in situ."

Well, I could put the booties on and walk away or stay and pummel Spears. Holding my bag out of the way with one hand while getting the covers over my boots was awkward. I held on to Haskins' elbow to steady myself. "Her name is Monica Spears. Make sure this intrusion is noted in the scene log," I instructed. "And put the deputies on alert. If I see her again, it won't go well for her."

He turned his attention to Spears. "I'm going to have to ask you to return to the media staging area, ma'am." Annoyed by his politeness, I stomped toward the woods. Dense trees and over-grown brush prevented any deviation from the path, which was discernible only where muddy ruts cut their way through knee-high grass. I heard Rourke and Haskins gaining on me with their longer strides.

My first instinct was to walk on the edge of the path, to avoid damaging possible footprints, but it was too late for that. At least two-dozen sets of tracks crisscrossed the trail. Most of the prints had clear tread patterns, indicating those who left them hadn't been wearing shoe coverings. Either the tracks were already there when investigators arrived or crime scene protocol had been egregiously violated. With Haskins running the show, my money was on the former. Did one set of prints belong to Allison Brightwell? Had she been forced to walk along the trail? I suspected she'd been barefoot, forced to strip before he marched her toward her fate. Had anyone bothered to look for barefoot prints before scores of more tracks were added to the mess? For that matter, *was* the victim Allison Brightwell? I hoped she was a nameless, faceless girl whose plans and dreams I didn't know.

Distracted, I hadn't prepared myself for what I might see in the clearing.

Holy Christ.

Some are worse. Some you can't prepare for.

CHAPTER TWENTY

December 19

6:48 p.m.

Church Hill, Maryland

39°8'32.43"N, 75°58'7.09"W

THE WHITE CANVAS pop-up tent bathed in light in the center of the small clearing was the kind of thing you'd erect for a backyard barbeque. Beneath it, a small female body was strung up on some sort of wooden frame.

The smell of burnt flesh was almost overpowering, but I couldn't rule out that I was imagining it. "Jesus Christ, what—"

"Damn. Sorry, I should have warned you," Haskins said.

The smaller of the two people in hooded Tyvek suits approached us and, by way of greeting, offered a box of nitrile gloves. *Fuentes.*

Haskins and Rourke each took a pair. I found a pair of size smalls in my bag and put them on.

The tall bulky man crouching in front of the frame slowly got to his feet, the effort accompanied by a series of snap-crackle-pops. "We're done here, so you won't need to suit up unless you want a close look," he said as he lumbered over to us. "Shane

Leffler, forensic investigator with the Office of the Chief Medical Examiner." Per protocol, we didn't shake hands.

Voice raised over the humming generators, I said, "Likewise. I'm Special Agent Regan Ross, this is—"

"Sheridan Rourke." Rourke didn't shake hands either. Her focus was elsewhere. "What's that she's tied to?"

Haskins answered, "It's a drying frame. Hunters use them to stretch—"

"—deer hides," I realized, and must've said. Each of the victim's wrists and ankles was bound to a corner of the frame, which had been erected next to a small hunting shack.

I forced myself to focus on everything but the body, beginning with the frame. A cross-bar was supported by two side posts, thick limbs lashed together with some sort of twine and wire. The wire showed no signs of rust, indicating limited exposure to the elements. There was no loose dirt or other signs of digging at the base of the posts. The ends of the wood were dark and worn, indicating it hadn't been recently cut.

"The frame has been here for a while. The wire lashing hasn't," I said.

Haskins nodded his agreement. "Hopefully, we can determine that for sure when we locate the owner."

"You know who that is?" I asked.

"One of the deputy sheriffs thinks it belongs to Sam Meyer. He owns the motel and restaurant in town," Haskins said.

"Shady Hill? The shithole we're staying in?" I asked.

"Yeah. He and his wife are apparently on a cruise. We're trying to reach them."

"All those footprints on the trail, geocachers?" I asked.

Haskins nodded. "At least a dozen, based on the cache log Fuentes found in the pellet stove inside the shack. They're holding the log and contents at the evidence tent until you've had a chance to examine them."

Haskins cut his eyes quickly toward Leffler, indicating the M.E. investigator's lack of the requisite need to know. I had questions, lots of them. What was in the cache? When was it first placed? Who exactly was this college student and was there a connection with either victim? What names were in the log? Not to mention, what clues might be on the geocache websites? We had to assume the killer placed the cache at the scene before the murder, to entice geocachers to the location to pre-contaminate the scene. Letting it go for the moment, I focused on the victim.

In life, she could've graced the cover of *Women's Fitness*. Her head hung forward, long dark hair obscuring her face and most of her chest. Her hair was longer than Allison's had been in the picture I'd seen, but a similar color. Whether the young woman I was looking at had been more or less sun-bronzed than Allison was impossible to say. Postmortem transformation had begun the moment her heart stopped, what the M.E. would call hypostasis in his report, pooling of blood in the extremities caused by gravity. In this case, the victim had been fully suspended, causing purplish-red legs and feet.

She was wearing a thin gold chain with a small charm around her left ankle, just below the bindings. A closer look would require donning a Tyvek suit. Maybe not. I removed the camera from my bag and used it to zoom in on the anklet. The charm was a gold crab identical to the one Rachel McAlester had been wearing on her wrist. "It's Allison."

Leffler started to caution us to wait for a definitive ID, but when I informed them of Rachel's matching bracelet, everyone was quiet.

Please, Agent Ross, I need you to promise me...

"Preliminarily, the rope looks like the same type used on Abbott," Haskins informed us.

"She was gagged with her panties, and the ligature marks on her neck are similar to those on Abbott. The tension was from behind, and he probably used a steel cable, but that's the M.E.'s call," Leffler said, tucking his notebook under his arm.

There was nothing over the frame that would facilitate the kind of pulley used at the Garrett Farm. I quickly scanned the exterior of the shack and could see no evidence that anything had been attached to it. "Did he change his M.O.?" I wondered aloud.

"Maybe," Haskins said. "But there are ATV tracks all through here, including behind the frame. It's possible he rigged something. The cable around her neck could have been over the frame and run through something attached to the ATV. He could've stood in front of her and managed it."

Or, he was sitting on the ATV, put it in reverse and… Jesus.

Leffler confirmed the tension had been from behind. If he'd been in front of her or standing or sitting on a four-wheeler, he would've had to loop the cable over the top of the frame. There wasn't a single scratch on the wood. I said, "There's nothing around the frame to attach a cable to that would give him the same kind of rig he used with Abbott. I'm not sure I buy that he used an ATV. If he did, he would have had to use a truck or trailer to get it here. The ATV tracks could belong to geocachers or hunters and have nothing to do with this crime. He could have parked his vehicle at the edge of the woods and marched her in here."

"And changed his M.O. with regard to the manner of strangulation," Rourke added. "Shorter timeline as well. He didn't hold her as long, perhaps not at all. It may mean something has become more important to him, something that trumps M.O. regarding tolerance for risk."

"Signature," I offered. "The cache."

The contents of the cache intrigued me, but I had work to do at the scene. I adjusted the camera strap across my chest and got the handheld GPS out of my bag as Leffler and Fuentes began carefully removing Allison Brightwell from the tanning frame, preserving as much of the rope and knots as possible. I walked around the hunting shack to get a general impression of the area.

Without a GPS, machete, and hours of free time to hack through the dense woods, the ATV trail was the only way in or out. I recorded coordinates and took some three-hundred-and-sixty-degree photos from the shack. The inside of the shack was equipped for not more than a couple nights of primitive camping, with a small stove in the corner, a card table, and three folding chairs. The scene had told me about all it was going to until I could put everything into the GIS and analyze it.

With coughing fits slowing me down, the walk back to the tents took longer than it should have. As we entered the heated tent, Fuentes, Graham, and a couple of techs from the Evidence Response Team were arranging evidence bags on a long folding table. The cache container was a simple blue plastic box, like a large pencil case, which had been placed inside a gallon size Ziploc bag. Smooth surfaces. A forensic dream. So, why didn't I feel optimistic?

"Three partial prints. Two should be good enough for comparison," Graham informed us. She and Fuentes were trying to get warm near a portable heater in the corner while the rest of us donned fresh gloves.

"Probably belong to geocachers," Haskins said. "We know this guy is too careful for that."

I picked up an evidence bag and studied the item inside through clear plastic. The silver coin, a centennial piece I'd never seen before, featured a male American Indian. "Anyone know what this is?" There were "nopes" and "not-yets" all around, but I was assured they would find out as soon as they were back in the land of reliable Wi-Fi. Rourke picked up a bag containing a postcard, which naturally had me a bit spooked.

"Greetings from the Williams Family. Panama City, Florida. Happy geocaching," she read.

"An entire family's worth of prints to slog through. Awesome," I muttered.

"We found plenty of candy wrappers to analyze, too, probably dropped by the Williams kids who haven't quite mastered the concept of Leave No Trace," Graham said around her disposable cup of lukewarm coffee.

I read the description on the label of the third bag aloud. "Silver chain with silver pendant, St. Michael. Inscribed with numbers. Engraving on reverse."

"Which one is St. Michael?" Haskins asked me, as if I was the only Catholic in the vicinity. Not that I made a habit of profiling people, but our colleagues' surnames were Rourke, Graham, and Fuentes. Given that I hadn't been to mass in twenty years, he was probably barking up the wrong tree.

"St. Michael the Archangel is the leader of the Army of God, protector of the Church. He's also the angel of death, charged with carrying souls to heaven after weighing them on the balanced scales," Fuentes informed us.

"He protected God against Lucifer's rebellion," Graham added.

Wisdom resounded from the faithful contingent.

"Patron saint of soldiers and first responders," Rourke said, her voice almost mechanical. Her eyes were wide as she watched the necklace slide out of the plastic pouch and into my palm. I told myself it'd been a long day and she probably just needed food and a hot shower. I should've known better. My attention was on the medal as I moved to the other side of the table where someone had clamped a lamp.

"Yeah," Graham said, "lots of cops wear them."

"Looks like a buff angel wielding a sword, standing on the head of what looks like a, what is that, a dragon?" I asked.

"Lucifer," Fuentes offered. Twenty years of rust. I'd apparently confused the Bible with *Game of Thrones*.

"Well, that makes more sense," I said. "There's a banner

below the Mike vs. Lucifer scene with four numbers engraved on it. Looks like four-oh-" It clicked. Four-oh-two-nine. The numbers handwritten on the postcard. O'Donnell's constable number. Sheridan was grey.

"Protect my..." she trailed off, her lips moving without sound.

"Sheridan, you okay?" *Asinine, Ross. Clearly, she isn't.*

"Turn it over," she said, pale enough to summon the Archangel. I flipped the medallion over and read the inscription in the center of the medal, *Protect my heart.*

"Sheridan, look at me." She did, for a moment, before her eyes suddenly rolled back in her head.

"Rob!"

We were moving, but not fast enough.

She was already falling.

CHAPTER TWENTY-ONE

December 19
7:51 p.m.
Church Hill, Maryland
39°8'42.61"N, 75°58'7.09"W

THE TENT MUST'VE been seventy-five degrees, but Rourke was shivering under a parka loaned by a deputy sheriff. Haskins had reached her in time to break her fall, and she'd come around fairly quickly, insisting she was fine. Fuentes and Graham had stayed with her while Haskins rounded up creature comforts. I retrieved Ripley from the K-9 tent, and the dog had followed willingly enough sans leash. She made a beeline for Rourke. Rourke began to stroke Ripley's head absently, and soon the dog's head rested contentedly on her mistress' knee. As Rourke settled into the folding chair, I realized we were alone. Haskins' doing, I was sure.

Rourke's reaction to the medal had been puzzling. Clearly, there was a personal connection. One possibility kept surfacing, but only Rourke could confirm it or provide another explanation. She hadn't acknowledged me, was clearly focusing all of her attention on keeping it together. I filled a Styrofoam cup with the good stuff from the CNN tent and handed it to her. She attempted a smile, which made me feel worse for what I was about to do. She'd been absently fingering the beads on her necklace since she sat down. She wasn't ready. Concerned colleague or investigator. I couldn't be both.

Damn you, Rob.

I cleared my throat, said, "Four-oh-two-nine. Grace O'Donnell's constable number." It wasn't gentle. Ripley's head snapped up at "Grace" and only relaxed when Rourke settled her hand between the dog's ears. The next bit I wasn't sure about. *Lead and hope she follows.* "O'Donnell was your—"

"Partner."

Ambiguous. She'd worked with O'Donnell on the Belfast Strangler cases, and they could have been constables at the same time, professional partners.

Finally, she met my eyes. "*Partner* in every sense of the word."

"How long?"

"Eleven years. Fifteen all told, but we took a break while I was in San Diego." Her voice waivered slightly, and I had the feeling if I let on I felt terrible for her, she'd lose it.

"Well, as I've said before, he could've gotten her constable's number through some creative cold calling. And anyone with a credit card could have ordered a medallion online and had it engraved. It doesn't necessarily mean—"

"Aye, Regan, it does. She didn't *display* it. There are hundreds of versions. And you're forgetting the inscription. We were the only ones who… Well, he couldn't have known."

"Four years is a long time apart. How do you know Grace never took the necklace off during that time?" I asked.

"According to her, she didn't."

"It's possible someone could've been close enough to get a good look," I suggested.

She gave me a look that could cut glass. Kid gloves would get us nowhere. "In the four years you were apart, are you telling me *you* weren't intimate with anyone?"

"No."

"No you weren't or no you—"

"I'm not naïve, Regan, but I also can't imagine Grace playing show and bloody tell with something so personal."

"You gave it to her? You had it inscribed?" I asked.

"Aye, when we were both probationary constables."

She closed her eyes. "I've always thought it so bloody ironic that the St. Michael, meant to invoke protection, would go missing the day she was killed."

Pieces were sliding into place, but not quickly enough.

"Grace would always take it off and hang it on the handle of the armoire in the bedroom. Every night. That morning, it wasn't there. She insisted I must've moved it. Not once I'd done in eleven years, mind you. We were both meant to be at the station, and instead we were ransacking the flat searching for it. She wouldn't let it go."

She was hunched over her coffee, not looking at me. I waited.

"I told her to go on, promised to find it and bring it to HQ. Grace was deadly superstitious. She didn't want to leave without it, and I just wanted to look for it in peace without listening to her prattle on. I lost my temper, was practically pushing her out of the flat. Ripley sensed something was off. She was going mental, trying to claw her way through the door. I assumed she was reacting to the tension between us. I should've paid attention, should've realized the threat was outside."

Jesus. Was she saying she was with Grace moments before she was killed?

"As if it's not bad enough to have her taken from me, those last ten minutes were spent in anger. Do you know what my final words to her were? Words that replay over and over, words I can never take back. 'Just go!' That's what I said to her. 'Just go!'"

"I'm sorry, Sheridan."

We pretended to give a shit about our coffee. After a respectful beat I said, "Just so I'm tracking here, you're saying you believe that the man who killed Jennifer Abbott, Allison Brightwell, and the others is the same man who planted the bomb that killed Grace O'Donnell?"

"Don't you?" she asked, finally looking at me. Her eyes were dry and as intense as I'd seen them.

"Hell, I don't know. Why was it assumed Grace was killed in a terrorist attack? Was that based on the signature of the explosive device?"

"No, that assumption was based on the fact that when a cop gets blown to bits, a track suit-wearing moke doesn't exactly top the suspect list. It would've required knowledge of her schedule, her patterns. A carefully planned attack, not one of opportunity."

"Was the device like ones used in similar attacks?" I asked.

"Aye."

"So, if he's not associated with a dissident group, then where the hell did he learn how to make the device?"

"The world wide feckin' web. There's loads of information and he's clever."

"It doesn't make sense to me. A car bomb suggests retaliation or a political agenda. It's so impersonal. The man who killed the Belfast women, Abbott, Brightwell, he's meticulous, hands-on, not exactly the kind of guy who would plant a bomb and leave things to chance."

"True, Regan, but it's about motivation. With Grace, he wasn't feeding a fantasy."

"Then why? Explain it to me. Why did he specifically target Inspector O'Donnell?"

"Grace was the lead investigator. She knew Ballinger wasn't our man and she was actively pursuing other leads. He must've felt she was getting close."

"You're saying he killed her because he was being *practical?*"

"Why not? It plays right into his psychopathy. Think, Regan. What motivates him? At his core, what does he desire more than anything?"

"Control," I said. "He needs to feel in control."

"Aye, and doing away with the one person he believed might be on to him, if that's not exercising control, I don't know what is."

"But he didn't stop there. He baited *you* here, to the States, bided his time, waited for an opportunity. He must've planned this from the beginning. Why else take her St. Michael medal? Why *you*, Sheridan? Why go through all of this trouble, take all these risks, to fuck with *you?*"

"Why do serial offenders take risks? What does risk correlate to?" she prompted.

"Gratification. Pleasure."

"Aye, pleasure. I've no doubt he's getting his jollies at the thought of me discovering Grace's medal. And I've played right into his hands, haven't I?"

"Why didn't you tell me about you and Grace sooner?"

"What difference would it have made?"

"None. I mean, I guess that's my point. I hope you don't think... I wouldn't judge you."

She huffed, leaned back, and crossed her arms. However I'd insulted her was lost on me. She didn't seem inclined to elaborate.

"Listen, forget it," I said. "If I offended you in some way, I'm sorry. I'm just trying to make sense of this."

"Offend me? No. It's just that I wonder, Regan, if you don't find the personal questions a wee hypocritical?"

It felt unfair. My personal business had absolutely nothing to do with the investigation, while hers obviously did, but, hell, maybe she had a point. I hadn't exactly been forthcoming with personal information. She'd just been through a real head-wringer.

I felt like shit all around, and I could only imagine how she felt. No more questions.

"Listen, it's been a shit day," I conceded. "Why don't we head back to the motel? You can take a hot bath and try to get some sleep."

She nodded once and dumped the full contents of her cup onto the ground. Not much changed during the drive. She looked away from me the whole time, gazed out the window, and occasionally wiped her eyes. There were things I wanted to say, but I wouldn't get it right. She needed space, time to process, and I, for one, needed a drink.

CHAPTER TWENTY-TWO

December 19

8:47 p.m.

Centreville, Maryland

39°2'25.44"N, 76°4'17.17"W

IF DURING, SAY, a beer run, you suddenly realized you'd left a meatball sub or shotgun shells off your list, the Shady Hill Liquor Store had you covered. You could also get your Lotto action on or choose from a wide selection of live bait. On my way to the deli counter, I passed a large wall cooler full of Styrofoam containers hand-labeled in black Sharpie: minnows; bloodworms; night crawlers; even grubs. The merchandise on the shelves was eclectic, to say the least, and I decided this would be my first stop in the event of an apocalyptic survival situation.

Swallowing was painful, and I wasn't particularly keen on the thought of eating, but I figured Rourke might be up for a late dinner after thawing out and having some time to herself. The deli counter was a no-frills affair. An older man with unkempt facial hair pulled himself away from the *What's Up, Eastern Shore* magazine he'd been perusing, plucked a stubby pencil and well-used notepad from his shirt pocket, licked the tip of the pencil, and waited expectantly for my order. The tongue action, several mysterious stains on his shirtfront, and six or seven flies buzzing around the cold cuts prompted me to smile apologetically and inquire where I might find the non-perishables. The place was a far cry from Whole Foods, and by the time I got to the wine and spirits aisle, my basket contained two cans of Campbell's soup, a box of Wheat Thins, cold medicine, and Twizzlers.

I pegged Rourke for a wine drinker, for no other reason than wine seemed a bit classier than my go-to's, beer or Bushmills. What was that old adage? *In vino veritas*? Here's some *veritas*: the entirety of what I know about wine could be written in longhand on a cork. It was made from grapes and gave me a headache. In a pinch, it could save you from choking to death on lethal baked goods. Supposedly, it improved with age, but was that actually true, or just a saying? Wasn't there also something about even or odd years and wine regions? This was why I drank beer. Selecting a six pack did not require an almanac. One would think that the decision would've been simplified by Shady Hill's meager stock, but half the bottles had screw caps and probably tasted worse than the Robitussin in my basket. Time to use a lifeline. My raw throat would've given me away in a heartbeat. Thank God for text messaging.

Hey, Erin. Need a wine recommendation.

You don't drink wine.

Correct.

My phone vibrated. *Damnit.*

"Hey."

"What's wrong with your voice?" Erin asked.

"I've been outside all day. Just hoarse."

"You're buying the wine. Does that mean he's cooking for you? Or is this nightcap wine?"

"What? There is no *he*. It's for a colleague, a colleague whom I'm pretty sure doesn't drink beer."

"Male colleague?"

"No."

"Damn."

"Erin, *wine?*"

"Honestly, Regan, that's like asking for advice on shoes when I haven't seen the dress. It depends on the pairing. Will the wine accompany food of some sort?"

Case in point: an almanac *and* a carefully planned menu. Pairings? Shit. "A light dinner," I said. "Soup."

"That's incredibly vague. What kind of base, chicken or beef? You know, I had a glass of Jadot Santenay Clos de Malte Blanc the other night, 2013 I believe. It was lovely."

"Well, mademoiselle, that sounds fucking expensive," I said.

"You should be able to get a bottle for under fifty dollars."

Right, because fifty bucks is not at all expensive for a bottle of wine.

"I'm in a convenience store, Erin. Lovely is a stretch. I'll settle for under twenty bucks and drinkable."

"Why the hell are you buying wine in a convenience store?"

"Oh, you know, two birds, one stone. Keno was calling." A coughing fit threatened, which would lead to a rundown of my symptoms, diagnosis, and doctor's orders. She sounded tired and, in an effort to deflect, I told her so.

"Mitral valve repair went a little long. Coppola makes a decent merlot for about fifteen dollars, but I'm not sure a gas station would carry it. Do they at least have a J. Lohr?"

I had to actually dust off a few bottles to read the labels, and finally one earned a response that wasn't disapproving. "Get the Barefoot," my sister advised. "A decent budget wine that should pair nicely with just about anything."

"Sold. Thanks."

"You're welcome." Because she just couldn't help herself, she added, "Gargle with warm salt water and get some rest."

"Yes, Doctor. Sorry, E, I have to go." I couldn't end the call fast enough and coughed my way to the register.

The counter was covered with Plexiglas. Underneath it was a muddled collage of business cards—everything from auto detailing to tax services. A handwritten index card centered amid the display caught my attention. *Hunting Leases Available.* I wondered if the listed phone number belonged to Sam Meyer or—I accessed idle mental files—Eddie Garrett. More to the point, I wondered if the killer had seen that phone number and, at some point, dialed it. The cashier asked to see my ID, and as I fished it out of my wallet, I made a mental note to mention to Haskins that this was worth a follow-up. Hunting leases seemed to be a common denominator.

* * *

A potpourri of high-end bath products hit me as soon as I stepped into the room. Rourke was on her bed, knees drawn to her chest, with Ripley curled up beside her. Her eyes were red and swollen, but mine probably were, too, and I hadn't been crying, so I wasn't going to jump to conclusions.

"The deli at the convenience store practically screamed 'Get your E. coli here!' so I had to abort mission on a sandwich, but there's some canned soup and crackers in the bag if you're hungry. I grabbed you a bottle of wine, which is probably sketchy, too. Help yourself. I'm gonna take a shower."

She mumbled her thanks, but didn't stir as I gathered an armful of flannel and fleece and headed into the bathroom. The hot water made every abrasion evident, some I hadn't been aware of. The heat was heavenly until the steam prompted a violent expulsion of a half-gallon of mucus. Not so divine. Unwilling to relinquish the warmth, I stayed under the water until it turned lukewarm. My teeth were chattering before I stepped out of the shower. Things didn't improve much once I was dry and clothed, even with the addition of a sweatshirt and socks to my usual PJ ensemble. I opened the door and followed the liberated steam into the room.

Rourke was in the same position I'd left her. I felt her watching me as I took a couple of generous swigs of cough syrup and curled up in one of the chairs like an old, decrepit cat. "You're sick," she said, sounding more like herself. She was holding a plastic cup of wine, I realized, and I noticed the mangled synthetic cork on the table in front of me.

"Shit, I forgot to get a corkscrew. How did—"

"I improvised." I couldn't imagine anything in that motel room that would do the job.

"That cough is horrid," she said. It was exactly the kind of thing Erin would say, except she'd be more clinical about it, adding words like *moist* and *productive*.

"Just a cold."

"Not likely. I considered summoning an exorcist." She was up, stripping the blanket from my bed. I didn't protest when she cocooned me in it, or when she declared I needed to eat something. She was probably right, but I didn't have the energy to heat the soup, and I wasn't about to swallow scratchy crackers. Besides, my hands were trapped inside my warm pupa. "Maybe later," I said, teeth chattering.

"At least some broth."

She heated a mug of soup and brought it to me. Was it her natural thoughtfulness at work, or did I look that pathetic? Either way, at least she didn't seem inclined to hold a grudge.

"Thanks." The warm mug felt nice in my freed hands. The soup soothed my throat and ignited my hunger. By the time Rourke had prepped her own dinner, my mug was almost empty and I was considering a Twizzler.

We were quiet for a while, which was fine with me. Having finally gotten warm, I was dozing off when the gunk in my chest decided intermission was over. I grudgingly trudged my way to the bathroom and, after fifteen minutes of hacking and spitting expectorated green sludge into the toilet, my lungs felt like they'd been worked over with a sander.

When I came out of the bathroom, Rourke was sitting on her bed almost exactly like she had been earlier, and I feared some kind of emotional regression. I collected the blanket from my chair and was remaking my bed when I noticed Rourke's necklace with the silver beads, the one I'd never seen her take off, coiled in a clear plastic cup on the nightstand. Wine dregs ringed the bottom of the cup.

She habitually rolled her fingers over the beads, and I chalked it up to one of those things people do when they're nervous, or bored, or in deep thought. I should've realized there was more to it. She'd given an engraved medal to Grace O'Donnell, who'd faithfully worn it around her neck for a decade and a half. Sheridan Rourke wouldn't wear something around her own neck that didn't mean something. If she didn't want me to ask, she should've been less conspicuous about it. "You want to tell me what this is about?"

"Not particularly, but I suppose it's inevitable." She was massaging her forehead like she had a headache. She sighed deeply, and I couldn't tell whether she was summoning strength or accepting defeat. I didn't particularly relish the thought of being the reason for either. Finally, she said, "Eighteen beads. One for every month."

Since Grace's death? No, that was over two years ago.

"I carried a chip for a while, but it's easily forgotten in a pocketbook. The beads are more—"

Oh. Hell.

No idea what to say, I emptied the bottle into the sink. I collected her necklace and focused on rinsing the beads.

"Just leave it, Regan."

Her first drink in a year and a half.

I couldn't bring myself to look at her, even in the mirror. "I'm sorry, Sheridan. This was my fault."

She snorted. "Hardly. I'd say dislodging a cork with a pair of tweezers demonstrates how bloody determined I was. I wanted a drink. I had a drink. It's as simple and complicated as that."

"Okay, but..." *But what?* Yeah, I'd fucked up, read her wrong.

My mistake had been assuming Rourke's strategy for dealing with pain and grief was the same as mine, hold it in until you can't. "Would it help to talk to someone? A friend or, *someone?*" *Someone who has a clue and knows what to say. Someone who isn't me.*

She settled back on the bed and glanced at the phone. "I thought of calling my sponsor, but it's three thirty in the morning in the UK."

"Isn't that what sponsors are for, the middle-of-the-night call?" I asked.

"Aye, but my sponsor, Jamie, is Grace's cousin. They were as close as sisters. I don't want to upset her. Not yet, anyway. I'm not ready to have that conversation with her."

I suspected this was the same Jamie she'd been talking to when we were en route to the kennel.

"You wouldn't have to give her details, just tell her that you had a lapse," I said.

"Jamie knows me well enough to sense there's more to it. She'd get straight to the heart of it, and I won't do that to her."

Maybe what she needed, I realized, was for me to stop guessing what the hell she needed. "What can I do, Sheridan? Or, *not* do. What do you need?"

"To sleep, but that's not going to happen any time soon. If I could just stop thinking about it for a moment."

"I'm sorry you're stuck with me. And I'm sorry if I've been an asshole."

"Listen, Regan, I get it. You feel like shite. You shouldn't. This was the result of a weak moment at the end of a horrid day. Tomorrow is Day One. I don't intend to beat myself up over it."

"No, that's not—"

"Trust me, Regan, it has fuck-all to do with you."

"Okay, but that's not what I meant. Earlier tonight, when you asked me if the questions felt, how did you put it, a wee hypocritical?"

Eyes closed, she shook her head. "No, that wasn't fair of me, personally or professionally. You were doing your job. Honestly, I'm glad you were the one asking."

"It wasn't exactly a field day for me, you know. The last thing I wanted to do was make it worse for you."

"I know that. Even at the time, I knew it. I reacted badly and I'm sorry."

"Please don't apologize. I'm screwing this up. What I'm trying to say is that I haven't been intentionally keeping secrets. I mean, there are plenty of things I don't talk about, but that's because I don't spend a lot of time thinking about them."

"Are you saying you're willing to try? It's fine if you're not."

"Well, you probably want to know why Monica Spears is obsessed with me, and I'm sure you have questions about my connection to Lockerbie," I said.

She studied me for a moment, and I got the impression she was trying to gauge how forthcoming I was going to be. "Your hand. You were burned?"

She thinks I got the scars in Lockerbie. Well, why wouldn't she?

"Yeah." Surprising myself, I extended my hand across the short divide between our beds. I told myself it wasn't a big deal when she tentatively turned my hand over. She trailed two fingers along my palm, avoiding the freshly injured area. With the exception of medical professionals, only one other person had ever touched my scars. She pushed my sleeve up and traced the scars to their end, halfway between wrist and elbow.

"Does it ever hurt?" she asked.

"No, not really," I replied, letting out the breath I'd been holding.

"Is this the extent of it?" she asked.

"No." When I pulled my hand back, I wasn't sure what to do with it. Rourke sat back, waiting. I stuffed my hands into the pocket of my hoodie. "Full thickness burns over twenty-eight percent of my body. Let's just say my dreams of being a bikini model went up in flames."

She studied me and looked... sympathetic? Curious?

"You want to know how it happened?" I asked.

"Only if you feel comfortable talking about it."

"I have no problem telling you about it, Sheridan, but you have to understand something."

She nodded.

"You seem to have the impression I've been holding things back. Maybe I have, but not always intentionally. What details I do remember are sketchy."

"When we were discussing violent behavior and brain injuries, I noticed you touch the scar over your eye. Does the memory loss have to do with that?" she asked.

"*I* think so. The Army shrink pushed the repressed memory theory pretty hard."

"I see. Sorry I interrupted."

The only way was to jump right in. "In 2007, the Chinook helicopter I was on was hit by an SA-7."

"An SA-7 is some kind of rocket?" she asked. She'd been expecting a story about Lockerbie and her confusion was obvious.

I nodded. "Heat-seeking, shoulder-fired missile. They were a dime a dozen in Iraq. We were heading to Baghdad, eleven passengers, plus the pilots. Four of us were from my unit, most of the others were on their way to catch a flight home. The Chinook went down in the village of Hasi, just south of Fallujah."

Rourke was silent.

"The chopper broke apart, but I'm not sure if that was before or after impact. One minute the pilots are yelling in my headset, the next I'm face-down in the sand, still strapped into my seat, ass on fire. Literally. I'm sitting here talking to you, so obviously I managed to get out of the seat, but I can't tell you how because I don't remember."

"You burned your hand getting yourself out?"

"No. I was told my gloves weren't damaged when the medics arrived at the crash scene."

"Then how was your hand burned?"

"Apparently, I broke away from my rescuers and attempted to pull one of my fellow soldiers from the burning fuselage. I have no memory of that at all."

"Jaysus, Regan."

"I was later told that I was covering a piece of shrapnel impaled in my thigh with my right hand while all that was going on, which prevented it from being burned, too. What was left of my left glove had to be surgically removed."

"And you don't remember any of this?" she asked.

"Fragments, but I don't know if it's memory or dreams, or something in between. It's not something I can rely on."

The ten minutes before that were crystal clear, but she'd only asked about the scars on my hand and I wasn't above getting off on a technicality.

"How many survived?"

"Two," I said.

"Monica Spears said you were the third woman to receive the Silver Star in almost seven decades. If I'm not mistaken, that honor is reserved for valor in combat. You said once that you've never killed anyone outside of a war zone. I understand you not wanting to talk about it, and maybe you can't, but something tells me there's more to the story."

"There's always more to the story. But no one will ever know all of the details of this one, including me. It's been a long day and the cold medicine is kicking in."

"Of course," she said, and I could tell she wasn't going to hold it against me. "How does it feel to talk about it?"

"God, you sound like a shrink," I said.

She smiled, which I was glad to see.

"I don't know. I don't feel much of anything except tired."

"Well, that's almost true for me, too," she said. "Thank you."

"You're welcome."

By the time I cleaned off the table, brushed my teeth, turned off the lights, retrieved my blanket and a glass of water, and burrowed beneath the covers, Rourke was still and I couldn't tell if she was awake. After a few minutes, she casually trailed a hand along Ripley's side. I imagined the dog trying to get to Grace just before the apartment door blew apart. Was that how she'd lost an eye?

"Sheridan?"

Her pillow muffled a faint, "Mm?"

We'll get the son of bitch was on the tip of my tongue, but wanting something didn't make it true.

"Good night."

The sleepy sigh might've come from Rourke or Ripley. A few minutes later, I drifted off listening to their slow, measured breaths rising and falling together.

CHAPTER TWENTY-THREE

December 20
3:31 a.m.
Centreville, Maryland
39°2'25.27"N, 76°4'16.25"W

THE AWAKENING WAS sudden, which was nothing new. The coughing was different this time, though, not the lingering dream-induced kind laden with phantom smoke, but the real thing, deep and violent. My throat was on fire. Everything ached. *Where the hell am I?* Watery eyes scanned the dark space, searching for clues in a room lit only by the faint yellow light seeping in and around the drapes. My eyes finally adjusted and I made out a form sleeping in the other bed. *Definitely not my bedroom. A person. A dog. Rourke. Ripley. Motel.*

Face buried in the crook of my elbow, I stifled a series of deep coughs as I felt my way one-handed to the bathroom. Once behind the closed door, I was completely wracked by whatever backwoods country croup I'd contracted. I took a tentative sip of tap water. Another. The pain brought tears to my eyes, but God, I was thirsty. Another round of coughing was imminent, and I sat on the toilet lid, waiting. So much for the 12-hour cough medicine. I thought there might be a bottle of Tylenol in the Tahoe, possibly a few cough drops. I left the bathroom light on so I could see enough to avoid crashing into anything. I was halfway across the room when a noise caused me to freeze. A murmur. For a moment, I stood there listening. Rourke was moaning in her sleep.

The comforter, which obviously hadn't lived up to its name, was on the floor. I tried to imagine the amount of thrashing it had taken for the sheets and blanket to become so twisted around her legs. There was no way to free her legs from the blanket without waking her, so I picked up the comforter and gently laid it over her. Ripley, who'd been curled at the foot of the bed, resettled.

I'd shed my sweatshirt at some point during the night. Tank top and flannel pants weren't exactly stepping-out clothes, but I reasoned I was only going to the parking lot. I slipped on my running shoes, not bothering with socks, grabbed my car keys off the nightstand, and was halfway to the door when the time bomb in my chest went off. I practically threw myself out into the cold, deserted parking lot.

My glove box had evolved into a mobile medicine cabinet, and I found a bottle of Tylenol and three cough drops, which had melded with the wrapper. I scraped as much gelatinous cherry Halls from the wax paper as I could and hoped for the best. I'd taken two steps toward the motel when I realized I'd forgotten the room key. The door automatically locked when it closed, but I double-checked just to make certain. Yep, I was screwed. I didn't want to wake Rourke, but my arms were bare and I could see my breath. Fuck.

Haskins' light was on. I saw movement through the gap in the curtains. Dismissing the idea of waking Rourke, I knocked on his door. The curtain moved to the side for a moment, briefly framing his sleepy face. When the door opened, I started rambling before noticing he had his cellphone to his ear. *Who the hell is he talking to at zero dark thirty?* His tone was professional, not personal, and somehow this mattered. He was still wearing the same clothes he'd worn all day, minus the tie. He motioned for me to come in as he ended the call.

"Jesus," he said, tossing the phone on the bed. "Were you running? It's freezing."

My teeth were chattering, yet I'd sweat through my shirt.

"Yes, Rob. I like to jog alone, in the dark, in my PJs, braless, at—what time is it?"

"Almost four. And do you really want to get into your questionable decisions when it comes to jogging?"

"Touché. How am I sweating? I'm fucking freezing."

His hand felt cool against my forehead.

"You're burning up," he announced, and for the second time in a few hours someone was wrapping me in a blanket. This time it was followed by a hug and back rub.

"I just took some Tylenol."

He sat us both on the edge of his bed and continued rubbing my back. His shirt was rumpled, his hair slightly mussed, like he'd been running his hands through it, something he did when he was anxious. "You haven't slept, have you?" I asked.

"I dozed off for an hour or so. Feel any warmer?"

I nodded.

"Why are you up? You should be in bed."

In the midst of explaining, I started coughing and held onto the back of a chair for support.

"Okay, Typhoid Mary, I'm not a doctor, but that sounds bad. You can take a shower if you want. Might loosen up the gunk in your chest."

"Yeah, I just might take you up on that."

"Want a clean shirt? Not that I mind that look."

My white tank top was completely soaked. I might've been embarrassed if I didn't feel like death warmed over, or if the man hadn't seen me naked. I took him up on the shirt offer.

Alone in the bathroom, I inhaled the subtle fragrances trapped in the soft t-shirt cotton that made up his familiar scent: a hint of fabric softener, his body wash, and the dye-free, organic cologne, the kind I'd given him last Christmas. Violent hacking interrupted my olfactory trip down Better Days Boulevard. The defective cough drops had lasted all of ten minutes. I ran the bath as hot as I could stand it. The warm steam helped, and I stayed in the tub for a long time, periodically adding hot water for as long as the motel's water heater obliged. My skin was bright pink when I finally emerged from the bathroom wearing Haskins' shirt, which hit me at mid-thigh.

"Thanks for—"

He was snoring. I turned off the lamp on the nightstand and crawled under the covers, trying not to wake him. I was convinced I'd succeed when he asked, "Feel any better?"

"Damn. I tried to be stealthy."

"I'm a light sleeper."

"I know. And yeah, I feel a little better, thanks."

He rolled over to face me and tucked an arm under his pillow. There was just enough light coming in through the crack in the curtains to make out the planes of his face. He was grinning. "The pavement definitely won that round. I won't say I told you so."

"You're an ass. You and Rourke rehearse that line?"

He reached out and gently touched my scabbed chin. "Does it hurt?"

"Comparatively, no," I said.

We were quiet for a moment. I might've drifted off.

"I'd forgotten how good you look in my shirt." It was almost a whisper.

Heat spread across my cheeks. When I turned my head into the pillow, a tendril of hair fell across my face. He gently tucked it behind my ear, and I shifted closer to him, seeking his warmth. Strong arms wrapped around me and for a while I forgot about everything else. As I drifted off, I was only aware of our thumping hearts, mine rabbit-wild, his slow and steady. Like it had all the time in the world.

CHAPTER TWENTY-FOUR

December 20
8:32 a.m.
Centreville, Maryland
39°2'25.27"N, 76°4'16.25"W

FACE BURIED IN a pillow, vaguely aware of a familiar masculine scent, it took a moment to realize the pounding wasn't entirely in my head. I rolled onto my side just in time to catch a glimpse of Rob Haskins, shirtless, toothbrush hanging from his mouth. My eyes settled on his socks, where elves danced in festive poses. He was reaching for the motel room doorknob. *His room. Shit!* Thoughts of subtly vacating the bed and hiding weren't timely enough to be actionable. Rourke had stepped into the room, and she and Haskins were exchanging good mornings.

While I was sure my bed head invited speculation, the look Rourke gave me was *relief.* "Hey," I said dumbly, eyes searching the room for my pants. Haskins pointed to them, folded on a chair. Cheeks burning with more than fever, I shoved my legs in too quickly and was reminded of the abrasions on my knees. Why was I embarrassed? I was, after all, a grown woman. Nothing happened, but so what if it had? So what if we'd been having wild gorilla sex all night? More power to us! We were two single, consenting adults, and I had no reason to—'"

"Your room key, pocketbook, and phone were in the room and you weren't. I was concerned," Rourke said.

"Sorry. I went out to the truck and locked myself out. I didn't want to wake you. Haskins' light was on. I fell asleep." To her credit, she didn't mention the suspicious circumstantial evidence.

"So, you haven't seen this, then?" She held up a folded newspaper.

"Seen what?" I asked, taking the paper from her.

"I'm sorry, Regan. It was left at the doorstep. When you weren't in the room, I thought maybe you'd already seen it."

I didn't have to open the paper to discover what she was referring to. The article spanned the entire front page of the *Baltimore Sun*. Photos of Jennifer Abbott and Allison Brightwell were practically thumbnails, while I was prominently featured. The left-hand photo was from my Virginia Tech ROTC days, dirty, sweaty, and obviously in the middle of a training exercise. *G.I. Fucking Jane.* My official FBI headshot was on the right. It took a moment for the headline to register: *War Hero Hunts Eastern Shore Serial Killer.* Monica Spears was apparently working freelance, selling her story to the highest bidder.

Spears summarized my early days in surprisingly vague terms, only saying I was orphaned at the age of six and raised by my aunt in Virginia. There was nothing about Lockerbie and no mention of Erin. This was a teaser, Spears' way of telling me the documentary or podcast or what the fuck ever was going to happen with or without me. With an entire page of copy to work with, she'd covered as much territory as possible in broad strokes.

The first paragraph contrasted Pentagon policy on women in combat versus reality, pointing to the shifting nature of war and dissolving "front lines." She'd thrown in some stats for good measure, comparing female casualties in Afghanistan and Iraq to previous conflicts. Her summary was utter bullshit: *Captain Ross was* awarded a medal for gallantry in action that she never should have been in a position to earn in the first place, according to policy. What about the nurses, medics, and convoy drivers, women who, like me, were in a fucking combat zone where *anything* could, and did, happen? Policy had fuck-all to do with it.

Spears had included a summary of the medal citation plucked from the newspaper article she'd wrapped the medals in before mailing them to me. *Finding herself in the most perilous conditions, under fire, while her fellow Americans lay dying around her, Capt. Regan Elane Ross' bravery, unselfish actions and first aid rendered under fire represented the finest traditions of heroism in combat.* There were few details about my injuries and extended stint at the Army medical center. She glossed over my transition to the FBI and touched on my role with the Baltimore F.O. on the Sanchez case.

She mentioned my partnership with a foreign forensic psychologist, but didn't identify Rourke by name. Several times, she quoted "an anonymous Defense Department source" and "FBI colleagues." The former probably referred to heavily redacted Army records. I suspected the Bureau source was Eberley, who would sell me out at the bat of a lash or twinge of the loin. As I skimmed the last paragraph through a haze of red, the impact hit home. Erin would read about certain things for the first time, details that should've come from me. Lanie probably would, too. *Goddamnit.*

I'd missed Rourke's exit. Haskins, fully dressed, was reading the copy of the *Sun* that had been left at his door. I needed to do something, to not think about Monica Spears or the tens of thousands of people reading about me as they drank their morning coffee, or how my head ached and my throat burned. What I really wanted was to crawl into a deep, dark hole. I was sliding my feet into my shoes when Haskins threw the newspaper into the trash.

"Regan, I—"

"We have a new data point and I've got work to do," I said and was out the door before he had a chance to say another word.

The room was empty. Rourke had left a note saying she'd gone for a run, and I was thankful. It meant I didn't have to talk or try to be polite or anything else I wasn't up for. I threw a sweatshirt over Haskins' t-shirt, downed a dose of Robitussin and a bottle of water, sat at my makeshift workstation, and booted my laptop.

After transferring GPS data from the Brightwell crime scene to the GIS software, I pulled up the overhead image of the Eastern Shore and stared at the new data point, the third red point of a narrow, stretched triangle. The magic number was five. We weren't there yet. The location where Lenore Zimmerman spotted the van, the likely place where Brightwell was abducted, would make four, but the data hadn't been validated. Garbage in, garbage out. The van might've been completely legit and unrelated. Brightwell could've been ambushed two miles down the road. We just didn't know. *Meanwhile, her killer is already hunting his next victim, scouting a place to kill. There's probably already another cache.*

My head pounded and I couldn't think. It was time for the machine to do some work. First, I selected a distance decay model. This model was based on the generally accepted notion that offenders typically travel limited distances to commit crimes. Next, I selected models based on offender type. He was a local, a member of the community—a marauder, rather than a commuter. The system would use marauder and distance decay algorithms that included specific predictor factors.

The probability output resembled an amorphous polychromatic organism viewed at high magnification with the all-important red nucleus in the middle. In other words, it looked like unicorn vomit with a Skittle in the middle. The display itself didn't mean anything without the underlying statistical correlations, or what Haskins would call the "mojo." Violet indicated low, or "cold," probability. Red was "hot," high probability. What did this mean? Well, I could say with some confidence that our guy would likely choose a location in the warm-to-hot area to abduct, hold, or kill his next victim.

After adding a map overlay for spatial context, the hot zone covered the town of Chestertown, including the entire Washington College campus, most of the town's waterfront along the Chester River, and part of Kingstown, Chestertown's across-the-river neighbor. There were a few marinas within the red area and several additional possibilities in the warm zone. The area was large, but it was a manageable starting point.

As the jeopardy surface slowly emerged from the printer, I decided to call Haskins. No phone. I'd forgotten it during my hasty exit from Haskins' room. My call from the landline went unanswered. Email would have to do. I sent him a quick note urging him to call my room phone. It was midmorning. Food was probably a good idea. The bed was calling my name. *Just for a little while.* For the next three hours, I dreamed of dark, abstract things.

* * *

Had the motel not called to offer fresh towels and cleaning service, I might've slept all day. Rourke's running shoes were on top of her suitcase. The fragrance of her botanical shower gel lingered, indicating she'd showered, changed clothes, and departed again. My head felt moderately better. My stomach demanded food, but a shower was definitely in order. I'd just lathered my hair when the motel room door slammed. Someone called my name.

"In here!"

After two knocks the bathroom door opened enough for Rourke to talk through the gap. "Regan? Haskins is with me. We need to speak to you."

Something was up.

"I'm getting out. Give me a minute." Rinsing, drying, and dressing were frantic. My shirt was half-buttoned when I stepped out of the bathroom, towel-drying my hair. Rourke and Haskins' rigid postures and should-you-tell-her-or-should-I expressions were making me more anxious by the second.

"What is it?" Fingers combed through my Medusa nest.

Rourke was the first speak. "Your sister called. Your niece, she…" She cut her eyes to Haskins.

"Jesus, would someone just please tell me what the hell is going on? Rob?"

He wouldn't meet my eyes. *Protocol.* Something terrible had happened and he was working out how much to tell me.

Haskins hedged. "Your sister will know more."

"Know more about *what*? Christ, it's *me*. Just tell me!"

"We don't know exactly. They were taking her into surgery." He glanced at his watch. "About twenty minutes ago."

"Surgery? For *what*? For fuck's sake, Rob. What the hell has happened?"

"GSW."

"She's been *shot*?" It was a whisper.

"I'm sorry, Regan. That's all we know."

"Lanie's been *shot*?"

"Where is she?"

"Baltimore. She's at Hopkins," he said.

He kept talking and Rourke chimed in, but I was on autopilot, grabbing gun, bag, keys, running, barely aware of the gravel and glass under my bare feet. Doors slammed, my fingers gripping the wheel. Rourke was in the passenger's seat, squeezing my arm hard enough to bruise.

Not safe, not thinking clearly, let me drive, your shoes, not safe, please, your shoes, not safe, you'reupsetReganyourshoesstopletmedriveplease.

Words swirled like vapor as the gearshift slammed into drive.

CHAPTER TWENTY-FIVE

December 20
1:48 p.m.
Baltimore, Maryland
39°17'45.20"N, 76°35'30.05"W

"FUCKING BALTIMORE TRAFFIC!" I screamed, flipping the siren on because apparently the flashing red and blue lights weren't a big enough clue. Rourke's colorful explicative was punctuated by a yelp from Ripley as the Tahoe jumped the curb, almost clipping a minivan, without slowing down. When we stopped in front of the ER, I threw the Tahoe into park and sprinted toward the entrance without closing the door. My loose, untied shoes caused me to nearly bust my ass twice en route to the emergency bay.

"I'll park the car and find you!" Rourke yelled behind me, as if I'd given her a choice.

Two strides inside the ER, the dueling odors of sickness and antiseptic hit me. Patients and anxious family members filled the waiting room. A few were pacing, some were taking their frustrations out on the vending machines. Children wailed. Every fiber screamed *leave now*, but Lanie was there, somewhere, fighting for her life. *Please, God, let her still be fighting.* Two men were calmly drinking coffee in the middle of the chaos. *Baltimore's finest.* If my niece had been shot, there would be cops, though these two weren't necessarily there because of Lanie. A police presence in an ER in a city like Baltimore was commonplace. The investigator in me wanted to find out what the hell happened, but Lanie's condition concerned me more than what caused it.

A youngish nurse, *Martin, Julie, RN* according to her nametag, was manning the admin desk. She looked up from whatever she'd been reading on her monitor and her eyes registered the letters on my jacket. "You here about the two GSWs?"

"*Two?*"

"Two females brought in together. One was just pronounced. The other's in surgery," she informed me.

My fingernails dug into the counter. "Elane Ross—is she—"

"In surgery."

Thank Christ. "Condition?"

"Critical. GSWs to the head usually are, not to mention the beating she took. She didn't look good."

NoNoNoNo

"We won't know anything until the surgeons update the family. You're welcome to wait over there with the other detectives. I'll let you all know as soon as we know something," Julie assured me.

She'd assumed I was there as an investigator.

"I need to speak to Dr. Erin Ross right now."

"I can have her paged, but she's—"

"Page her. Please. I'll be over there with the detectives."

While kneeling to tie my shoes, I caught a sideways glimpse of the detectives. They were watching me, undoubtedly wondering what a Fed was doing there. My nerves weren't up for a pissing match. My approach was deliberate, my question directed at the older detective. "The GSW, Elane Ross. You guys know what happened to her?"

I caught Rourke's hurried entrance in my periphery and waved her over without taking my eyes off the detectives. My hand blindly searched pockets for my credentials. Nothing. Badge, ID, keys, were all in the Tahoe. "Elane Ross is my niece. I'm just trying to find out what the hell happened."

His eyes softened. "Oh, hell. I'm sorry. Listen, we're going to—"

"What exactly *did* happen to her? She was shot and beaten? How?"

The detectives' eyes shifted to Rourke. Skipping a lengthy explanation, I said, "My colleague, Sheridan Rourke."

The younger half of the duo eyed Sheridan up and down, then ogled me for good measure. His eyes settled on my chest.

"Up here, Detective," I said. He set his jaw.

Ignoring him, I shifted my focus to the senior, more professional BPD representative, who informed me that four assailants had jumped Lanie and Ren Saito.

"And Miss Saito is…?" I asked.

"I'm sorry," he said and seemed to mean it. "She was hit twice in the chest. She didn't make it."

"Where did this happen?" My voice sounded tinny and foreign.

"Western District, near Lyndhurst Park. They'd just left a tattoo shop. It looks like they cut down a narrow alley behind the building to get to their vehicle, where they were approached by at least four black males."

"What vehicle?" I asked, wondering if my Jeep might still be near the scene or in police impound.

"A Saturn," he said.

"Was anything stolen?"

"Purses, cellphones, but we suspect the primary intent was sexual assault."

"Why do you say that?" Rourke asked.

"The perps attempted to force them into an abandoned row house. That area is a maze of them."

Stars flitted across my vision. Rourke grasped my elbow, whispered, "You okay?"

My nod apparently wasn't convincing. She kept her hand on my elbow. "If it's a tight cluster of houses, it suggests the perpetrators are familiar with the area. They knew which house was vacant," I said. "Please tell me you've got these fuckers in custody."

"Working on it. We've got a twelve-year-old wit who got a good look, says they tried to drag the girls into a basement. Frankly, I'm surprised we got that much out of anyone in that neighborhood."

"Could this have been gang-related, some kind of initiation?" Rourke asked.

"Maybe, or could be four thugs who saw two pretty girls and decided to act on some nasty thoughts."

"What stopped them?" Rourke asked.

"An ass kicking," the young detective said, finally engaging in something besides tit gawking.

His partner asked, "Agent Ross, does your niece know martial arts?"

"Yes. Why?"

"Because our wit says she put some quote 'Bruce Lee moves' on her assailants."

"Well, Lanie wouldn't have gone anywhere willingly, and she would have fought for her friend. I'm sure she knew damn well what would have happened to them in that building."

"Well, there's plenty of evidence corroborating what our young witness says. She definitely put up a fight," the older detective informed us.

"What evidence?" I asked.

"A couple of teeth imbedded in her knuckles. She hit them hard enough to break her hands. If they hadn't shot her, they'd probably be the ones in surgery."

Salty saliva flooded my mouth and bile rose, prompting me to lean forward and breathe through my nose.

You will not get sick.

Rourke steered me to a chair. Once we were seated, she asked the detectives, "So, what are you doing to find the others?"

"We've got a BOLO out. According to the witness, the one who pulled the trigger is tall and thin, wearing a Ravens jacket, which won't exactly set him apart around here. Lots of gold in his teeth, though his grill may not be so pretty now."

"She notice any vehicles?" Rourke asked.

"No. They fled on foot, which, again, points to them being from the neighborhood."

"Any cameras?" I asked.

"I don't fucking believe it," the other detective said in a low voice, staring incredulously over my head. "Everybody sit tight. I don't want him to take off."

I had to turn around in my seat to see what they were staring at. Just inside the ER entrance, a tall black man in a Ravens jacket staggered toward the admin desk, his right arm across his chest, his left holding his jaw. One eye was swollen shut. Blood leaked from his nose, and when he grimaced in pain, I saw a flash of gold and two gaping holes where his front teeth should've been.

"Wait 'til they take him to an examination room," the older detective quietly instructed.

Nurse Julie was escorting him to a triage room when a guttural sound caused all motion and sound to freeze, as if someone had pushed pause. My body vibrated like a high-tension wire. Rourke tried to grab my wrist, but I was already running. We slammed into the wall and landed in a heap. I drove the heel of my hand into his ruined nose. *Motherfucker!* He bucked, swung at me. My knees dug into his sides, anchoring me. His blows landed on my forearms, and when he screamed, I put all my weight into his nose, imagining cartilage invading his sinus cavity. *Hurt! Die, you piece of shit!* He bucked, clawed at my face. I clamped down on the fleshy part of his palm and he howled. I tasted blood.

An arm wrapped around my waist and hauled me up as a chorus of voices yelled my name. Erin was standing in front of me, shaking my shoulders, saying something. The words meant nothing. I could only focus on her blood-soaked sweater.

CHAPTER TWENTY-SIX

December 20

3:05 p.m.

Baltimore, Maryland

39°17'45.20"N, 76°35'30.05"W

"SHE'S BEEN DRAGGIN' her arse since yesterday and refuses to go to clinic," Rourke said.

"Why am I not surprised?" Erin said as she peeled off the ruined sweater. There were dark streaks across her abdomen where the blood had soaked through. Oblivious, she pulled on a scrub shirt.

After rinsing and spitting Listerine into the sink for the third time, I tossed the paper cup into the hole in the exam room counter. "Satisfied?"

"You're up to date on your vaccinations? Hep?" Erin asked me.

"Hepatitis? Yeah, why?" *Shit.* "Shit!"

"Do you have any breaks in the mucosa? Mouth ulcer? Cut? If you do, the Listerine would've stung."

"It does anyway," I said. "It's like gargling jet fuel." My tongue explored my cheek and gums for possible points of deadly disease intrusion. "I don't think so. What about HIV? He's probably a goddamned junkie."

"Oral transmission is rare," Erin informed me. "You probably have nothing to worry about."

She must've detected my skepticism. "I'll draw some blood, and we'll test to make sure. What happened to your chin and hands? They're scabbed over. That didn't just happen."

It was so low on the scale of things we should be worried about, so absurd, I laughed.

"Well, I'm so glad you're amused. This entire situation is obviously hysterical."

"I'm sorry," I said. "I'm fine."

"You're quite clearly not fine. You look like hell," she said, scrubbing her hands at the sink.

"Is that your clinical diagnosis, Doctor?"

"Not a diagnosis; an observation. You're pale, feverish, weak."

"I'm not weak." It sounded lame.

"Oh, no? Dr. Rourke tells me you had a presyncope episode in the waiting area."

"*Pre-sin-what?* Can we go back to me looking like hell? At least I know what that means. You do know Sheridan's not an M.D., right?"

"Quiet," she instructed, fitting a blood pressure cuff around my bicep. "Try to relax."

"This isn't—"

"Regan, for God's sake. Shut your gob."

Erin watched the cuff deflate. Scowling, she jotted something on a notepad.

"Can I speak now?"

She nodded.

"Lanie?"

Erin's eyes stayed on whatever she was writing. She was pale. "Still in surgery," she said, removing the BP cuff from my arm.

"GSW? My God, Erin. Her head?"

"What I know at this point is that the bullet entered about here." She touched a spot above my left ear. "Just above the acoustic meatus, her ear hole—"

"Jesus."

"—and exited the right cheek," she finished.

"Wait, but that's good, right? If it came out her cheek, the trajectory was downward. It probably missed her—"

"Bullets tend to bounce around, and there will be bone fragments from the point of penetration, at the least."

"What's the worst case?" I asked.

"Cranial swelling, possible hearing loss, and significant nerve damage, and loss of the use of the muscles on the left side of the face. Bone fragments could cause neurological damage, infection, or both." Her tone was clinical. She was discussing a hypothetical case. Either it hadn't hadn't sunk in yet or she was compartmentalizing.

She continued, "There are other injuries. Impacted fracture of the right ulna and at the neck of the fourth metacarpal in both hands."

"Boxer's fractures," I said. "From striking something hard with a closed fist." *Something like a jaw. Has she seen the x-rays? Does she know about the teeth embedded in Lanie's knuckles?*

"She's got three fractured ribs, too," she added. "Any of those injuries could cause infection, but all of that is secondary to the cranial trauma. We won't know the extent of the damage until she wakes up. We may not know the long-term effects for months."

If there was a just God, the gangbanger I'd jumped in the ER was in a world of hurt.

Erin held a thermometer in one hand and the monitor it was attached to in the other.

"Shouldn't a nurse be doing this?"

"You *want* a nurse to do this?"

"No, I just—"

"The fewer people who know you're in here right now, the better. The chief of trauma and Baltimore PD want to talk to you about the stunt you just pulled."

"Great."

"Speaking of whom, I promised to speak to them after we got you to a room. I'll be back in few," Rourke said and disappeared behind a sliding curtain. She'd been sitting so quietly in the corner behind me, I'd forgotten she was there.

Erin slipped the thermometer under my tongue, and when it beeped a few seconds later, she checked the readout and pronounced, "One oh one point five."

She rummaged in the cabinets and produced a hospital gown.

"No fucking way."

"Regan—"

"I mean it, Erin. I'm not putting it on. Never again."

"Fine, but at least remove your gun and shirt so I can examine you properly."

My firearm. Jesus. The scene in the ER could've been so much worse. *What the fuck is wrong with you, Ross?*

Once the holster was off my belt, I hesitated. Removing my shirt meant revealing secrets I'd hidden from Erin for seven years. The reason still escaped me, but probably had something to do with why I'd run from Rob Haskins.

"Regan, please, your shirt."

"For fuck's sake, Erin, I'm not even wearing a bra."

"You're the one who won't put a gown on. Either take your shirt off and allow me to examine you properly, or I'll find another doctor to do it."

"Fine!"

My eyes stayed on the buttons until the shirt slid off my shoulders. When she gasped, it took everything in me to sit there, staring at the floor tiles while her expert eyes examined the many scars across my chest and abdomen. When she touched the circle of puckered flesh just below my right clavicle, I flinched. She tried again, tentatively.

Just breathe. She needs to do this. She needs to know.

She reached over my shoulder and gently probed until her fingers froze on the raised flesh where the round had entered my body. "Were you not wearing body armor?" It was a whisper.

Not at that point.

"No."

"For God's sake, why not?"

The question was simple. The answer was not, and would just lead to more questions. My jaw was quivering. "Erin—"

"Shh." It was so gentle it hurt. Tears spilled over. I kept my hands in my lap and let them fall. She placed one hand on my shoulder while the other moved the stethoscope over my chest. I was shivering.

"Deep breath."

I complied, fighting the cough that threatened.

She repositioned the stethoscope. "Again."

She reached over my shoulder and placed the instrument against my back. We repeated the process.

"You're congested."

"I could've told you that. With my shirt on."

She retrieved a tongue depressor from a canister on the counter and a pointy flashlight from the wall.

"Open."

She proceeded to examine my throat.

"Throat sore?"

"Uh-huh," I said around the tongue depressor.

"There's some redness," she informed me while palpitating the glands in my throat.

"Any soreness?"

"A little."

"What's your normal weight?"

"I don't know? Why?"

"You do know. Based on your height and usual amount of muscle mass, I'm going to say it's probably about one-fifteen. That about right?"

"In college, maybe. About one-ten since."

"Get onto the scale."

"Erin, I'm not getting—"

"My nerves are shot and I cannot…Get onto the goddamn scale, Regan."

I slid off the table and walked to the scale, my back in full view.

"Oh, *Regan*."

Standing there, motionless, while she palpated the burn scars across my lower back down to the waistband of my jeans was one of the hardest things I'd ever done. Over the years, I'd convinced myself that it was easier for both of us to let her believe my hand was the extent of it. Stupid.

"Skin grafts?" Her voice was barely audible.

I nodded.

"How many surgeries?"

"Six." A hot tear made its way toward my neck. Irritated, I swiped at it with the back of my hand.

"Is there more?"

"Some."

She took a ragged breath behind me, and a trembling hand reached past me to manipulate the slide on the scale.

"A hundred and one."

"What?"

"Your weight. A hundred and one with shoes."

A shrug. "So I've lost a few pounds, what's the big deal?"

"It's more than a few pounds, Regan. For someone who doesn't weigh much to begin with, it's significant."

The curtain slid open enough for Rourke to enter. At the sight of my bare back, she dropped her eyes and retreated to her seat in the corner.

"Can I put my shirt on now?"

Erin was pinching the bridge of her nose. She nodded.

Buttoning my shirt was a challenge with shaky hands. I'd just clipped the holster onto my belt when Erin asked, "When was your last menstrual cycle?"

Rourke stood, said, "I'll just wait outside."

"No. It's fine." It was sharper than necessary, and my eyes stayed on Erin. "What does my period have to do with anything?"

Erin crossed her arms, did her best authoritative doctor pose.

"I don't know. A while."

"What does 'a while' mean, Regan?"

"A couple of months maybe."

"Any chance you're pregnant?"

Cue sarcastic eye roll.

"I'll take that as a no," she said.

"Not likely."

"But it's possible."

"*Highly* unlikely. I'd have to be six months along," I said.

"Well, your workup will tell us for sure. And if you're not, then something else is causing the amenorrhea."

"Ameno—what?"

"Amenorrhea. Cessation of menstrual cycle. In your case, probably caused by the drastic weight loss. Your body fat has to be in the single digits, low even by male athlete standards. How often are you exercising?"

"I run three or four miles and spend a couple of hours in the Hapkido gym."

"Every day?"

"Until recently, yeah, pretty much."

She sighed and added something to her shorthand list of the ways I'd been sabotaging my health.

"What, is working out not healthy now?" I asked.

"Not if you're overdoing it."

Rourke chimed in. "If you're exercising beyond your body's ability to recover, it could cause some psychological symptoms, moodiness, irritability, altered sleep patterns, depression."

Great. They were ganging up on me.

"And over-exercising would definitely contribute to your compromised immune system," Erin added. "You need to cut back on the exercise or consume more calories. Are you taking vitamins or any kind of supplement?"

"No."

"You need to take a multivitamin daily. Short-term, what you need most is rest. You're not allergic to anything, are you?"

"You know I'm not."

"Well, I'm certainly not going to assume anything when it comes to your health, Regan, because clearly there's plenty I'm not privy to. You could have developed any number of allergies in the last seven years."

Touché.

"How have you been sleeping?" she asked.

She'll see right through it if you lie.

"Not well." *What with the nightmares and sleepwalking and all.*

"Well, your immune system is compromised. Have you had a flu shot?"

When the hell had I had time to get a flu shot?

"No."

"My God, Regan. That's just irresponsible."

"I have the flu?"

"It appears so."

"Fuck. Well, write me a prescription for an antibiotic or something and let me get the hell out of here so I can see Lanie when she's out of surgery."

"First of all, influenza is a viral infection. Antibiotics are ineffective, and it's too late for Tamiflu. You're highly contagious. You won't be able to be in the same room with her until you're asymptomatic."

"How long with that take?" I asked.

"It'll probably get worse before it gets better. Three or four days, minimum. You're going to my house and you're going to stay in bed."

"This fucking blows. Where's my jacket anyway?"

"You managed to shed it during the *altercation*," Rourke interjected. "The detective nicked it as soon as he got the chance. I suspect he's using it as leverage to force you to have a word before you leave."

"Fantastic."

Erin chimed in. "I don't think you realize how bad this could be, Regan. Freddie Gray protesters were burning buildings three blocks from here a few months ago, and you just attacked a black man in a crowded ER. For all we know, the video has already gone viral."

"There's a fucking *video*?" I asked.

"There's video of *everything* these days," Erin said.

It hadn't even occurred to me.

"Have you had a flu shot, Dr. Rourke?" Erin asked.

"Please, just Sheridan. And no. I haven't had a chance."

"Probably a good idea since hard-head here has been spreading her germs around. I can take care of it right now."

"Sure. Thank you, Dr. Ross."

"Sheridan, please call me Erin. And it's no problem. Could you see that my infuriatingly stubborn sister goes straight to my house and gets lots of fluids and rest?"

"I'm not three, you know. Lanie was shot, for God's sake. I'm not going anywhere."

"Once she's out of surgery, she'll be in the ICU. They're going to keep her sedated. You're sick. You can't go into her room anyway.

Go home and go to bed. The sooner you're over this, the sooner you can see her."

"Erin is right. I'm sure she'll let us know the minute there's any news about your niece," Rourke added.

"Fine. But make sure the detectives have my number. I want to know the minute they know anything. And call me the second there's any news about Lanie."

"You know I will." She didn't sound quite as detached. The stress was starting to take its toll. "I'm just going to get the flu vaccine and some ibuprofen for Patient of the Year."

When she was gone I told Rourke, "Looks like I'll be in Baltimore for the next few days. I'm not leaving until I know Lanie's okay. That doesn't mean you're stuck too. My Jeep should be parked either at Erin's or on campus. You should take it and head back to Centreville."

"I'll check in with Special Agent Haskins, but I don't think I need to rush back," she said.

"Listen, there's a printout in the motel room, a probability map. Tell Haskins to focus on the red areas, then work his way out. Cross-check addresses within the hot zone against DMV records."

"Do we limit it to vans or include trucks as well?" she asked.

"We shouldn't exclude trucks at this point. Mrs. Zimmerman's mysterious van may have nothing to do with the killer. What else do we know? What's another limiting factor?"

"Well, he wouldn't have been on the Eastern Shore from April to August 2013, because he was in the Belfast area," Rourke suggested.

"Right. I don't think he'll have a criminal record in the U.S. Publicly, he would have stayed under the radar. What else? Bobby at Boater's World said the guy looks like he spends time in a gym. That might be something. Chestertown and Centreville are small towns. How many gyms could there be?"

"A manageable number, I'd wager," she said.

"A cross-check of addresses in the hot zone against local gym membership records might be helpful, but there's not enough for probable cause, and the gym might not share member info without a warrant. Still, it's worth a shot."

"True. He might have a home gym, though," Rourke suggested.

"Sure, he could. But he targets young, athletic women. A gym would be a good place to scout for victims."

"Aye, I think you're right. I'm just going to let Ripley stretch her legs and take care of her personals. Be back in fifteen."

Erin returned with Motrin and a syringe.

"Where's Sheridan?"

"She went to let Ripley out. She'll be back in a few."

"Ripley?"

"Big, black, one-eyed dog. Will they let you see Lanie?"

She shook her head. "Not until she's awake."

"Then you should go home, too. You look wrecked."

"I'm sure I do, but I have some paperwork to finish."

Erin found a plastic bag in one of the cabinets and began stuffing the bloody sweater into it.

"My God. Was that Lanie's blood?"

"No. Ren's."

"You were with her?"

She nodded, still staring at the bag, trying to decide what to do with it. "It was a fluke, really. I shouldn't even have been in the ER, but they ice the sidewalks in front of the emergency bay more carefully, and I just thought it'd be a safer route. Anyway, I was there when they brought her in. When I heard GSW to the chest, I offered to help. The damage was just… We'd barely gotten the liver lac under control when her BP tanked. I had to open her up right there in the goddamned ER. Her heart was just shredded, Regan. It's a miracle she had a pulse at all when they brought her in. She never had a chance. Damnit, I completely forgot about this." She pulled a small plastic bag from the pocket of her jeans.

Oh shit. "It's okay. Give it to me and I'll hand it over."

"I know you're feverish and probably a little delirious, but you have to realize how ridiculous that is, Regan. You know better than I do, the fewer links in the chain of custody, the better. And you should have nothing to do with evidence or anything else having to do with this investigation, especially after the shit you just pulled out there."

"You're absolutely right, but neither should you. Erin, a defense attorney would have a field day with this."

"I know the protocol, Regan. This is not the first time I've extracted a bullet."

"No, but it's the first time you've pulled one out of your daughter's friend."

"Shit."

"Yeah."

"I'll give it to Julie Martin and have her sign it over. She was with me in the ER the whole time."

"Do it as soon as possible. Did you know Ren well?"

"No, not really. She and Lanie had just started hanging out recently. They have, *had,* a couple of classes together. They beat her so badly, Regan. I held her heart right here," she said, cupping her hands. "I didn't realize it was her until she was already gone. How could they do that to them, Regan?" Her voice broke. "Lanie has to be okay. She *has* to be."

"She will be," I assured her, taking her hands in mine.

"I have to tell you, Regan, honestly, I'm glad she's a fighter like her aunt."

"Erin, I…"

When her eyes searched mine, I couldn't say the words.

"Yeah, Regan. I know. Me, too."

CHAPTER TWENTY-SEVEN

December 23

Flu-ville, Delirium

39°19'58.90"N, 76°36'52.58"W

MY FEVER FINALLY broke after days of delirious half-sleep. I'd been vaguely aware of Erin and Rourke's presence at my bedside, administering meds and pushing soup and fluids. It was taking a long time to summon the energy to get out of bed. I'd been listening to the house noises, wondering what day it was, whether it was morning or evening. Voices and other audible clues beyond the door were drowned out by the vaporizer's gurgles and hisses. Finally, I climbed out of my nest of blankets and ambled to the kitchen on weak fawn's legs.

Rourke was leaning into Erin, saying something to her in a low voice. She seemed to be comforting her. When they realized I was standing there, they both sat up straighter. Rourke quickly removed her hand from Erin's arm. I'd evidently intruded on something.

"It's alive," Erin said. Her posture gave her away. She was exhausted.

"Barely," I mumbled, trudging to the fridge. Standing there with the door open staring at the contents didn't help me remember what I'd wanted. My stomach was growling, but anything substantial was probably a bad idea. "How's Lanie?"

"The oral surgery went well. She's recovering nicely."

"Wait, what surgery?"

"The bullet shattered two teeth, exposing the roots. She was in pain and it made sense to go ahead with the procedure."

"So, she's awake? What does she remember?" I asked, selecting a carton of orange juice.

"Most of it, I think. She's devastated about Ren. It's hard for her to talk because of the damage to her teeth and jaw and sutures in her tongue."

"Goddamnit." My hand was trembling as I poured the juice into a glass, and I didn't think it had much to do with low blood sugar. "I slept through the anniversary, didn't I? Fuck, I'm sorry."

"Don't worry about it. I was at the hospital anyway. Sheridan kept me company."

It was the first time we hadn't spent December twenty-first together in years.

"Can I see her?" I asked.

"Let her sleep tonight and see her first thing in the morning. You need to take it easy. Besides, Tabitha will be here any minute. She'll want to see you."

"Oh, shit. It's the twenty-third?"

"Yes, Rip Van Winkle, it's the twenty-third. I offered to pick her up at BWI, but she insisted on taking a cab." She paused, added, "You might want to take a shower before she gets here. Sheridan washed the clothes you were wearing. There are a few things in Lanie's closet I'm sure will fit you."

Rourke appeared to be wearing the same jeans I'd last seen her in. I hadn't seen the sweater before. *Erin's?*

"Or," I said, "I could just go back to bed."

"You can't avoid her forever, Regan. It's been almost two years. She misses you. Don't act like a child."

"Sheridan, take my Jeep and escape while you still can."

* * *

After blow-drying my hair and actually styling it, I spent about fifteen minutes choosing one of four sweaters in Lanie's closet. Procrastination tactics. My aunt was on the other side of the door, and I wasn't ready for her. Tabitha reinvented herself more often than the Material Girl, and one never knew what the hell to expect. Just when we acclimated to one incarnation, she was on to whatever she thought her new "beau" was into. Since I'd last seen her, she'd remarried and moved to Texas, which opened up a range of possibilities.

A check of my phone revealed twelve unread emails, seven texts, four voicemails, three missed calls, and a partridge in a pear tree. My call to Haskins went straight to voicemail. I sent him a text letting him know I was back among the living. Communication with the rest of the world could wait.

The three of them were having coffee in the living room, and my aunt was loudly complaining about baggage fees. As soon as she saw me, she came at me in an all-out blitz, giving me only a second to take in her getup. I registered a spray of pink fringe and enough turquoise to anchor a ship before Tabitha pulled me into a crushing embrace.

"Good Lord, Honey, doesn't anyone eat around here?" My aunt was stronger than her thin frame suggested and the hug was as over-the-top as her recently acquired Texas twang. She rocked us back and forth, tightening the vise with each sway. My ribs protested and I pulled away. She held on, squeezed my biceps, and leaned back, evaluating. "Hell, I'm not kiddin'. We're gonna have to get some meat on these bones, Regan Elane Ross. A light breeze could blow you over."

It took a while to process the pink leather and what it might mean. Clothing preferences were usually the first clue about the current man in her life, which was husband number four? Five? Had she actually ever married the Italian investment broker? Current spouse, Wyatt or Winston or something, came from oil money and owned land. Whenever someone mentioned him, the *Dallas* theme played in my head. Though the western flair was new, leather wasn't. A few years ago, Tabitha was briefly engaged to a rock musician. She apparently hadn't gotten the memo that no one, with the possible exception of Joan Jett, could rock leather pants after menopause. Somehow though, the pink version was worse—Annie Oakley doused in Pepto. The bedazzled pink boots were especially cringe-worthy.

For years, our aunt managed to convince anyone who didn't know better that she was my and Erin's sister, rather than our *mother's* sister. In her mid-fifties, that bit of fiction was now nearly impossible to sell. She tried too hard, even though she didn't need to. My aunt was an attractive woman, quite possibly beautiful— there's no telling what's under the seven layers of Revlon.

Tabitha settled back on the couch and picked up the conversation they'd apparently been having before I joined them. "Well, I just don't understand what she was doing down *there,*" she drawled, and I wondered what image of "down there" she had.

"She'd been to a tattoo shop," Erin informed her. "She probably didn't think twice about it during the daytime. According to the police, most of the serious crime in that area occurs at night."

"Hell, that's true anywhere. *Most* serious crimes occur during hours of darkness, but it's more about opportunity than time of day. If no one's going to witness the crime, or talk if they do…" I hadn't really meant to say it out loud. "Sorry."

"Well, I'll tell you one thing, I would love to get my hands on the sonsabitches who did this to my niece."

*Grand*niece. No one mentioned I'd beaten her to it.

"When can she come home?" Tabitha asked.

"Hopefully, the day after tomorrow."

"Really? That seems soon," I said.

"It's just a matter of wound care and managing her meds. She'll be more comfortable in her own room."

"She's going to require weeks of care. She can't even use her damn hands," I pointed out.

"I'm aware of that, Regan. I'm on a leave of absence from the hospital."

"Well, I told Wesley I'm staying as long as I'm needed, so count me in," my aunt declared. Cue *Dallas* theme earworm and visions of Uncle Wesley all alone at Southfork. Erin could probably use the help, but an open-ended visit was an exhausting prospect. After an awkward pause, Tabitha said, "Well, hell, if Lanie's gonna be home for Christmas, we better do somethin' about deckin' these halls. No offense, Honey, but this house is about as festive as a funeral parlor."

CHAPTER TWENTY-EIGHT

December 23

11:56 a.m.

Baltimore, Maryland

39°19'58.90"N, 76°36'52.58"W

TABITHA WANTED TO catch up with Erin and undoubtedly discuss me behind my back, so Rourke and I ended up on attic duty. We found the fake tree easily enough. The shape and size of the box simplified things. The ornaments and lights were a different story. We'd discovered the one exception to my sister's insistence on organization and cleanliness. The attic looked like Sanford and Son's overflow.

"Can't we just string some macaroni or popcorn or something?" I suggested. "This could take all night."

"Something tells me your aunt would have none of that."

"I'm sorry Tabitha subjected you to the third degree." Tabitha had basically asked enough questions of Rourke to learn her biography, as well as the complete history of Britain.

"Don't be. She's lovely."

I choked on a lungful of dust.

"A bit eccentric, yes, but she seems like a warm person," Rourke added.

"If you say so."

"You at least have to give her some credit for raising you and Erin."

"She took us in. She kept us from being separated and going into foster care. She put a roof over our heads and Lucky Charms on the table, and for that I will always be grateful. But to be clear, there wasn't a lot of *raising* going on."

The twenty-second box contained an assortment of bird feeders. "This is ridiculous. How is Erin doing? Is she getting any sleep?"

"Not much. She insists on being there, can't bear the thought of Lanie waking up and being alone. She's allowed me to sit with Lanie long enough for her to eat something and shower, but I've been bouncing back and forth between here and Centreville, so she's been on her own a lot of the time. It'll be easier, I think, once she's able to care for her here. I'm sure having Tabitha here will be a great help."

"Anything new happening with the case? I feel like I've been asleep for a year."

"Not really," she muttered, closing a box of trophies.

"Let me see that." I reopened the box and lifted out a familiar, faded Rockbridge High School soccer jersey. An examination of a few of the trophies confirmed it. They were all there, all thirteen years' worth. "What the hell?"

"Lanie's?"

I shook my head. "Mine. Now, if I didn't feel the need to keep all this shit, what in God's name would possess Erin to? I don't understand her sometimes. She needs to hire a nurse to help out, at least a few hours a day."

"I suggested that."

"What'd she say?" I asked, moving a box marked "Lampshades" out of my path.

"Said she'd think about it."

"That's a no." A green plastic container looked promising. "Christmas lights! Bingo! Tree, lights, and enough ornaments to cover the front of the tree. We'll put it in the corner so the backside is hidden. Mission accomplished."

We'd all eaten a healthy serving of Aunt Tabitha's "famous" New Mexico soup and managed to get the tree assembled and one strand of lights on when Haskins called. No hello, no how are you feeling, the first thing he asked was, "Have you talked to Spielman?"

"No, why?" I headed to Lanie's room.

"I don't know what's going on, Regan. He called yesterday and said that you'd be taking some time off."

"Well, I've been sick—"

"He said he was suspending BAU support."

"I have no idea what you're talking about. Exactly what did he say?"

"That you would be on leave for a couple of weeks, that I shouldn't discuss the case with you until further notice. He apologized, said it was out of his hands. Call him, Regan."

* * *

"What the fuck, Harry?" Not the smartest way to begin a conversation with your boss, but my give-a-damn was busted.

"I was going to ask how you're doing, but it sounds like the fever might've fried your brain. You want to try again, Ross?"

"Sir, would you mind telling me why you've withdrawn BAU support?"

"Well, Jesus, Ross, you attacked a man."

"I didn't—"

"Sounds like he got off lucky, though he'll probably have

a permanent impression of your teeth in his hand, from what I hear." He sighed. "Hell, I'm not sure I wouldn't have done the same thing."

"So, why am I being punished?"

"Your timing, for one thing. You're a white federal law enforcement officer and you beat a black man. In downtown Baltimore, no less. If you'd pulled that shit in the middle of the ER, there would've been witnesses, video probably. The whole thing would've gone viral and your career would probably already be over. Thank Christ you didn't pull your weapon on the SOB, or you'd be looking at aggravated assault. I'll do what I can, but there's going to be backlash."

"Shit. Will I be charged?"

"Hard to say. For a felony charge, they'd have to show serious physical injury. That's hard to do because he was pretty messed up when he came in and hadn't been examined yet. But they've got you for simple battery if they choose to pursue it. The Bureau will have to take disciplinary action of some sort. You know how it works. The Office of Professional Responsibility will investigate."

"It wasn't premeditated," I assured him. "I wasn't planning on—"

"Doesn't matter. You threw fuel on a fire that's been burning for a long time. Look, I get it, Ross. He almost killed your niece and you lost it."

You did lose it. You totally lost it. "Yeah."

"I spoke to Dr. Rourke and your sister. They feel the situation with your niece has left you, well, volatile, and I agree. The process will take some time, and in the meantime, you don't need to be in any situations that could—"

What in the hell had Sheridan and Erin told him? *Volatile? Take some time? What was he saying?*

"Harry, I'm *fine.*"

"I've scheduled an appointment for you. All you have to do is show up. January first is the earliest she can see you, and that's a miracle," he says. "It'll stay off the record."

"Earliest who can see me?"

"Dr. Hannah Bloom. Her office is in Baltimore, the Inner Harbor."

"A fucking *shrink*?"

"A psychotherapist, Ross. A damn good one."

"No way. I need to get back to work."

"I must not be making myself clear, because it sounds like you think you have an option."

"You can't force me to see a shrink."

"The OPR board sure as hell can. You want to wait until it's mandated and you have to see a Bureau psychiatrist, fine. You can go that route. Or, you can see Dr. Bloom off the books. She's good, Ross, and I'm telling you, it's better if you get out in front of this thing. January first, ten o'clock. I'll email you the address."

"So, I'm what, on leave for the next two weeks? What the hell am I supposed to do?"

"You're on administrative leave, with pay. It's the holidays. Spend it with your family, find a warm beach. I don't give a damn. But you will not discuss the investigation with Haskins, Dr. Rourke, or anybody else, and you're not authorized to use any Bureau assets. No phone, no laptop, no credentials, no weapons. I won't make you turn everything in, but you better tell me right now that you're goddamn clear on how this is going to go."

"*Fine.*"

"Try again, Special Agent Ross."

"*Okay.* I get it, Jesus."

"Try harder."

"Yes, Sir. I understand."

But I didn't. I didn't understand at all.

CHAPTER TWENTY-NINE

December 24

7:34 a.m.

Baltimore, Maryland

39°17'46.05"N, 76°35"33.21"W

AFTER A SLEEPLESS night at a Holiday Inn Express near the hospital, I fought through Christmas Eve morning traffic and crowds of procrastinators at two different stores. Still, I managed to make it to Lanie's room four minutes after the start of visiting hours. Had a nurse not directed me there, I probably would've walked right past her room. It was virtually impossible to reconcile the broken thing lying in the bed with my niece. Swelling had transformed her normally angular and delicate features into the face of a stranger. Her ivory skin was barely discernible under the various shades of purple and blue. They'd removed her piercings, leaving nothing familiar. Gauze covered her left ear and right cheek. Auburn stubble covered the left side of her head where they'd shaved it prior to surgery. One arm was casted from her hand to halfway up her forearm, the other to just above her elbow, leaving only the tips of her fingers exposed. I'd inventoried her injuries in my mind, imagined what she would look like. This was so much worse. For the first time, I understood what Erin must've felt when I'd shut her out. To be kept away from Lanie would kill me.

I watched her sleep for a few minutes while my conversation with Harry and the ensuing blowup with Erin and Rourke replayed over and over. "I'm sorry you're off the investigation, but I'm not sorry for being honest with your supervisor," Rourke had said. Erin claimed she was speaking objectively as a physician. She said it would be detrimental to my health if I didn't take some time off. *You need to rest.* The two of them had repeated it like a chorus. Rourke had provided Harry her "honest professional opinion," and now I was going to spend the next two weeks doing what? Drinking mai tais on a beach? Fuck that.

It didn't surprise me coming from Erin, but Rourke's part in barring me from doing my job felt like betrayal. *You don't know me. You don't know what I need. How could you do this to me? How could you not have my back? I'm volatile? I'm fine. I need to do my job. I trusted you.* That had been the soundtrack in my head, but I'd actually only said two words to her—two words I wouldn't apologize for. Erin had come to Rourke's defense, either because she thought I was being a bitch, or because of whatever was developing between them, or both. Either way, her claim of objectivity was a farce. Honestly, the only thing I felt bad about was not saying goodbye to Aunt Tabitha, because it could damn well be another two years before I saw her again.

Lanie stirred. It took a moment for her eyes to focus. When she saw me, she smiled, or at least tried to.

"Hey," I said, my voice was husky with emotion.

"Hi," she managed. Moving her mouth was obviously painful.

"You don't need to talk, Lane."

She tried to say something, but gave up, clearly frustrated.

"Are you in pain? Want me to call a nurse?" The casts made

it impossible for her to push a call button, and I understood why Erin wanted her at home.

She nodded. I pushed the call button to summon a nurse. "Your hair's already growing back, but I gotta say, you're totally rocking the punk look. Very badass."

She smiled a little, but it was fleeting, and her eyes welled.

"What's wrong, Lane?"

"So-rry," she said.

"Sorry for *what?*"

"Shhhould unt—"

"No, don't do that. *You* weren't the ones looking for trouble, okay? And don't ever be sorry for trying to defend yourself. You're smart enough to know what they would've done to you. Listen to me, okay? I know you're thinking about Ren, replaying it over and over, considering what you should or shouldn't have done, but goddamn it, Lanie, don't you blame yourself. This was not your fault. You hear me?"

How many times had I heard those words?

She nodded and turned her head into the pillow to wipe her eyes.

"Good morning, Sleeping Beauty!" a large, energetic African American nurse said as he entered the room carrying a plastic tray of vials. "You must be ready for your morning cocktail."

"I know I am," I said.

He smiled, but didn't take his eyes off his task as he introduced three different liquids to Lanie's IV drip. Once he was satisfied with the results, he directed his full attention on my niece. "Your eyes look better this morning, Miss Elane. Not as swollen."

When he finally looked at me, I tried to guess his age. Early thirties, maybe. About my age. His teeth were Crest commercial worthy. "DeJon Fountenot," he said, pronouncing it Day-Zhyahn, not at all like the mustard. "I have the privilege of taking care of Miss Elane on the dayshift. Let me guess. Sister?"

"Aunt. Regan."

"Nice to meet you, Miss Regan. So that would make you Dr. Ross' sister?"

"Yep."

"I was expecting to see her here."

"I'm sure you will soon enough." I nodded toward the IV stand. "What'd you give her?"

"Antibiotics, something for the pain, and something for nausea."

"Nausea from the pain meds?"

He nodded. "She'll probably sleep for a while when they kick in. You're looking great, Miss Elane. You just keep on healing up," he said, giving her foot a squeeze. "She needs anything else, just hit the button and I'll be here in two shakes."

"Thanks, DeJon."

When he was gone, I rummaged in my bag and found the iPhone and ear buds. "So, it was pretty shitty that your purse was taken and you lost your phone and all your music. Your mom can activate service for you once you're home. In the meantime, I transferred a couple hundred songs on here for you. I think you'll find I've totally hooked you up."

She was smiling, and if it hurt, she didn't show it.

"I figured this is way better than hospital sounds and bad TV."

I warned her about Aunt Tabitha's latest fixation with western wear and let her know she was lucky to be drugged up for the impending reunion. When her eyes got droopy, I said, "Listen, Lane, I'm going away for a while. You're going to be at home, in your own bed. You'll be in good hands. Just keep getting better, okay?"

She gave me a dopey nod. I set the music to shuffle, turned the volume down low, and placed the phone on the pillow next to her good ear. On my way out, I stopped at the nurses' station and handed DeJon the small box I'd not wrapped, but marked as a gift with a bow swiped from one of the packages under Erin's tree. "Dejon, do me a favor and please see that Lanie gets this."

"You got it, Miss Regan."

The contents of the box and the implications would infuriate my sister. A gift that would keep on giving.

CHAPTER THIRTY

December 24

5:35 p.m.

Claytor Lake, Virginia

36°59'24.46"N, 80°41'49.04"W

A S TEMPTING AS it was to find a warm beach and stay drunk for two weeks, it seemed a sacrilege to celebrate the birth of Christ in such a state. Besides, making any sort of plans, travel or otherwise, was too much trouble. After picking Stella up from my imposed-upon neighbor, I quickly grabbed some clothes and every blanket in the house, stuffed it all into the Porsche, and started driving. The sun was setting when I arrived at Claytor Lake. The view of Mack Creek from the back porch of the cabin was proof enough that a little spontaneity was a good thing. After being confined inside the pet carrier for four hours, Stella was ready to try her claws on for size. Tail high, she trotted into the high grass near the water's edge. I supposed, at some point, I'd discover some poor gutted critter on the cabin's welcome mat. Oh well, c'est la vie.

Our mother's grandparents built the cabin just before the Civil War. The modern version was the result of numerous remodels and upgrades. We called the cabin home one summer when Tabitha was between beaus and lacking in liquid assets. There had been no "lounge entertainer" positions within a two-hundred-mile radius, and she was damned if she'd ever sling hash again in this lifetime. She'd been equally adamant in her refusal to spend the guardianship money bequeathed to her on rent. So, she moved the three of us into five hundred square feet of "rustic heaven" for what she called "our big country adventure."

Erin hadn't so much objected to the cabin's quaint remoteness as the lack of TV, phone, and other teenagers. We had a canoe, two kayaks, and a private pier. Mack Creek was full of trout, bass, and crappie. From day one, the cabin was paradise to me. Blacksburg was only a half-hour drive, and having the perfect place to cram for exams or escape the stress of college life might've contributed to my decision to attend Virginia Tech.

The last time I was at the cabin was Memorial Day, summer before last. I spent the long weekend replacing the wood floors after watching a series of videos on YouTube. Had I actually planned out my agenda for the next two weeks, I might've considered another renovation project. On the other hand, the Carrera wasn't exactly designed for hauling home improvement supplies. The Porsche wasn't my first choice, but the use of Bureau assets was verboten while on admin leave. I could drive an hour or so to a hardware store, but it was too late for internet DIY support. The cabin offered no modern technical amenities. No LAN, no Wi-Fi, no landline, no TV, no cell reception.

Some might consider me cut off from the rest of the world, but I preferred to think of it as blissful solitude. The downside, of course, was that in the event of an emergency, I was on my own. I'd brought a shotgun, which would address a couple of contingencies.

I had enough provisions to last a week and could make the hour drive into town when I ran low. The cabin was heated by a wood-burning stove in the middle of the combination kitchen/

den. There hadn't been room in the Carrera for firewood, but there was a small stack next to the stove and another small pile on the back porch. It would last through the night, and I added stockpiling wood to tomorrow's to-do list.

The alarm clock was the obnoxious kind with jangling bells, and a film of dust on both sides of the glass face made it hard to read the faded roman numerals. Part of me didn't want to even consider time during the next seven days. On the other hand, it would be easy to become temporally disoriented, and I had an appointment I might decide to keep.

Deciding to track the days the way of the imprisoned and marooned, I tore off a piece of butcher paper and stuck the improvised calendar to the fridge with a Hokies magnet. During the warmer months, Claytor Lake offered plenty of activities to keep one busy and entertained, but options were limited in winter.

Determined not to be undone by sloth or boredom, I tore off a larger sheet of butcher paper and documented the following rules, which I tacked next to the front door:

Rule 1: Thou shall not get into bed any later than 2300.

Rule 2: Thou shall not get out of bed any later than 0600.

Rule 3: Thou shall exercise a minimum of two hours per day.

Rule 4: Thou shall not imbibe in alcoholic beverages prior to 1700; thou shall not imbibe to the extent that thou can't adhere to Rule 2.

Rule 5: Thou shall shower at least once daily and immediately after following Rule 3.

Rule 6: Thou shall ~~keep a journal meditate~~ sit still and think positive thoughts for thirty minutes each day.

Once Stella and I had full stomachs, I added two logs to the fire. We settled on the couch under a pile of blankets, and I had the notion that maybe this resting business wasn't so terrible after all.

On Christmas morning, I woke at five thirty. After dragging fallen logs to the cabin, I chopped wood and scrubbed every surface in the place. Few serious or negative thoughts entered my mind while I was cleaning, so I considered that adherence to Rule 6. I showered and had a beer before turning in at nine o'clock. Day One was a success.

Day Two: I was again bright-eyed and bushy-tailed at five thirty. After making myself some eggs, I sat still in the middle of the floor and tried not to fidget for about ten minutes. After jogging a mile and half to the nearest blacktop, I ran along Eanes Ferry Road for a couple of miles, then reversed course and headed back. After following Rule 5, it was a quarter after seven. I was at a loss. The place was clean and there was nothing to be done. *What would Laura Ingalls do? No livestock to feed, no crops to harvest, no candles to make. Not helpful.* I found a deck of cards and played solitaire for a while. Ate an apple. Listened to the radio. Took a two-hour nap. Spent a ridiculously long time making tuna salad. Went for another run. Took another shower. Ate a sandwich. It was five o'clock, and I was kicking myself for not considering some sort of project. I was never going to make it a week.

Day Three went about the same. I ran farther, cleaned out the fridge, and made spaghetti. Everything changed on Day Four, when I decided that just because I couldn't talk to anyone about the investigation didn't mean I couldn't think about it. I probably should've made it a rule, but that ship had sailed. I didn't have my laptop or any of the case files, but I had plenty in my head and plenty of paper. Thinking led to writing, which led to more thinking, which led to less sleeping, less eating, less everything else.

I stopped tracking the days. I stopped following the rules. There was no light bulb moment, no new insight, nothing that would help the investigation. Hell, if some great illumination had occurred, I wasn't allowed to do anything about it. Harry, Haskins, Rourke, and Erin would all be dragged into the mess I'd made. That could be avoided, I realized. I created new lists. Reasons to quit. Reasons not to. At some point, I decided the smart thing was to cash out, quit my life, and live at the cabin. Between my inheritance, savings, 401K, and what I could get for the Porsche, I could live simply and never have to work again. If I got bored, Tomaro Security was probably hiring. A feasible plan formed. I spent days and nights scrawling pros and cons on sheets of butcher paper while my thoughts kept returning to eight murdered women and a killer on the hunt.

At some point, I woke up on the cold tile floor. The fire had been reduced to smoldering ash. After days of thinking, writing, sketching, mapping, I'd finally slept. I didn't know what day it was, how much time had passed. It was dark. I moved to the couch, piled blankets on, and went back to sleep. The next time I woke, the cabin was filled with light. I brewed some coffee and took a mug to the back porch. The temperature was mild—fifties, I guessed. It was a day meant for doing something. The lake wasn't frozen over and I wondered if my old kayak would still float.

* * *

Claytor Lake was the result of the damming of the New River, which, despite its name, is the oldest river in North America, winding over three hundred miles through Virginia, West Virginia, and North Carolina. After two hours of paddling, I felt like I'd traveled the entire distance. My arms told me that if I didn't stop soon, I might not have the strength to get myself to shore. I hadn't seen anyone else on the water, but most of the larger craft would be docked and winterized for another three months.

After ferrying cross-current, I paddled the kayak through thin ice along the shoreline and used the blade to push as far up onto the bank as possible. After tossing the small cooler and dry bag I'd brought with me ashore, I leapt after them, managing to keep my boots mostly dry. All the exercise had me ravenous, and I scarfed down a sandwich. Using my jacket as a pillow, I lay down. The sun felt heavenly on my face. A mental map formed, a bird's-eye view of the New River.

I visualized my route downstream from Claytor Lake. The map gradually transitioned, the river's bends straightened. This was a different river. As I flew lower, I could make out small lines along the shore. Piers. Boats looked like bugs on the surface of the Chester River, white wake trailing. *What does your mental map look like? What kind of place do you like? Rural. Wooded. Farmland. Hunting land. The Eastern Shore and Belfast area are more alike than different. What's your connection to Maryland? Why are you there? Where were you for almost two years? What were you doing? Was there water there too? How did you know about the Garrett Farm and the hunting shack? Do you hunt other things, besides young, dark-haired women? Or do you just look for places to hide things, hide yourself, until you're ready for us to see? Where are you now?*

I woke to a quick succession of loud cracks. *Semi-automatic. Move!*

Heart pounding, mouth dry. Thirsty, God, so thirsty. More pops, small explosions overhead. Move! But I can't. Heat. Pain. Move! The screams are familiar somehow. Go, Ross. Find him. Get up! Move! Jesus. Jesus, there's so much blood. This isn't possible. Help him. Gunfire, so close! Move! I can't. He's dying, Ross. You're letting him die.

My eyes opened to a rocket screaming through the night sky. Instinctively, I scrambled for the nearest cover, crouching low in the sparse, leafless brush. The sound of lapping water was disorienting. The sky exploded into a shower of green and another whistling flame raced toward the stars. A distant boom was followed by a sizzling cascade of blue tracers falling back to earth. *Beautiful.*

Beautiful.

They're beautiful, Lanie. Not the little ones from the roadside stand, but the big aerials all the way from China. Close your eyes. Electric chrysanthemums, blue, red, purple, green filling the whole sky. Can you see them?

I can see them, Aunt Regan.

Happy birthday, kiddo.

No small arms fire. No mortars. No chaos. No screaming. No dying. Just a small-town fireworks show and some kids across the river with Black Cats and bottle rockets.

Shit.

Happy New Year.

CHAPTER THIRTY-ONE

December 24

7:30 p.m.

Claytor Lake, Virginia

36°59'24.46"N, 80°41'49.04"W

DEHYDRATED AND UTTERLY sapped of energy, it took me almost four hours to paddle back. I smelled the smoke before I got to shore, and the last few yards were a frantic scramble of paddling, dragging, and sprinting. Once I made it inside the cabin, it took several seconds for my mind to process that there was no emergency. The roaring fire was intentional and contained, and the person responsible for my panic was sitting calmly on the couch with my cat curled in her lap.

Thirst temporarily overrode anger. I stomped to the fridge, grabbed a jug of water, and started chugging. Half the gallon was gone and the front of my jacket was soaked when I finally paused. "How'd you find me?" My throat was raw and speaking was painful. Rourke started to reply, but the answer came to me and I didn't give her a chance.

"Sonofabitch!" I slammed the jug down onto the counter and grabbed a steak knife from the block on the counter. Her eyes went wide, but I didn't give a damn how she might interpret things. The darkness didn't slow me down. I had the driver's door open before she reached me. "Give me your phone," I demanded.

"What?"

"Give me your goddamn phone, Sheridan."

Reluctantly, she handed it over and I used the screen's backlight to see what I was doing. "Goddamnit! You had no right to track me," I said, working the serrated blade over the stitching. "Vincent had no right!"

"Regan, please stop! You're not making sense. Who's Vincent?"

I snorted. "Right, like you don't know."

"You're not being rational and you're going to ruin the seat. Regan, please just stop and talk to me."

"Go to hell." I pulled the seam apart and reached inside, feeling along the bottom of the seat pad. Nothing.

"Erin said you loved this place and came here often while you were at university. It's the only place we could think of. Think, Regan! I wouldn't know how to track you, and I don't know anyone named Vincent."

The device was imbedded in the top of the seat pad and came out after some prying. I stared at it, finding its size hard to believe. Even with the waterproof plastic casing, it wasn't much bigger than a memory card for a digital camera. Too late, I understood that it was true. Rourke couldn't know about the GPS device. She'd never met Vincent and wouldn't know how to contact him. I'd ripped the Porsche's seat open for nothing.

I wasn't thinking straight, which only made me more furious. I started to throw the GPS module, but thought better of it and stuffed it into the pocket of my jeans. The least I could do was return it to Vincent. I slammed the car door and started walking fast, back to the cabin. "What are you doing here, Sheridan?"

She followed me. "Everyone is worried. You can't just go off the grid for a week and expect that no one will be bothered."

Oh, but I could.

"What I expected is that *I* wouldn't be bothered. Isn't this what all of you wanted, for me to fucking *rest*? I didn't realize I was required to check in." I didn't hold the screen door open and it sprang back on her, not that I cared. I went straight for the bottle of Bushmills and poured two generous fingers, not giving a damn that I was drinking in front of her.

"This," she motioned to the sheets of butcher paper covering the walls, "Isn't resting and you know it. This looks *manic*. Can you imagine what went through my mind when I saw this? Your car, ID, everything was here, but you weren't. I relaxed for a moment when I found the shotgun, but then I thought you might've taken another firearm with you. It scared me, Regan."

"You looked pretty fucking content to me." I downed the whiskey and poured more.

"I found the drag marks and your footprints where you put the kayak in. I expected you'd turn up. I wasn't going to leave until I knew you were safe."

"Well, I'm safe."

"I'm relieved to see that you are."

"How's Lanie?"

"Much better. She's anxious to see you. Did you draw this from memory?" She was standing in front of maps of Northern Ireland and the Eastern Shore, and it reminded me of that first day in my office when she'd studied the murder board.

I screwed the cap on the bottle, put it away. "It's all I have out here. Memory, time, colored pencils. It might need updating, though. I've been out of the loop. Is there anything I should add? Any more data points?"

As expected, she hesitated, seemed conflicted.

"Right. You're not supposed to discuss the case with me."

"I'm sorry. You know I would if—"

"So, why are you here?"

"Like I said, we were concerned."

"Well, Dr. Rourke, you can report back to Erin that I'm fine. I'll be seeing the shrink tomorrow as ordered. I haven't blown my head off, drowned in the river, or left the country. I've managed to limit my axe-wielding to the woodpile. So, if there's nothing else, I'd appreciate it if you'd leave me the hell alone. I'm tired."

She nodded. "Right, well, I need to be going anyway. I've an early flight tomorrow." She pointed to my Pros and Cons list. "It isn't like you to give up. You can rationalize it all you want, but you're better than that, and I think you know it."

"Yeah, well, it's my life and my business."

"Take care of yourself, Regan. A lot of people are counting on you."

The words echoed long after she was gone.

CHAPTER THIRTY-TWO

January 1

10:03 a.m.

Baltimore, Maryland

39°17'10.29"N, 76°36'34.42"W

D R. HANNAH BLOOM'S office glowed with natural light. The open, contemporary space was inviting, and obviously designed by someone with impeccable taste. Erin would approve. The impressive view from the eighth floor should've made it easier to forget where I was, but I was having a hard time focusing on anything except the large geologic object that sat between the doctor and me. Someone's idea of a practical joke, surely. It was the largest geode I'd ever seen. Technically, it was half a geode, encased in Plexiglas to both protect it and render it functional as a coffee table.

The halved spheroid mineral mass, easily three feet in diameter, revealed the most breathtaking layers of shimmering azurite, prismatic crystals, chaotic swirls, and rings of gold and blues ranging from deep midnight to a hue so electric it fluoresced. There were plenty of reasons to stare at it, and everyone who sat on Bloom's couch for the first time probably did, but I was fascinated for another reason. If there was a more apropos symbol of my dead mother, I couldn't imagine it. Dr. Bloom balanced a notepad on her crossed thighs and slipped a pen, the expensive kind people give as graduation gifts, from one of the deep pockets of her cashmere sweater. Bloom hadn't taken her eyes off me since I sat down.

She had Rourke's gift for being the most well-put-together person in the room. Or maybe I just made it particularly easy. I'd done well to shower and put on cleanish clothes. My face was red and swollen from falling asleep in the sun, my nose and cheeks blistered and painful. Had I bothered to brush my hair before throwing it into a sloppy ponytail? I thought so, but probably looked like a feral creature recently introduced to civilization. "Are you anxious, Regan?"

Anxious was the wrong word. More like thrown for a fucking loop. My mother may as well have been sitting between us.

Say something, Ross.

"I'm not, really," I said. "I was just wondering why you would take on a charity case, especially on a holiday."

"What makes you think you're a charity case?"

"Are you getting paid for this?"

"Well, no, but pro bono is—"

"Semantics. I'm not sure how Harry Spielman got you to agree to this, but the fact is, if he hadn't pulled strings, neither of us would be here."

"Do you not want to be here, Regan?"

"I'm not trying to be rude or difficult, Dr. Bloom. I'm sure you're good at what you do, but it's not like being here is really a choice."

She raised an eyebrow.

"Right, we always have a choice," I said, punctuating with finger quotes. "But they're all shitty ones."

"Okay, let's talk about these shitty choices. If you had decided not to show up today, what would be the consequences?"

"According to Harry, I'd be putting myself even more at the mercy of the OPR board. That's the Office of—"

"Professional Responsibility," she finished. "I was on staff at the Bureau for several years and I'm familiar with how OPR investigations work."

Well, that explained how Harry knew her.

Bloom continued. "So, if I understand the situation correctly, your supervisor believes the OPR will look favorably on the fact that you're seeking help to deal with the issues going on in your life? Is that right?"

"Yeah, that's about it. So, where do we start? Do we jump right to me attacking the gangbanger in the ER or go all the way back to childhood? How does this work?"

"Well, before we begin, I want to make sure that you understand that whatever you tell me here is confidential, unless you tell me that you're hurting a child, an elder or dependent adult, or—"

"Or plan to off myself. Yep, got it. I haven't hurt, or planned to hurt, anyone lately. Except maybe, for a second, the obnoxious hipster at Starbucks earlier, but she was neither a minor nor elderly, and I'm pretty sure everyone in line wanted to kill her. One shouldn't have that many specific dietary concerns over a fucking latte."

God, Ross. You don't have to say everything that comes into your head. Maybe you shouldn't have slammed a double espresso right before your first therapy session.

Her expression was unreadable, and I was curious what she was writing on that fancy notepad.

Don't think about that. And for God's sake, don't look at the geode.

My eyes wandered to the wall of windows behind Bloom, and I squinted against the light.

"So, I'd like to get to know you a bit. What was your childhood like? What's your family life like? Are you married? Do you have children?"

I snorted. "Sorry. These just sound a lot like first date questions, the shit people conveniently leave out of their Tinder profiles."

She smiled. "Well, we're not following a script here. You may start with whatever you'd like."

"Okay. Well, there's no significant other. Never been married. No kids. I have a sister, a niece, and an aunt. That's the extent of my family, unless we're counting my father's Scottish cousins with whom we have no contact. My parents were killed when I was six. I guess we should start there, unless you're interested in the prologue."

Her nod was open to interpretation. I focused on her pen, which was in constant motion.

"In the beginning, things were great. And that sounds biblical. I mean, we were happy *before*."

"Who is we?"

"My parents, sister Erin, and I. My father, Cailean Ross, taught physics and astronomy at the University of Edinburgh—that's where he met my mother Elane, an American doctoral candidate in the geology department. The two of them had a scandalous affair, evidently. They tied the knot in 1971, almost exactly eight months before Erin was born. I'll let you connect those dots.

"Mum traveled a lot for her work before I entered the picture. The house was full of rocks, minerals, crystals, baby food jars full of sand, from all over the world."

Which are all in boxes in your guestroom. What would she think about that?

"She stayed home with us until I was about five, then she started teaching at Heriot-Watt. Things were great. And then they were the opposite of great. Do you want to know how they died or what happened after?"

"Whatever you think is important, Regan. Is it hard for you to talk about how they died?"

As far as shit-that-probably-fucked-me-up, it was all important.

Without testing the water, I took a deep breath and dove in. "I blamed poor Mrs. Naughton at first. Believed it was all her fault they were dead." Interesting, I'd forgotten about that. Bloom raised a meticulously plucked eyebrow and waited for me to continue. I didn't.

"Mrs. Naughton?"

"The widow who lived three doors down."

"Where?"

"Lockerbie."

"You lived there?" she asked, quietly. "When was this?"

I shook my head. "We lived in Livingston, a suburb of Edinburgh. We were in Lockerbie visiting Da's cousins. This was in 1988."

"I see. Did it help to blame Mrs. Naughton?"

"Of course not. The only thing Ellie Naughton was guilty of was being lonely during the holidays."

"Have you ever talked about what happened, Regan?"

I hadn't. Not really. Erin had wanted details, was obsessed for a while, read everything she could find about the two hundred and fifty-nine people who'd died aboard Pan Am Flight 103. She could tell you about every one of them, where they were from, where they were going, the lives their deaths touched. I think it helped distract her from what was going on around us.

The newspapers were full of information about the passengers, and interviews with the families seemed to play on continuous loop on TV, but no one remembered the ones of us on the ground. One minute, we were going about our pre-holiday business, the next we were in the village of the damned. I'd always told Erin I hadn't seen anything, but I didn't necessarily believe that, even if I didn't remember what I saw. Dr. Bloom was waiting for an answer.

"No."

"Do you think you might be able to talk about it? If not, that's okay, we can move on to something else. Like I said, there's no script here."

I never had to see Hannah Bloom again. What did her opinion matter, ultimately, when my career and future weighed in the balance? I sat there for a while, eyes closed, just breathing. Bloom was patient. I concentrated on the sound of her Mont Blanc gliding over paper.

"It was four days before Christmas and bitterly cold. I wanted Da to carry me, to wrap me in his warm sheepskin coat. I was small for my age. *You're not a wee babe anymore, Bird.* That's what he called me, Little Bird. That was almost the last thing he said to me. I would've gladly settled for holding his hand, but I was carrying the steaming loaf of holiday cheer that was supposed to make Mrs. Naughton forget she had no one to spend Christmas with. My mother's banana bread was my favorite. Since that night, the smell of it sickens me."

I'd gone quiet, not sure where to go next.

Bloom said, "Often, when someone experiences trauma, certain senses kick in and can trigger those feelings."

"Certain smells, like the burning, I get. But fucking *banana bread*?" It was harsher than I'd intended. Her smile was warm and made me feel bad. I settled back in the plush blue cushions and closed my eyes again. Bloom's pen was busy.

"Erin stayed home because she was a teenager and had better things to do. The three of us marched down Sherwood Crescent, singing carols. I was thinking how lucky I was to have my parents all to myself when we felt the tremor. It was the impact from the wing section, but we couldn't know that. The crater was still smoldering two days later.

"Da saw them first, fluttering embers I thought were fireflies until I followed his gaze and watched a hunk of flaming wreckage strike the Flannigans' roof. The house just exploded. Da grabbed my arm, spun me around, and yelled for me to run toward the house. I did, I ran. I have this recurring dream. I'm still holding the bread when I look over my shoulder like Lot's wife. I'm not sure if I actually did that, saw that, or if it's what I imagine I would've seen."

* * *

We talked for a while about the years I'd bounced from one town, one school to the next as Tabitha followed a series of men all over Virginia. Erin had been at UVA, then Hopkins, and missed out on most of the crazy times. I told Bloom about the challenges of trying to take care of Lanie when my support system consisted of a woman who couldn't balance a checkbook. We moved on to Iraq. Bloom got roughly the same account Rourke had. It wasn't her style to press me on the details. That was probably why, almost an hour later, I was still talking.

"Your memory of that day seems fragmented. Are there certain details you wish you could remember?" Bloom asked.

I wanted to say no, but I was on a truth roll. "My friend died, he was killed, and it was just the two of us, and... people always say we should remember how people lived, not how they died. That's bullshit. We should remember how they died. *Someone* should."

"Tell me about your friend, Regan."

"His Iraqi name was Basim Abdul Hamid, but we called him Sly. This won't make any sense, but he looked like an Iraqi Sylvester Stallone. He was risking his life to work with us, had to be scared for his life, for his family's lives all the time, but he never stopped smiling. That's a special kind of bravery, you know? He wore these Buddy Holly glasses and was always doing these spot-on impressions of American celebrities. His Bush impersonation was the best. This goofy Iraqi doing George W."

I was laughing, then I wasn't.

"He shouldn't have died. I dream about it. A lot. It's always the same, but I don't know if it's all real."

The dream version was terrible, but it was also beautiful. This, I couldn't say out loud. Those last moments, kneeling over him, our blood mixing in the sand. His eyes were focused on mine. He was smiling. There was no fear, just peace. That moment, in the dream or memory, or whatever it was, was the closest to God I've ever felt.

Mesmerized by the neon blue swirls beneath the glass, I sat there for what seemed like an eternity. Bloom was silently writing notes, then finally asked, "Regan, have you ever in your life been as scared as you were that night in Lockerbie or when you were under attack in Iraq?"

I didn't have to think about it. "The moment I found out Lanie had been shot. Actually, I was pretty much in shock at that point, and I don't remember what I felt. Later, at the hospital, when I learned Lanie's condition was critical."

"Lanie is your niece?"

"Yes."

"Tell me about what happened in the ER. You attacked one of the men who almost killed her?"

"I don't know what happened. People describe it as snapping. Something did snap, I think, in my brain. One second I was forming coherent thoughts, the next, it was like watching a movie filmed through a filter, a red haze. My body hummed, like a current was running through me. And then I was on top of him. He was scared. I saw it in his eyes, smelled it in his sweat. When he screamed, it *excited* me. There's something wrong about that, I think. I was bent on hurting him. No, it was more than that. I wanted him to die. Nothing else mattered or even existed. I would've killed him. I lost it, which is bad enough, but the Bureau thinks I might again. They think I'm a liability."

"What do you think?"

"I don't know. Right now, when I'm rational, it doesn't seem possible that I'm capable of that. But I was capable. I *am* capable."

"Is that what scares you most? Are you afraid of losing control again?" she asked.

"Yes."

"If you could do it over, have that day in the ER back, what would you change?"

"To know that the piece of shit was going to walk in, for one thing. But if precognition isn't allowed in this hypothetical, then I guess I wish I'd been able to have a cool head, to think before I acted."

"And what would that have accomplished?"

"I would have been able to stop. I wouldn't have attacked him, and..."

"And?"

"And the Bureau wouldn't see me as a liability."

"Take that one isolated event away and the OPR would see you as the asset you've always been to the organization and to the people you serve, right?"

"I guess."

"Then that's your homework."

"*Homework?*"

"Yes. For next time, I want you to list at least two ways in which you're the opposite of a liability to the Bureau."

"So, I'm your client now? I thought this was a one-time thing."

"That's entirely up to you, Regan. Think about whether or not you found the session worthwhile. If so, give me a call and we'll set up regular sessions. It's not that complicated."

If that were true, it'd be a first.

CHAPTER THIRTY-THREE

January 1
6:48 p.m.
Baltimore, Maryland
39°19'58.89"N, 76°36'52.58"W

CURLED UP ON my sister's couch with Lanie and Ripley binge watching *Breaking Bad* was the perfect way to decompress after my session with Dr. Bloom. There was something about Walter White's complex layers of fictional drama that caused one to temporarily forget real-world catastrophes. Lanie's recovery was going astoundingly well. Her face had almost completely returned to its pretty, angular normality. The bruising had faded, and she'd decided on a buzz cut to allow her hair to grow in evenly. Erin had bought her a variety of hats to wear until it grew to a stylable length. She was sporting a rainbow-striped knit toboggan with a pompom on top.

It was hard to believe the girl leisurely sprawled on the sofa sucking on a Twizzler could barely talk a week before. She'd decided to return to Hopkins in the spring and live at home. If all went well, she'd move back on campus in the fall. If she was upset about having to put her enlistment plans on indefinite hold, she hadn't said. It was going on seven o'clock and Erin still hadn't returned from the hospital. Lanie informed me she wasn't surprised. Apparently, Erin had gone to work after Rourke left yesterday and had hardly been home since.

"She's probably just catching up," I suggested. "I doubt she's ever been away from work this long. Has Sheridan been staying here since I left, since Christmas?"

"She's been back and forth to the Eastern Shore, but she's been here most nights. She took her bags with her yesterday, though. Obviously, she's coming back for Ripley at some point, but Mom was vague and pissy when I asked when that might be. Your Jeep keys are on the kitchen counter, by the way. I'm starving."

"You know I don't cook. Pizza?"

"God, yes! Mom's been making me eat all this bland shit until my tongue is totally healed. She hasn't even let me have a Coke. It's ridiculous."

"Oh, well, maybe pizza isn't such a good idea. I can make toast and eggs. How about grilled cheese?"

"Oh my God, Aunt Regan, you can't mention pizza, and then not order it. That's just cruel."

"Okay, but my story is that it was all your idea and I didn't know you weren't supposed to have it." As I ordered, Lanie picked at the afghan blanket covering her legs. Something was bothering her. When Pizza Guy put me on hold, I asked, "What's wrong?"

"Nothing. I just want to know what's going on with Mom."

"What do you mean?"

"Well, there's *something* going on between her and Dr. Rourke. Don't tell me you haven't noticed. Seriously, I've never seen Mom like this. Sheridan leaves and she acts like someone stole her puppy."

Pizza Guy took my order and assured me our pie would be at the door within 45 minutes.

"Lanie, your mom has been through a lot the last couple of

weeks and I bailed on her. I'm sure she just misses having someone here to talk to."

"Yeah, but they hardly know each other. Then suddenly, they're—I don't even know. It's kinda crazy, right?"

"No, I don't think so. Sometimes people get close to each other fast, especially if things are crazy." *Like in war, or serial rape investigations, for example.*

"Speaking of crazy, did Erin totally freak about the Ducati?"

"It was epic. She and Sheridan were both there when DeJon gave me the box. When she realized what the key was for—friggin' bananas! Dr. Rourke was trying to play it cool, but I could tell she was about to crack up. Mom was so pissed she had to leave the room."

Erin's inevitable reaction wasn't the main reason I'd given Lanie my motorcycle. The physical therapy was going to be a bitch, physically and mentally. Lanie would need a reason to push through the pain, and I figured imagining herself on the Ducati might help. It had worked for me once.

The house phone rang, a friend of Lanie's, and I urged her to take the call. Not only was I having technology withdrawals, but I'd also been cut off from what had been going on in the world for the last week. I wasn't surprised to find Erin's computer screen unlocked. She never used a password at home. When the screensaver disappeared, I was looking at an email she'd left open. Though I immediately looked away, my brain had captured a snapshot. It was from Rourke and I got the gist. When Ripley nosed the office door open, it startled me. *Leave well enough alone. It's private and none of your business.* On the other hand, the glance had been so brief that it was entirely possible I'd misread or misinterpreted it. Ripley nudged past my leg, curled up under the desk, and rested her head on my foot. Damnit. This was why people should use passwords and log out of email accounts. Of course I read it. Who wouldn't?

Erin,

Please know that I'd give anything to be there with you. You were right, of course, but we both knew that. Eventually, I will have a choice, and I only hope you'll still want me to stay. Until then, I'm thinking of you. Always.

Sheridan

P.S. – Take care of my dog. And take care of yourself.

Well, if there'd been any doubt that Erin and Rourke had something going on, it was gone. This was just further proof that where my sister's personal life was concerned, I'd never had a clue.

I closed the email and navigated to the CNN website, looking for any new information on the Eastern Shore murders. I tried a couple of Maryland news channel sites. The general consensus seemed to be that the investigation had stalled. I brought up Google Maps and located the spot where Sam Meyer's hunting shack should've been, beneath the canopy of trees. The overhead shot had been taken in the warmer months, when full foliage had obscured the shack as well as the trail that led to it. The ATV path through the field was faintly visible if I zoomed in close enough, but it would be difficult to spot if someone wasn't specifically looking for it. The doorbell startled me. Lanie called my name. The next voice I heard belonged to Erin. Figuring that between the two of them they could handle the pizza delivery, I went back to what I was doing.

A quick search on a few other popular map sites produced the same results. Those sites used the same images, or at least ones captured when the tree canopy had been present. This all but confirmed what I'd expected. The only way the killer would know about the shack was if he'd been there or someone who had been there told him about it.

Erin's voice had gotten louder, and though I couldn't make out the words, I suspected she was lighting Lanie up about the pizza. I logged into my personal email account and sent Harry a quick message letting him know I'd spent what I thought was a productive two hours with Dr. Bloom. I basically begged him to let me go back to work. I considered calling Haskins, but I was sure he'd been instructed not to talk to me about the investigation, and it wouldn't be fair to put him in that position, so I was in limbo.

When I entered the kitchen, Erin was cutting Lanie's pizza into bite-sized pieces. My niece waited expectantly, a fork gripped between fingers and cast. My sister was still wearing scrubs, and I hated the way that made me feel. She looked exhausted. And sad.

"Hi," I said, brushing past her on my way to the fridge. I wanted a beer, would've settled for wine. She had only stocked water and juice. Was that out of consideration for Rourke? I grabbed a bottle of water, said, "The pizza was my idea. Sorry."

"Oh, I doubt it was entirely your idea." She cut her eyes to Lanie. "But it's here, and I'm sure everyone is famished."

Lanie was spearing pizza and shoveling it in as fast as Erin could cut it. "Let me do that," I offered. "You eat."

She hesitated briefly before handing me the pizza cutter. I multitasked, cutting Lanie's slice up while eating my own. Ripley sat next to Lanie's chair, eyeing each bite, waiting for something to be offered or dropped. Lanie, oblivious, was eating like it was her last meal. I discreetly held a pepperoni next to my knee. Ripley immediately locked onto her target and nimbly maneuvered around chairs and table legs to snatch it.

"You're not driving home tonight, are you?" Erin asked me. "It's getting late."

"Stella and all my stuff are still at the cabin. I have to go pack everything up before going home."

"I hope you're not planning to drive to the cabin tonight."

"I'd never make it, I'm wiped out. I, um, saw a therapist today."

"Really? That's... Wow, Regan. How did it go?"

"Okay, I guess. It was so weird, E. She had this, like, massive azurite geode in this glass case she uses as a coffee table."

"How strange. Did it feel like Mum was in the room?"

"God, it did. Totally fucking bizarre."

"I'm glad you went. How do you feel?"

"I'm too wiped out to feel anything right now."

"Well, all the shit'll get stirred up. When it does, don't fight it. Just let yourself process."

CHAPTER THIRTY-FOUR

January 2

Triangle, Virginia

38°32'40.87"N, 77°19'32.87"W

OF COURSE, ERIN was right. My session with Dr. Bloom stirred up all kinds of shit that my mind decided to "process" during the night. This led to unsettling dreams, and by four thirty, I'd given up on any kind of real sleep and decided to head to Claytor Lake. With nothing but the radio to entertain me during the drive, my mind swirled with pieces of my session with Dr. Bloom, fragments of memory, and random images. This evoked a range of emotions I hadn't been expecting. I took Erin's advice and didn't fight it. By the time I arrived at the cabin, I was emotionally raw and weepy and thankful to be able to concentrate on the physical tasks of packing up.

By the time I cleaned the cabin, secured it, and loaded the car, it was almost noon. It was just after four when I got back to Triangle. I freed and fed Stella, unpacked the Porsche, collected my mail, started laundry ops, fed myself, and showered. I checked my phone messages and work email. There was nothing significant after the twenty-third except an emailed memo from the OPR board informing me I was scheduled for an interview on January third at nine-thirty. Feeling blindsided, I spent the next three hours contemplating my future, going over all the pros and cons and plans I'd hashed out at the cabin.

Determined to refocus my energy on something productive, I decided to go through my mail and pay bills. This was a bad idea. Tucked inside a supermarket deals-of-the-week flier, I discovered a letter from the Law Office of Townes, Draper, Clemont & Associates. Apparently, the punk ass who'd shot my niece hadn't wasted any time finding himself an ambulance chaser. At least it wasn't a summons. It was too early for that anyway. To bring a suit against me, the attorney would need to have the asshole's medical bills in hand to assess appropriate damages. There hadn't been enough time to put together a proper demand package.

Mr. Temple Clemont suggested that given my "brutal, unprovoked attack" on his client, Mr. Devonte Brooks, which resulted in significant bodily harm, it would behoove me to settle the matter by fairly compensating the injured party for his pain and suffering to the tune of two hundred and fifty thousand dollars. Once fairly compensated, Mr. Brooks agreed to legally release me from any future civil action relating to the incident on the twentieth of December. Otherwise, he warned, Townes, Draper, Clemont, and every associate they could round up would sue my ass.

Mr. Clemont highly encouraged me to contact the firm immediately to arrange settlement. There was a note at the bottom of the page informing me that a copy of this letter had been sent to the Federal Bureau of Investigation's Office of Professional Responsibility. Fuck Townes. Fuck Draper. Fuck Clemont. Not one penny of mine would ever go to the piece of shit who tried to rape and kill my niece.

Feeling the need to channel my anger somewhere, I threw the last load of laundry into the dryer, changed clothes, and headed to Chang's. Master Lee Ho Chang was instructing a mostly young group of yellow belts in the main *do-jang*. He didn't stop what he was doing, but he smiled when he saw me and pointed toward the back of the building where the two smaller rooms were. One of them was dark and empty, and I was thankful to have the quiet, open space to myself. After twenty minutes of stretching and try- ing not to think about anything else, my muscles were loose, but my chest was still tight with anxiety.

For several months, I'd been intensely preparing to test for fourth *dan*. Successful rank advancement would qualify me to apply for instructor certification. My regular sessions with Master Chang had been derailed by a heavy travel schedule followed by a series of unfortunate events. Advancement to the next rank in Hapkido was cumulative, meaning I would have to demonstrate the stances, body movements, strikes, kicks, and self-defense techniques required for all previous black belt ranks in addition to those required for fourth *dan*. I focused on working through the forms for each *dan* for about forty minutes, then moved on to armed defense.

In Hapkido, pretty much anything tangible is considered a possible weapon. The lower ranks concentrate on mastery of tra- ditional combat implements: sticks, staffs, and swords, but as the practitioner progresses in his or her training, the arsenal widens. In addition to the aforementioned long weapons, Master Chang's weapons closet contained various lengths of rope, stones, fake knives and handguns, hand tools, silverware, books, and a bag of spare change. A quarter or nickel in Master Chang's hand was a dangerous projectile. As I reached for a medium-length staff, I heard Chang say, "Rope!"

He was standing in the center of the *do-jang*, having slunk in as quietly as a cat. I faced him and we bowed. In keeping with proper etiquette, I turned away from him to adjust my *do-bok* and straightened my belt. I selected a short length of rope and tried not to think about ligatures.

"Good to see you, Regan." Before I could reply, he moved into the ready position and instructed me to do the same. "*Joon-bi*!"

Once I was facing him and ready, he said, "*Shi-jak*!" *Begin.*

He varied his attacks as we sparred, moving in high and low, forcing me to anticipate and respond. He didn't offer much in the way of feedback, except "Good!" once when I took him to the ground. More than once, he reminded me to focus.

He noticed I was out of breath. "*Shwi-o.*"

After about twenty seconds of rest, he thrust his right, fisted, hand out. "Knife."

As soon as I nodded my understanding and came to attention, he commanded, "*Shi-jak*!"

He attacked with his imaginary weapon, and I used the rope to grab and twist the wrist of the knife hand, following this with various throws and strikes. Once, I misjudged. He feinted high, like he was going for my face, then crouched and drove the knife hand at me. My body was open to him and, were he holding a real knife, I would've been stabbed in the gut. He was not pleased. Nor was I.

He stood at attention. We bowed.

"Focus is out there," he said, pointing at the door. "We are here."

"I know, Master Chang. I'm sorry."

"Do not be sorry. Be *here.* Or be there. You choose now."

He instructed me to set the rope aside, and for the next half hour or so he attacked and I responded with various defensive counters. The last thing we worked on was a series of techniques, throws and joint locks, designed to turn an attacker's own force and momentum back on him. The bigger the attacker, the more momentum he or she had, and a skilled practitioner could redirect this momentum where she wanted it to go, away from the body or to the ground. Hapkido was perfect for a smaller person like me because an attacker's strength and size could be turned into a disadvantage. It had served Lanie well, too. When Chang decided I'd had enough, he simply nodded. We bowed. I left the *do-jang* spent and much calmer.

Once inside my car, I checked for missed calls or messages. There was a text from Haskins instructing me to call him ASAP. He answered on the first ring.

"Hey! Guess who I just talked to."

"Oh, how I just *love* guessing games," I said.

"Your boss must like you, Ross. He's apparently worked out some sort of compromise with the OPR, got authorization to have you assigned to the investigation as a consultant. No badge, no gun, but you're off the bench."

"You talked to Spielman?" I asked. Why hadn't Harry told me this himself? *Probably because he's been instructed not to speak to you until after your interview.*

"So, how soon can you get out here?" he asked.

"My fucking OPR interview is scheduled for tomorrow morning."

"Damn. Sam Meyer's meeting me in a couple of hours. I was hoping you'd be here."

"I could probably leave there early in the morning and make it to D.C. in plenty of time for the witch hunt."

"Then get your ass out here, Ross. We'll wait for you."

Within half an hour I'd showered, thrown some clothes into a bag, and was heading to the Shore.

CHAPTER THIRTY-FIVE

January 2
9:35 p.m.
Centreville, Maryland
39°2'25.46"N, 76°4'16.25"W

HASKINS AND A beer were waiting for me at the bar. Shady Hill was busy as usual. The patrons had apparently gotten over their New Year's hangovers and were ready for round two.

"Good to see you, Regan. You look better," Haskins said.

Better than what? Anything, I supposed, would be an improvement over my state the last time he'd seen me. "Thanks. Where's Meyer?" The Sam Adams tasted good.

"On his way. How's Lanie?"

"Good. Amazing, actually. So, what's going on with Rourke? She flew back to the UK?"

"Yeah, the PSNI managed to turn up three possible suspects based on her behavioral profile and your pretty rainbow map. She's helping them prepare for the interviews."

"Have you heard from her at all?" I asked.

He shook his head. "By the way, we've lost most of our real estate at the motel and I had to give up your room. We're down to my room and the one we're using as an office. You're booked at the Best Western in Grasonville, and I've already moved your bags."

"*You* packed up my stuff?"

"Dr. Rourke and I, yeah. The motel is only about fifteen minutes from here, but if it's a hassle, I've got plenty of room."

Not true. He barely had room to turn around. I was pretty sure sleepovers were a bad idea, but before I could say so, his gaze moved past me toward the door. I glanced over my shoulder. A tall, tanned man waved at us. The bartender slid Sam Meyer a bottle of Budweiser and a frosty mug without being asked. Ownership had its privileges. After introductions, Meyer led us to a private banquet room in the back of the restaurant. He didn't waste any time producing a list of people who had any business being on his land. It was clear the six or seven names he came up with would lead to more names and we had our work cut out for us.

"Do you lease to these people?" I asked him.

"Nope. I've never leased. A few friends and family hunt on my property and would know about the shack, but there's nothing formal about it."

"Based on the tax records, it looks like you've owned the property for about eighteen years. That about right?" Haskins ask.

"Yeah, but the Meyer family has owned it since right before the Depression. My brother and I built the shack about eight or nine years ago."

"He live around here?"

"Did. Goddamned prostate cancer got him three years ago," he said, punctuating with a generous pull of Bud.

Haskins asked him to go through the list. When Meyer nodded, Haskins pointed to the first name, Justin Meyer.

"My nephew. He blew his knee out his senior year of high school playing football, and it still gives him fits. I'm pretty sure he hasn't been hunting since, wouldn't have any reason to be out there." He pointed to the next name. "Karen Meyer is Justin's mom, my sister-in-law. She's not exactly the outdoorsy type. She's what you'd call high maintenance. Had a paintball party for Justin's birthday party out there one year, but other than that, nah, she wouldn't have any interest in it."

"How long's it been since Justin was out there?" I asked him. "Did he ever take friends hunting with him?"

"Well, let's see, he graduated five years ago, so it would have been before that. He usually hunted with his dad, but I suppose he could have brought a friend with him."

I worked down the list. "What about Peter Jensen?"

"Pete was a friend. He used to winterize my boat for me, never charged me for it. Told him he could hunt on the property any time, and he did."

"You're speaking in past tense," I said. "He no longer a friend or no longer around?"

"He passed a couple years ago."

Haskins jumped in. "He ever take anyone hunting with him?"

"Hell, it ain't a country club. I imagine most everybody who hunted brought somebody with 'em, and why would I care? You want to know who was with them or who they told about the shack, you'll have to ask them. I need another beer. And I haven't had a damn thing to eat. How about y'all?" My stomach reminded me I hadn't had a damn thing to eat either.

Meyer flagged down a waitress, called out, "Menus when you get a chance, Hon."

"You said Peter Jensen winterized your boat. Did he work on it, too, maybe have a shop somewhere?" I asked.

"Yeah, over in Kent Island. Jensen's Boat Sales and Service."

My back was to the door, so I didn't see our server until she was at the table.

Please, Agent Ross, I need you to promise me.

She handed out menus, which I ignored because I suddenly had a lead weight in my gut and no appetite. "Hi, Rachel."

"Hi, Agent Ross." She wouldn't meet my eyes. "What can I get for y'all?"

The guys ordered burgers and fries. "Nothing for me, thanks," I said.

"What happened to the business after Jensen died?" Haskins asked.

"It closed down," Meyer said. "I'm not sure if his son still owns it or not."

"Can I get y'all another beer?" Rachel asked. Her eyes were brimming.

Oblivious, Meyer and Haskins ordered another round. I didn't.

When she was out of earshot, Meyer said, "Goddamn shame. You know that girl hasn't missed a day of work since her friend died."

Haskins wouldn't be deterred. "Jensen has a son?"

"I never met him. He was in the military, I believe. The business was pretty successful, I think. Figured it would all go to the son after Pete died."

Unable to focus on anything being said, I excused myself and went to look for Rachel. A waitress pointed toward the back of the restaurant. The exit door opened to a cloud of cigarette smoke. I found myself standing in front of Deputy Chris Reynolds. It was the first time I'd seen him in civilian clothes and without a hat, so it took me a second to recognize him. He was lighting Rachel's cigarette, guarding the flame against the wind with a cupped hand. She exhaled a stream of smoke. "Sorry, I know I was rude, but I just needed some air. I saw you and... It just sneaks up on me sometimes."

"Of course it does. I understand. *I'm* sorry." I pulled a packet of Kleenex from my jacket and handed it to her.

"Thanks. You always seem to have tissues on you. I know it's none of my business, but it sounded like y'all were talking about the Jensen place, the one in Kent Island?"

"Yeah, you know it?"

She nodded. "I know Trig. I mean, I used to, before he joined the Marines. It's been a while."

"Trig?"

"Trig Jensen. His dad owned the boat place," she informed me.

"How do you know him, Rachel?"

"He's friends with my brother. They used to hang out in high school and when Trig would come home on leave."

"Does your brother still live around here?"

"Oh yeah, Jeremy's a shore boy. Still lives in Kent Island."

"Jeremy McAlester?"

She nodded.

"What's his address and phone number?" She pulled her phone from a back pocket and looked up the information. She gave it to me, and I saved it in my phone. "Does your brother hunt, Rachel?"

"Like I said, Agent Ross, Jeremy's a shore boy."

Reynolds piped up, "We all hunt."

I was about to ask if her brother ever hunted with Jensen when a waitress stuck her head out the door and let Rachel know she had an order up. Rachel quickly stubbed her cigarette out and hurried back inside.

When we were alone, Reynolds said, "Good to see you. We missed you around here."

"Oh, yeah. There was a family emergency."

"Everything okay now?"

"Getting there."

"Some guys and I are having a beer. You should join us. Trivia's about to start."

"Rain check?"

"I'm gonna hold you to that, Agent Ross."

"I'm sure you will, Deputy."

Haskins and Meyer had finished going through the short list of names when I rejoined them. I passed on the information about

Trig Jensen and wrote down Jeremy McAlester's address and phone number for Haskins. I must've looked as exhausted as I felt.

"Call it a night, Ross. Get some rest." Haskins didn't have to remind me that my interview with the OPR was in a few hours.

CHAPTER THIRTY-SIX

January 3

9:37 a.m.

Washington, D.C.

38°53'42.67"N, 77°1'30.27"W

THE WOMAN AND two men on the other side of the conference table made a great show of shuffling papers, preparing for what the Bureau called an "interview." I knew the score. The room was atypically pleasant for questioning a hostile witness. Was I hostile? I wasn't feeling so yet, but it was too soon to tell. It was my third visit to 935 Pennsylvania Avenue. I'd been there seven years ago for new employee orientation and once since for my official promotion photo op. It was my first foray to that part of the J. Edgar Hoover Building, what we cool kids called the "JEH."

An intern, Janelle, had escorted me to one of several conference rooms located within the Office of Professional Responsibility. Janelle's perky politeness was immediately belied by my interviewers' icy stoicism. She was busy arranging muffins that no one would eat on a tray at the far end of the table. Once satisfied, she aimed her pageant contestant grin at me and placed a sweating bottle of water onto the coaster in front of me. God bless her. I would've left a generous tip if we were at Olive Garden.

The trio across from me hadn't bothered to make eye contact, let alone introduce themselves. The contrast between them and our chipper hostess would be comical under different circumstances. How much did my interviewers know? Knowledge was power, after all, and it would be encouraging to think they might not have a monopoly. Of course, there were things they couldn't know, and wouldn't, unless I told them. We were in the investigation phase, still fact-finding, not—and this is an important distinction—fact-*giving*.

I deduced that the woman sitting between the two men was the unit chief. This assumption was based on two facts. First, she was significantly older than the gents, suggesting tenure. Second, she was holding my personnel file. Beyond that, she was a mystery aside from her obvious affinity for tweed: tweed skirt; jacket; and matching coat draped over the back of her chair. The anachronistic librarian façade wasn't fooling me for a second. She had probably been on the payroll since Al Capone's heyday and no one had the balls to question her. This did nothing to bolster my confidence in the system or this process, and for the hundredth time that morning, I considered handing them my letter of resignation. My hand was halfway to my bag when Tweedy said, "Good morning, Miss Ross. I'm Supervisory Special Agent Eleanor Williams, the Unit Chief of the OPR's Investigation Division."

Miss Ross? *What the hell?*

She continued, "The gentleman to my right is Dr. Bard Prescott, our staff psychologist."

Bard? Seriously?

"And this gentleman," she tilted her head to her left without breaking eye contact, "is Mr. Thomas Donovan, with the Office of General Counsel." A round of nodding ensued while I fixated on *Miss* Ross and the implications of a psychologist and attorney on the board.

"You understand, Miss Ross, this is merely a conduct investigation.

There are no criminal charges against you at this time." She emphasized the last three words. The second use of the civilian title didn't bode well and made me want to squirm, or cry, or hit someone, maybe all three. It wasn't easy to sit completely still and maintain eye contact with Supervisory Special Agent Eleanor Williams, especially when I knew she was trained to read the smallest tick or gesture.

"We're here to determine the facts so that we can proceed to the adjudication phase able to make an informed decision regarding whether or not disciplinary action is required," Williams added.

"I understand." My voice cracked. I reached for the bottle of water provided by Miss Congeniality. Where was she anyway? I could've used a friendly face.

Williams was staring at me over her bifocals, which I assumed meant she was expecting an answer. Unfortunately, I'd forgotten the question. *Calm the hell down, Ross. Jesus.*

"Right. The facts. What would you like to know?" I asked.

"Well, we'd like to hear your version of exactly what occurred in the Johns Hopkins emergency room on December twentieth and the events leading up to the incident." She stressed the last word as she adjusted her glasses, and it struck me as beyond absurd that she'd reduced it to an *incident.* I made an effort not to sigh, fidget, or roll my eyes.

"My *version?* You're implying there's more than one."

"Well, now, we won't know that until we hear what you have to say. We've already spoken to your supervisor."

Of course, they wouldn't hint at what Harry's *version* might be. He and Haskins were under a gag order. Rourke wasn't, simply because the OPR had no authority over her. We hadn't talked about it because she refused, but I was told she had declined to participate. If this thing went to court, which was a distinct possibility, she could be compelled to testify against me. *For* me? I had no idea, and it occurred to me that Rourke might not either.

Williams apparently didn't know what to make of whatever my

face was conveying, but decided to push it while I was visibly agitated. "We'll be speaking to your colleagues and those familiar with your actions on the date in question. Let's go back to the beginning. Why don't we start with the day Special Agent Haskins solicited your services?"

Solicited my services, as if Haskins is my john. That would make Harry my pimp.

I choked on my water while Williams flipped through her notes, which I suspected were more of a prop than anything. At least she hadn't reduced Rob to "Mr. Haskins."

"November fourteenth, correct?" she asked, as if she didn't damn well know.

"I was officially assigned on the sixteenth." This was true, though my involvement began about five minutes after Haskins' call on the fourteenth. It was just semantics, anyway. It was hard to pinpoint the exact date my life started turning to shit.

"Would you mind telling us how you came to be involved with the case?" Williams' feigned pleasantness didn't quite mask the judgment in her voice.

Cases. Plural. And yeah, as a matter of fact, I do. I didn't have a choice unless I was ready to play the resignation card. I wasn't. I wanted my goddamned credentials back. "Well, it's been a bizarre few weeks, but I'll tell you what I can remember."

Who was I kidding? A few weeks or a few decades, it wouldn't matter. I couldn't forget this shit if I tried. I gave them the gist. The rest they could get from my colleagues, witnesses, and the son of a bitch with my dental impression in his hand. Really, it came down to whether or not they considered what happened in the ER an isolated event. I wasn't necessarily the best person to answer that, and until told otherwise, I still had a job to do. Eleanor Williams peered at me over her bifocals, clearly unimpressed by the level of detail I'd provided. "Tell us exactly what happened during your altercation with Davonte Brooks."

"I really can't," I said.

"Can't or *won't?*"

"Both. But others were there, and I assume there's a police report and that you have it there in front of you. Talk to whomever you need to, get the facts, because it's important you understand what happened. You have to weigh my actions during five minutes of extreme stress against the rest of my seven years of service. I don't think there's anything else I can tell you that will help you reach a conclusion."

"One question, Agent Ross. Are you sorry for your actions?" Dr. Prescott asked.

"Well, I wish I hadn't done it, because then I wouldn't be here wasting everyone's time. Generally speaking, the consequences suck, and will continue to suck, but if you're asking if I feel bad about it or feel sorry for hurting him, then no, I'm not sorry."

"I see," Williams said. "We have a copy of a letter sent to you from a law firm in Baltimore. Have you decided how you plan to respond?"

"I just read it for the first time last night, and I haven't had a chance to decide anything. I'm not inclined to comply unless someone provides a compelling reason why I should." The shitbag was facing charges for murder and attempted murder, and the thought of a penny of my money going toward his defense made me want to puke.

For the first time, the attorney, Donovan, spoke. "It's not my purview to provide legal counsel in this forum, but if I may offer some advice, off the record?"

"I'm all ears," I said.

"There's a reason Mr. Brooks' legal team has not yet brought a suit against you. There are also reasons no criminal charges have been filed. I believe, at this point, it's in your best interest to wait and see how things play out."

"Sounds like a plan," I said.

CHAPTER THIRTY-SEVEN

January 3

11:41 a.m.

Chester, Maryland

38°58'26.94"N, 76°17'47.62"W

LIGHTS AND THE sporadic, if unwarranted, siren got me through D.C. traffic, and 50 East was smooth sailing. Once across the bridge, I navigated to Jeremy McAlester's apartment complex following Haskins' directions and found him there already, leaning against his car, waiting for me.

"Hey. I figured the Best Western continental breakfast isn't much to write home about," he said by way of greeting and handed me a smoothie. "Thought this might get you through the interview."

I'd had nothing but coffee and the water intern Janelle provided, and the frozen strawberry and banana was blissful.

"How'd it go?"

"About like I expected," I said, squeezing my eyes shut as if it would thaw my brain. I nodded toward the apartment building. "What's McAlester's story?"

"Well, there's a good chance he's asleep. He just pulled a double shift at the Anne Arundel Medical Center. The hood of his car was still warm when I got here about fifteen minutes ago, so maybe he hasn't crashed yet. Either way, expect him to be tired."

"What does he do at the hospital?"

"Pharmacy tech. He's been with them for eight years and, based on his employment records and his supervisor's glowing comments, Jeremy McAlester is a dream employee. Speeding ticket when he was seventeen, other than that, nada."

"You check his schedule for November and December?"

"Yep. No way he's our guy."

"But," I said, "he knows Trig Jensen. And Jensen may be our guy. You ready?"

Jeremy McAlester opened the door about five seconds after we knocked. He was holding something wrapped in a tortilla, wiped his mouth with the back of his hand. Mr. Squeaky Clean seemed surprised, though not particularly bothered, to have two Feds at his door. We had a seat on his IKEA sofa that'd seen better days and skipped past his employment history and what he'd been up to the last few months, because we already knew. He'd been working. A lot.

"Trying to buy a boat, a repo'd forty-foot Luhrs over in Grasonville," he explained. "I pick up extra shifts whenever I can." He ditched the breakfast burrito and casually sipped coffee from an Anne Arundel Community College mug.

Haskins got right to it. "You know Trig Jensen, Jeremy?"

"Sure. Trig and I've been buddies since middle school. We were roommates for a while before he joined the military."

"When was that?" Haskins asked.

"We graduated in 2002 and both worked at the lumber yard for about a year, then he enlisted. I haven't seen him much."

"When was the last time you saw Jensen?" I asked him.

"Hell, it's been a while, close to three years now, I guess. Shit, did something happen to him?"

"We'd just like to talk to him. He might be able to help us with something we're working on," Haskins said.

"He was home on leave when you saw him last?" I asked.

"No, he'd gotten out of the Corps and had been working in D.C. He got hired on with a shipping company in Baltimore. Crashed on my couch for a few days before he was scheduled to start with 'em."

"What kind of shipping company?" Haskins asked.

"One of those big outfits that ships all over the world. He was gonna be doing something on a container ship. He didn't say much about it, just that he was looking forward to traveling. He'd tried some kind of government desk job in D.C. for a few months and hated it. Trig is the kind of guy who goes nuts in a cubicle farm."

"Do you happen to remember the name of the shipping company?" I asked.

"No, not really. It had diamond or ruby or something like that in the name, I think."

"You and Trig ever go hunting?" Haskins asked.

"All the time. When we weren't working or fishing, we were hunting. His dad had a couple of nice boats. I mean, he had a lot of boats—he sold them—but he had a couple he'd let us take out."

I asked him if he and Jensen ever hunted on Sam Meyer's place.

"We hunted at a few different places. I'm not sure who actually owned the land."

"You two ever see a hunting shack in the woods?" I asked.

"Oh, yeah. This place out in Church Hill, off Hall Road. We went out there a few times. Spent the night in the shack once when a storm rolled in on us."

Haskins and I shared a look. Haskins asked, "You familiar with geocaching, Jeremy?"

"Sort of. Trig talked about it. It was something he started doing when he was stationed overseas."

"When he was a Marine?" I asked.

"Yeah, as a hobby. He liked to hike and said it was a fun, cheap way to sightsee and get a feel for a place."

CHAPTER THIRTY-EIGHT

January 3

4:55 p.m.

Locust Point

Baltimore, Maryland

39°16'26.19"N, 76°35"25.07"W

"PLACE IS KIND of a shithole, huh?" I commented as we climbed out of Haskins' sedan. The Ford was one of only four cars in the parking lot. It was getting dark, and just as I was about to mention the lack of security, floodlights bathed us in light. Video cameras mounted on the corners of the building swiveled to follow our approach.

"Don't judge a book by its cover, Ross. I think the word you're looking for is *industrial*. The fancy glass castles are on the other side of the harbor. Locust Point is where the actual work happens. Like all international cargo outfits, I'm sure Emerald Shipping puts its capital into logistics. Administrative offices are probably low on the priority list."

The office wasn't much more than a trailer, something you'd see at a construction site, and I wondered under my breath what their customers might think.

To further his point, he said, "They could put a picture of that," he pointed to the Baltimore World Trade Center across the Inner Harbor, "on their website and most customers wouldn't know the difference. Hell, ninety-nine percent of their business is probably conducted online or over the phone."

There was only one entrance on our side of the building, and a card scanner controlled access. Before we could ring the call buzzer, a sixtyish lady with short grey hair opened the door.

"Mrs. Galecki?" Haskins presumed.

"Yes, good morning. Glenna Galecki. C'mon in before this tricky door sets off the alarm."

Once inside, Haskins held up his credentials. "We appreciate your cooperation, Mrs. Galecki."

She made a disapproving sound. "It's just Glenna. Mrs. Galecki is my mother-in-law and I try to think about her as little as possible. My husband, Marty, would have met you himself, but he's down in South Carolina. Gotta tell you, we're all curious why the FBI is interested in our employee records."

"We appreciate it, Glenna," Haskins said. "We don't intend to take up too much of your time. We certainly don't need all of your employee records. A name came up during the course of an investigation, and we just want to make sure we're covering all our bases."

She eyed me closely as she led us down a hallway, then through a maze of cubicles, and finally to an office, where *Martin R. Galecki* was stenciled on the faux wood nameplate. The furniture and wood paneling was circa 1983, but the flat screen monitor on the desk and much larger model mounted on the wall added some modernity to the room. World maps, family and business photos, and digital clocks showing the local times in Baltimore and half a dozen countries covered the rest of the wall space.

Glenna made herself at home at her husband's desk and started up the computer. Without looking up, she said, presumably to me, "I read about you in the paper. This doesn't have anything to do with those awful killings across the bridge, does it? I just can't imagine—"

Haskins jumped in. "We don't know too much at this point. Like I said, a name came up, and we just need to tie up any loose ends."

"You can't discuss it. I understand. It's just unnerving to think someone at Emerald could... Well, Cheryl's our HR associate and could tell you about anyone you want to know about off the top of her head, but like most of our admin staff, she's gone for the day. All of our employee records are maintained electronically, and I can show you anything you need. If there's a problem with one of our employees, obviously you'll have our full cooperation."

"Thank you, Glenna. We appreciate that," Haskins said.

"Did you and your husband found the company?" I asked, even though the photos pretty much told the story.

"Oh no, that was all Marty. I was against it, to tell you the truth. The collateral took everything we had and a lot we didn't. I'm a retired CPA, and the financial aspects of starting a shipping company made me question it. But not Marty. He never doubted," she said, and there was an amused twinkle in her eye. "I'd been asking for an emerald ring for years. I just love emeralds, and it's my birthstone. Well, six years ago, Marty says to me, Honey, I finally got you that emerald. We started small, operating along the East Coast. Within three years, we were shipping to South America and Africa. Emerald Shipping is Marty's baby. The only thing I can take credit for is making sure the bills get paid and we're good with the IRS. So, how can I help you?"

"We're trying to locate Trig Jensen, and we believe he is or was employed by your company," Haskins explained.

"Name doesn't ring a bell, but that doesn't mean anything. I don't know any of the contracted crew," she told us. "Let's see here. Jensen, you said?"

"Yes, ma'am. Trig Jensen."

"Jefferson... Jennings... here he is. Trig L. Jensen. His initial contract is dated October 18, 2012. Looks like it was renewed twice."

"Do you have a home address and phone number for him?" I asked.

She did, and the Kent Island address included an apartment number.

"Mrs.—" I started to say, then caught myself. "Sorry, Glenna, I noticed the badge reader at the entrance. Do your company IDs have photos on them?"

"Yes, and all office employees are required to wear their security badges inside the building. They don't wear them on the ship, but we do have photos on file."

I asked her to print a copy of Jensen's photo, as well as his personal information, home address, phone number, and anything else I could think of that might help us locate him.

Haskins asked, "Jensen is under contract? So that means he's a crew member?"

"Mm-hm. Security specialist. Looks like he was promoted to team leader after nine months."

"A team leader is in charge of the security crew on a ship?" I asked.

"That's right. Those guys are all prior military, police, or port security," she informed us.

"How long are crew member contracts usually written for?" I asked.

"Marty or Cheryl could tell you specifically, but I know it depends on the job. Key personnel like the captain, senior officers, and engineers are typically two-year contracts. Other officers and security specialists are usually twelve months, and I believe the less skilled crewmembers sign six-month contracts."

Haskins said, "Glenna, we intend to speak to Jensen, but it would be great to have some information before we do. If you could tell us when he was and wasn't at sea from April 2013 to today, it would help us out a lot."

While she was typing, I asked how many ships the company operated.

"Six right now." She was studying something on the monitor. "But hopefully one more after this weekend. Marty's in Charleston negotiating the purchase of number seven."

It could take a while, I realized, depending on what kind of records they kept of crew assignments.

Glenna said, "I'm just looking at Jensen's crew log. He's been assigned to the *Chivor Gem* for almost his entire period of employment, since January 2013."

"Does the *She*—I'm sorry, what did you call it?" I asked.

"*Chivor Gem*," Haskins answered for her. "Chivor is an emerald mine in Columbia." Of course he would know that because it was just obscure enough to interest him.

"Are all the ships named after mines?" he asked.

"Five are. Our very first ship is the *Alisa Gem,* named after our daughter."

"Does the *Chivor Gem* travel the same route every trip, or does it vary?" I asked.

"I think it probably varies. Trips will have more or fewer stops in port for loading and unloading, depending on the scheduled shipment orders. But we don't have to guess," she added. "I can show you."

It was becoming evident that Glenna Do-Not-Call-Me-Mrs.-Galecki knew more about the operation of the company than she let on. She used a remote to turn on the wall-mounted monitor, and after a few keyboard strokes, a world map displayed. At least fifty blinking triangles, some blue, some green, some yellow, some red, moved forward every few seconds. Most of them moved. Some were static and appeared to be in port. We were looking at real-time ship tracking. "What do the different colors correlate to?" I asked.

"Ship types. Cargo, tanker, passenger... hang on a sec." More keys were pressed, and all but the yellow triangles disappeared. "Here we go. These are the cargo ships. But this is real-time and we want the trip history for the *Chivor*." She narrowed the search criteria, said, "This is the entire trip history."

A ship icon represented the *Chivor Gem*. Numerous overlapping tracks, represented by dotted lines, traced courses down the East Coast to the northern coast of South America, and up to the UK. Three or four tracks shot west to Africa and Spain.

"Why only a couple of tracks to Africa?" I asked.

"I suspect we added another ship to the fleet, probably the *Muzo Gem*, and she picked up the Africa route," Glenna explained.

Haskins asked, "You said Jensen's contract would have been for twelve months and it was renewed twice. So, he would have been under contract through this October?"

"Yes, that sounds right. The system tracks ship movements for each trip, and each trip is assigned a number. I can show you the trip history for a specific date range or locations on a specific date. I can also tell you the assigned crew for a particular trip. This will probably be easier if you give me specific dates to search."

"Do you have the date of the first one?" Haskins asked me, meaning the date the first victim, Dana Mullen, was found.

I instructed Glenna to search for trip history for the first week of April 2013, and when she did, a track showed us the *Chivor Gem's* route from Baltimore to Miami, with stops in Charleston and Savannah. "Was Jensen assigned to the crew for that trip?" I asked. Glenna confirmed that he was. When we repeated trip history searches for May through August of the same year, it became clear that Trig Jensen couldn't possibly have killed the women in Northern Ireland because he'd been at sea.

A query for the ninth through the fourteenth of November,

2015 showed that the *Chivor* had been docked at home, at Locust Point. Glenna informed us that on December seventeenth, the date Allison Brightwell had been abducted, the *Chivor* was at Port of Spain.

"That's in Spain?" I asked.

They responded in unison, "Trinidad and Tobago," and I, the *geographic* profiler, felt like a dumbass.

"Was Jensen assigned to the crew?" I asked.

Her fingernails clicked over the keys. "Nope, he's not on the crew manifest."

"When was his most recent trip?" I asked.

She spent a few minutes working backward through the trip histories and cross-checking crew manifests. Finally, she said, "March of 2014."

"Could he have been assigned to another ship?" I suggested.

"I don't think so. It shows him assigned to the *Alisa Gem* for his first three months, which makes sense. The *Alisa* only does domestic shipments, and most crewmembers train on domestics before being assigned to international routes. He transferred to the *Chivor* in January 2013 and hasn't been assigned to any other crews."

I said, "If his initial contract was signed in October 2012 and renewed twice, that would take his period of employment through last October. Why wasn't he assigned to any trips for the last seven months of his contract?"

Glenna didn't know, but suggested the captain might.

"Who captained the *Chivor Gem* on Jensen's last trip?" Haskins asked her.

After checking the manifest, Glenna reported, "Gregory Bowman."

"Where is Captain Bowman now?" he wanted to know.

More clicking and typing. "Captaining the *Chivor*. She's in the North Atlantic."

"The ship has satellite phones, right?" I asked.

"Of course. All of them do."

"Well, let's give Captain Bowman a ring, shall we?" Haskins suggested.

Glenna was game, but after fifteen minutes of trying to link up with the *Chivor*, we learned a new word, *bombogenesis*. This was what meteorologists called it when a seemingly innocuous storm decided to rapidly turn into a badass. It had to do with cold air masses hitting warm ocean water, or something to that effect. What it meant, among other things, was that satellite communication with a ship in the North Atlantic was a no-go.

We couldn't talk to Captain Bowman until the storm calmed or the ship was in port, which wasn't going to happen for many hours, if not days. Ol' Marty was apparently driving back from Charleston, and calls to him went straight to voicemail. Essentially, with regard to Trig Jensen and what he may or may not have to do with our investigation, we were dead in the water. This, admittedly, might not be the most appropriate figure of speech, considering.

We gave Glenna our contact information and asked her to email Bowman and request he contact us as soon as possible. She assured us she would have her husband call us as well. We left with Jensen's employee photo, last known address and phone number, but not much else. As we walked to the car, my stomach growled, which gave me an idea. I suggested, in my best pirate voice, "Arr, me hearty, what do you say we head across the harbor where be yar favorite galley, the Rusty Scupper, savvy?"

"Ha-harr! Weigh anchor, Lass!" Haskins said, hitting the gas and kicking up gravel. When his phone rang, we were momentarily hopeful that something might be going our way for once, but when he saw the display he shook his head.

"Haskins," he answered. He squeezed the steering wheel. It was bad.

"Where?"

Shit.

"We're on our way."

He sped for other reasons as dinner at the Scupper was forgotten. I asked him to drop me off at Jeremy McAlester's place on the way, because the Tahoe was still there and I would need my gear. We hardly spoke during the hour drive as a single thought played on loop. *Too late. Again.*

CHAPTER THIRTY-NINE

January 3

7:08 p.m.

Queenstown, Maryland

38°59'12.89"N, 76°9'4.59"W

A QUEEN ANNE'S COUNTY sheriff's deputy had discovered Rachel McAlester's Isuzu Rodeo at a self-storage complex off MD-301, about seven miles southwest of Centreville. When Rachel had failed to show for her shift and calls went straight to voicemail, Sam Meyer phoned it in as a possible missing person. Normally, the Sheriff's Office would've told him the usual; she's an adult, she'll turn up eventually, just give it some time. Given the circumstances, a BOLO had gone out immediately. A team of deputies and state troopers tasked with checking every storage unit were finishing up when we arrived. Investigator Santos informed us they hadn't found anything to connect Rachel to the storage units. There was no reason that anyone could think of for her to have been there, other than to meet her abductor. The owners of U-Store-It hadn't deemed it prudent to install security cameras at their establishment, and I couldn't imagine why anyone would choose to store anything of value at a place secured by a single padlock on the gate.

The driver's door of the Rodeo was open, as it had been found, leaving little doubt Rachel had been taken against her will. He kept Allison Brightwell for two days before killing her. Everyone was thinking the same thing, though no one said it: *We don't have much time.* Why would he target Rachel McAlester, someone with a close connection to a victim and who would be especially wary and aware of her surroundings? Was it a coincidence that Rachel disappeared shortly after telling us about the connection between her brother and Trig Jensen? Wondering was allowed. Dwelling was not. We had another data point. That was what I needed to focus on.

For half an hour I recorded coordinates, took photos, noted ingress and egress routes, and measured distance to MD-301, the nearest major highway. There was one way in and out of the storage complex. After the scene had told me everything it was going to, I let Haskins know I was heading back to the motel. When he slipped the room key from his wallet and handed it to me, we both knew it would be many hours before I saw him again.

* * *

Haskins was usually a tidy person, and I decided to cut him some slack because he'd been living and working in the cramped motel room for weeks. I made a mental note to suggest he have the staff come in and clean, because it had obviously been a while. I made room for my laptop on the folding table that served as his desk, and when it finished booting up, I uploaded the coordinates and measurements I'd collected at the storage complex.

Alone with my thoughts, I started to ask myself the wrong questions. *Why would he choose McAlester? Why has he changed his M.O., his timeline? What would Rourke say? His motivation is different. He had another reason to take McAlester. He may kill her more quickly. Because he's being practical. No, Ross. Do your job.*

I did, for a while. The location where Rachel's car had been found became a new data point. I removed the data point associated with where I thought Allison *might* have been abducted, so that I was dealing solely with verified data. The system ran, mathematical magic worked behind the curtain. Waiting and silence put me in dangerous territory. I started thinking about the OPR board, asking what-ifs. *What if the Bureau pulls me off the case before we find Rachel? What if my employment is terminated and I can't even know what's going on? Don't think about that.*

The geoprofile was finally displayed. I wasn't able to tell if the jeopardy surface was much different than the previous one until I laid it over a map and converted it to a 3-D rendering. It was different. The area was still concentrated in the Chestertown area, but the hot zone was smaller. This was good, but we still needed to narrow down the search criteria.

As I waited for it to finish printing, I thought about ways to narrow the search within the hot zone. Vehicle registrations. I got an idea and made a note to tell Haskins. I was so tired. Just a little while, I told myself, but I fell asleep almost immediately after curling up on his bed. Hours later, my foot was being lifted, and through cracked eyelids, I watched Haskins remove my boots. A few minutes later, we were both lying beneath a blanket. His breath tickled the fine hairs on the back of my neck, and when I shivered, strong arms pulled me closer.

"Hey," I rasped.

"Hey." He sounded too tired to read anything into it.

"Anything?" I asked.

"No, not really. She met him sometime before her shift would have started, so it was still light out. No one saw a damn thing. We're thinking it has to be someone she knows."

We were silent for a while, and I listened to his breathing. It didn't change. He was still awake.

"What's the story with your socks?" I asked.

"What? Seriously, you're asking about my socks *now*?"

"Do you order them online or buy them from the mall or—"

"If you have to know, my mother sends them. A new pair every month."

"Your mom the ACLU attorney?"

"She says they're to remind me not to take myself too seriously."

"Oh my God, that's... I don't even know what to say."

"That's a first. It's three o'clock in the morning, Regan."

"Rob, I think I'm going to need a lawyer."

"You have one."

"You can't represent me," I pointed out.

"No, but I can advise you, and if you actually do need an attorney at some point, I'll call my old man."

"Since when are you on speaking terms?" I asked.

"We're not. But the son of a bitch is the best defense attorney I know. Don't worry about it right now. You haven't been arrested or served. You know the process takes time. Go to sleep, Regan."

Eventually, I did.

CHAPTER FORTY

January 4

7:16 a.m.

Centreville, Maryland

39°2'25.27"N, 76°4'17.95"W

THE PHONE AWAKENED us, but that's probably overstating it. We untangled and stumbled our way through mutual disorientation. When Haskins finally answered, his voice was heavy with sleep.

"Captain Bowman, thank you for calling," he said, pantomiming he needed something to write with and on. After some rummaging, I found him a notebook and pen and decided to make do with the back of an envelope for my own notes. When he put the phone on speaker, I caught, "If you find Trig Jensen, you tell him he's welcome back on my crew. Unless he's killed someone, of course," he added, chuckling. At Haskins' silence, he sobered. "He hasn't, has he?"

"Not that we're aware of, Captain. We just need to ask him some questions. Emerald Shipping records indicate that Jensen was last at sea with you in March?"

"Sounds about right. The months kind of run together, but it was spring, I think."

Haskins wanted to know if something happened that caused Jensen not to be assigned to the *Chivor* after March 2014.

"It's the damnedest thing. I can usually see it coming, but not with Trig. He was always squared away, reliable, you know? He'd been with us for a long time, always seemed to enjoy being part of the crew. It surprised the hell out of me when he quit."

"Jensen resigned?"

"Yeah, last spring."

Haskins asked, "There was no indication he wanted to leave the company before that?"

"None. His resignation letter said something about personal issues back home, his father being sick or something. It was sudden. The thing that surprises me is that he didn't talk to me about it."

"Is there anybody else he might have discussed it with? Was he particularly close to anyone on the crew?"

"If he told anybody, it would be Deck. He and his Wonder Twin were joined at the hip."

"Wonder Twin?" Haskins asked.

"Declan Lynch. Everybody called him Deck. He and Trig could be brothers, and they played it up. One of them would shave his head or grow his beard out and the other would do the same. Half the time, we had to look twice to tell them apart. They even started talking alike, mimicking each other's accents."

On the back of my envelope, I wrote: *Declan Lynch. Employment records.*

Seeing my note, Haskins asked, "Is Declan Lynch a member of the security team, too?"

"No, he was a motorman."

"Is that like a mechanic?"

"Yeah, engine mechanic, certified welder." *Welder.* I underlined it three times, wrote: *welding torch.*

"Captain, you happen to know where Lynch is from?"

"He's Irish. We picked him up at Bangor Marina."

Bangor Marina was only a couple of miles from where Colleen Byrne's body had been found.

"You're using past tense. Declan Lynch is no longer a member of your crew?"

"Nope. Couldn't tell you where he is or what he's up to, Special Agent Haskins. He and Trig Jensen walked off my ship ten months ago and I haven't seen or heard from them since."

"Walked off where?"

"Sáu Luís," he said. "Brazil."

* * *

While Haskins updated Interpol, I called Emerald Shipping. Glenna wasn't in, I was told, but HR Associate Cheryl was more than willing to help. I grilled her about a certain employee from Northern Ireland who was competent with a welding torch.

"Declan Lynch's initial contract date is September seventeenth, 2013. It wasn't renewed," she informed me.

"What's the termination date?" I asked.

"September seventeenth, 2014."

"Are there any additional notes in his records regarding why he didn't serve out his contract?"

"None that I see here."

"What's his listed address and phone number?" I asked.

Having upgraded to a legal pad, I jotted the information down as she read off a Lisburn, Northern Ireland, address and a phone number. Something told me they would be dead ends, and I was much more interested in Lynch's employee photo, which Cheryl promised to fax. I thanked her and ended the call. Haskins was still on the phone with Interpol, and I gathered from his side of the conversation he was discussing which types of Notice should be issued. He mentioned a diffusion, or direct assistance from an Interpol member country—in this case, Brazil. The momentum the new information had generated made it impossible for me to sit idle, and I decided to call Rourke.

My timing sucked. She was boarding a plane, probably juggling bags, and was muttering under her breath. She started to say something about interviews, but it was interrupted by a sidebar with a flight attendant. I couldn't get a word in edgewise before she told me she had to go, said she'd send the audio files, which I assumed were suspect interviews. She was off the line before I could tell her about Declan Lynch.

When Haskins hung up, I stopped pacing and we caught each other up. Interpol was issuing a virtual rainbow of notices, he informed me: green, red, and even purple.

"I don't even remember what a Purple Notice is," I admitted.

"It provides specific M.O. information," he explained. "Details about the branding, the torching, and ligatures. The thought is that we may be able to make the connection if he's killed similarly in another country."

"Like Brazil," I said.

"Yeah. Interpol is coordinating with the Brazilians for direct assistance since we know Declan Lynch was there, and they're initiating a missing person search for Trig Jensen. His fingerprints are on file because of his military service and prior employment with the Department of Homeland Security. Once they're in the international database, they'll be able to compare to any John Does. They're also going to see what they can find regarding a branding iron. It's a long shot, but there are a lot of cattle ranches in Brazil. The Brazil connection also makes us wonder about the coin left in the cache. Is he just pointing us to his connection to Brazil, or—"

"—or are there more victims there?" I filled him in on what Cheryl had been able to tell me about Lynch and informed him that Rourke was somewhere over the Atlantic, oblivious about suspect number one.

"She's coming back here?" he asked.

"She didn't say, but I assume so." Erin probably knew, was probably picking her up at the airport. I started to call her to find out when Rourke's plane was scheduled to land, but my phone pinged and I got sidetracked. As promised, there were five audio files from Rourke. Before I could even read her message, one of the attachment filenames got my attention: *lynch.wav*.

CHAPTER FORTY-ONE

January 4

7:57 a.m.

Centreville, Maryland

39°2'25.27"N, 76°4'17.95"W

W E HUDDLED OVER my laptop, and I adjusted the volume as a voice that reminded me of Bono's said, "Interview with Jacqueline Marie Finley, Saturday the second of January, 2016. PSNI Musgrave Station, 60 Victoria Street, Belfast. Time is seventeen-fifty. Inspector Art Harris speaking. Also present are Chief Inspector Barry King and Dr. Sheridan Rourke."

Formalities out of the way, there was a slight pause before Harris asked, "Now, for the record, are you speaking to us voluntarily today, Mrs. Finley?"

All we knew about this interview subject, based on Rourke's brief email, was that she was female and somehow associated with Declan Lynch.

"Aye," a female voice said on a long exhale, and I imagined a stream of smoke.

"All right, then, Jackie. What's the nature of your relationship with Declan Bryce Lynch?"

"Declan's my brother," she said, then added, "half-brother, actually." Her accent was Ulster, like Rourke's, but the similarity stopped there. It was like comparing Snow White's voice to the hag with a poisoned apple, though realistically, Jackie Finley probably wasn't much older than I.

"Same mother or father?" Inspector Harris asked.

"Mother. Couldn't say who his father is. Mum never said and Declan never knew."

"You were raised with Declan?"

"Aye, until I was fifteen and went to live with my da."

"Why was that, Jackie?"

"He finally turned up." There was a pause as she inhaled a lungful of toxins. "He was practically a stranger, but that was better than the alternative."

"Things were bad at home between you and your mum?"

"Bad? Aye, bad like the devil himself is bad. It was a feckin' nightmare."

"But Declan stayed there with her after you left?"

I heard a quiet, "Christ," followed by another long exhale.

Rourke's voice broke the silence. "Jackie, I know it's difficult, but if you could tell us more about that, about your brother's experience."

"I got out, yeah? Turns out, my da's all right. Sometimes, I even managed to forget about her. But I thought about Declan. He was nine when I left. He always had it worse, and after I left, I knew she'd really hit the bottle. And when she drank, she always went after him. He would hide, but that just got her worked up. She'd drink, get angrier, and go after him."

"Go after him how, Jackie?" Inspector Harris asked.

"He was afraid of the dark. His closet had no bulb, and she would lock him in there for ages. But that was after she…"

Rourke said, gently, "Go on, Jackie. What did she do?"

"Fire and water. He was afraid of those, too. Cigarettes, lighters, she'd heat forks and spoons on the stove burner. She was smart about it, never did it in places people would see. Groin, arse, bottom of his feet. She stuffed a dishcloth into his mouth so the neighbors wouldn't hear."

"You're doing great, Jackie," Rourke assured her. "What else?"

"When she decided he'd had enough, she'd put him into the tub, make him sit in cold water for ages. She'd dunk his head under over and over."

It was quiet, and Haskins and I actually jumped when Jackie blew her nose. Inspector Harris wisely let Rourke continue the questioning because, so far at least, it seemed like Jackie was responding to her. "What did she do to you, Jackie?"

"She yelled, would slap me sometimes, yank me up by the hair, but nothing much more than that. She was different with me, normal sometimes. Gentle even, not often, but enough to keep me off balance, braiding my hair, asking about my day."

"Did anyone ever suspect Declan was being abused? A doctor? Someone at school? Was it ever reported?" Rourke asked.

"Only once that I know of. The neighbors heard screaming and called the police. It took ages for anyone to come, and when they did, they did fuck-all about it. Ma gave them some bollocks about a slasher film being on the telly and the volume being up. The neighbors had it all wrong. They swallowed it, didn't bat a feckin' eye."

"Where's your mother now, Jackie?"

"The Greer House on Kings Road, you know, one of those care facilities for geriatrics and invalids. That's her, for definite. Can't do anything now but drool and piss herself."

"What happened?" Rourke asked.

"About six or seven years ago, she got good and wrecked one night and took a header down the cellar stairs, snapped her neck. It's fittin', right? Trapped in that broken body. Good riddance, I say, but do ya want to hear the most pathetic thing? Declan visited her at Greer every day until he left."

"When did he leave?" Inspector Harris asked.

"Headed out on a merchant ship a couple years ago and I haven't heard from him since, except a couple of cards in the mail."

"Do you have the postcards, Jackie?" Inspector Harris asked.

"I think so."

"Before he left, he was living in Donaghadee?"

"Aye, he worked at an engine shop, rented a flat in the village by the harbor."

Donaghadee, I wrote. *Dana Mullen found there.* I tapped the notepad to get Haskins' attention.

The interview lasted a few more minutes, but there was nothing else that would tell us much about Declan Lynch we didn't already know.

"Jesus Christ," Haskins murmured. "It always seems to be the mother with these guys."

"It starts there, but I bet you dollars to donuts Jackie Finley is small-boned, was probably once athletic before she started smoking a pack a day. Bet she's got long, dark hair like her mother. The woman he fantasizes about killing is a composite of his mother and his sister."

"Why the sister? Because she didn't save him from Mommy Dearest?"

"No, because she got out. He was in hell and he was all alone. He resents her for that."

CHAPTER FORTY-TWO

January 4
9:41 a.m.
Centreville, Maryland
39°2'25.46"N, 76°4'16.25"W

EVEN AFTER A trip to the Grasonville Best Western for a shower and change of clothes, I'd managed to beat the rest of the task force to the meeting. My hair was still damp and I'd opted for jeans and a sweater because my nicer clothes had been in a suitcase for days and looked slept in. Though I normally wouldn't dress down while "on duty," technically, I wasn't. What did consultants wear, anyway?

Because the real estate at the Shady Hill Motel had been relinquished, we were meeting in Sam Meyer's banquet room. Haskins and I huddled in a corner, beneath a mounted stag head. He'd just spent ten minutes on the phone with Cheryl and was frustrated because the employee photo she'd faxed was the wrong one. The one associated with his employee record, but wrong, all the same.

"She confirmed that this—" He held up the printed photo of Trig Jensen, "Is the picture on file for Declan Lynch. I don't understand how it's possible. They have pictures on their security badges; how would someone not realize he had his buddy's photo on his badge?"

"No," I reminded him, "remember what Glenna said. Only the office staff are required to wear their badges. Crewmembers don't wear them aboard ship and they rarely go into the office. Besides, Lynch and Jensen look enough alike that no one's going to notice the photo, let alone question it. Lynch and Jensen are joined at the hip, right? The Wonder Twins. Lynch knows what Jensen knows. Jensen is a member of the security staff and probably has access to employee records. How hard do you think it would be for Lynch to get Jensen's administrative password?"

"Not very," he admitted.

"Right, and if he's remotely IT savvy and doesn't want his picture on file, deleting or editing information in the system would be easy enough. It just sucks that we still don't have a photo of our suspect. You'd think Jackie Finley would have a picture of her brother. The PSNI's got to help us out here. I wish Rourke was still on the ground there because she might be able to light a fire under someone's ass."

"The PSNI assures me they're on it, and Marty Galecki sent out a company-wide email asking all employees to check to see if anyone may have a personal photo of Lynch," he said.

"I wouldn't hold my breath. He would have been careful about making sure he wasn't captured on camera. There are two possibilities. Either he killed Jensen and assumed his identity or they're working together and both of them killed Jennifer Abbott and Allison Brightwell. If that's the case, we've had it all wrong, but I don't think so. This has always felt like a single offender to me."

"Since Lynch likely stole Jensen's identity, that's where we need to start," he said. "How would he do that?"

"The captain said Jensen would have had identification and passport with him, all his important documents. So, if Lynch kills Jensen in Brazil, he catches a flight to the States using Jensen's passport. They look enough alike to be brothers. What luck, right? He's leaving Belfast because the heat is on, he hires on with Emerald Shipping, and his crewmate could be his brother. He had six months at sea with the guy to work out a plan, prepare to *become* him. His new life fell right into his lap."

"So," Haskins said, "we need to figure out what he did when he got to the States. What steps did he take to set up his new life here in Maryland? I figure these guys," he nodded past me, "can help us with that."

Detective Santos and another investigator in plain clothes I didn't recognize flanked Sheriff Banks. Reynolds and two fellow deputies rounded out the Kent County contingent. Sheriff Wagner had three detectives with him, and the MSP was also well represented. It was almost the same crew as the first task force meeting, except Graham, Fuentes, and Rourke were absent and I was swimming alone in a pool of testosterone.

Haskins got everyone's attention and relayed the new information regarding Trig Jensen and Declan Lynch to the group. He summarized Lynch's history of systematic parental abuse. "Interpol and the Brazilian authorities are working the international connections, but we need to focus on where he is now. We need to know everything we can about the steps Lynch would have taken once he arrived in Maryland."

An MSP investigator said, "We've determined that Trig Jensen was the sole beneficiary of his father's estate. The real estate was rented, but Peter Jensen owned the rest of the assets outright."

"What happened to the inventory?" Haskins asked.

"In December 2012, Trig sold off all the boat inventory and maintenance equipment at auction through a broker," he told us.

"That's a couple months after Jensen went to work for Emerald Shipping," I added.

"So," Haskins said, "he's got all this money in the bank from the auction sales, plus his salary, which wasn't too shabby. Lynch gets his account numbers, passport, and driver's license. Once Jensen is out of the picture, he returns to Maryland, cleans out the accounts. He's flush with cash, ready to set up shop somewhere."

"Probably somewhere near this red area," I said, holding up a copy of the probability map.

"That's a pretty big area," someone in the back said.

"I agree," I said. "So, we need to narrow it down."

Haskins jumped in, "We believe our suspect owns an older model Ford van, '88 to '97. I've asked Sheriff Wagner to provide us with DMV information for vehicles previously registered to Peter Jensen. Sheriff?"

"Well, the Motor Vehicle Administration information is limited because it's been some time since the registrations were active, and it's likely that some of these vehicles were included in the auction lot. Tracking down titles has been a bit of a challenge. But we managed to catch a break. The marina where Jensen Boat Sales and Service operated requires all marina business owners and anyone with a boat slip in the marina to provide their vehicle information to the marina office."

Jesus, spit it out, man.

"Since Peter Jensen fell into both categories, we found his information in the marina records. He kept an F-350 that he probably used to tow boats, a pickup truck, and a van at the marina. His boat slip lists two boats, a seventeen-foot Whaler and a thirty-four-foot Sea Ray."

This meant nothing to me because I know zero about boats. I was more interested in the van and asked Wagner if he had the make, model, and year.

He checked his notes, evidently unaware that this was the most important information in his possession. "A 1992 Ford Econoline."

Haskins said, "All right, it's a pretty safe bet Declan Lynch now owns this van, maybe the trucks and boats, too, and has registered them under a new name."

"Probably using an address somewhere in this hot zone, the red area," I added.

Haskins said, "So, what we need is a new list showing addresses for all Ford vans, years 1988 to 1997, within the red area indicated on Agent Ross' geoprofile."

"Actually," I said, "we shouldn't just limit it to the hot zone. We should include all addresses within the colored areas, but prioritize the list based on zones. That way, the most likely addresses will be higher on the list."

"This is going to take some time," Sheriff Banks said.

"It will, but I can help," I said. The Queen Anne's Sheriff's Office was the closest location with database access. "Sheriff Wagner, if you can give me access to a computer and a couple of folks who know their way around DMV records, I think we can handle this pretty quickly."

"Whatever you need, Agent Ross."

Haskins told the group not to go too far, and I headed to the Sheriff's Office with a plan.

CHAPTER FORTY-THREE

January 4

10:05 a.m.

Centreville, Maryland

39°2'25.46"N, 76°4'16.25"W

THE SHERIFF WANTED to assign me two detectives, but I had another idea. Admin specialists Kerri and Lara were used to working independently on short deadlines and spent their days immersed in databases and records. They also didn't hen peck a keyboard like the guys tended to do. In two hours, the three of us compiled a targeted, prioritized address list based on registrations for vehicles within the high probability areas. Since the physical search would be divided among the task force members, we created several separate, unique lists, dividing up the high priority addresses first, then working from higher to lower probability. Kerri printed off the lists for me and I hurried back to our antler-adorned temporary command center.

Everyone was wound-up, and Haskins wasted no time issuing lists and instructions. The plan was for the teams to cover the entire jeopardy surface area, using the prioritized address lists. We were looking for a van at one of the addresses matching our suspect vehicle criteria.

"We don't have a photo of our suspect, Declan Lynch, yet, but we should have one soon and we'll get those distributed," Haskins informed the group. "In the meantime, I can tell you he looks a lot like the man in the photo Special Agent Ross is passing out."

Trig Jensen was sporting a beard in the picture I handed out, which wasn't ideal. A deputy had been dispatched to Jeremy McAlester's apartment to get a photo of a clean-shaven Jensen. We were still waiting on the PSNI to obtain and provide a photo of Lynch. It was frustrating, but we couldn't afford to wait.

"What's the procedure if we find a van at one of these addresses?" Santos asked.

"Run the tag," Haskins instructed. "If a warrant doesn't come back, then it's just a tap and rap. Homeowner comes to the door, we're looking for someone who looks like he could be this guy's brother. Find anyone who might be our guy, radio it in, sit tight and keep an eye on him, and we'll go from there. We'll be using the tactical channel so we don't interfere with routine comms. All teams check in on the half hour. Any questions?"

There weren't any. Everyone was ready. Haskins decided I should partner with Deputy Reynolds because I didn't have access to DMV records and Chris did.

We headed out on a wing and a prayer, in search of a van.

CHAPTER FORTY-FOUR

January 4

3:22 p.m.

Chestertown, Maryland

39°13'10.35"N, 76°4'3.42"W

OUR SEARCH TOOK longer than it probably should've. I instructed Reynolds to detour to check out every van that could possibly be a match. It would be my shit luck to be sitting next to Declan Lynch at a red light while we were focused on the next address on the list. Our first stop, Washington College, wasn't one of our assigned addresses, but it fit with the target backcloth and I wasn't inclined to leave any unturned stones. Every van on campus was a newer model and bore the seal of the college. To Reynolds' credit, he didn't complain or question.

The homes located at the first two addresses didn't have a garage, and we saw no vehicles near the property like the one we were looking for. The third was more promising because a dark blue Ford van that had seen better days was parked in the driveway. We ran the plates, learned the registered owner was Charles Kinnear, thirty-five years old. The van's year was good, Reynolds informed me, 1992. I waited in the car like a good little consultant while he handled the tap and rap. The man who came to the door looked older than thirty-five, and his massive gut and grease-stained shirt said he probably wasn't our guy. He might've been able to pass for Trig Jensen's beer-guzzling gear head cousin, but definitely not his brother.

Reynolds was smiling when he got back into the car. "Next!"

I read off the address.

"That's going to be on the water," he said, and he was right. It turned out to be an old warehouse on the Chester River. There was no van, but warehouses caused me to imagine all sorts of nefarious activity. It warranted a closer look. Reynolds balked at the suggestion, citing lack of probable cause and Haskins' instructions that I was to stay in the car.

"There's cause to be curious," I countered, "and that's not illegal. There could be a vehicle inside. It's cool with me if you want to stay in the car, but I'm going to have a look. Gimme your flashlight."

He cocked his head and made no move to comply.

"May I please borrow your flashlight, Deputy?" I asked.

When I opened my door, he said, "Hell, if you're going, I guess I'm going. I swear, FBI agents are crazy."

"There you go again with your generalizations," I said, taking his flashlight. The flashlight beam revealed a plethora of windows, but most of the lower ones had been painted over. "What is this place?" I wondered aloud.

"Used to be a crab house, but that was a while back. I don't think it's anything now. Looks vacant."

"Crab house? That local slang for a brothel?" I asked, earning a chuckle. Reynolds had lightened up.

"So, if it's nothing now, why's there a satellite dish mounted on the side of the building?" I asked. We walked along the side of the warehouse and I stopped at the electric meter. The dials were spinning.

"Somebody's paying the electric bill," I said. Vacant wasn't the impression I was getting.

We continued toward the rear of the building, and I noticed the pier where a small yacht was docked there. I walked a wider arc to try to get a look at the side of the craft. I didn't see any lettering, couldn't tell the manufacturer, but I was getting a feeling. "That look like a thirty-four footer to you?"

"Yeah," Reynolds said, then added, "it might be a Sea Ray, too. I'll be damned."

The boat had me curious, but I jogged back toward the building, motivated to see what was inside. Methodically, I started examining windows, looking for one with peeling paint or... Ah ha! A broken pane. Damnit. Of course, it was too high for me to reach.

"Let me guess, you want me to boost you up?"

"Pretty please, for old time's sake?" I asked, handing him the flashlight.

Shaking his head, he returned the Maglite to the loop on his duty belt. After sighing dramatically, he squatted, interlaced his hands, and I stepped up. The windowpane was covered with years of grime, both inside and out, and it took a second to make out the dark shapes inside the warehouse bay. "We're getting pretty good at this. We should quit our jobs and join Cirque du—son of a bitch, Reynolds, there's a van in there with—"

I was falling. As soon as my feet hit the ground, hands that should've been catching me, breaking my fall, were in my hair, jerking me back.

My face collided into the building and the sound of crunching cartilage registered an instant before the pain. Stars exploded.

What the fuck is hap—

"You just had to look, didn't you?" His voice was different, the accent both foreign and familiar. Too late, I understood.

When he wrenched my head again, I threw my hip back and twisted left. As I thrust my elbow, he slammed me against the building, pinning me with his weight. My face ground against the worn wood and peeling paint. Chris Reynolds had my neck in a vise grip and was lifting me off my feet. *No, not Chris Reynolds.*

Declan Lynch.

My head slammed into the windows. Again. I heard the crunch of cartilage. Pain radiated from my nose. Again.

Then, black.

CHAPTER FORTY-FIVE

DARK.

Cold.

Open your eyes.

Why is it so dark?

Pain. Where? Head. Neck. Face. Everywhere.

My nose throbbed with each heartbeat.

Heartbeat. You're alive.

Sleep.

No! Stay awake. What do you hear?

Nothing.

Not nothing. There are sounds.

Focus.

Rushing pulse, chattering teeth, a low rumbling.

A motor. A boat. You're on a boat.

Pain flared and my eyes squeezed shut. Mistake! A wave of nausea rolled over me. Bile burned my throat.

No, you won't be sick.

My left hand reached to my face, and my right moved with it.

A familiar sound, metal, jangling. *Handcuffs.*

My hands explored my face. Blood, sticky in places. Either I was still bleeding or I hadn't been there long enough for it to dry. Turning my neck was painful, but something else caused a fresh surge of panic, a tight band of pressure against my throat. Stiff tendrils brushed my jaw. *Wires.* My fingers explored the thick collar around my throat. The wires were connected to a plastic box the size of a deck of cards. *What the fuck?*

There's a fucking bomb on your neck. You will not freak the fuck out. You will stay calm and work through this.

I was on my back, knees bent, toes against something hard. My ankles were bound, and a detail tried to surface, but it was lost in the pounding in my head.

Every muscle screamed with the slightest movement, and I wanted to cry out.

Don't! He'll hear you and it's what he wants.

I shoved a fist into my mouth and fought against the deepest urge to scream.

Calm the hell down. Where are you? Think!

I touched my bound wrists to my chest, moved trembling hands down the length of my body. An alarm sounded in the back of my brain. I'd been stripped to my underwear.

Like the others. He'll remove your panties, too, later. Just like he did before, with the others. *To muffle your screams, and you will scream. No! Stop it!*

Focus!

My shoulders were wedged against something hard. I reached forward and my hands slid over a smooth surface. *Plastic? Fiberglass?*

You're on a boat, in a box. A live well. This is why he likes them small. So they'll fit in tight spaces.

There were other reasons, too. It was hard to breathe. I couldn't get enough air. Something warm and wet dripped from my nose, ran down my cheek. My tongue moved over dry, swollen lips.

Calm down! Breathe, Ross. Reynolds put you in here because... No, not Reynolds. Lynch. *He's taking you, where?*

It was the million fucking dollar question. It had been all along.

Some place that's isolated and accessible by boat.

I listened and tried to think, visualized the Chester River. *North or south?*

How will they know where I am?

They won't. You're on your own.

The boat was slowing, turning.

Are we entering a stream, an inlet? Are we stopping? What will he do to me?

Don't scream. No one will hear you. What are you going to do once you're out of this box? What did the others do? Did they have a plan? When did they realize it wouldn't work?

It seemed like hours before we stopped, but pain had distorted my sense of time. Water lapped against the sides of the boat as it rocked, waves of nausea rippled through my gut.

What's the plan, Ross?

Don't give him what he wants. He wants you to be afraid.

I was. The violent shivering wasn't all from the cold. I would be found with the same marks left on Jennifer and Allison, from the bolts holding the plastic casing together. It was how he'd kept them subdued. It was why Allison, who could've outrun him, didn't try.

You won't run either. You're going to end up just like her. Like all of them. No!

When he opened the live well, I did what I said I wouldn't. I panicked, turned into the girl who begged for her life. The girl who would die just like the others.

Stop it! That's not helpful. Keep your mouth shut and just breathe.

He untied my feet because he wanted me to walk. He was gentle when he pulled me up and out of the storage well, like he didn't want to hurt me. I almost expected him to say, "Careful there, watch your step," and I wanted to laugh, cry, scream. The galley was dark, and I wondered if that was so other boats wouldn't notice us. Were there any other boats near us?

Well, you were wrong. He's not short. He's Paul Fucking Bunyan's kid brother, and he's been right in front of you the whole time. How did you not see?

His height required him to bend over to move through the galley. He was no longer wearing the uniform of a deputy because he was no longer Chris Reynolds. He was a black shadow. He was Declan Lynch or whoever he became when he was feeding his dark fantasies. My legs were stiff, and I stumbled going up the steps. Things didn't improve once we were on deck. Waves rocked the boat against the pier, and there was nothing to hold onto. The wind tore through me, and I wanted desperately to be below deck. My neck ached and it was difficult to turn my head.

Say something! What are you thinking? What do you want from me?

I'm so cold.

My jaw ached from being clamped shut, but I wouldn't open my mouth until I thought of something to say that wouldn't make things worse.

You'll die if you leave this boat.

Force him to detonate the thing on your neck. Someone might see the explosion. It would be quick. No pain. No, this isn't a fucking Die Hard movie. Besides, they might not find Rachel alive and she's—Rachel!

She's got to be here, somewhere. Maybe he's already killed her, torched her. Maybe he wants me to see what he's done, a last reminder of what he's going to do to me.

He nudged my shoulder, urging me to step up and onto a pier that had seen better days. Half the planks were missing, and those that weren't were buckled. Maybe it would collapse. It wouldn't be the worst thing if it collapsed and we ended up in the icy water. It might give me a chance, but the planks and pilings held up, and before I could contemplate jumping, I was stumbling on numb feet into the thick woods.

It was so cold, and my bare feet hurt as we walked over pine needles and brush toward something terrible. I was running out of time. The others didn't know what lay in front of them, but I did. I wouldn't be getting back on the boat. It would happen there, in the woods, and he wouldn't be quick about it.

No, you can't let that happen.

You won't let him put a brand to your skin. They—Haskins—can't find you with your underwear in your mouth and your face burned off. Fuck that. It ends here.

When I stopped, he almost walked into me. "Keep moving," he said and shoved my shoulder. I was expecting it and shifted my weight. He seemed surprised when I was able to keep my balance. I didn't budge. Anger flashed.

"No," I said, my left foot automatically moving back as I shifted into a defensive stance.

"I said keep moving, b—"

"You're going to have to make me, you piece of shit." His nostrils flared, and I thought I'd scored a point. Just as suddenly, the mask slid back into place. The corner of his mouth turned up.

"Nice try, Agent Ross. You're trying to make me angry so I'll do something impulsive. The sooner you realize you're not the one in control here, the easier it'll be."

"Oh, sure, you're in control. Declan Lynch, the big man. That's why you need to cuff me and put a fucking bomb on my neck. Is that why you pick the small ones? They make you feel big and powerful? Pussy."

"Shut your fucking mouth and walk. Move!"

"Fuck you!" I punctuated with double birds. "Guess what, Deck? I know your secrets. Jackie and I had a nice little chat." Not exactly true, but he hesitated at the mention of his sister.

"Inside, you're what you've always been, just a s-s-scared little boy. You can hide your scars, Declan, but I see them as clearly as you see mine." My teeth chattered so violently I could barely hear myself. "You think this is the worst thing you can do to me? It's not. Dying, pain at the hands of a stranger, isn't the worst thing. But you know that, don't you? You know d-damn well what the worst thing is. And Jackie left you to bear it alone, didn't she? She got out and left you there with your mother, who gave you nothing but cruel words and ugly scars. But you still loved her, didn't you? Never a single kind word for you, but all you wanted was, for one goddamn s-s-second, to n-not feel pathetic."

"Shut up!" The backpack slid from his shoulders. I scanned the area for a weapon, for anything that might help me.

"But did you really love her? Or d-did you go to that nursing home every day and whisper hateful things into her ear because she was trapped in that b-b-broken body and, for once, couldn't hurt you? Is there some sick part of you that misses it—the heat against your skin, the icy water? Did you get off on it? When your body was changing, when you were becoming a man, did you get hard when your mum touched that hot metal to the most private parts? When women put their lustful hands on you, did you think of that, think of her? Killing gets you off, t-too, but it's never quite the same is it, Declan?"

"You bitch cops. You think you're so smart, the lot of you. Inspector O'Donnell thought she was smart, too. It took 'em three days to collect all her crispy parts from Lisburn Road." He was rummaging in the bag, and he was shaking, breathing hard.

I kept spitting out whatever words came to mind, praying something would push the right button. "Jackie thinks it's pathetic that you still love your dear old mum. But do you? Is it love or hate? Do you even know the d-difference? You helped her drunk ass d-d-down those stairs, didn't you, Declan? Huh? D-d-did you give Mummy a little push?"

He faced me, holding the detonator in one hand, a length of rope in the other. His eyes told me everything I needed to know. He was off his plan. It would end there, but he wouldn't use the detonator unless I ran, maybe not even then. He'd worked too hard for this. I'd be his last for a while, and he wanted to take his time with me. I was so dizzy, and I couldn't feel my feet, and my head, and—oh God, oh Jesus, I wouldn't be able to run.

No, you're not going to run.
I don't have the strength for—
You can. Find it.

He was close. So close.
Twigs snapped under his boots.
Focus. Be there or be here. Choose now.
I'm sorry, Erin.
Forgive me.

Fireflies.
A perfect night for magical things.
Where they land, flames erupt. For a moment, it is beautiful.
Holy Mary, Mother of God, pray for us sinners.
Cailean? Mum's voice.
Now and at the hour of our death.
A warm whisper.
Be brave now, Little Bird.

CHAPTER FORTY-SIX

February 10

11:48 a.m.

Baltimore, Maryland

39°17'10.29"N, 76°36'34.42"W

OKAY, YES, I'LL concede hot tea was a smarter choice. But I was tired of making "therapeutic" choices. I wanted coffee, damnit. Admittedly, I was mesmerized by the ritualistic preciseness of Dr. Bloom's process as she squeezed fresh lemon juice into the steaming water. Next, she used a wooden dipper to collect honey from a small ceramic pot and added a healthy dollop to the brew. I appreciated the effort and decided that even if it tasted like last week's dishwater, I'd find a way to get it down.

"Thanks," I rasped, and accepted the offered mug with the hand and arm that weren't encased in plaster and velcroed to my body. "I don't understand why you can't do it," I said to Bloom in a strange new voice I'd never get used to. Speaking was difficult, occasionally painful, and what my damaged larynx produced sounded like Clint Eastwood with a head cold. Rob found it sexy, which was ridiculous. According to Dr. Patricia Quince, my otolaryngologist, the effects may be permanent and I was looking at surgery at some point. Trish, as she insisted I call her, was a close friend of Erin's and one of several surgeons overseeing my care. In case it's not obvious, I was pretty banged up.

Lynch, a.k.a. Chris Reynolds, was also receiving top-notch treatment from the Hopkins surgical staff. Erin reported that Ripley had reduced his arm to a hunk of meat. Vascular repairs hadn't gone well, and he'd likely end up with a stump. If he got a new arm it wouldn't be one of those shiny Terminator ones. Metal appendages were prohibited in lockup. Lynch's boyish good looks were also a thing of the past, I was told. According to my media-obsessed niece, his face looked like it'd gone through a cheese grater. This had apparently been my doing, not Ripley's. The only explanation I could come up with was the handcuff chain.

My face fared much better thanks to Dr. Oh, Chief of Plastics and Reconstructive Surgery. The sutures and deep abrasions that covered my scalp, left side of my face and ear, the splinted nose, and bruising in various stages of healing left me looking like something assembled in a lab. Dr. Oh assured me I'd look almost good as new once everything healed. The neck brace had come off the week before, thank God.

"It's not that I *can't*, Regan," Bloom said, and she was talking about hypnotherapy. It was the reason I was in her office for the second time in a week. I'd asked her to help me remember, because if my track record was any indication, I'd never get there on my own. The nightmares, I supposed, were my mind's way of processing what happened, and I liked to think there was a less terrifying way. Convincing Bloom had not been easy. A shaft of sunlight fell across my face and she moved to the window to adjust the blinds. Her back to me, she said, "I don't believe it's in your best interest. Not yet, anyway."

"And driving myself fucking nuts trying to remember *is*?" I asked, gingerly leaning forward to place my mug on the Plexiglas tabletop without jarring my shoulder.

As usual, my snarkiness had zero effect. She calmly explained, "The dissociation is your mind's way of protecting itself. Part of your brain closed itself off from the present. I'm inclined to think your mind knows what it can handle and what it can't, and that we'd be wise to respect that."

"My mind doesn't know what it knows. That's the problem. Look, I get it, you're afraid of opening up a can of worms," I said. "But I'm not. This—" I waved my good arm and invited the room's Zen to provide some backup, "Is a safe place. I mean, hell, if I'm not safe remembering here, with you, then when will I ever be?"

Continuing our recently established routine, she made the rounds, gathered pillows. "In my experience, during the course of recovered memory therapy, the event can come back suddenly. Memories that aren't necessarily targeted, like Iraq and Lockerbie, could all come back at once. That's probably too much for anyone to process. On top of that, you're still healing from your injuries." She gently tucked a soft suede pillow beneath my broken wing. "And under the influence of narcotic pain medication." She positioned the others until I was surrounded in plushness. "It's not a good idea."

"I'm pretty much off the hard stuff these days, rarely take anything stronger than Motrin. And the memories, or whatever they are, come up whenever they damn well please anyway," I reminded her. "The dreams and random images we've been talking about, the panic attack at CVS, wouldn't it be better to deal with them in therapy, where we have some control?"

"You've said before that you don't know what you actually remember and what you imagine you did. The truth is, Regan, you'll probably never know. The news coverage is inescapable, and I'm sure you've read about the so-called expert reconstruction of the event. Naturally, what you 'recall' is going to be a composite of imagination, memory, and versions you've heard or read. I believe I can best serve you by helping you work on being okay with that."

"That sounds great, in theory. I'm sure it's textbook

psychotherapy protocol, but I've gone through this for twenty-five years and I'm trying to tell you I can't do it again. I can't move on without knowing what the hell happened," I said.

"Why? What do you hope to gain by remembering? There's no evidentiary or investigative value. You're safe, Rachel McAlester is safe, and Declan Lynch is in custody. There are witnesses and plenty of physical evidence to prove exactly what he did to you. Why not spend your energy on healing, in every sense of the word?" She sat, crossed her legs, and balanced her pad of paper on her knee, managing to look both relaxed and attentive. It was a skill she shared with Rourke.

"You sound like Erin. If I never hear the word 'heal' again, it'll be too soon." My voice had given out, as it randomly tended to do, and most of the words came out in a stage whisper. She looked at me sympathetically, which made me want to scream. Screaming would be bad.

"Do you need to take a break?" she asked.

I shook my head.

"Okay, then let's talk about what's going on at home. How's your support system?"

I snorted. "Well, it's more like a support *circus*. My niece is obsessed with the media coverage, is watching it or talking about it twenty-four seven. I don't see how she has time to attend classes. Meanwhile, my sister and aunt hover over me to the point I can barely take a shit in peace."

She smiled. "It sounds like you need a vacation from your convalescence. Is it difficult for you to let others take care of you?"

"Yeah, but I have been, even though it's unnecessary at this point. The pain isn't so bad, and except for dressing myself and stupid hygiene stuff, I can manage pretty well on my own."

I'd been letting Erin take care of me because she needed to, and maybe because of what I'd denied her seven years ago. Plus, it gave her something to focus on besides the Sheridan Situation. *Sheridan*.

Were it not for her… It all came down to the tracking device, which no one would've even known about if she hadn't gone out to the cabin to check on me. She thought to contact Vincent, though she only had a first name to go on. Between her, Haskins, and Harry they made the connection to Tomaro Security. It occurred to me umpteen times a day that I was only alive because of the smart people in my life who gave a damn. Luck, fate, or whatever you want to call it, might've played a part, too.

They had no way of knowing where the tracking device might be. What were the chances it would still be in the back pocket of my favorite jeans? What were the odds I'd be wearing those jeans? The only thing that didn't surprise me was that Vincent's custom protective casing survived my washing machine and dryer, because Vincent didn't do anything half-assed. It was a long shot at best, and I thanked Christ they hadn't dismissed it.

The jeans were on the boat in a garbage bag with the rest of clothes and "Chris Reynolds'" uniform, which enabled Vincent to track the boat. Ripley picked up my scent from the clothes, blazed a trail right to me, and launched herself at Lynch, who found out precisely what "subdue" meant.

Declan Lynch had all but succeeded in strangling the life out of me. Sheridan was the first to reach me, and by that time I wasn't breathing and barely had a pulse. According to Erin's translation of the medical records, Sheridan breathed for me, kept my heart going until the med flight crew could take over. This would not have been an easy feat because my throat was so damaged and swollen they could barely establish an airway.

I owed my life to Sheridan Rourke. Maybe this was the reason, or maybe it was because she'd been there for Erin in all the ways that mattered right after. Their relationship had evolved into something I was pretty sure distance wouldn't diminish, though the PSNI seemed intent on testing that theory.

As one of the PSNI's primary liaisons with Interpol, Sheridan was in South America helping the São Luís authorities determine if two Jane Does could be tied to Lynch. They had both been marked with the same brand as Abbott and Brightwell. The Brazilian government was also still searching for Trig Jensen, but I had no expectation that his body would ever be found.

When Rourke wrapped up in Brazil, she was due in Belfast because the PSNI had five cases of its own to close, six counting Grace O'Donnell. Understandably, Rourke had recused herself from that aspect of the investigation. Ripley's constant presence at my sister's side was a welcome reminder that at some point, Sheridan would be back. In the meantime, if Erin wanted to feed me lentil soup and wipe my ass, I'd find a way to live with it.

"It's good that you have people around you who are taking care of you, but it's understandable that you might need a break," Bloom said. "You're going to realize that you need different things at different times. One day, you might need solitude, space to reflect. Other days, you may be comforted by the energy of those around you. Just trust how you're feeling."

"My, um, friend Rob wants me to stay at his place and I'm considering it." Haskins had been busy tying up loose ends and had hardly been home in weeks. He was pretty good at gauging my moods and he had no problem giving me space. Plus, he'd been keeping Stella at his place, and they'd managed not to kill each other. That little miracle boded well. "I'm supposed to have an answer for him by the time he picks me up," I told Dr. Bloom.

Erin didn't know about this because I saw no reason to bring it up until I'd made a decision. I wasn't sure how she'd take it. Bloom had an odd look on her face, and I thought she was reacting to *friend*, wondering if it might be more. It probably was.

"Is this friend Robert Haskins?" she asked, and I understood how she'd made the connection. He'd been all over the news, despite his best efforts. Cameras loved him.

"Yeah," I said, and my voice was particularly husky. I told

myself it was because of all the talking and took a sip of tea to make the point.

"It might not be a bad thing to be with someone who has an idea of what you went through, someone who was there," she suggested.

Someone who saw me as broken as a person can be. Someone who thought he was too late. Someone who thought I was dead and won't let me forget it.

"How do things stand with the OPR?" she asked.

"There won't be any criminal charges. The ER staff who witnessed the *incident* say they can't distinguish between the injuries Lanie and I inflicted. Baltimore PD is backing me up, swearing the guy made a move to flee, then resisted arrest when I took him to the ground. Not exactly how I remember it, but we all know my memory can't be trusted."

She smiled.

"Based on those accounts, there's no criminal offense to charge me with or grounds for a civil case, and I get the impression the OPR thinks I've been punished enough."

"Well, that's good. It sounds like things are working out well," she said.

"Yeah, but there's a catch. The Bureau thinks I need a break from exclusively working violent crime. I've been highly encouraged to transfer out of the BAU."

"Under the circumstances, I can't say I disagree. What do they have in mind?" she asked.

"Hell, everybody has something in mind. Rob has been offered an ASAC job in Dallas. He'll report after things calm down here, probably late summer. He asked me to go with him. The Bureau will sign off on the transfer, under the condition that I serve as the Dallas F.O.'s NCAVC coordinator. So, there's that. Harry wants me to stay at Quantico and stand up the geographic profiling training program, which I'm not opposed to. There's also an open position in the Counterterrorism Division at headquarters that kind of intrigues me, and D.C. would be close to Erin and Lanie."

"Lots of options. Which way are you leaning?" she asked.

"I have no idea."

"Well," she said, "if you decide to take the Dallas job, I'll be glad to help you find another therapist."

Oh, God. I hadn't thought about having to see someone else. Who else would know tea was what I needed? Who else could relax me almost to the point of sleep with her patient Mont Blanc gliding over monogrammed paper? Who else would surround me with calming reminders of my mother? No one.

When I didn't reply, she added, "Even if you stay at the Academy, you'll probably want to find someone closer. Baltimore is quite a drive for you. I believe Dr. Klein is still on staff at Quantico. He's quite good."

"No."

"Well, if you'd like to see someone in private practice, I can certainly recommend—"

"No, I mean, I don't want to see someone closer. Can we not talk about this right now?"

"Sure, Regan. There's no rush. You have plenty of time to decide."

There's no way in hell I'd be able to start all over, go through all of my shit again, with another shrink. My mental health, and any chance of getting back to work in the near future, depended on my seeing Dr. Hannah Bloom on a regular basis. This complicated the decision I had to make.

"Right," I said, and it was lost in a yawn that engaged my entire upper body, including my shoulder that was only five days post-op. Wincing, I resettled against the cushions.

"You're tired," she said, glancing at her watch. "And your throat probably needs a rest. Why don't we call it a day?"

I nodded and she insisted I relax and finish my tea, which was just fine with me. I asked her to open the blinds, and when she did, I squinted against the harsh sunlight. She watched me for a moment, and I didn't know how to interpret her expression. I was anticipating a question when she said, "I'll have the receptionist send Special Agent Haskins in when he arrives."

She stepped out, leaving me in the bright, quiet space. Light flashed on blue crystal. *Was that a wink, Mum?*

The sunlight was burnt-orange warmth against my closed eyelids. It felt nice. There were things I'd intended to discuss with Bloom, but I supposed it could wait a week. Certain thoughts kept coming up, affecting my sleep, despite the Trazadone. *Reynolds.*

How did I not know? Hell, I'd even considered that rain check, would've happily had a beer with the guy. If I hadn't been completely blind, maybe Allison Brightwell would be alive. Maybe Rachel McAlester wouldn't be facing a lifetime of therapy and trust issues. Hindsight was a bitch. Bloom would point out that no one else saw it either and all the other shit people say to try to make you feel better. I didn't feel any better. The Bureau might've had a point. Maybe I did need a change.

Bloom hadn't asked about those last moments, when the lights were going out. It was impossible to say what was real. There was no bright tunnel, no winged hosts beckoning me toward the light. But my father's sweet pipe tobacco, the feel of his scratchy beard against my cheek as he whispered into my ear seemed plenty real. Maybe my mother's high clear voice singing "Joy to the World" had just been the wind in the pines. Maybe it was all like Bloom said, a composite of memory and imagination twenty-plus years in the making, the last spark of a dying mind. There was no telling. The feeling, the need to be my father's brave little bird, that had been real. Maybe it was enough.

When I opened my eyes, it took a few moments to adjust to the intense brightness. Eventually, I let my gaze wander down past the window where boats crowded the harbor, flags waved, and sails were full of wind. Three dozen or so people leisurely strolled along the brick-paved waterfront. It was midmorning and the restaurant patios and souvenir shops were mostly empty. A few people stopped to watch a group of buskers drum on five-gallon buckets.

A mother was pushing a boy and girl, twins maybe, but they didn't look very much alike, in a double stroller. They'd stopped near the *USS Constellation*, a restored Civil War era sloop moored at the dock, and the ship had the boy's full attention. Mom was rooting around in her purse for something. The dark-haired girl tugged on the balloon string tied to her wrist. As Mom scrubbed the boy's face with a napkin, the wind proved too much for the purple Mylar and its tether broke.

The girl's face contorted in disbelief—*No!* She stretched her chubby arm as high as she could, but the red ribbon was swiftly carried away, beyond her reach. *It's okay, sweetie, we'll get another one,* Mom was saying. She wanted *this* one, *hers*, and sad eyes followed as it drifted high over the sparkling bay. Blonde brother looked on with red, freshly scrubbed cheeks, as she raised desperate, pleading hands to the sky.

Let it go, kid. Just let it go.

The harbor scene reminded me of a postcard in an evidence bag, and this stirred up a bevy of emotions that left me chilled despite the room's natural warmth. I turned my attention to my mug and downed the dregs. The honey had settled on the bottom, and was particularly sweet. The tea wasn't terrible. Not saying I wouldn't rather have coffee, but I could get used to it.

The knock on the door startled me. From the sound of it, whoever was on the other side was having almost as much trouble opening the door as I was extracting myself from the nest of pillows. Haskins finally entered, and the mystery was solved. He was holding two Starbucks cups, one small, the other a venti. I hoped the large one was for me, but knew better. Goddamned therapeutic choices.

"Hey," I rasped.

"So, it's decaf because I figure you'll want a nap before your interview with Spears. Two creams, right?"

He knew perfectly well I preferred two creamers in my java, and yes, I was voluntarily meeting with Monica Spears. No, hell hadn't frozen over. She'd jumped on the true-crime serial podcast bandwagon. Season One: The Belfast Strangler. I'd agreed to provide a sanitized account of my involvement once the criminal process had run its course. She'd agreed to limit the scope of that afternoon's interview to my professional area of expertise. I'd speak to her only under the condition of a legally binding agreement, which Haskins drafted and witnessed, stating that my background, personal life, and family were strictly off-limits. That way, at least I had recourse to sue her ass if she tried to make it about me.

The main reason I'd agreed to talk to her was that I was starved for information. The people in my circle wouldn't talk to me about the investigation or the status of the prosecution's case for many reasons—personal, professional, and legal—and I wouldn't complicate things by asking.

The UK had decided not to extradite Lynch. Any day now, the federal prosecutor would charge him with the kidnapping and attempted murder of a federal agent. Spears shared this tidbit, which hadn't been released publicly, as a show of good faith. A conviction for the attempt on my life carried a maximum sentence of twenty years. I had no problem with the idea of Lynch sitting in a federal penitentiary while the Maryland D.A. strengthened his case, even if meant testifying sooner rather than later. I was ready, and Spears assured me that when it was Rachel McAlester's turn, she would be too.

Rachel spent twenty-six terrifying hours in Lynch's underground bunker, thinking about what he was going to do to her. If that hadn't broken her, maybe she was strong enough to stand up to him in court. Exactly why Lynch had targeted Rachel was still in question. Maybe it was because she'd known Trig Jensen and he thought she might be able to connect him to Jensen. In that case, her brother may have been in jeopardy too. In all likelihood, if I hadn't found that van and forced Lynch to deviate from his plan, Rachel would be his latest victim.

As for why Lynch had baited Sheridan to Maryland, I suspected he saw her as another female who thought she was smarter than him and he was determined to prove she wasn't. But there were two sides of that coin. Part of Declan Lynch enjoyed the attention of an intelligent woman and felt the loss of that after he killed Grace O'Donnell. It was partly why he left the geocaches. As Sheridan pointed out more than once, his primary motivation was the need for control. Beyond the practical aspect of the caches, contaminating the crime scenes, they were a way to bait us, to lead us where he wanted us to go. A game of manipulation.

He'd prepared a geocache to leave with Rachel's body, apparently. It had been found in the warehouse in Chestertown. I could only imagine what the contents might be because those details were being intentionally withheld from me. Haskins was making sure of it, and his diligence led me to believe there was something in that cache he thought I needed protection from, something personal. I wouldn't press him on it, but Monica Spears and I had an agreement. Say what you will about the woman, and I'd said plenty, but her competence and tenacity were beyond question. So, the lines between enemy and ally had become blurred. For the time being, I was okay with that.

Haskins patiently held the door for me. Before taking the offered cup of Sumatran manna, I plucked two feline hairs from the front of his burgundy sweater. There were a half dozen more in less conspicuous places.

"So, I think I have an answer for you," I said.

"Is that right?" He was grinning, waiting for me to say it—for my benefit, not his. Because, of course, he knew. He'd always known.

AUTHOR'S NOTES

ALTHOUGH A WORK of fiction, certain aspects of this narrative are inspired by real-world events. One of these is the tragedy that occurred on December 21, 1988, when Pan Am Flight 103 was destroyed by a bomb in the skies over the United Kingdom. The explosion killed all 259 people on board, including 189 Americans.

Debris from the aircraft hit the ground in the Sherwood Crescent neighborhood of Lockerbie, Scotland, at more than 500 miles per hour, creating a massive crater. Still full of jet fuel, a section of plane ignited, sending a massive inferno through nearby homes. Regan Ross' fragmented memory of that night is my imagining of the confusion and terror that the residents of that neighborhood, quiet and peaceful only moments before, must have felt. My work of fiction is in no way meant to diminish or dishonor the memory of those who lost their lives in this horrible terrorist attack. While crafting this story and accompanying Regan on her dark journey into that inferno, the names and faces of those Lockerbie residents were never far from my thoughts.

Dora and Maurice Henry
Jack and Rosalind Somerville and their children, Paul and Lyndsey
Kathleen and Thomas Flannigan and daughter Joanne
Mary Lancaster
Jean Murray

ACKNOWLEDGEMENTS

I am incredibly grateful to my family and friends for their unwavering support over the last few years as I've endeavored to bring this story to you. First and foremost, I am grateful for my parents, who happen to be the best people I know. They are, and have always been, my staunchest supporters even as my career aspirations and creative passions have changed over the years as abruptly as the east Texas weather. For that and so much more, thank you Mom and Dad.

This novel took fledgling form as my MFA thesis, and I lucked out with a phenomenal advisor. Thank you, Amina Cain, for your candid, constructive, and always encouraging feedback that made me believe the story and characters within that very rough first draft were worth all the revisions and rewrites and, ultimately, that *Jeopardy Surface* could be worthy of publication.

Many thanks to all my friends and colleagues who were patient and kind enough to answer my myriad random questions and share their technical expertise and professional insights over the last seven years.

Were it not for Sara Clark, this novel would've never been finished and Regan Ross would be perpetually drinking shitty coffee in a motel room in eastern Maryland. Thank you, Sara, for being my first reader, editor, publisher, soul sister, and dearest friend in this world. I would be lost without you.

CPSIA information can be obtained
at www.ICGtesting.com
Printed in the USA
FFOW02n0413150217
32425FF